DOVER · THRIFT · EDITIONS

The Mabinogion

TRANSLATED BY

LADY CHARLOTTE E. GUEST

DOVER PUBLICATIONS, INC.
Mineola, New York

DOVER THRIFT EDITIONS

GENERAL EDITOR: STANLEY APPELBAUM
EDITOR OF THIS VOLUME: ADAM FROST

Copyright

Published in Canada by General Publishing Company, Ltd., 30 Lesmill Road, Don Mills, Toronto, Ontario.

Published in the United Kingdom by Constable and Company, Ltd., 3 The Lanchesters, 162–164 Fulham Palace Road, London W6 9ER.

Bibliographical Note

This Dover edition, first published in 1997, contains the unabridged and unaltered text of Lady Charlotte Guest's original introduction to and translation of *The Mabinogion*, as published by J. M. Dent & Sons, Ltd., London, 1906 (see Note for earlier publishing history). The Note was prepared specially for this edition. Lady Guest's original end notes that accompanied the 1906 edition have been omitted.

Library of Congress Cataloging-in-Publication Data

Mabinogion. English.
The mabinogion / translated by Lady Charlotte E. Guest.
p. cm. — (Dover thrift editions)
Contents: Pwyll Prince of Dyved — Branwen the daughter of Llyr — Manawyddan the son of Llyr — Math the son of Mathonwy — The dream of Maxen Wledig — Llud and Llevelys — Kilhwch and Olwen — The dream of Rhonabwy — The lady of the fountain — Peredur the son of Evrawc — Geraint the son of Erbin — Taliesin.
ISBN 0-486-29541-9 (pbk.)
1. Mabinogion — Translations into English. 2. Welsh prose literature — To 1550 — Translations into English. 3. Arthurian romances — Translations into English. 4. Tales, Medieval — Translations into English. 5. Tales — Wales — Translations into English. I. Schreiber, Charlotte, Lady, 1812–1895. II. Title. III. Series.
PB2363.M2S37 1997
891.6'631 — dc21

96-49016
CIP

Manufactured in the United States of America
Dover Publications, Inc., 31 East 2nd Street, Mineola, N.Y. 11501

Note

IN THE THIRTEENTH OR FOURTEENTH CENTURY, when the tales which comprise *The Mabinogion* were first written down in *The Red Book of Hergest*, Wales still possessed a special class of professional storytellers, or "bards." It was a highly regimented class, and those wishing to enter the bardic ranks were required not only to undergo a formal training in composition, but to learn as well a common body of traditional stories (*Mabinogi*) such as are found here. These stories had circulated orally for countless years, some perhaps since before Christianity came to Wales, and as time passed and new bards were taught the traditional lore, the stories naturally evolved and changed; words were altered, passages were forgotten or replaced, and changes in customs and beliefs were reflected. It is now impossible to ascribe to any tale a specific date of composition, much less a specific author, for the differences in subject and style among the stories show that they are the work of many hands.

The reader can, however, elicit from these differences some sense of the order in which the stories were written. The so-called Four Branches of the Mabinogi, the first four pieces in this volume, are imbued with a distinct Celtic or pre-Christian mood and are probably the offspring of early Welsh myths; the stories of Maxen Wledig and Llud and Llevelys are set in Roman Britain and most likely stem from that period; the five Arthurian tales, from *Kilhwch and Olwen* through *Geraint*, are the most modern of the stories, and (as Lady Guest proposes in her introduction) bear the strongest connection to the literature of the European continent. The story of Taliesin — taken by the translator from a later manuscript — stands by itself among the tales, not only because of its separate source but because of its manner of composition: it is marked by its linking of verse (perhaps composed in the sixth century by Taliesin himself) with prose passages that give some narrative cohesion to the poetry. The manuscript breaks off before the completion.

What unites all of these pieces is their weaving together of fact and fiction, of history and fantasy. Many of the stories are given specific settings, whether it be in time—*The Dream of Rhonabwy*, for example, is set during the reign of Madawc (1132–1160), although Rhonabwy's dream takes him back to King Arthur's court—or in place—usually in Wales. Indeed, the tales are rich in Welsh lineages and place-names, as well as allusions to actual historical events. There is always, however, an underlying sense of the mythical in these stories, a sense that there is a strong connection between the tangible world and a shadowy and magical otherworld. This admixture of the real and the fantastic has come to be viewed as a primary characteristic of Celtic literature, and it is what makes the stories continue to seem so vibrant today.

The Red Book of Hergest, from which this translation was made, is part of the collection of Jesus College, Oxford, and has therefore always been of limited availability to any but scholars. Prior to 1849, when, after eleven years of work, Lady Charlotte E. Guest (1812–1895) completed her three-volume edition of *The Mabinogion* (published by Longman, London, between 1841 and 1850), no other complete English translation had been made, and even those who knew Welsh were most likely unfamiliar with the *Red Book*'s contents. The first edition met the needs of both the student and the lay reader, including not only the translation, but the text in Welsh and extensive explanatory notes as well. A one-volume edition, without the Welsh text, appeared in 1877, and Lady Guest's translation has retained its popularity ever since. Readers will find that the century and a half that have passed since the first publication of Guest's *Mabinogion* have not diminished her work, and the translation remains as timeless as the stories themselves.

Contents

Original Introduction

WHILST engaged on the Translations contained in these volumes, and on the Notes* appended to the various Tales, I have found myself led unavoidably into a much more extensive course of reading than I had originally contemplated, and one which in great measure bears directly upon the earlier Mediæval Romance.

Before commencing these labours, I was aware, generally, that there existed a connexion between the Welsh Mabinogion and the Romance of the Continent; but as I advanced, I became better acquainted with the closeness and extent of that connexion, its history, and the proofs by which it is supported.

At the same time, indeed, I became aware, and still strongly feel, that it is one thing to collect facts, and quite another to classify and draw from them their legitimate conclusions; and though I am loth that what has been collected with some pains, should be entirely thrown away, it is unwillingly, and with diffidence, that I trespass beyond the acknowledged province of a translator.

In the twelfth and thirteenth centuries there arose into general notoriety in Europe, a body of "Romance," which in various forms retained its popularity till the Reformation. In it the plot, the incidents, the characters, were almost wholly those of Chivalry, that bond which united the warriors of France, Spain, and Italy, with those of pure Teutonic descent, and embraced more or less firmly all the nations of Europe, excepting only the Slavonic races, not yet risen to power, and the Celts, who had fallen from it. It is not difficult to account for this latter omis-

* These explanatory notes have been omitted from the Dover Thrift Edition.

sion. The Celts, driven from the plains into the mountains and islands, preserved their liberty, and hated their oppressors with fierce, and not causeless, hatred. A proud and free people, isolated both in country and language, were not likely to adopt customs which implied brotherhood with their foes.

Such being the case, it is remarkable that when the chief romances are examined, the name of many of the heroes and their scenes of action are found to be Celtic, and those of persons and places famous in the traditions of Wales and Brittany. Of this the romances of Ywaine and Gawaine, Sir Perceval de Galles, Eric and Enide, Mort d'Arthur, Sir Lancelot, Sir Tristan, the Graal, &c., may be cited as examples. In some cases a tendency to triads, and other matters of internal evidence, point in the same direction.

It may seem difficult to account for this. Although the ancient dominion of the Celts over Europe is not without enduring evidence in the names of the mountains and streams, the great features of a country, yet the loss of their prior language by the great mass of the Celtic nations in Southern Europe (if indeed their successors in territory be at all of their blood), prevents us from clearly seeing, and makes us wonder, how stories, originally embodied in the Celtic dialects of Great Britain and France, could so influence the literature of nations to whom the Celtic languages were utterly unknown. Whence then came these internal marks, and these proper names of persons and places, the features of a story usually of earliest date and least likely to change?

These romances were found in England, France, Germany, Norway, Sweden, and even Iceland, as early as the beginning of the thirteenth and end of the twelfth century. The Germans, who propagated them through the nations of the North, derived them certainly from France. Robert Wace published his Anglo-Norman Romance of the Brut d'Angleterre about 1155. Sir Tristan was written in French prose in 1170; and The Chevalier au Lion, Chevalier de l'Epée, and Sir Lancelot du Lac, in metrical French, by Chrestien de Troyes, before 1200.

From these facts it is to be argued that the further back these romances are traced, the more clearly does it appear that they spread over the Continent from the North-west of France. The older versions, it may be remarked, are far more simple than the later corruptions. In them there is less allusion to the habits and usages of Chivalry, and the Welsh names and elements stand out in stronger relief. It is a great step to be able to trace the stocks of these romances back to Wace, or to his country and age. For Wace's work was not original. He himself, a native of Jersey, appears to have derived much of it from the "Historia Britonum" of Gruffydd ab Arthur, commonly known as

"Geoffrey of Monmouth," born 1128, who himself professes to have translated from a British original. It is, however, very possible that Wace may have had access, like Geoffrey, to independent sources of information.

To the claims set up on behalf of Wace and Geoffrey, to be regarded as the channels by which the Cymric tales passed into the Continental Romance, may be added those of a third almost contemporary author. Layamon, a Saxon priest, dwelling, about 1200, upon the banks of the upper Severn, acknowledges for the source of his British history, the *English* Bede, the *Latin* Albin, and the *French* Wace. The last-named however is by very much his chief, and, for Welsh matters, his only avowed authority. His book, nevertheless, contains a number of names and stories relating to Wales, of which no traces appear in Wace, or indeed in Geoffrey, but which he was certainly in a very favourable position to obtain for himself. Layamon, therefore, not only confirms Geoffrey in some points, but it is clear, that, professing to follow Wace, he had independent access to the great body of Welsh literature then current. Sir F. Madden has put this matter very clearly, in his recent edition of Layamon. The Abbé de la Rue, also, was of opinion that Gaimar, an Anglo-Norman, in the reign of Stephen, usually regarded as a translator of Geoffrey of Monmouth, had access to a Welsh independent authority.

In addition to these, is to be mentioned the English version of Sir Tristrem, which Sir Walter Scott considered to be derived from a distinct Celtic source, and not, like the later Amadis, Palmerin, and Lord Berners's Canon of Romance, imported into English literature by translation from the French. For the Auntours of Arthur, recently published by the Camden Society, their Editor, Mr. Robson, seems to hint at a similar claim.

Here then are various known channels, by which portions of Welsh and Armoric fiction crossed the Celtic border, and gave rise to the more ornate, and widely-spread romance of the Age of Chivalry. It is not improbable that there may have existed many others. It appears then that a large portion of the stocks of Mediæval Romance proceeded from Wales. We have next to see in what condition they are still found in that country.

That Wales possessed an ancient literature, containing various lyric compositions, and certain triads, in which are arranged historical facts or moral aphorisms, has been shown by Sharon Turner, who has established the high antiquity of many of these compositions.

The more strictly Romantic Literature of Wales has been less fortunate, though not less deserving of critical attention. Small portions only of it have hitherto appeared in print, the remainder being still hidden in the obscurity of ancient Manuscripts: of these the chief is supposed to be the Red Book of Hergest, now in the Library of Jesus College, Oxford, and of the fourteenth century. This contains, besides poems, the prose romances known as Mabinogion. The Black Book of Caermarthen, preserved at Hengwrt, and considered not to be of later date than the twelfth century, is said to contain poems only.[1]

The Mabinogion, however, though thus early recorded in the Welsh tongue, are in their existing form by no means wholly Welsh. They are of two tolerably distinct classes. Of these, the older contains few allusions to Norman customs, manners, arts, arms, and luxuries. The other, and less ancient, are full of such allusions, and of ecclesiastical terms. Both classes, no doubt, are equally of Welsh root, but the former are not more overlaid or corrupted, than might have been expected, from the communication that so early took place between the Normans and the Welsh; whereas the latter probably migrated from Wales, and were brought back and re-translated after an absence of centuries, with a load of Norman additions. Kilhwch and Olwen, and the dream of Rhonabwy, may be cited as examples of the older and purer class; the Lady of the Fountain, Peredur, and Geraint ab Erbin, of the later, or decorated.

Besides these, indeed, there are a few tales, as Amlyn and Amic, Sir Bevis of Hamtoun, the Seven Wise Masters, and the story of Charlemagne, so obviously of foreign extraction, and of late introduction into Wales, not presenting even a Welsh name, or allusion, and of such very slender intrinsic merit, that although comprised in the Llyvr Coch, they have not a shadow of claim to form part of the Canon of Welsh Romance. Therefore, although I have translated and examined them, I have given them no place in these volumes.

There is one argument in favour of the high antiquity in Wales of many of the Mabinogion, which deserves to be mentioned here. This argument is founded on the topography of the country. It is found that Saxon names of places are very frequently definitions of the nature of the locality to which they are attached, as Clifton, Deepden, Bridgeford, Thorpe, Ham, Wick, and the like; whereas those of Wales are more frequently commemorative of some event, real or supposed, said to have happened on or near the spot, or bearing allusion to some person renowned in the story of the country or district. Such are "Lyn y Morwynion," the Lake of the Maidens; "Rhyd y Bedd," the Ford of the

[1] It is also stated, that there is in the Hengwrt Library, a MS. containing the Graal in Welsh, as early as the time of Henry I. I had hoped to have added this to the present collection; but the death of Col. Vaughan, to whom I applied, and other subsequent circumstances, have prevented me from obtaining access to it.

Grave; "Bryn Cyfergyr," the Hill of Assault; and so on. But as these names could not have preceded the events to which they refer, the events themselves must be not unfrequently as old as the early settlement in the country. And as some of these events and fictions are the subjects of, and are explained by, existing Welsh legends, it follows that the legends must be, in some shape or other, of very remote antiquity. It will be observed that this argument supports *remote* antiquity only for such legends as are connected with the greater topographical features, as mountains, lakes, rivers, seas, which must have been named at an early period in the inhabitation of the country by man. But there exist, also, legends connected with the lesser features, as pools, hills, detached rocks, caves, fords, and the like, places not necessarily named by the earlier settlers, but the names of which are, nevertheless, probably very old, since the words of which they are composed are in many cases not retained in the colloquial tongue, in which they must once have been included, and are in some instances lost from the language altogether, so much so as to be only partially explicable even by scholars. The argument applies likewise, in their degree, to camps, barrows, and other artificial earthworks.

Conclusions thus drawn, when established, rest upon a very firm basis. They depend upon the number and appositeness of the facts, and it would be very interesting to pursue this branch of evidence in detail. In following up this idea, the names to be sought for might thus be classed: —

I. Names of the great features, involving proper names and actions.

Cadair Idris and Cadair Arthur both involve more than a mere name. Idris and Arthur must have been invested with heroic qualifications to have been placed in such "seats."

II. Names of lesser features, as "Bryn y Saeth," Hill of the Dart; "Llyn Llyngclys," Lake of the Engulphed Court; "Ceven y Bedd," the Ridge of the Grave; "Rhyd y Saeson," the Saxons' Ford.

III. Names of mixed natural and artificial objects, as "Coeten Arthur," Arthur's Coit; "Cerrig y Drudion," the Crag of the Heroes; which involve actions. And such as embody proper names only, as "Cerrig Howell," the Crag of Howell; "Caer Arianrod," the Camp of Arianrod; "Bron Goronwy," the Breast (of the Hill) of Goronwy; "Castell mab Wynion," the Castle of the son of Wynion; "Nant Gwrtheyrn," the Rill of Vortigern.

The selection of names would demand much care and discretion. The translations should be indisputable, and, where known, the connexion of a name with a legend should be noted. Such a name as "Mochdrev," Swine-town, would be valueless unless accompanied by a legend.

It is always valuable to find a place or work called after an individual, because it may help to support some tradition of his existence or his actions. But it is requisite that care be taken not to push the etymological dissection too far. Thus, "Caer Arianrod" should be taken simply as the "Camp of Arianrod," and not rendered the "Camp of the silver circle," because the latter, though it might possibly have something to do with the reason for which the name was borne by Arianrod herself, had clearly no reference to its application to her camp.

It appears to me, then, looking back upon what has been advanced: —

I. That we have throughout Europe, at an early period, a great body of literature, known as Mediæval Romance, which, amidst much that is wholly of Teutonic origin and character, includes certain well-marked traces of an older Celtic nucleus.

II. Proceeding backwards in time, we find these romances, their ornaments falling away at each step, existing towards the twelfth century, of simpler structure, and with less encumbered Celtic features, in the works of Wace, and other Bards of the Langue d'Oil.

III. We find that Geoffrey of Monmouth, Layamon, and other early British and Anglo-Saxon historians, and minstrels, on the one hand, transmitted to Europe the rudiments of its after romance, much of which, on the other hand, they drew from Wales.

IV. Crossing into Wales we find, in the Mabinogion, the evident counterpart of the Celtic portion of the continental romance, mixed up, indeed, with various reflex additions from beyond the border, but still containing ample internal evidence of a Welsh original.

V. Looking at the connexion between divers of the more ancient Mabinogion, and the topographical nomenclature of part of the country, we find evidence of the great, though indefinite, antiquity of these tales, and of an origin, which, if not indigenous, is certainly derived from no European nation.

It was with a general belief in some of these conclusions, that I commenced my labours, and I end them with my impressions strongly confirmed. The subject is one not unworthy of the talents of a Llwyd or a Prichard. It might, I think, be shown, by pursuing the inquiry, that the Cymric nation is not only, as Dr. Prichard has proved it to be, an early offshoot of the Indo-European family, and a people of unmixed descent, but that when driven out of their conquests by the later nations, the names and exploits of their heroes, and the compositions of their bards, spread far and wide among the invaders, and affected intimately their tastes and literature for many centuries, and that it has strong claims to be considered the cradle of European Romance.

C. E. G.

DOWLAIS, *August 29th, 1848.*

The Mabinogion

PWYLL PRINCE OF DYVED

PWYLL Prince of Dyved was lord of the seven Cantrevs of Dyved; and once upon a time he was at Narberth his chief palace, and he was minded to go and hunt, and the part of his dominions in which it pleased him to hunt was Glyn Cuch. So he set forth from Narberth that night, and went as far as Llwyn Diarwyd. And that night he tarried there, and early on the morrow he rose and came to Glyn Cuch, when he let loose the dogs in the wood, and sounded the horn, and began the chase. And as he followed the dogs, he lost his companions; and whilst he listened to the hounds, he heard the cry of other hounds, a cry different from his own, and coming in the opposite direction.

And he beheld a glade in the wood forming a level plain, and as his dogs came to the edge of the glade, he saw a stag before the other dogs. And lo, as it reached the middle of the glade, the dogs that followed the stag overtook it and brought it down. Then looked he at the colour of the dogs, staying not to look at the stag, and of all the hounds that he had seen in the world, he had never seen any that were like unto these. For their hair was of a brilliant shining white, and their ears were red; and as the whiteness of their bodies shone, so did the redness of their ears glisten. And he came towards the dogs, and drove away those that had brought down the stag, and set his own dogs upon it.

And as he was setting on his dogs he saw a horseman coming towards him upon a large light-grey steed, with a hunting horn round his neck, and clad in garments of grey woollen in the fashion of a hunting garb. And the horseman drew near and spoke unto him thus. "Chieftain," said he, "I know who thou art, and I greet thee not." "Peradventure," said Pwyll, "thou art of such dignity that thou shouldest not do so." "Verily," answered he, "it is not my dignity that prevents me." "What is it then, O Chieftain?" asked he. "By Heaven, it is by reason of thine own ignorance and want of courtesy." "What discourtesy, Chieftain, hast thou seen in me?" "Greater discourtesy saw I never in man," said he, "than to drive away the dogs that were killing the stag and to set upon it thine own. This was discourteous, and though I may not be revenged upon thee, yet I declare to Heaven that I will do thee more dishonour than the value of an hundred stags." "O Chieftain," he replied, "if I have done ill I will redeem thy friendship." "How wilt thou redeem it?" "According as thy dignity may be, but I know not who thou art?" "A crowned king am I in the land whence I come." "Lord," said he, "may the day prosper with thee, and from what land comest thou?" "From Annwvyn,"[1] answered he; "Arawn, a King of Annwvyn, am I." "Lord," said he, "how may I gain thy friendship?" "After this manner mayest thou," he said. "There is a man whose dominions are opposite to mine, who is ever warring against me, and he is Havgan, a King of Annwvyn, and by ridding me of this oppression, which thou canst easily do, shalt thou gain my friendship." "Gladly will I do this," said he. "Show me how I may." "I will show thee. Behold thus it is thou mayest. I will make firm friendship with thee; and this will I do. I will send thee to Annwvyn in my stead, and I will give thee the fairest lady thou didst ever behold to be thy companion, and I will put my form and semblance upon thee, so that not a page of the chamber, nor an officer, nor any other man that has always followed me shall know that it is not I. And this shall be for the space of a year from to-morrow, and then we will meet in this place." "Yes," said he; "but when I shall have been there for the space of a year, by what means shall I discover him of whom thou speakest?" "One year from this night," he answered, "is the time fixed between him and me that we should meet at the Ford; be thou there in my likeness, and with one stroke that thou givest him, he shall no longer live. And if he ask thee to give him another, give it not, how much soever he may entreat thee, for when I did so, he fought with me next day as well as ever before." "Verily," said Pwyll, "what shall I do concerning my kingdom?" Said Arawn, "I will cause that no one in all thy dominions, neither man nor woman, shall know that I am not thou, and I will go there in thy stead." "Gladly then," said Pwyll, "will I set forward." "Clear shall be thy path, and nothing shall detain thee, until thou come into my dominions, and I myself will be thy guide!"

So he conducted him until he came in sight of the palace and its dwellings. "Behold," said he, "the Court and the kingdom in thy power. Enter the Court, there is no one there who will know thee, and when thou seest what service is done there, thou wilt know the customs of the Court."

---

[1] Hades.

So he went forward to the Court, and when he came there, he beheld sleeping-rooms, and halls, and chambers, and the most beautiful buildings ever seen. And he went into the hall to disarray, and there came youths and pages and disarrayed him, and all as they entered saluted him. And two knights came and drew his hunting-dress from about him, and clothed him in a vesture of silk and gold. And the hall was prepared, and behold he saw the household and the host enter in, and the host was the most comely and the best equipped that he had ever seen. And with them came in likewise the Queen, who was the fairest woman that he had ever yet beheld. And she had on a yellow robe of shining satin; and they washed and went to the table, and sat, the Queen upon one side of him, and one who seemed to be an Earl on the other side.

And he began to speak with the Queen, and he thought, from her speech, that she was the seemliest and most noble lady of converse and of cheer that ever was. And they partook of meat, and drink, with songs and with feasting; and of all the Courts upon the earth, behold this was the best supplied with food and drink, and vessels of gold and royal jewels.

And the year he spent in hunting, and minstrelsy, and feasting, and diversions, and discourse with his companions until the night that was fixed for the conflict. And when that night came, it was remembered even by those who lived in the furthest part of his dominions, and he went to the meeting, and the nobles of the kingdom with him. And when he came to the Ford, a knight arose and spake thus. "Lords," said he, "listen well. It is between two kings that this meeting is, and between them only. Each claimeth of the other his land and territory, and do all of you stand aside and leave the fight to be between them."

Thereupon the two kings approached each other in the middle of the Ford, and encountered, and at the first thrust, the man who was in the stead of Arawn struck Havgan on the centre of the boss of his shield, so that it was cloven in twain, and his armour was broken, and Havgan himself was borne to the ground an arm's and a spear's length over the crupper of his horse, and he received a deadly blow. "O Chieftain," said Havgan, "what right hast thou to cause my death? I was not injuring thee in anything, and I know not wherefore thou wouldest slay me. But, for the love of Heaven, since thou hast begun to slay me, complete thy work." "Ah, Chieftain," he replied, "I may yet repent doing that unto thee, slay thee who may, I will not do so." "My trusty Lords," said Havgan, "bear me hence. My death has come. I shall be no more able to uphold you." "My Nobles," also said he who was in the semblance of Arawn, "take counsel and know who ought to be my subjects." "Lord," said the

Nobles, "all should be, for there is no king over the whole of Annwvyn but thee." "Yes," he replied, "it is right that he who comes humbly should be received graciously, but he that doth not come with obedience, shall be compelled by the force of swords." And thereupon he received the homage of the men, and he began to conquer the country; and the next day by noon the two kingdoms were in his power. And thereupon he went to keep his tryst, and came to Glyn Cuch.

And when he came there, the King of Annwvyn was there to meet him, and each of them was rejoiced to see the other. "Verily," said Arawn, "may Heaven reward thee for thy friendship towards me. I have heard of it. When thou comest thyself to thy dominions," said he, "thou wilt see that which I have done for thee." "Whatever thou hast done for me, may Heaven repay it thee."

Then Arawn gave to Pwyll Prince of Dyved his proper form and semblance, and he himself took his own; and Arawn set forth towards the Court of Annwvyn; and he was rejoiced when he beheld his hosts, and his household, whom he had not seen so long; but they had not known of his absence, and wondered no more at his coming than usual. And that day was spent in joy and merriment; and he sat and conversed with his wife and his nobles. And when it was time for them rather to sleep than to carouse, they went to rest.

Pwyll Prince of Dyved came likewise to his country and dominions, and began to inquire of the nobles of the land, how his rule had been during the past year, compared with what it had been before. "Lord," said they, "thy wisdom was never so great, and thou wast never so kind or so free in bestowing thy gifts, and thy justice was never more worthily seen than in this year." "By Heaven," said he, "for all the good you have enjoyed, you should thank him who hath been with you; for behold, thus hath this matter been." And thereupon Pwyll related the whole unto them. "Verily, Lord," said they, "render thanks unto Heaven that thou hast such a fellowship, and withhold not from us the rule which we have enjoyed for this year past." "I take Heaven to witness that I will not withhold it," answered Pwyll.

And thenceforth they made strong the friendship that was between them, and each sent unto the other horses, and greyhounds, and hawks, and all such jewels as they thought would be pleasing to each other. And by reason of his having dwelt that year in Annwvyn, and having ruled there so prosperously, and united the two kingdoms in one day by his valour and prowess, he lost the name of Pwyll Prince of Dyved, and was called Pwyll Chief of Annwvyn from that time forward.

* * *

Once upon a time, Pwyll was at Narberth his chief palace, where a feast had been prepared for him, and with him was a great host of men. And after the first meal, Pwyll arose to walk, and he went to the top of a mound that was above the palace, and was called Gorsedd Arberth. "Lord," said one of the Court, "it is peculiar to the mound that whosoever sits upon it cannot go thence, without either receiving wounds or blows, or else seeing a wonder." "I fear not to receive wounds and blows in the midst of such a host as this, but as to the wonder, gladly would I see it. I will go therefore and sit upon the mound."

And upon the mound he sat. And while he sat there, they saw a lady, on a pure white horse of large size, with a garment of shining gold around her, coming along the highway that led from the mound; and the horse seemed to move at a slow and even pace, and to be coming up towards the mound. "My men," said Pwyll, "is there any among you who knows yonder lady?" "There is not, Lord," said they. "Go one of you and meet her, that we may know who she is." And one of them arose, and as he came upon the road to meet her, she passed by, and he followed as fast as he could, being on foot; and the greater was his speed, the further was she from him. And when he saw that it profited him nothing to follow her, he returned to Pwyll, and said unto him, "Lord, it is idle for any one in the world to follow her on foot." "Verily," said Pwyll, "go unto the palace, and take the fleetest horse that thou seest, and go after her."

And he took a horse and went forward. And he came to an open level plain, and put spurs to his horse; and the more he urged his horse, the further was she from him. Yet she held the same pace as at first. And his horse began to fail; and when his horse's feet failed him, he returned to the place where Pwyll was. "Lord," said he, "it will avail nothing for any one to follow yonder lady. I know of no horse in these realms swifter than this, and it availed me not to pursue her." "Of a truth," said Pwyll, "there must be some illusion here. Let us go towards the palace." So to the palace they went, and they spent that day. And the next day they arose, and that also they spent until it was time to go to meat. And after the first meal, "Verily," said Pwyll, "we will go the same party as yesterday to the top of the mound. And do thou," said he to one of his young men, "take the swiftest horse that thou knowest in the field." And thus did the young man. And they went towards the mound, taking the horse with them. And as they were sitting down they beheld the lady on the same horse, and in the same apparel, coming along the same road. "Behold," said Pwyll, "here is the lady of yesterday. Make ready, youth, to learn who she is." "My lord," said he, "that will I gladly do." And thereupon the lady came opposite to them. So the youth mounted his horse; and before he had settled himself in his saddle, she passed by, and there was a clear space between them. But her speed was no greater than it had been the day before. Then he put his horse into an amble, and thought that notwithstanding the gentle pace at which his horse went, he should soon overtake her. But this availed him not; so he gave his horse the reins. And still he came no nearer to her than when he went at a foot's pace. And the more he urged his horse, the further was she from him. Yet she rode not faster than before. When he saw that it availed not to follow her, he returned to the place where Pwyll was. "Lord," said he, "the horse can no more than thou hast seen." "I see indeed that it avails not that any one should follow her. And by Heaven," said he, "she must needs have an errand to some one in this plain, if her haste would allow her to declare it. Let us go back to the palace." And to the palace they went, and they spent that night in songs and feasting, as it pleased them.

And the next day they amused themselves until it was time to go to meat. And when meat was ended, Pwyll said, "Where are the hosts that went yesterday and the day before to the top of the mound?" "Behold, Lord, we are here," said they. "Let us go," said he, "to the mound, to sit there. And do thou," said he to the page who tended his horse, "saddle my horse well, and hasten with him to the road, and bring also my spurs with thee." And the youth did thus. And they went and sat upon the mound; and ere they had been there but a short time, they beheld the lady coming by the same road, and in the same manner, and at the same pace. "Young man," said Pwyll, "I see the lady coming; give me my horse." And no sooner had he mounted his horse than she passed him. And he turned after her and followed her. And he let his horse go bounding playfully, and thought that at the second step or the third he should come up with her. But he came no nearer to her than at first. Then he urged his horse to his utmost speed, yet he found that it availed nothing to follow her. Then said Pwyll, "O maiden, for the sake of him whom thou best lovest, stay for me." "I will stay gladly," said she, "and it were better for thy horse hadst thou asked it long since." So the maiden stopped, and she threw back that part of her headdress which covered her face. And she fixed her eyes upon him, and began to talk with him. "Lady," asked he, "whence comest thou, and whereunto dost thou journey?" "I journey on mine own errand," said she, "and right glad am I to see thee." "My greeting be unto thee," said he. Then he thought that the beauty of all the maidens, and all the ladies that he had ever seen, was as nothing compared to her beauty. "Lady," he said, "wilt thou tell me aught concerning thy purpose?" "I will tell thee," said she. "My chief quest was to seek thee." "Behold," said Pwyll, "this is to me the most pleasing quest on which thou couldst have come; and wilt thou tell me who thou art?" "I will tell thee, Lord," said she. "I am Rhiannon, the daughter of Heveydd Hên, and they sought to give me to a husband against my will. But no husband would I have, and that because of my love for thee, neither will I yet have one unless thou reject me. And hither have I come to hear thy answer." "By Heaven," said Pwyll, "behold this is my answer. If I might choose among all the ladies and damsels in the world, thee would I choose." "Verily," said she, "if thou art thus minded, make a pledge to meet me ere I am given to another." "The sooner I may do so, the more pleasing will it be unto me," said Pwyll, "and wheresoever thou wilt, there will I meet with thee." "I will that thou meet me this day twelvemonth at the palace of Heveydd. And I will cause a feast to be prepared, so that it be ready against thou come." "Gladly," said he, "will I keep this tryst." "Lord," said she, "remain in health, and be mindful that thou keep thy promise; and now I will go hence." So they parted, and he went back to his hosts and to them of his household. And whatsoever questions they asked him respecting the damsel, he always turned the discourse upon other matters. And when a year from that time was gone, he caused a hundred knights to equip themselves and to go with him to the palace of Heveydd Hên. And he came to the palace, and there was great joy concerning him, with much concourse of people and great rejoicing, and vast preparations for his coming. And the whole Court was placed under his orders.

And the hall was garnished and they went to meat, and thus did they sit; Heveydd Hên was on one side of Pwyll, and Rhiannon on the other. And all the rest according to their rank. And they ate and feasted and talked one with another, and at the beginning of the carousal after the meat, there entered a tall auburn-haired youth, of royal bearing, clothed in a garment of satin. And when he came into the hall, he saluted Pwyll and his companions. "The greeting of Heaven be unto thee, my soul," said Pwyll, "come thou and sit down." "Nay," said he, "a suitor am I, and I will do mine errand." "Do so willingly," said Pwyll. "Lord," said he, "my errand is unto thee, and it is to crave a boon of thee that I come." "What boon soever thou mayest ask of me, as far as I am able, thou shalt have." "Ah," said Rhiannon, "wherefore didst thou give that answer?" "Has he not given it before the presence of these nobles?" asked the youth. "My soul," said Pwyll, "what is the boon thou askest?" "The lady whom best I love is to be thy bride this night; I come to ask her of thee, with the feast and the banquet that are in this place." And Pwyll was silent because of the answer which he had given. "Be silent as long as thou wilt," said

Rhiannon. "Never did man make worse use of his wits than thou hast done." "Lady," said he, "I knew not who he was." "Behold this is the man to whom they would have given me against my will," said she. "And he is Gwawl the son of Clud, a man of great power and wealth, and because of the word thou hast spoken, bestow me upon him lest shame befall thee." "Lady," said he, "I understand not thine answer. Never can I do as thou sayest." "Bestow me upon him," said she, "and I will cause that I shall never be his." "By what means will that be?" asked Pwyll. "In thy hand will I give thee a small bag," said she. "See that thou keep it well, and he will ask of thee the banquet, and the feast, and the preparations which are not in thy power. Unto the hosts and the household will I give the feast. And such will be thy answer respecting this. And as concerns myself, I will engage to become his bride this night twelvemonth. And at the end of the year be thou here," said she, "and bring this bag with thee, and let thy hundred knights be in the orchard up yonder. And when he is in the midst of joy and feasting, come thou in by thyself, clad in ragged garments, and holding thy bag in thy hand, and ask nothing but a bagful of food, and I will cause that if all the meat and liquor that are in these seven Cantrevs were put into it, it would be no fuller than before. And after a great deal has been put therein, he will ask thee whether thy bag will ever be full. Say thou then that it never will, until a man of noble birth and of great wealth arise and press the food in the bag with both his feet, saying, 'Enough has been put therein;' and I will cause him to go and tread down the food in the bag, and when he does so, turn thou the bag, so that he shall be up over his head in it, and then slip a knot upon the thongs of the bag. Let there be also a good bugle horn about thy neck, and as soon as thou hast bound him in the bag, wind thy horn, and let it be a signal between thee and thy knights. And when they hear the sound of the horn, let them come down upon the palace." "Lord," said Gwawl, "it is meet that I have an answer to my request." "As much of that thou hast asked as it is in my power to give, thou shalt have," replied Pwyll. "My soul," said Rhiannon unto him, "as for the feast and the banquet that are here, I have bestowed them upon the men of Dyved, and the household, and the warriors that are with us. These can I not suffer to be given to any. In a year from to-night a banquet shall be prepared for thee in this palace, that I may become thy bride."

So Gwawl went forth to his possessions, and Pwyll went also back to Dyved. And they both spent that year until it was the time for the feast at the palace of Heveydd Hên. Then Gwawl the son of Clud set out to the feast that was prepared for him, and he came to the palace, and was received there with rejoicing. Pwyll, also, the Chief of Annwvyn, came to the orchard with his hundred knights, as Rhiannon had commanded him, having the bag with him. And Pwyll was clad in coarse and ragged garments, and wore large clumsy old shoes upon his feet. And when he knew that the carousal after the meat had begun, he went towards the hall, and when he came into the hall, he saluted Gwawl the son of Clud, and his company, both men and women. "Heaven prosper thee," said Gwawl, "and the greeting of Heaven be unto thee." "Lord," said he, "may Heaven reward thee, I have an errand unto thee." "Welcome be thine errand, and if thou ask of me that which is just, thou shalt have it gladly." "It is fitting," answered he. "I crave but from want, and the boon that I ask is to have this small bag that thou seest filled with meat." "A request within reason is this," said he, "and gladly shalt thou have it. Bring him food." A great number of attendants arose and began to fill the bag, but for all that they put into it, it was no fuller than at first. "My soul," said Gwawl, "will thy bag be ever full?" "It will not, I declare to Heaven," said he, "for all that may be put into it, unless one possessed of lands, and domains, and treasure, shall arise and tread down with both his feet the food that is within the bag, and shall say, 'Enough has been put therein.' " Then said Rhiannon unto Gwawl the son of Clud, "Rise up quickly." "I will willingly arise," said he. So he rose up, and put his two feet into the bag. And Pwyll turned up the sides of the bag, so that Gwawl was over his head in it. And he shut it up quickly and slipped a knot upon the thongs, and blew his horn. And thereupon behold his household came down upon the palace. And they seized all the host that had come with Gwawl, and cast them into his own prison. And Pwyll threw off his rags, and his old shoes, and his tattered array; and as they came in, every one of Pwyll's knights struck a blow upon the bag, and asked, "What is here?" "A Badger," said they. And in this manner they played, each of them striking the bag, either with his foot or with a staff. And thus played they with the bag. Every one as he came in asked, "What game are you playing at thus?" "The game of Badger in the Bag," said they. And then was the game of Badger in the Bag first played.

"Lord," said the man in the bag, "if thou wouldest but hear me, I merit not to be slain in a bag." Said Heveydd Hên, "Lord, he speaks truth. It were fitting that thou listen to him, for he deserves not this." "Verily," said Pwyll, "I will do thy counsel concerning him." "Behold this is my counsel then," said Rhiannon; "thou art now in a position in which it behoves thee to satisfy suitors and minstrels; let him give unto them in thy stead, and take a pledge from him that he will never seek to revenge that which has been done to him. And this will be punishment enough." "I will do this gladly," said the man in the bag. "And gladly will I accept it," said Pwyll, "since it is the counsel of Heveydd and Rhiannon." "Such then is our counsel," answered they. "I accept it," said Pwyll. "Seek thyself sureties." "We will be for him," said Heveydd, "until his men be free to answer for him." And upon this he was let out of the bag, and his liegemen were liberated. "Demand now of Gwawl his sureties," said Heveydd, "we know which should be taken for him." And Heveydd numbered the sureties. Said Gwawl, "Do thou thyself draw up the covenant." "It will suffice me that it be as Rhiannon said," answered Pwyll. So unto that covenant were the sureties pledged. "Verily, Lord," said Gwawl, "I am greatly hurt, and I have many bruises. I have need to be anointed; with thy leave I will go forth. I will leave nobles in my stead, to answer for me in all that thou shalt require." "Willingly," said Pwyll, "mayest thou do thus." So Gwawl went towards his own possessions.

And the hall was set in order for Pwyll and the men of his host, and for them also of the palace, and they went to the tables and sat down. And as they had sat that time twelvemonth, so sat they that night. And they ate, and feasted, and spent the night in mirth and tranquillity. And the time came that they should sleep, and Pwyll and Rhiannon went to their chamber.

And next morning at the break of day, "My Lord," said Rhiannon, "arise and begin to give thy gifts unto the minstrels. Refuse no one to-day that may claim thy bounty." "Thus shall it be gladly," said Pwyll, "both to-day and every day while the feast shall last." So Pwyll arose, and he caused silence to be proclaimed, and desired all the suitors and the minstrels to show and to point out what gifts were to their wish and desire. And this being done, the feast went on, and he denied no one while it lasted. And when the feast was ended, Pwyll said unto Heveydd, "My Lord, with thy permission I will set out for Dyved to-morrow." "Certainly," said Heveydd, "may Heaven prosper thee. Fix also a time when Rhiannon may follow thee." "By Heaven," said Pwyll, "we will go hence together." "Willest thou this, Lord?" said Heveydd. "Yes, by Heaven," answered Pwyll.

And the next day, they set forward towards Dyved, and journeyed to the palace of Narberth, where a feast was made ready for them. And there came to them great numbers of the chief men and the most noble ladies of the land, and of these there was none to whom Rhiannon did not give some rich gift, either a bracelet, or a ring, or a precious stone. And they ruled the land prosperously both that year and the next.

And in the third year the nobles of the land began to be sorrowful at seeing a man whom they loved so much, and who was moreover their lord and their foster-brother, without an heir. And they came to him.

And the place where they met was Preseleu, in Dyved. "Lord," said they, "we know that thou art not so young as some of the men of this country, and we fear that thou mayest not have an heir of the wife whom thou hast taken. Take therefore another wife of whom thou mayest have heirs. Thou canst not always continue with us, and though thou desire to remain as thou art, we will not suffer thee." "Truly," said Pwyll, "we have not long been joined together, and many things may yet befall. Grant me a year from this time, and for the space of a year we will abide together, and after that I will do according to your wishes." So they granted it. And before the end of a year a son was born unto him. And in Narberth was he born; and on the night that he was born, women were brought to watch the mother and the boy. And the women slept, as did also Rhiannon, the mother of the boy. And the number of the women that were brought into the chamber was six. And they watched for a good portion of the night, and before midnight every one of them fell asleep, and towards break of day they awoke; and when they awoke, they looked where they had put the boy, and behold he was not there. "Oh," said one of the women, "the boy is lost!" "Yes," said another, "and it will be small vengeance if we are burnt or put to death because of the child." Said one of the women, "Is there any counsel for us in the world in this matter?" "There is," answered another, "I offer you good counsel." "What is that?" asked they. "There is here a stag-hound bitch, and she has a litter of whelps. Let us kill some of the cubs, and rub the blood on the face and hands of Rhiannon, and lay the bones before her, and assert that she herself hath devoured her son, and she alone will not be able to gainsay us six." And according to this counsel it was settled. And towards morning Rhiannon awoke, and she said, "Women, where is my son?" "Lady," said they, "ask us not concerning thy son, we have nought but the blows and the bruises we got by struggling with thee, and of a truth we never saw any woman so violent as thou, for it was of no avail to contend with thee. Hast thou not thyself devoured thy son? Claim him not therefore of us." "For pity's sake," said Rhiannon; "the Lord God knows all things. Charge me not falsely. If you tell me this from fear, I assert before Heaven that I will defend you." "Truly," said they, "we would not bring evil on ourselves for any one in the world." "For pity's sake," said Rhiannon, "you will receive no evil by telling the truth." But for all her words, whether fair or harsh, she received but the same answer from the women.

And Pwyll the Chief of Annwvyn arose, and his household, and his hosts. And this occurrence could not be concealed, but the story went forth throughout the land, and all the nobles heard it. Then the nobles came to Pwyll, and besought him to put away his wife, because of the great crime which she had done. But Pwyll answered them, that they had no cause wherefore they might ask him to put away his wife, save for her having no children. "But children has she now had, therefore will I not put her away; if she has done wrong, let her do penance for it."

So Rhiannon sent for the teachers and the wise men, and as she preferred doing penance to contending with the women, she took upon her a penance. And the penance that was imposed upon her was, that she should remain in that palace of Narberth until the end of seven years, and that she should sit every day near unto a horse-block that was without the gate. And that she should relate the story to all who should come there, whom she might suppose not to know it already; and that she should offer the guests and strangers, if they would permit her, to carry them upon her back into the palace. But it rarely happened that any would permit. And thus did she spend part of the year.

Now at that time Teirnyon Twryv Vliant was Lord of Gwent Is Coed, and he was the best man in the world. And unto his house there belonged a mare, than which neither mare nor horse in the kingdom was more beautiful. And on the night of every first of May she foaled, and no one ever knew what became of the colt. And one night Teirnyon talked with his wife: "Wife," said he, "it is very simple of us that our mare should foal every year, and that we should have none of her colts." "What can be done in the matter?" said she. "This is the night of the first of May," said he. "The vengeance of Heaven be upon me, if I learn not what it is that takes away the colts." So he caused the mare to be brought into a house, and he armed himself, and began to watch that night. And in the beginning of the night, the mare foaled a large and beautiful colt. And it was standing up in the place. And Teirnyon rose up and looked at the size of the colt, and as he did so he heard a great tumult, and after the tumult behold a claw came through the window into the house, and it seized the colt by the mane. Then Teirnyon drew his sword, and struck off the arm at the elbow, so that portion of the arm together with the colt was in the house with him. And then did he hear a tumult and wailing, both at once. And he opened the door, and rushed out in the direction of the noise, and he could not see the cause of the tumult because of the darkness of the night, but he rushed after it and followed it. Then he remembered that he had left the door open, and he returned. And at the door behold there was an infant boy in swaddling-clothes, wrapped around in a mantle of satin. And he took up the boy, and behold he was very strong for the age that he was of.

Then he shut the door, and went into the chamber where his wife was. "Lady," said he, "art thou sleeping?" "No, lord," said she, "I was asleep, but as thou camest in I did awake." "Behold, here is a boy for thee if thou wilt," said he, "since thou hast never had one." "My lord," said she, "what adventure is this?" "It was thus," said Teirnyon; and he told her how it all befell. "Verily, lord," said she, "what sort of garments are there upon the boy?" "A mantle of satin," said he. "He is then a boy of gentle lineage," she replied. "My lord," she said, "if thou wilt, I shall have great diversion and mirth. I will call my women unto me, and tell them that I have been pregnant." "I will readily grant thee to do this," he answered. And thus did they, and they caused the boy to be baptized, and the ceremony was performed there; and the name which they gave unto him was Gwri Wallt Euryn, because what hair was upon his head was as yellow as gold. And they had the boy nursed in the Court until he was a year old. And before the year was over he could walk stoutly. And he was larger than a boy of three years old, even one of great growth and size. And the boy was nursed the second year, and then he was as large as a child six years old. And before the end of the fourth year, he would bribe the grooms to allow him to take the horses to water. "My lord," said his wife unto Teirnyon, "where is the colt which thou didst save on the night that thou didst find the boy?" "I have commanded the grooms of the horses," said he, "that they take care of him." "Would it not be well, lord," said she, "if thou wert to cause him to be broken in, and given to the boy, seeing that on the same night that thou didst find the boy, the colt was foaled and thou didst save him?" "I will not oppose thee in this matter," said Teirnyon. "I will allow thee to give him the colt." "Lord," said she, "may Heaven reward thee; I will give it him." So the horse was given to the boy. Then she went to the grooms and those who tended the horses, and commanded them to be careful of the horse, so that he might be broken in by the time that the boy could ride him.

And while these things were going forward, they heard tidings of Rhiannon and her punishment. And Teirnyon Twryv Vliant, by reason of the pity that he felt on hearing this story of Rhiannon and her punishment, inquired closely concerning it, until he had heard from many of those who came to his court. Then did Teirnyon, often lamenting the sad history, ponder within himself, and he looked steadfastly on the boy, and as he looked upon him, it seemed to him that he had never beheld so great a likeness between father and son, as between the boy and Pwyll the Chief of Annwvyn. Now the semblance of Pwyll was well known to him, for he had of yore been one of his followers. And thereupon he became grieved for the wrong that he did, in keeping with him a boy whom he knew to be the son of another man. And the first time that he was alone with his wife, he told her that it was not right that they should keep the boy with them, and suffer so excellent a lady as Rhiannon to be punished so greatly on his account, whereas the boy was the son of Pwyll the Chief of Annwvyn. And Teirnyon's wife agreed with him, that they should send the boy to Pwyll. "And three things, lord," said she, "shall we gain thereby. Thanks and gifts for releasing Rhiannon from her punishment; and thanks from Pwyll for nursing his son and restoring him unto him; and thirdly, if the boy is of gentle nature, he will be our foster-son, and he will do for us all the good in his power." So it was settled according to this counsel.

And no later than the next day was Teirnyon equipped, and two other knights with him. And the boy, as a fourth in their company, went with them upon the horse which Teirnyon had given him. And they journeyed towards Narberth, and it was not long before they reached that place. And as they drew near to the palace, they beheld Rhiannon sitting beside the horse-block. And when they were opposite to her, "Chieftain," said she, "go no further thus, I will bear every one of you into the palace, and this is my penance for slaying my own son and devouring him." "Oh, fair lady," said Teirnyon, "think not that I will be one to be carried upon thy back." "Neither will I," said the boy. "Truly, my soul," said Teirnyon, "we will not go." So they went forward to the palace, and there was great joy at their coming. And at the palace a feast was prepared, because Pwyll was come back from the confines of Dyved. And they went into the hall and washed, and Pwyll rejoiced to see Teirnyon. And in this order they sat. Teirnyon between Pwyll and Rhiannon, and Teirnyon's two companions on the other side of Pwyll, with the boy between them. And after meat they began to carouse and to discourse. And Teirnyon's discourse was concerning the adventure of the mare and the boy, and how he and his wife had nursed and reared the child as their own. "And behold here is thy son, lady," said Teirnyon. "And whosoever told that lie concerning thee, has done wrong. And when I heard of thy sorrow, I was troubled and grieved. And I believe that there is none of this host who will not perceive that the boy is the son of Pwyll," said Teirnyon. "There is none," said they all, "who is not certain thereof." "I declare to Heaven," said Rhiannon, "that if this be true, there is indeed an end to my trouble." "Lady," said Pendaran Dyved, "well hast thou named thy son Pryderi,[1] and well becomes him the name of Pryderi son of Pwyll Chief of Annwvyn." "Look you," said Rhiannon, "will not his own name become him better?" "What name has he?" asked Pendaran Dyved. "Gwri Wallt Euryn is the name that we gave him." "Pryderi," said

[1] The word "Pryder" or "Pryderi" means anxiety.

Pendaran, "shall his name be." "It were more proper," said Pwyll, "that the boy should take his name from the word his mother spoke when she received the joyful tidings of him." And thus was it arranged.

"Teirnyon," said Pwyll, "Heaven reward thee that thou hast reared the boy up to this time, and, being of gentle lineage, it were fitting that he repay thee for it." "My lord," said Teirnyon, "it was my wife who nursed him, and there is no one in the world so afflicted as she at parting with him. It were well that he should bear in mind what I and my wife have done for him." "I call Heaven to witness," said Pwyll, "that while I live I will support thee and thy possessions, as long as I am able to preserve my own. And when he shall have power, he will more fitly maintain them than I. And if this counsel be pleasing unto thee, and to my nobles, it shall be that, as thou hast reared him up to the present time, I will give him to be brought up by Pendaran Dyved, from henceforth. And you shall be companions, and shall both be foster-fathers unto him." "This is good counsel," said they all. So the boy was given to Pendaran Dyved, and the nobles of the land were sent with him. And Teirnyon Twryv Vliant, and his companions, set out for his country, and his possessions, with love and gladness. And he went not without being offered the fairest jewels and the fairest horses, and the choicest dogs; but he would take none of them.

Thereupon they all remained in their own dominions. And Pryderi, the son of Pwyll the Chief of Annwvyn, was brought up carefully as was fit, so that he became the fairest youth, and the most comely, and the best skilled in all good games, of any in the kingdom. And thus passed years and years, until the end of Pwyll the Chief of Annwvyn's life came, and he died.

And Pryderi ruled the seven Cantrevs of Dyved prosperously, and he was beloved by his people, and by all around him. And at length he added unto them the three Cantrevs of Ystrad Tywi, and the four Cantrevs of Cardigan; and these were called the Seven Cantrevs of Seissyllwch. And when he made this addition, Pryderi the son of Pwyll the Chief of Annwvyn desired to take a wife. And the wife he chose was Kicva, the daughter of Gwynn Gohoyw, the son of Gloyw Wallt Lydan, the son of Prince Casnar, one of the nobles of this Island.

And thus ends this portion of the Mabinogion.

BRANWEN THE DAUGHTER OF LLYR

HERE IS THE SECOND PORTION OF THE MABINOGI

BENDIGEID VRAN, the son of Llyr, was the crowned king of this island, and he was exalted from the crown of London. And one afternoon he was at Harlech in Ardudwy, at his Court, and he sat upon the rock of Harlech, looking over the sea. And with him were his brother Manawyddan the son of Llyr, and his brothers by the mother's side, Nissyen and Evnissyen, and many nobles likewise, as was fitting to see around a king. His two brothers by the mother's side were the sons of Eurosswydd, by his mother, Penardun, the daughter of Beli son of Manogan. And one of these youths was a good youth and of gentle nature, and would make peace between his kindred, and cause his family to be friends when their wrath was at the highest; and this one was Nissyen; but the other would cause strife between his two brothers when they were most at peace. And as they sat thus, they beheld thirteen ships coming from the south of Ireland, and making towards them, and they came with a swift motion, the wind being behind them, and they neared them rapidly. "I see ships afar," said the king, "coming swiftly towards the land. Command the men of the Court that they equip themselves, and go and learn their intent." So the men equipped themselves and went down towards them. And when they saw the ships near, certain were they that they had never seen ships better furnished. Beautiful flags of satin were upon them. And behold one of the ships outstripped the others, and they saw a shield lifted up above the side of the ship, and the point of the shield was upwards, in token of peace. And the men drew near that they might hold converse. Then they put out boats and came towards the land. And they saluted the king. Now the king could hear them from the place where he was, upon the rock above their heads. "Heaven prosper you," said he, "and be ye welcome. To whom do these ships belong, and who is the chief amongst you?" "Lord," said they, "Matholwch, king of Ireland, is here, and these ships belong to him." "Wherefore comes he?" asked the king, "and will he come to the land?" "He is a suitor unto thee, lord," said they, "and he will not land unless he have his boon." "And what may that be?" inquired the king. "He desires to ally himself with thee, lord," said they, "and he comes to ask Branwen the daughter of Llyr, that, if it seem well to thee, the Island of the Mighty may be leagued with

Ireland, and both become more powerful." "Verily," said he, "let him come to land, and we will take counsel thereupon." And this answer was brought to Matholwch. "I will go willingly," said he. So he landed, and they received him joyfully; and great was the throng in the palace that night, between his hosts and those of the Court; and next day they took counsel, and they resolved to bestow Branwen upon Matholwch. Now she was one of the three chief ladies of this island, and she was the fairest damsel in the world.

And they fixed upon Aberffraw as the place where she should become his bride. And they went thence, and towards Aberffraw the hosts proceeded; Matholwch and his host in their ships; Bendigeid Vran and his host by land, until they came to Aberffraw. And at Aberffraw they began the feast and sat down. And thus sat they. The King of the Island of the Mighty and Manawyddan the son of Llyr on one side, and Matholwch on the other side, and Branwen the daughter of Llyr beside him. And they were not within a house, but under tents. No house could ever contain Bendigeid Vran. And they began the banquet and caroused and discoursed. And when it was more pleasing to them to sleep than to carouse, they went to rest, and that night Branwen became Matholwch's bride.

And next day they arose, and all they of the Court, and the officers began to equip and to range the horses and the attendants, and they ranged them in order as far as the sea.

And behold one day, Evnissyen, the quarrelsome man of whom it is spoken above, came by chance into the place, where the horses of Matholwch were, and asked whose horses they might be. "They are the horses of Matholwch king of Ireland, who is married to Branwen, thy sister; his horses are they." "And is it thus they have done with a maiden such as she, and moreover my sister, bestowing her without my consent? They could have offered no greater insult to me than this," said he. And thereupon he rushed under the horses and cut off their lips at the teeth, and their ears close to their heads, and their tails close to their backs, and wherever he could clutch their eyelids, he cut them to the very bone, and he disfigured the horses and rendered them useless.

And they came with these tidings unto Matholwch, saying that the horses were disfigured, and injured so that not one of them could ever be of any use again. "Verily, lord," said one, "it was an insult unto thee, and as such was it meant." "Of a truth, it is a marvel to me, that if they desire to insult me, they should have given me a maiden of such high rank and so much beloved of her kindred, as they have done." "Lord," said another, "thou seest that thus it is, and there is nothing for thee to do but to go to thy ships." And thereupon towards his ships he set out.

And tidings came to Bendigeid Vran that Matholwch was quitting the Court without asking leave, and messengers were sent to inquire of him wherefore he did so. And the messengers that went were Iddic the son of Anarawd, and Heveydd Hir. And these overtook him and asked of him what he designed to do, and wherefore he went forth. "Of a truth," said he, "if I had known I had not come hither. I have been altogether insulted, no one had ever worse treatment than I have had here. But one thing surprises me above all." "What is that?" asked they. "That Branwen the daughter of Llyr, one of the three chief ladies of this island, and the daughter of the King of the Island of the Mighty, should have been given me as my bride, and that after that I should have been insulted; and I marvel that the insult was not done me before they had bestowed upon me a maiden so exalted as she." "Truly, lord, it was not the will of any that are of the Court," said they, "nor of any that are of the council, that thou shouldest have received this insult; and as thou hast been insulted, the dishonour is greater unto Bendigeid Vran than unto thee." "Verily," said he, "I think so. Nevertheless he cannot recall the insult." These men returned with that answer to the place where Bendigeid Vran was, and they told him what reply Matholwch had given them. "Truly," said he, "there are no means by which we may prevent his going away at enmity with us, that we will not take." "Well, lord," said they, "send after him another embassy." "I will do so," said he. "Arise, Manawyddan son of Llyr, and Heveydd Hir, and Unic Glew Ysgwyd, and go after him, and tell him that he shall have a sound horse for every one that has been injured. And beside that, as an atonement for the insult, he shall have a staff of silver, as large and as tall as himself, and a plate of gold of the breadth of his face. And show unto him who it was that did this, and that it was done against my will; but that he who did it is my brother, by the mother's side, and therefore it would be hard for me to put him to death. And let him come and meet me," said he, "and we will make peace in any way he may desire."

The embassy went after Matholwch, and told him all these sayings in a friendly manner, and he listened thereunto. "Men," said he, "I will take counsel." So to the council he went. And in the council they considered that if they should refuse this, they were likely to have more shame rather than to obtain so great an atonement. They resolved therefore to accept it, and they returned to the Court in peace.

Then the pavilions and the tents were set in order after the fashion of a hall; and they went to meat, and as they had sat at the beginning of the feast, so sat they there. And Matholwch and Bendigeid Vran began to discourse; and behold it seemed to Bendigeid Vran, while they talked, that Matholwch was not so cheerful as he had been before. And he thought that the chieftain might be sad, because of the smallness of the atonement which he had, for the wrong that had been done him. "Oh, man," said Bendigeid Vran, "thou dost not discourse to-night so cheerfully as thou wast wont. And if it be because of the smallness of the atonement, thou shalt add thereunto whatsoever thou mayest choose, and to-morrow I will pay thee the horses." "Lord," said he, "Heaven reward thee." "And I will enhance the atonement," said Bendigeid Vran, "for I will give unto thee a cauldron, the property of which is, that if one of thy men be slain to-day, and be cast therein, to-morrow he will be as well as ever he was at the best, except that he will not regain his speech." And thereupon he gave him great thanks, and very joyful was he for that cause.

And the next morning they paid Matholwch the horses as long as the trained horses lasted. And then they journeyed into another commot, where they paid him with colts until the whole had been paid, and from thenceforth that commot was called Talebolion.

And a second night sat they together. "My lord," said Matholwch, "whence hadst thou the cauldron which thou hast given me?" "I had it of a man who had been in thy land," said he, "and I would not give it except to one from there." "Who was it?" asked he. "Llassar Llaesgyvnewid; he came here from Ireland with Kymideu Kymeinvoll, his wife, who escaped from the Iron House in Ireland, when it was made red hot around them, and fled hither. And it is a marvel to me that thou shouldst know nothing concerning the matter." "Something I do know," said he, "and as much as I know I will tell thee. One day I was hunting in Ireland, and I came to the mound at the head of the lake, which is called the Lake of the Cauldron. And I beheld a huge yellow-haired man coming from the lake with a cauldron upon his back. And he was a man of vast size, and of horrid aspect, and a woman followed after him. And if the man was tall, twice as large as he was the woman, and they came towards me and greeted me. 'Verily,' asked I, 'wherefore are you journeying?' 'Behold, this,' said he to me, 'is the cause that we journey. At the end of a month and a fortnight this woman will have a son; and the child that will be born at the end of the month and the fortnight will be a warrior fully armed.' So I took them with me and maintained them. And they were with me for a year. And that year I had them with me not grudgingly. But thenceforth was there murmuring, because that they were with me. For, from the beginning of the fourth month they had begun to make themselves hated and to be disorderly in the land; committing outrages, and molesting and harassing the nobles and ladies; and thenceforward my people rose up and besought me to part with them, and they bade me to choose between them and my dominions. And I applied to the council of my country to know what should be done concerning them; for of their own free will they would not go, neither could they be compelled against their will, through fighting. And [the people of the country] being in this strait, they caused a chamber to be made all of iron. Now when the chamber was ready, there came there every smith that was in Ireland, and every one who owned tongs and hammer. And they caused coals to be piled up as high as the top of the chamber. And they had the man, and the woman, and the children, served with plenty of meat and drink; but when it was known that they were drunk, they began to put fire to the coals about the chamber, and they blew it with bellows until the house was red hot all around them. Then was there a council held in the centre of the floor of the chamber. And the man tarried until the plates of iron were all of a white heat; and then, by reason of the great heat, the man dashed against the plates with his shoulder and struck them out, and his wife followed him; but except him and his wife none escaped thence. And then I suppose, lord," said Matholwch unto Bendigeid Vran, "that he came over unto thee." "Doubtless he came here," said he, "and gave unto me the cauldron." "In what manner didst thou receive them?" "I dispersed them through every part of my dominions, and they have become numerous and are prospering everywhere, and they fortify the places where they are with men and arms, of the best that were ever seen."

That night they continued to discourse as much as they would, and had minstrelsy and carousing, and when it was more pleasant to them to sleep than to sit longer, they went to rest. And thus was the banquet carried on with joyousness; and when it was finished, Matholwch journeyed towards Ireland, and Branwen with him, and they went from Aber Menei with thirteen ships, and came to Ireland. And in Ireland was there great joy because of their coming. And not one great man or noble lady visited Branwen unto whom she gave not either a clasp, or a ring, or a royal jewel to keep, such as it was honourable to be seen departing with. And in these things she spent that year in much renown, and she passed her time pleasantly, enjoying honour and friendship. And in the meanwhile it chanced that she became pregnant, and in due time a son was born unto her, and the name that they gave him was Gwern the son of Matholwch, and they put the boy out to be foster-nursed, in a place where were the best men of Ireland.

And behold in the second year a tumult arose in Ireland, on account of the insult which Matholwch had received in Cambria, and the payment made him for his horses. And his foster-brothers, and such as were nearest unto him, blamed him openly for that matter. And he might have no peace by reason of the tumult until they should revenge upon him this disgrace. And the vengeance which they took was to drive away Branwen from the same chamber with him, and to make her cook for the Court; and they caused the butcher after he had cut up the meat to come to her and give her every day a blow on the ear, and such they made her punishment.

"Verily, lord," said his men to Matholwch, "forbid now the ships and the ferry boats and the coracles, that they go not into Cambria, and such as come over from Cambria hither, imprison them that they go not back for this thing to be known there." And he did so; and it was thus for not less than three years.

And Branwen reared a starling in the cover of the kneading trough, and she taught it to speak, and she taught the bird what manner of man her brother was. And she wrote a letter of her woes, and the despite with which she was treated, and she bound the letter to the root of the bird's wing, and sent it towards Britain. And the bird came to this island, and one day it found Bendigeid Vran at Caer Seiont in Arvon, conferring there, and it alighted upon his shoulder and ruffled its feathers, so that the letter was seen, and they knew that the bird had been reared in a domestic manner.

Then Bendigeid Vran took the letter and looked upon it. And when he had read the letter he grieved exceedingly at the tidings of Branwen's woes. And immediately he began sending messengers to summon the island together. And he caused sevenscore and four countries to come unto him, and he complained to them himself of the grief that his sister endured. So they took counsel. And in the council they resolved to go to Ireland, and to leave seven men as princes here, and Caradawc, the son of Bran, as the chief of them, and their seven knights. In Edeyrnion were these men left. And for this reason were the seven knights placed in the town. Now the names of these seven men were, Caradawc the son of Bran, and Heveydd Hir, and Unic Glew Ysgwyd, and Iddic the son of Anarawc Gwalltgrwn, and Fodor the son of Ervyll, and Gwlch Minascwrn, and Llassar the son of Llaesar Llaesgygwyd, and Pendaran Dyved as a young page with them. And these abode as seven ministers to take charge of this island; and Caradawc the son of Bran was the chief amongst them.

Bendigeid Vran, with the host of which we spoke, sailed towards Ireland, and it was not far across the sea, and he came to shoal water. It was caused by two rivers; the Lli and the Archan were they called; and the nations covered the sea. Then he proceeded with what provisions he had on his own back, and approached the shore of Ireland.

Now the swineherds of Matholwch were upon the seashore, and they came to Matholwch. "Lord," said they, "greeting be unto thee." "Heaven protect you," said he, "have you any news?" "Lord," said they, "we have marvellous news, a wood have we seen upon the sea, in a place where we never yet saw a single tree." "This is indeed a marvel," said he; "saw you aught else?" "We saw, lord," said they, "a vast mountain beside the wood, which moved, and there was a lofty ridge on the top of the mountain, and a lake on each side of the ridge. And the wood, and the mountain, and all these things moved." "Verily," said he, "there is none who can know aught concerning this, unless it be Branwen."

Messengers then went unto Branwen. "Lady," said they, "what thinkest thou that this is?" "The men of the Island of the Mighty, who have come hither on hearing of my ill-treatment and my woes." "What is the forest that is seen upon the sea?" asked they. "The yards and the masts of ships," she answered. "Alas," said they, "what is the mountain that is seen by the side of the ships?" "Bendigeid Vran, my brother," she replied, "coming to shoal water; there is no ship that can contain him in it." "What is the lofty ridge with the lake on each side thereof?" "On looking towards this island he is wroth, and his two eyes, one on each side of his nose, are the two lakes beside the ridge."

The warriors and the chief men of Ireland were brought together in haste, and they took counsel. "Lord," said the nobles unto Matholwch, "there is no other counsel than to retreat over the Linon (a river which is in Ireland), and to keep the river between thee and him, and to break down the bridge that is across the river, for there is a loadstone at the bottom of the river that neither ship nor vessel can pass over." So they retreated across the river, and broke down the bridge.

Bendigeid Vran came to land, and the fleet with him by the bank of the river. "Lord," said his chieftains, "knowest thou the nature of this river, that nothing can go across it, and there is no bridge over it?" "What," said they, "is thy counsel concerning a bridge?" "There is none," said he, "except that he who will be chief, let him be a bridge. I will be so," said he. And then was that saying first uttered, and it is still used as a proverb. And when he had lain down across the river, hurdles were placed upon him, and the host passed over thereby.

And as he rose up, behold the messengers of Matholwch came to him, and saluted him, and gave him greeting in the name of Matholwch, his kinsman, and showed how that of his goodwill he had merited of him nothing but good. "For Matholwch has given the kingdom of Ireland to Gwern the son of Matholwch, thy nephew and thy sister's son. And this he places before thee, as a compensation for the wrong and despite that has been done unto Branwen. And Matholwch shall be maintained wheresoever thou wilt, either here or in the Island of the Mighty." Said Bendigeid Vran, "Shall not I myself have the kingdom? Then peradventure I may take counsel concerning your message. From this time until then no other answer will you get from me." "Verily," said they, "the best message that we receive for thee, we will convey it unto thee, and do thou await our message unto him." "I will wait," answered he, "and do you return quickly."

The messengers set forth and came to Matholwch. "Lord," said they, "prepare a better message for Bendigeid Vran. He would not listen at all to the message that we bore him." "My friends," said Matholwch, "what may be your counsel?" "Lord," said they, "there is no other counsel than this alone. He was never known to be within a house, make therefore a house that will contain him and the men of the Island of the Mighty on the one side, and thyself and thy host on the other; and give over thy kingdom to his will, and do him homage. So by reason of the honour thou doest him in making him a house, whereas he never before had a house to contain him, he will make peace with thee." So the messengers went back to Bendigeid Vran, bearing him this message.

And he took counsel, and in the council it was resolved that he should accept this, and this was all done by the advice of Branwen, and lest the country should be destroyed. And this peace was made, and the house was built both vast and strong. But the Irish planned a crafty device, and the craft was that they should put brackets on each side of the hundred pillars that were in the house, and should place a leathern bag on each bracket, and an armed man in every one of them. Then Evnissyen came in before the host of the Island of the Mighty, and scanned the house with fierce and savage looks, and descried the leathern bags which were around the pillars. "What is in this bag?" asked he of one of the Irish. "Meal, good soul," said he. And Evnissyen felt about it until he came to the man's head, and he squeezed the head until he felt his fingers meet together in the brain through the bone. And he left that one and put his hand upon another, and asked what was therein. "Meal," said the Irishman. So he did the like unto every one of them, until he had not left alive, of all the two hundred men, save one only; and when he came to him, he asked what was there. "Meal, good soul," said the Irishman. And he felt about until he felt the head, and he squeezed that head as he had done the others. And, albeit he found that the head of this one was armed, he left him not until he had killed him. And then he sang an Englyn: —

"There is in this bag a different sort of meal,
The ready combatant, when the assault is made
By his fellow-warriors, prepared for battle."

Thereupon came the hosts unto the house. The men of the Island of Ireland entered the house on the one side, and the men of the Island of the Mighty on the other. And as soon as they had sat down there was concord between them; and the sovereignty was conferred upon the boy. When the peace was concluded, Bendigeid Vran called the boy unto him, and from Bendigeid Vran the boy went unto Manawyddan, and he was beloved by all that beheld him. And from Manawyddan the boy was called by Nissyen the son of Eurosswydd, and the boy went unto him lovingly. "Wherefore," said Evnissyen, "comes not my nephew the son of my sister unto me? Though he were not king of Ireland, yet willingly would I fondle the boy." "Cheerfully let him go to thee," said Bendigeid Vran, and the boy went unto him cheerfully. "By my confession to Heaven," said Evnissyen in his heart, "unthought of by the household is the slaughter that I will this instant commit."

Then he arose and took up the boy by the feet, and before any one in the house could seize hold of him, he thrust the boy headlong into the blazing fire. And when Branwen saw her son burning in the fire, she strove to leap into the fire also, from the place where she sat between her two brothers. But Bendigeid Vran grasped her with one hand, and his shield with the other. Then they all hurried about the house, and never was there made so great a tumult by any host in one house as was made by them, as each man armed himself. Then said Morddwydtyllyon, "The gadflies of Morddwydtyllyon's Cow!" And while they all sought their arms, Bendigeid Vran supported Branwen between his shield and his shoulder.

Then the Irish kindled a fire under the cauldron of renovation, and they cast the dead bodies into the cauldron until it was full, and the next day they came forth fighting-men as good as before, except that they were not able to speak. Then when Evnissyen saw the dead bodies of the men of the Island of the Mighty nowhere resuscitated, he said in his heart, "Alas! woe is me, that I should have been the cause of bringing the men of the Island of the Mighty into so great a strait. Evil betide me if I find not a deliverance therefrom." And he cast himself among the dead bodies of the Irish, and two unshod Irishmen came to him, and, taking him to be one of the Irish, flung him into the cauldron. And he stretched himself out in the cauldron, so that he rent the cauldron into four pieces, and burst his own heart also.

In consequence of that the men of the Island of the Mighty obtained such success as they had; but they were not victorious, for only seven men of them all escaped, and Bendigeid Vran himself was wounded in the foot with a poisoned dart. Now the seven men that escaped were Pryderi, Manawyddan, Gluneu Eil Taran, Taliesin, Ynawc, Grudyen the son of Muryel, and Heilyn the son of Gwynn Hen.

And Bendigeid Vran commanded them that they should cut off his head. "And take you my head," said he, "and bear it even unto the White Mount, in London, and bury it there, with the face towards France. And a long time will you be upon the road. In Harlech you will be feasting seven years, the birds of Rhiannon singing unto you the while. And all that time the head will be to you as pleasant company as it ever was when on my body. And at Gwales in Penvro you will be fourscore years, and you may remain there, and the head with you uncorrupted, until you open the door that looks towards Aber Henvelen, and towards Cornwall. And after you have opened that door, there you may no longer tarry, set forth then to London to bury the head, and go straight forward."

So they cut off his head, and these seven went forward therewith. And Branwen was the eighth with them, and they came to land at Aber Alaw, in Talebolyon, and they sat down to rest. And Branwen looked towards Ireland and towards the Island of the Mighty, to see if she could descry them. "Alas," said she, "woe is me that I was ever born; two islands have been destroyed because of me!" Then she uttered a loud groan, and there broke her heart. And they made her a foursided grave, and buried her upon the banks of the Alaw.

Then the seven men journeyed forward towards Harlech, bearing the head with them; and as they went, behold there met them a multitude of men and of women. "Have you any tidings?" asked Manawyddan. "We have none," said they, "save that Caswallawn the son of Beli has conquered the Island of the Mighty, and is crowned king in London." "What has become," said they, "of Caradawc the son of Bran, and the seven men who were left with him in this island?" "Caswallawn came upon them, and slew six of the men, and Caradawc's heart broke for grief thereof; for he could see the sword that slew the men, but knew not who it was that wielded it. Caswallawn had flung upon him the Veil of Illusion, so that no one could see him slay the men, but the sword only could they see. And it liked him not to slay Caradawc, because he was his nephew, the son of his cousin. And now he was the third whose heart had broke through grief. Pendaran Dyved, who had remained as a young page with these men, escaped into the wood," said they.

Then they went on to Harlech, and there stopped to rest, and they provided meat and liquor, and sat down to eat and to drink. And there came three birds, and began singing unto them a certain song, and all the songs they had ever heard were unpleasant compared thereto; and the birds seemed to them to be at a great distance from them over the sea, yet they appeared as distinct as if they were close by, and at this repast they continued seven years.

And at the close of the seventh year they went forth to Gwales in Penvro. And there they found a fair and regal spot overlooking the ocean; and a spacious hall was therein. And they went into the hall, and two of its doors were open, but the third door was closed, that which looked towards Cornwall. "See, yonder," said Manawyddan, "is the door that we may not open." And that night they regaled themselves and were joyful. And of all they had seen of food laid before them, and of all they had heard of, they remembered nothing; neither of that, nor of any sorrow whatsoever. And there they remained fourscore years, unconscious of having ever spent a time more joyous and mirthful. And they were not more weary than when first they came, neither did they, any of them, know the time they had been there. And it was not more irksome to them having the head with them, than if Bendigeid Vran had been with them himself. And because of these fourscore years, it was called "the Entertaining of the noble Head." The entertaining of Branwen and Matholwch was in the time that they went to Ireland.

One day said Heilyn the son of Gwynn, "Evil betide me, if I do not open the door to know if that is true which is said concerning it." So he opened the door and looked towards Cornwall and Aber Henvelen. And when they had looked, they were as conscious of all the evils they had ever sustained, and of all the friends and companions they had lost, and of all the misery that had befallen them, as if all had happened in that very spot; and especially of the fate of their lord. And because of their perturbation they could not rest, but journeyed forth with the head towards London. And they buried the head in the White Mount, and when it was buried, this was the third goodly concealment; and it was the third ill-fated disclosure when it was disinterred, inasmuch as no invasion from across the sea came to this island while the head was in that concealment.

And thus is the story related of those who journeyed over from Ireland.

In Ireland none were left alive, except five pregnant women in a cave in the Irish wilderness; and to these five women in the same night were born five sons, whom they nursed until they became grown-up youths. And they thought about wives, and they at the same time desired to possess them, and each took a wife of the mothers of their companions, and they governed the country and peopled it.

And these five divided it amongst them, and because of this partition are the five divisions of Ireland still so termed. And they examined the land where the battles had taken place, and they found gold and silver until they became wealthy.

And thus ends this portion of the Mabinogi, concerning the blow given to Branwen, which was the third unhappy blow of this island; and concerning the entertainment of Bran, when the hosts of sevenscore countries and ten went over to Ireland to revenge the blow given to Branwen; and concerning the seven years' banquet in Harlech, and the singing of the birds of Rhiannon, and the sojourning of the head for the space of fourscore years.

MANAWYDDAN THE SON OF LLYR

HERE IS THE THIRD PORTION OF THE MABINOGI

WHEN the seven men of whom we spoke above had buried the head of Bendigeid Vran, in the White Mount in London, with its face towards France; Manawyddan gazed upon the town of London, and upon his companions, and heaved a great sigh; and much grief and heaviness came upon him. "Alas, Almighty Heaven, woe is me," he exclaimed, "there is none save myself without a resting-place this night." "Lord," said Pryderi, "be not so sorrowful. Thy cousin is king of the Island of the Mighty, and though he should do thee wrong, thou hast never been a claimant of land or possessions. Thou art the third disinherited prince." "Yea," answered he, "but although this man is my cousin, it grieveth me to see any one in the place of my brother Bendigeid Vran, neither can I be happy in the same dwelling with him." "Wilt thou follow the counsel of another?" said Pryderi. "I stand in need of counsel," he answered, "and what may that counsel be?" "Seven Cantrevs remain unto me," said Pryderi, "wherein Rhiannon my mother dwells. I will bestow her upon thee and the seven Cantrevs with her, and though thou hadst no possessions but those Cantrevs only, thou couldst not have seven Cantrevs fairer than they. Kicva, the daughter of Gwynn Gloyw, is my wife, and since the inheritance of the Cantrevs belongs to me, do thou and Rhiannon enjoy them, and if thou ever desire any possessions thou wilt take these." "I do not, Chieftain," said he; "Heaven reward thee for thy friendship." "I would show thee the best friendship in the world if thou wouldst let me." "I will, my friend," said he, "and Heaven reward thee. I will go with thee to seek Rhiannon and to look at thy possessions." "Thou wilt do well," he answered. "And I believe that thou didst never hear a lady discourse better than she, and when she was in her prime none was ever fairer. Even now her aspect is not uncomely."

They set forth, and, however long the journey, they came at length to Dyved, and a feast was prepared for them against their coming to Narberth, which Rhiannon and Kicva had provided. Then began Manawyddan and Rhiannon to sit and to talk together, and from their discourse his mind and his thoughts became warmed towards her, and he thought in his heart he had never beheld any lady more fulfilled of grace and beauty than she. "Pryderi," said he, "I will that it be as thou didst say." "What saying was that?" asked Rhiannon. "Lady," said Pryderi, "I did offer thee as a wife to Manawyddan the son of Llyr." "By that will I gladly abide," said Rhiannon. "Right glad am I also," said Manawyddan; "may Heaven reward him who hath shown unto me friendship so perfect as this."

And before the feast was over she became his bride. Said Pryderi, "Tarry ye here the rest of the feast, and I will go into Lloegyr to tender my homage unto Caswallawn the son of Beli." "Lord," said Rhiannon, "Caswallawn is in Kent, thou mayest therefore tarry at the feast, and wait until he shall be nearer." "We will wait," he answered. So they finished the feast. And they began to make the circuit of Dyved, and to hunt, and to take their pleasure. And as they went through the country, they had never seen lands more pleasant to live in, nor better hunting grounds, nor greater plenty of honey and fish. And such was the friendship between those four, that they would not be parted from each other by night nor by day.

And in the midst of all this he went to Caswallawn at Oxford, and tendered his homage; and honourable was his reception there, and highly was he praised for offering his homage.

And after his return, Pryderi and Manawyddan feasted and took their ease and pleasure. And they began a feast at Narberth, for it was the chief palace; and there originated all honour. And when they had ended the first meal that night, while those who served them ate, they arose and went forth, and proceeded all four to the Gorsedd of Narberth, and their retinue with them. And as they sat thus, behold, a peal of thunder, and with the violence of the thunderstorm, lo there came a fall of mist, so thick that not one of them could see the other. And after the mist it became light all around. And when they looked towards the place where they were wont to see cattle, and herds, and dwellings, they saw nothing now, neither house, nor beast, nor smoke, nor fire, nor man, nor dwelling; but the houses of the Court empty, and desert, and uninhabited, without either man or beast within them. And truly all their companions were lost to them, without their knowing aught of what had befallen them, save those four only.

"In the name of Heaven," cried Manawyddan, "where are they of the Court, and all my host beside these? Let us go and see." So they came into the hall, and there was no man; and they went on to the castle, and to the sleeping-place, and they saw none; and in the mead-cellar and in the kitchen there was nought but desolation. So they four feasted, and hunted, and took their pleasure. Then they began to go through the land and all the possessions that they had, and they visited the houses and dwellings, and found nothing but wild beasts. And when they had consumed their feast and all their provisions, they fed upon the prey they killed in hunting, and the honey of the wild swarms. And thus they passed the first year pleasantly, and the second; but at the last they began to be weary.

"Verily," said Manawyddan, "we must not bide thus. Let us go into Lloegyr, and seek some craft whereby we may gain our support." So they went into Lloegyr, and came as far as Hereford. And they betook themselves to making saddles. And Manawyddan began to make housings, and he gilded and coloured them with blue enamel, in the manner that he had seen it done by Llasar Llaesgywydd. And he made the blue enamel as it was made by the other man. And therefore is it still called Calch Lasar [blue enamel], because Llasar Llaesgywydd had wrought it.

And as long as that workmanship could be had of Manawyddan, neither saddle nor housing was bought of a saddler throughout all Hereford; till at length every one of the saddlers perceived that they were losing much of their gain, and that no man bought of them, but him who could not get what he sought from Manawyddan. Then they assembled together, and agreed to slay him and his companions.

Now they received warning of this, and took counsel whether they should leave the city. "By Heaven," said Pryderi, "it is not my counsel that we should quit the town, but that we should slay these boors." "Not so," said Manawyddan, "for if we fight with them, we shall have evil fame, and shall be put in prison. It were better for us to go to another town to maintain ourselves." So they four went to another city.

"What craft shall we take?" said Pryderi. "We will make shields," said Manawyddan. "Do we know anything about that craft?" said Pryderi. "We will try," answered he. There they began to make shields, and fashioned them after the shape of the good shields they had seen; and they enamelled them, as they had done the saddles. And they prospered in that place, so that not a shield was asked for in the whole town, but such as was had of them. Rapid therefore was their work, and numberless were the shields they made. But at last they were marked by the craftsmen, who came together in haste, and their fellow-townsmen with them, and agreed that they should seek to slay them. But they received warning, and heard how the men had resolved on their destruction. "Pryderi," said Manawyddan, "these men desire to slay us." "Let us not endure this from these boors, but let us rather fall upon them and slay them." "Not so," he answered; "Caswallawn and his men will hear of it, and we shall be undone. Let us go to another town." So to another town they went.

"What craft shall we take?" said Manawyddan. "Whatsoever thou wilt that we know," said Pryderi. "Not so," he replied, "but let us take to making shoes, for there is not courage enough among cordwainers either to fight with us or to molest us." "I know nothing thereof," said Pryderi. "But I know," answered Manawyddan; "and I will teach thee to stitch. We will not attempt to dress the leather, but we will buy it ready dressed and will make the shoes from it."

So he began by buying the best cordwal that could be had in the town, and none other would he buy except the leather for the soles; and he associated himself with the best goldsmith in the town, and caused him to make clasps for the shoes, and to gild the clasps, and he marked how it was done until he learnt the method. And therefore was he called one of the three makers of Gold Shoes; and, when they could be had from him, not a shoe nor hose was bought of any of the cordwainers in the town. But when the cordwainers perceived that their gains were failing (for as Manawyddan shaped the work, so Pryderi stitched it), they came together and took counsel, and agreed that they would slay them.

"Pryderi," said Manawyddan, "these men are minded to slay us." "Wherefore should we bear this from the boorish thieves?" said Pryderi. "Rather let us slay them all." "Not so," said Manawyddan, "we will not slay them, neither will we remain in Lloegyr any longer. Let us set forth to Dyved and go to see it."

So they journeyed along until they came to Dyved, and they went forward to Narberth. And there they kindled fire and supported themselves by hunting. And thus they spent a month. And they gathered their dogs around them, and tarried there one year.

And one morning Pryderi and Manawyddan rose up to hunt, and they ranged their dogs and went forth from the palace. And some of the dogs ran before them and came to a small bush which was near at hand; but as soon as they were come to the bush, they hastily drew back and returned to the men, their hair bristling up greatly. "Let us go near to the bush," said Pryderi, "and see what is in it." And as they came near, behold, a wild boar of a pure white colour rose up from the bush. Then the dogs, being set on by the men, rushed towards him; but he left the bush and fell back a little way from the men, and made a stand against the dogs without retreating from them, until the men had come near. And when the men came up, he fell back a second time, and betook him to flight. Then they pursued the boar until they beheld a vast and lofty castle, all newly built, in a place where they had never before seen either stone or building. And the boar ran swiftly into the castle and the dogs after him. Now when the boar and the dogs had gone into the castle, they began to wonder at finding a castle in a place where they had never before seen any building whatsoever. And from the top of the Gorsedd they looked and listened for the dogs. But so long as they were there they heard not one of the dogs nor aught concerning them.

"Lord," said Pryderi, "I will go into the castle to get tidings of the dogs." "Truly," he replied, "thou wouldst be unwise to go into this castle, which thou hast never seen till now. If thou wouldst follow my counsel, thou wouldst not enter therein. Whosoever has cast a spell over this land has caused this castle to be here." "Of a truth," answered Pryderi, "I cannot thus give up my dogs." And for all the counsel that Manawyddan gave him, yet to the castle he went.

When he came within the castle, neither man nor beast, nor boar nor dogs, nor house nor dwelling saw he within it. But in the centre of the castle floor he beheld a fountain with marble work around it, and on the margin of the fountain a golden bowl upon a marble slab, and chains hanging from the air, to which he saw no end.

And he was greatly pleased with the beauty of the gold, and with the rich workmanship of the bowl, and he went up to the bowl, and laid hold of it. And when he had taken hold of it his hands stuck to the bowl, and his feet to the slab on which the bowl was placed, and all his joyousness forsook him, so that he could not utter a word. And thus he stood.

And Manawyddan waited for him till near the close of the day. And late in the evening, being certain that he should have no tidings of Pryderi or of the dogs, he went back to the palace. And as he entered, Rhiannon looked at him. "Where," said she, "are thy companion and thy dogs?" "Behold," he answered, "the adventure that has befallen me."

And he related it all unto her. "An evil companion hast thou been," said Rhiannon, "and a good companion hast thou lost." And with that word she went out, and proceeded towards the castle according to the direction which he gave her. The gate of the castle she found open. She was nothing daunted, and she went in. And as she went in, she perceived Pryderi laying hold of the bowl, and she went towards him. "Oh, my lord," said she, "what dost thou do here?" And she took hold of the bowl with him; and as she did so her hands became fast to the bowl, and her feet to the slab, and she was not able to utter a word. And with that, as it became night, lo, there came thunder upon them, and a fall of mist, and thereupon the castle vanished, and they with it.

When Kicva the daughter of Gwynn Gloyw saw that there was no one in the palace but herself and Manawyddan, she sorrowed so that she cared not whether she lived or died. And Manawyddan saw this. "Thou art in the wrong," said he, "if through fear of me thou grievest thus. I call Heaven to witness that thou hast never seen friendship more pure than that which I will bear thee, as long as Heaven will that thou shouldst be thus. I declare to thee that were I in the dawn of youth I would keep my faith unto Pryderi, and unto thee also will I keep it. Be there no fear upon thee, therefore," said he, "for Heaven is my witness that thou shalt meet with all the friendship thou canst wish, and that it is in my power to show thee, as long as it shall please Heaven to continue us in this grief and woe." "Heaven reward thee," she said, "and that is what I deemed of thee." And the damsel thereupon took courage and was glad.

"Truly, lady," said Manawyddan, "it is not fitting for us to stay here, we have lost our dogs, and we cannot get food. Let us go into Lloegyr; it is easiest for us to find support there." "Gladly, lord," said she, "we will do so." And they set forth together to Lloegyr.

"Lord," said she, "what craft wilt thou follow? Take up one that is seemly." "None other will I take," answered he, "save that of making shoes, as I did formerly." "Lord," said she, "such a craft becomes not a man so nobly born as thou." "By that however will I abide," said he.

So he began his craft, and he made all his work of the finest leather he could get in the town, and, as he had done at the other place, he caused gilded clasps to be made for the shoes. And except himself all the cordwainers in the town were idle, and without work. For as long as they could be had from him, neither shoes nor hose were bought elsewhere. And thus they tarried there a year, until the cordwainers became envious, and took counsel concerning him. And he had warning thereof, and it was told him how the cordwainers had agreed together to slay him.

"Lord," said Kicva, "wherefore should this be borne from these boors?" "Nay," said he, "we will go back unto Dyved." So towards Dyved they set forth.

Now Manawyddan, when he set out to return to Dyved, took with him a burden of wheat. And he proceeded towards Narberth, and there he dwelt. And never was he better pleased than when he saw Narberth again, and the lands where he had been wont to hunt with Pryderi and with Rhiannon. And he accustomed himself to fish, and to hunt the deer in their covert. And then he began to prepare some ground, and he sowed a croft, and a second, and a third. And no wheat in the world ever sprung up better. And the three crofts prospered with perfect growth, and no man ever saw fairer wheat than it.

And thus passed the seasons of the year until the harvest came. And he went to look at one of his crofts, and behold it was ripe. "I will reap this to-morrow," said he. And that night he went back to Narberth, and on the morrow in the grey dawn he went to reap the croft, and when he came there he found nothing but the bare straw. Every one of the ears of the wheat was cut from off the stalk, and all the ears carried entirely away, and nothing but the straw left. And at this he marvelled greatly.

Then he went to look at another croft, and behold that also was ripe. "Verily," said he, "this will I reap to-morrow." And on the morrow he came with the intent to reap it, and when he came there he found nothing but the bare straw. "Oh, gracious Heaven," he exclaimed, "I know that whosoever has begun my ruin is completing it, and has also destroyed the country with me."

Then he went to look at the third croft, and when he came there, finer wheat had there never been seen, and this also was ripe. "Evil betide me," said he, "if I watch not here to-night. Whoever carried off the other corn will come in like manner to take this. And I will know who it is." So he took his arms, and began to watch the croft. And he told Kicva all that had befallen. "Verily," said she, "what thinkest thou to do?" "I will watch the croft to-night," said he.

And he went to watch the croft. And at midnight, lo, there arose the loudest tumult in the world. And he looked, and behold the mightiest host of mice in the world, which could neither be numbered nor measured. And he knew not what it was until the mice had made their way into the croft, and each of them climbing up the straw and bending it down with its weight, had cut off one of the ears of wheat, and had carried it away, leaving there the stalk, and he saw not a single stalk there that had not a mouse to it. And they all took their way, carrying the ears with them.

In wrath and anger did he rush upon the mice, but he could no more come up with them than if they had been gnats, or birds in the air, except one only, which though it was but sluggish, went so fast that a man on foot could scarce overtake it. And after this one he went, and he caught it and put it in his glove, and tied up the opening of the glove with a string, and kept it with him, and returned to the palace. Then he came to the hall where Kicva was, and he lighted a fire, and hung the glove by the string upon a peg. "What hast thou there, lord?" said Kicva. "A thief," said he, "that I found robbing me." "What kind of thief may it be, lord, that thou couldst put into thy glove?" said she. "Behold I will tell thee," he answered. Then he showed her how his fields had been wasted and destroyed, and how the mice came to the last of the fields in his sight. "And one of them was less nimble than the rest, and is now in my glove; to-morrow I will hang it, and before Heaven, if I had them, I would hang them all." "My lord," said she, "this is marvellous; but yet it would be unseemly for a man of dignity like thee to be hanging such a reptile as this. And if thou doest right, thou wilt not meddle with the creature, but wilt let it go." "Woe betide me," said he, "if I would not hang them all could I catch them, and such as I have I will hang." "Verily, lord," said she, "there is no reason that I should succour this reptile, except to prevent discredit unto thee. Do therefore, lord, as thou wilt." "If I knew of any cause in the world wherefore thou shouldst succour it, I would take thy counsel concerning it," said Manawyddan, "but as I know of none, lady, I am minded to destroy it." "Do so willingly then," said she.

And then he went to the Gorsedd of Narberth, taking the mouse with him. And he set up two forks on the highest part of the Gorsedd. And while he was doing this, behold he saw a scholar coming towards him, in old and poor and tattered garments. And it was now seven years since he had seen in that place either man or beast, except those four persons who had remained together until two of them were lost.

"My lord," said the scholar, "good day to thee." "Heaven prosper thee, and my greeting be unto thee. And whence dost thou come, scholar?" asked he. "I come, lord, from singing in Lloegyr; and wherefore dost thou inquire?" "Because for the last seven years," answered he, "I have seen no man here save four secluded persons, and thyself this moment." "Truly, lord," said he, "I go through this land unto mine own. And what work art thou upon, lord?" "I am hanging a thief that I caught robbing me," said he. "What manner of thief is that?" asked the scholar. "I see a creature in thy hand like unto a mouse, and ill does it become a man of rank equal to thine to touch a reptile such as this. Let it go forth free." "I will not let it go free, by Heaven," said he; "I caught it robbing me, and the doom of a thief will I inflict upon it, and I will hang it." "Lord," said he, "rather than see a man of rank equal to thine at such a work as this, I would give thee a pound which I have received as alms, to let the reptile go forth free." "I will not let it go free," said he, "by Heaven, neither will I sell it." "As thou wilt, lord," he answered; "except that I would not see a man of rank equal to thine touching such a reptile, I care nought." And the scholar went his way.

And as he was placing the crossbeam upon the two forks, behold a priest came towards him upon a horse covered with trappings. "Good day to thee, lord," said he. "Heaven prosper thee," said Manawyddan; "thy blessing." "The blessing of Heaven be upon thee. And what, lord, art thou doing?" "I am hanging a thief that I caught robbing me," said he. "What manner of thief, lord?" asked he. "A creature," he answered, "in form of a mouse. It has been robbing me, and I am inflicting upon it the doom of a thief." "Lord," said he, "rather than see thee touch this reptile, I would purchase its freedom." "By my confession to Heaven, neither will I sell it nor set it free." "It is true, lord, that it is worth nothing to buy; but rather than see thee defile thyself by touching such a reptile as this, I will give thee three pounds to let it go." "I will not, by Heaven," said he, "take any price for it. As it ought, so shall it be hanged." "Willingly, lord, do thy good pleasure." And the priest went his way.

Then he noosed the string around the mouse's neck, and as he was about to draw it up, behold, he saw a bishop's retinue with his sumpter-horses, and his attendants. And the bishop himself came towards him. And he stayed his work. "Lord bishop," said he, "thy blessing." "Heaven's blessing be unto thee," said he; "what work art thou upon?" "Hanging a thief that I caught robbing me," said he. "Is not that a mouse that I see in thy hand?" "Yes," answered he. "And she has robbed me." "Aye," said he, "since I have come at the doom of this reptile, I will ransom it of thee. I will give thee seven pounds for it, and that rather than see a man of rank equal to thine destroying so vile a reptile as this. Let it loose and thou shalt have the money." "I declare to Heaven that I will not set it loose." "If thou wilt not loose it for this, I will give thee four-and-twenty pounds of ready money to set it free." "I will not set it free, by Heaven, for as much again," said he. "If thou wilt not set it free for this, I will give thee all the horses that thou seest in this plain, and the seven loads of baggage, and the seven horses that they are upon." "By Heaven, I will not," he replied. "Since for this thou wilt not, do so at what price soever thou wilt." "I will do so," said he. "I will that Rhiannon and Pryderi be free," said he. "That thou shalt have," he answered. "Not yet will I loose the mouse, by Heaven." "What then wouldst thou?" "That the charm and the illusion be removed from the seven Cantrevs of Dyved." "This shalt thou have also; set therefore the mouse free." "I will not set it free, by Heaven," said he. "I will know who the mouse may be." "She is my wife." "Even though she be, I will not set her free. Wherefore came she to me?" "To despoil thee," he answered. "I am Llwyd the son of Kilcoed, and I cast the charm over the seven Cantrevs of Dyved. And it was to avenge Gwawl the son of Clud, from the friendship I had towards him, that I cast the charm. And upon Pryderi did I revenge Gwawl the son of Clud, for the game of Badger in the Bag, that Pwyll Pen Annwvyn played upon him, which he did unadvisedly in the Court of Heveydd Hên. And when it was known that thou wast come to dwell in the land, my household came and besought me to transform them into mice, that they might destroy thy corn. And it was my own household that went the first night. And the second night also they went, and they destroyed thy two crofts. And the third night came unto me my wife and the ladies of the Court, and besought me to transform them. And I transformed them. Now she is pregnant. And had she not been pregnant thou wouldst not have been able to overtake her; but since this has taken place, and she has been caught, I will restore thee Pryderi and Rhiannon; and I will take the charm and illusion from off Dyved. I have now told thee who she is. Set her therefore free." "I will not set her free, by Heaven," said he. "What wilt thou more?" he asked. "I will that there be no more charm upon the seven Cantrevs of Dyved, and that none shall be put upon it henceforth." "This thou shalt have," said he. "Now set her free." "I will not, by my faith," he answered. "What wilt thou furthermore?" asked he. "Behold," said he, "this will I have; that vengeance be never taken for this, either upon Pryderi or Rhiannon, or upon me." "All this shalt thou have. And truly thou hast done wisely in asking this. Upon thy head would have lighted all this trouble." "Yea," said he, "for fear thereof was it, that I required this." "Set now my wife at liberty." "I will not, by Heaven," said he, "until I see Pryderi and Rhiannon with me free." "Behold, here they come," he answered.

And thereupon behold Pryderi and Rhiannon. And he rose up to meet them, and greeted them, and sat down beside them. "Ah, Chieftain, set now my wife at liberty," said the bishop. "Hast thou not received all thou didst ask?" "I will release her gladly," said he. And thereupon he set her free.

Then Llwyd struck her with a magic wand, and she was changed back into a young woman, the fairest ever seen.

"Look around upon thy land," said he, "and then thou wilt see it all tilled and peopled, as it was in its best state." And he rose up and looked forth. And when he looked he saw all the lands tilled, and full of herds and dwellings. "What bondage," he inquired, "has there been upon Pryderi and Rhiannon?" "Pryderi has had the knockers of the gate of my palace about his neck, and Rhiannon has had the collars of the asses, after they have been carrying hay, about her neck."

And such had been their bondage.

And by reason of this bondage is this story called the Mabinogi of Mynnweir and Mynord.

And thus ends this portion of the Mabinogi.

MATH THE SON OF MATHONWY

THIS IS THE FOURTH PORTION OF THE MABINOGI

MATH the son of Mathonwy was lord over Gwynedd, and Pryderi the son of Pwyll was lord over the one-and-twenty Cantrevs of the South; and these were the seven Cantrevs of Dyved, and the seven Cantrevs of Morganwc, the four Cantrevs of Ceredigiawn, and the three of Ystrad Tywi.

At that time, Math the son of Mathonwy could not exist unless his feet were in the lap of a maiden, except only when he was prevented by the tumult of war. Now the maiden who was with him was Goewin, the daughter of Pebin of Dôl Pebin, in Arvon, and she was the fairest maiden of her time who was known there.

And Math dwelt always at Caer Dathyl, in Arvon, and was not able to go the circuit of the land, but Gilvaethwy the son of Don, and Eneyd the son of Don, his nephews, the sons of his sisters, with his household, went the circuit of the land in his stead.

Now the maiden was with Math continually, and Gilvaethwy the son of Don set his affections upon her, and loved her so that he knew not what he should do because of her, and therefrom behold his hue, and his aspect, and his spirits changed for love of her, so that it was not easy to know him.

One day his brother Gwydion gazed steadfastly upon him. "Youth," said he, "what aileth thee?" "Why," replied he, "what seest thou in me?" "I see," said he, "that thou hast lost thy aspect and thy hue; what, therefore, aileth thee?" "My lord brother," he answered, "that which aileth me, it will not profit me that I should own to any." "What may it be, my soul?" said he. "Thou knowest," he said, "that Math the son of Mathonwy has this property, that if men whisper together, in a tone how low soever, if the wind meet it, it becomes known unto him." "Yes," said Gwydion, "hold now thy peace, I know thy intent, thou lovest Goewin."

When he found that his brother knew his intent, he gave the heaviest sigh in the world. "Be silent, my soul, and sigh not," he said. "It is not thereby that thou wilt succeed. I will cause," said he, "if it cannot be otherwise, the rising of Gwynedd, and Powys, and Deheubarth, to seek the maiden. Be thou of glad cheer therefore, and I will compass it."

So they went unto Math the son of Mathonwy. "Lord," said Gwydion, "I have heard that there have come to the South some beasts, such as were never known in this island before." "What are they called?" he asked. "Pigs, lord." "And what kind of animals are they?" "They are small animals, and their flesh is better than the flesh of oxen." "They are small, then?" "And they change their names. Swine are they now called." "Who owneth them?" "Pryderi the son of Pwyll; they were sent him from Annwvyn, by Arawn the king of Annwvyn, and still they keep that name, half hog, half pig." "Verily," asked he, "and by what means may they be obtained from him?" "I will go, lord, as one of twelve, in the guise of bards, to seek the swine." "But it may be that he will refuse you," said he. "My journey will not be evil, lord," said he; "I will not come back without the swine." "Gladly," said he, "go thou forward."

So he and Gilvaethwy went, and ten other men with them. And they came into Ceredigiawn, to the place that is now called Rhuddlan Teivi, where the palace of Pryderi was. In the guise of bards they came in, and they were received joyfully, and Gwydion was placed beside Pryderi that night.

"Of a truth," said Pryderi, "gladly would I have a tale from some of your men yonder." "Lord," said Gwydion, "we have a custom that the first night that we come to the Court of a great man, the chief of song recites. Gladly will I relate a tale." Now Gwydion was the best teller of tales in the world, and he diverted all the Court that night with pleasant discourse and with tales, so that he charmed every one in the Court, and it pleased Pryderi to talk with him.

And after this, "Lord," said he unto Pryderi, "were it more pleasing to thee, that another should discharge my errand unto thee, than that I should tell thee myself what it is?" "No," he answered, "ample speech hast thou." "Behold then, lord," said he, "my errand. It is to crave from thee the animals that were sent thee from Annwvyn." "Verily," he replied, "that were the easiest thing in the world to grant, were there not a covenant between me and my land concerning them. And the covenant is that they shall not go from me, until they have produced double their number in the land." "Lord," said he, "I can set thee free from those words, and this is the way I can do so; give me not the swine to-night, neither refuse them unto me, and to-morrow I will show thee an exchange for them."

And that night he and his fellows went unto their lodging, and they took counsel. "Ah, my men," said he, "we shall not have the swine for the asking." "Well," said they, "how may they be obtained?" "I will cause them to be obtained," said Gwydion.

Then he betook himself to his arts, and began to work a charm. And he caused twelve chargers to appear, and twelve black greyhounds, each of them white-breasted, and having upon them twelve collars and twelve leashes, such as no one that saw them could know to be other than gold. And upon the horses twelve saddles, and every part which should have been of iron was entirely of gold, and the bridles were of the same workmanship. And with the horses and the dogs he came to Pryderi.

"Good day unto thee, lord," said he. "Heaven prosper thee," said the other, "and greetings be unto thee." "Lord," said he, "behold here is a release for thee from the word which thou spakest last evening concerning the swine; that thou wouldst neither give nor sell them. Thou mayest exchange them for that which is better. And I will give these twelve horses, all caparisoned as they are, with their saddles and their bridles, and these twelve greyhounds, with their collars and their leashes as thou seest, and the twelve gilded shields that thou beholdest yonder." Now these he had formed of fungus. "Well," said he, "we will take counsel." And they consulted together, and determined to give the swine to Gwydion, and to take his horses and his dogs and his shields.

Then Gwydion and his men took their leave, and began to journey forth with the pigs. "Ah, my comrades," said Gwydion, "it is needful that we journey with speed. The illusion will not last but from the one hour to the same to-morrow."

And that night they journeyed as far as the upper part of Ceredigiawn, to the place which, from that cause, is called Mochdrev still. And the next day they took their course through Melenydd, and came that night to the town which is likewise for that reason called Mochdrev between Keri and Arwystli. And thence they journeyed forward; and that night they came as far as that Commot in Powys, which also upon account thereof is called Mochnant, and there tarried they that night. And they journeyed thence to the Cantrev of Rhos, and the place where they were that night is still called Mochdrev.

"My men," said Gwydion, "we must push forward to the fastnesses of Gwynedd with these animals, for there is a gathering of hosts in pursuit of us." So they journeyed on to the highest town of Arllechwedd, and there they made a sty for the swine, and therefore was the name of Creuwyryon given to that town. And after they had made the sty for the swine, they proceeded to Math the son of Mathonwy, at Caer Dathyl. And when they came there, the country was rising. "What news is there here?" asked Gwydion. "Pryderi is assembling one-and-twenty Cantrevs to pursue after you," answered they. "It is marvellous that you should have journeyed so slowly." "Where are the animals whereof you went in quest?" said Math. "They have had a sty made for them in the other Cantrev below," said Gwydion.

Thereupon, lo, they heard the trumpets and the host in the land, and they arrayed themselves and set forward and came to Penardd in Arvon.

And at night Gwydion the son of Don, and Gilvaethwy his brother, returned to Caer Dathyl; and Gilvaethwy took Math the son of Mathonwy's couch. And while he turned out the other damsels from the room discourteously, he made Goewin unwillingly remain.

And when they saw the day on the morrow, they went back unto the place where Math the son of Mathonwy was with his host; and when they came there, the warriors were taking counsel in what district they should await the coming of Pryderi, and the men of the South. So they went in to the council. And it was resolved to wait in the strongholds of Gwynedd, in Arvon. So within the two Maenors they took their stand, Maenor Penardd and Maenor Coed Alun. And there Pryderi attacked them, and there the combat took place. And great was the slaughter on both sides; but the men of the South were forced to flee. And they fled unto the place which is still called Nantcall. And thither did they follow them, and they made a vast slaughter of them there, so that they fled again as far as the place called Dol Pen Maen, and there they halted and sought to make peace.

And that he might have peace, Pryderi gave hostages, Gwrgi Gwastra gave he and three-and-twenty others, sons of nobles. And after this they journeyed in peace even unto Traeth Mawr; but as they went on together towards Melenryd, the men on foot could not be restrained from shooting. Pryderi dispatched unto Math an embassy to pray him to forbid his people, and to leave it between him and Gwydion the son of Don, for that he had caused all this. And the messengers came to Math. "Of a truth," said Math, "I call Heaven to witness, if it be pleasing unto Gwydion the son of Don, I will so leave it gladly. Never will I compel any to go to fight, but that we ourselves should do our utmost."

"Verily," said the messengers, "Pryderi saith that it were more fair that the man who did him this wrong should oppose his own body to his, and let his people remain unscathed." "I declare to Heaven, I will not ask the men of Gwynedd to fight because of me. If I am allowed to fight Pryderi myself, gladly will I oppose my body to his." And this answer they took back to Pryderi. "Truly," said Pryderi, "I shall require no one to demand my rights but myself."

Then these two came forth and armed themselves, and they fought. And by force of strength, and fierceness, and by the magic and charms of Gwydion, Pryderi was slain. And at Maen Tyriawc, above Melenryd, was he buried, and there is his grave.

And the men of the South set forth in sorrow towards their own land; nor is it a marvel that they should grieve, seeing that they had lost their lord, and many of their best warriors, and for the most part their horses and their arms.

The men of Gwynedd went back joyful and in triumph. "Lord," said Gwydion unto Math, "would it not be right for us to release the hostages of the men of the South, which they pledged unto us for peace? for we ought not to put them in prison." "Let them then be set free," saith Math. So that youth, and the other hostages that were with him, were set free to follow the men of the South.

Math himself went forward to Caer Dathyl. Gilvaethwy the son of Don, and they of the household that were with him, went to make the circuit of Gwynedd as they were wont, without coming to the Court. Math went into his chamber, and caused a place to be prepared for him whereon to recline, so that he might put his feet in the maiden's lap. "Lord," said Goewin, "seek now another to hold thy feet, for I am now a wife." "What meaneth this?" said he. "An attack, lord, was made unawares upon me; but I held not my peace, and there was no one in the Court who knew not of it. Now the attack was made by thy nephews, lord, the sons of thy sister, Gwydion the son of Don, and Gilvaethwy the son of Don; unto me they did wrong, and unto thee dishonour." "Verily," he exclaimed, "I will do to the utmost of my power concerning this matter. But first I will cause thee to have compensation, and then will I have amends made unto myself. As for thee, I will take thee to be my wife, and the possession of my dominions will I give unto thy hands."

And Gwydion and Gilvaethwy came not near the Court, but stayed in the confines of the land until it was forbidden to give them meat and drink. At first they came not near unto Math, but at the last they came.

"Lord," said they, "good day to thee." "Well," said he, "is it to make me compensation that ye are come?" "Lord," they said, "we are at thy will." "By my will I would not have lost my warriors, and so many arms as I have done. You cannot compensate me my shame, setting aside the death of Pryderi. But since ye come hither to be at my will, I shall begin your punishment forthwith."

Then he took his magic wand, and struck Gilvaethwy, so that he became a deer, and he seized upon the other hastily lest he should escape from him. And he struck him with the same magic wand, and he became a deer also. "Since now ye are in bonds, I will that ye go forth together and be companions, and possess the nature of the animals whose form ye bear. And this day twelve-month come hither unto me."

At the end of a year from that day, lo there was a loud noise under the chamber wall, and the barking of the dogs of the palace together with the noise. "Look," said he, "what is without." "Lord," said one, "I have looked; there are there two deer, and a fawn with them." Then he arose and went out. And when he came he beheld the three animals. And he lifted up his wand. "As ye were deer last year, be ye wild hogs each and either of you, for the year that is to come." And thereupon he struck them with the magic wand. "The young one will I take and cause to be baptized." Now the name that he gave him was Hydwn. "Go ye and be wild swine, each and either of you, and be ye of the nature of wild swine. And this day twelvemonth be ye here under the wall."

At the end of the year the barking of dogs was heard under the wall of the chamber. And the Court assembled, and thereupon he arose and went forth, and when he came forth he beheld three beasts. Now these were the beasts that he saw; two wild hogs of the woods, and a well-grown young one with them. And he was very large for his age. "Truly," said Math, "this one will I take and cause to be baptized." And he struck him with his magic wand, and he became a fine fair auburn-haired youth, and the name that he gave him was Hychdwn. "Now as for you, as ye were wild hogs last year, be ye wolves each and either of you for the year that is to come." Thereupon he struck them with his magic wand, and they became wolves. "And be ye of like nature with the animals whose semblance ye bear, and return here this day twelvemonth beneath this wall."

And at the same day at the end of the year, he heard a clamour and a barking of dogs under the wall of the chamber. And he rose and went forth. And when he came, behold, he saw two wolves, and a strong cub with them. "This one will I take," said Math, "and I will cause him to be baptized; there is a name prepared for him, and that is Bleiddwn. Now these three, such are they: —

The three sons of Gilvaethwy the false,
The three faithful combatants,
Bleiddwn, Hydwn, and Hychdwn the Tall."

Then he struck the two with his magic wand, and they resumed their own nature. "Oh men," said he, "for the wrong that ye did unto me sufficient has been your punishment and your dishonour. Prepare now precious ointment for these men, and wash their heads, and equip them." And this was done.

And after they were equipped, they came unto him. "Oh men," said he, "you have obtained peace, and you shall likewise have friendship. Give your counsel unto me, what maiden I shall seek." "Lord," said Gwydion the son of Don, "it is easy to give thee counsel; seek Arianrod, the daughter of Don, thy niece, thy sister's daughter."

And they brought her unto him, and the maiden came in. "Ha, damsel," said he, "art thou the maiden?" "I know not, lord, other than that I am." Then he took up his magic wand, and bent it. "Step over this," said he, "and I shall know if thou art the maiden." Then stepped she over the magic wand, and there appeared forthwith a fine chubby yellow-haired boy. And at the crying out of the boy, she went towards the door. And thereupon some small form was seen; but before any one could get a second glimpse of it, Gwydion had taken it, and had flung a scarf of velvet around it and hidden it. Now the place where he hid it was the bottom of a chest at the foot of his bed.

"Verily," said Math the son of Mathonwy, concerning the fine yellow-haired boy, "I will cause this one to be baptized, and Dylan is the name I will give him."

So they had the boy baptized, and as they baptized him he plunged into the sea. And immediately when he was in the sea, he took its nature, and swam as well as the best fish that was therein. And for that reason was he called Dylan, the son of the Wave. Beneath him no wave ever broke. And the blow whereby he came to his death, was struck by his uncle Govannon. The third fatal blow was it called.

As Gwydion lay one morning on his bed awake, he heard a cry in the chest at his feet; and though it was not loud, it was such that he could hear it. Then he arose in haste, and opened the chest: and when he opened it, he beheld an infant boy stretching out his arms from the folds of the scarf, and casting it aside. And he took up the boy in his arms, and carried him to a place where he knew there was a woman that could nurse him. And he agreed with the woman that she should take charge of the boy. And that year he was nursed.

And at the end of the year he seemed by his size as though he were two years old. And the second year he was a big child, and able to go to the Court by himself. And when he came to the Court, Gwydion noticed him, and the boy became familiar with him, and loved him better than any one else. Then was the boy reared at the Court until he was four years old, when he was as big as though he had been eight.

And one day Gwydion walked forth, and the boy followed him, and he went to the Castle of Arianrod, having the boy with him; and when he came into the Court, Arianrod arose to meet him, and greeted him and bade him welcome. "Heaven prosper thee," said he. "Who is the boy that followeth thee?" she asked. "This youth, he is thy son," he answered. "Alas," said she, "what has come unto thee that thou shouldst shame me thus? wherefore dost thou seek my dishonour, and retain it so long as this?" "Unless thou suffer dishonour greater than that of my bringing up such a boy as this, small will be thy disgrace." "What is the name of the boy?" said she. "Verily," he replied, "he has not yet a name." "Well," she said, "I lay this destiny upon him, that he shall never have a name until he receives one from me." "Heaven bears me witness," answered he, "that thou art a wicked woman. But the boy shall have a name how displeasing soever it may be unto thee. As for thee, that which afflicts thee is that thou art no longer called a damsel." And thereupon he went forth in wrath, and returned to Caer Dathyl and there he tarried that night.

And the next day he arose and took the boy with him, and went to walk on the seashore between that place and Aber Menei. And there he saw some sedges and seaweed, and he turned them into a boat. And out of dry sticks and sedges he made some Cordovan leather, and a great deal thereof, and he coloured it in such a manner that no one ever saw leather more beautiful than it. Then he made a sail to the boat, and he and the boy went in it to the port of the castle of Arianrod. And he began forming shoes and stitching them, until he was observed from the castle. And when he knew that they of the castle were observing him, he disguised his aspect, and put another semblance upon himself, and upon the boy, so that they might not be known. "What men are those in yonder boat?" said Arianrod. "They are cordwainers," answered they. "Go and see what kind of leather they have, and what kind of work they can do."

So they came unto them. And when they came he was colouring some Cordovan leather, and gilding it. And the messengers came and told her this. "Well," said she, "take the measure of my foot, and desire the cordwainer to make shoes for me." So he made the shoes for her, yet not according to the measure, but larger. The shoes then were brought unto her, and behold they were too large. "These are too large," said she, "but he shall receive their value. Let him also make some that are smaller than they." Then he made her others that were much smaller than her foot, and sent them unto her. "Tell him that these will not go on my feet," said she. And they told him this. "Verily," said he, "I will not make her any shoes, unless I see her foot." And this was told unto her. "Truly," she answered, "I will go unto him."

So she went down to the boat, and when she came there, he was shaping shoes and the boy stitching them. "Ah, lady," said he, "good day to thee." "Heaven prosper thee," said she. "I marvel that thou canst not manage to make shoes according to a measure." "I could not," he replied, "but now I shall be able."

Thereupon behold a wren stood upon the deck of the boat, and the boy shot at it, and hit it in the leg between the sinew and the bone. Then she smiled. "Verily," said she, "with a steady hand did the lion aim at it." "Heaven reward thee not, but now has he got a name. And a good enough name it is. Llew Llaw Gyffes be he called henceforth."

Then the work disappeared in seaweed and sedges, and he went on with it no further. And for that reason was he called the third Gold-shoemaker. "Of a truth," said she, "thou wilt not thrive the better for doing evil unto me." "I have done thee no evil yet," said he. Then he restored the boy to his own form. "Well," said she, "I will lay a destiny upon this boy, that he shall never have arms and armour until I invest him with them." "By Heaven," said he, "let thy malice be what it may, he shall have arms."

Then they went towards Dinas Dinllev, and there he brought up Llew Llaw Gyffes, until he could manage any horse, and he was perfect in features, and strength, and stature. And then Gwydion saw that he languished through the want of horses and arms. And he called him unto him. "Ah, youth," said he, "we will go to-morrow on an errand together. Be therefore more cheerful than thou art." "That I will," said the youth.

Next morning, at the dawn of day, they arose. And they took way along the sea coast, up towards Bryn Aryen. And at the top of Cevn Clydno they equipped themselves with horses, and went towards the Castle of Arianrod. And they changed their form, and pricked towards the gate in the semblance of two youths, but the aspect of Gwydion was more staid than that of the other. "Porter," said he, "go thou in and say that there are here bards from Glamorgan." And the porter went in. "The welcome of Heaven be unto them, let them in," said Arianrod.

With great joy were they greeted. And the hall was arranged, and they went to meat. When meat was ended, Arianrod discoursed with Gwydion of tales and stories. Now Gwydion was an excellent teller of tales. And when it was time to leave off feasting, a chamber was prepared for them, and they went to rest.

In the early twilight Gwydion arose, and he called unto him his magic and his power. And by the time that the day dawned, there resounded through the land uproar, and trumpets and shouts. When it was now day, they heard a knocking at the door of the chamber, and therewith Arianrod asking that it might be opened. Up rose the youth and opened unto her, and she entered and a maiden with her. "Ah, good men," she said, "in evil plight are we." "Yes, truly," said Gwydion, "we have heard trumpets and shouts; what thinkest thou that they may mean?" "Verily," said she, "we cannot see the colour of the ocean by reason of all the ships, side by side. And they are making for the land with all the speed they can. And what can we do?" said she. "Lady," said Gwydion, "there is none other counsel than to close the castle upon us, and to defend it as best we may." "Truly," said she, "may Heaven reward you. And do you defend it. And here may you have plenty of arms."

And thereupon went she forth for the arms, and behold she returned, and two maidens, and suits of armour for two men, with her. "Lady," said he, "do you accoutre this stripling, and I will arm myself with the help of thy maidens. Lo, I hear the tumult of the men approaching." "I will do so, gladly." So she armed him fully, and that right cheerfully. "Hast thou finished arming the youth?" said he. "I have finished," she answered. "I likewise have finished," said Gwydion. "Let us now take off our arms, we have no need of them." "Wherefore?" said she. "Here is the army around the house." "Oh, lady, there is here no army." "Oh," cried she, "whence then was this tumult?" "The tumult was but to break thy prophecy and to obtain arms for thy son. And now has he got arms without any thanks unto thee." "By Heaven," said Arianrod, "thou art a wicked man. Many a youth might have lost his life through the uproar thou hast caused in this Cantrev to-day. Now will I lay a destiny upon this youth," she said, "that he shall never have a wife of the race that now inhabits this earth." "Verily," said he, "thou wast ever a malicious woman, and no one ought to support thee. A wife shall he have notwithstanding."

They went thereupon unto Math the son of Mathonwy, and complained unto him most bitterly of Arianrod. Gwydion showed him also how he had procured arms for the youth. "Well," said Math, "we will seek, I and thou, by charms and illusion, to form a wife for him out of flowers. He has now come to man's stature, and he is the comeliest youth that was ever beheld." So they took the blossoms of the oak, and the blossoms of the broom, and the blossoms of the meadow-sweet, and produced from them a maiden, the fairest and most graceful that man ever saw. And they baptized her, and gave her the name of Blodeuwedd.

After she had become his bride, and they had feasted, said Gwydion, "It is not easy for a man to maintain himself without possessions." "Of a truth," said Math, "I will give the young man the best Cantrev to hold." "Lord," said he, "what Cantrev is that?" "The Cantrev of Dinodig," he answered. Now it is called at this day Eivionydd and Ardudwy. And the place in the Cantrev where he dwelt, was a palace of his in a spot called Mur y Castell, on the confines of Ardudwy. There dwelt he and reigned, and both he and his sway were beloved by all.

One day he went forth to Caer Dathyl, to visit Math the son of Mathonwy. And on the day that he set out for Caer Dathyl, Blodeuwedd walked in the Court. And she heard the sound of a horn. And after the sound of the horn, behold a tired stag went by, with dogs and huntsmen following it. And after the dogs and the huntsmen there came a crowd of men on foot. "Send a youth," said she, "to ask who yonder host may be." So a youth went, and inquired who they were. "Gronw Pebyr is this, the lord of Penllyn," said they. And thus the youth told her.

Gronw Pebyr pursued the stag, and by the river Cynvael he overtook the stag and killed it. And what with flaying the stag and baiting his dogs, he was there until the night began to close in upon him. And as the day departed and the night drew near, he came to the gate of the Court. "Verily," said Blodeuwedd, "the Chieftain will speak ill of us if we let him at this hour depart to another land without inviting him in." "Yes, truly, lady," said they, "it will be most fitting to invite him."

Then went messengers to meet him and bid him in. And he accepted her bidding gladly, and came to the Court, and Blodeuwedd went to meet him, and greeted him, and bade him welcome. "Lady," said he, "Heaven repay thee thy kindness."

When they had disaccoutred themselves, they went to sit down. And Blodeuwedd looked upon him, and from the moment that she looked on him she became filled with his love. And he gazed on her, and the same thought came unto him as unto her, so that he could not conceal from her that he loved her, but he declared unto her that he did so. Thereupon she was very joyful. And all their discourse that night was concerning the affection and love which they felt one for the other, and which in no longer space than one evening had arisen. And that evening passed they in each other's company.

The next day he sought to depart. But she said, "I pray thee go not from me to-day." And that night he tarried also. And that night they consulted by what means they might always be together. "There is none other counsel," said he, "but that thou strive to learn from Llew Llaw Gyffes in what manner he will meet his death. And this must thou do under the semblance of solicitude concerning him."

The next day Gronw sought to depart. "Verily," said she, "I will counsel thee not to go from me to-day." "At thy instance will I not go," said he, "albeit, I must say, there is danger that the chief who owns the palace may return home." "To-morrow," answered she, "will I indeed permit thee to go forth."

The next day he sought to go, and she hindered him not. "Be mindful," said Gronw, "of what I have said unto thee, and converse with him fully, and that under the guise of the dalliance of love, and find out by what means he may come to his death."

That night Llew Llaw Gyffes returned to his home. And the day they spent in discourse, and minstrelsy, and feasting. And at night they went to rest, and he spoke to Blodeuwedd once, and he spoke to her a second time. But, for all this, he could not get from her one word. "What aileth thee?" said he, "art thou well?" "I was thinking," said she, "of that which thou didst never think of concerning me; for I was sorrowful as to thy death, lest thou shouldst go sooner than I." "Heaven reward thy care for me," said he, "but until Heaven take me I shall not easily be slain." "For the sake of Heaven, and for mine, show me how thou mightest be slain. My memory in guarding is better than thine." "I will tell thee gladly," said he. "Not easily can I be slain, except by a wound. And the spear wherewith I am struck must be a year in the forming. And nothing must be done towards it except during the sacrifice on Sundays." "Is this certain?" asked she. "It is in truth," he answered. "And I cannot be slain within a house, nor without. I cannot be slain on horseback nor on foot." "Verily," said she, "in what manner then canst thou be slain?" "I will tell thee," said he. "By making a bath for me by the side of a river, and by putting a roof over the cauldron, and thatching it well and tightly, and bringing a buck, and putting it beside the cauldron. Then if I place one foot on the buck's back, and the other on the edge of the cauldron, whosoever strikes me thus will cause my death." "Well," said she, "I thank Heaven that it will be easy to avoid this."

No sooner had she held this discourse than she sent to Gronw Pebyr. Gronw toiled at making the spear, and that day twelvemonth it was ready. And that very day he caused her to be informed thereof.

"Lord," said Blodeuwedd unto Llew, "I have been thinking how it is possible that what thou didst tell me formerly can be true; wilt thou show me in what manner thou couldst stand at once upon the edge of a cauldron and upon a buck, if I prepare the bath for thee?" "I will show thee," said he.

Then she sent unto Gronw, and bade him be in ambush on the hill which is now called Bryn Kyvergyr, on the bank of the river Cynvael. She caused also to be collected all the goats that were in the Cantrev, and had them brought to the other side of the river, opposite Bryn Kyvergyr.

And the next day she spoke thus. "Lord," said she, "I have caused the roof and the bath to be prepared, and lo! they are ready." "Well," said Llew, "we will go gladly to look at them."

The day after they came and looked at the bath. "Wilt thou go into the bath, lord?" said she. "Willingly will I go in," he answered. So into the bath he went, and he anointed himself. "Lord," said she, "behold the animals which thou didst speak of as being called bucks." "Well," said he, "cause one of them to be caught and brought here." And the buck was brought. Then Llew rose out of the bath, and put on his trowsers, and he placed one foot on the edge of the bath and the other on the buck's back.

Thereupon Gronw rose up from the hill which is called Bryn Kyvergyr, and he rested on one knee, and flung the poisoned dart and struck him on the side, so that the shaft started out, but the head of the dart remained in. Then he flew up in the form of an eagle and gave a fearful scream. And thenceforth was he no more seen.

As soon as he departed Gronw and Blodeuwedd went together unto the palace that night. And the next day Gronw arose and took possession of Ardudwy. And after he had overcome the land, he ruled over it, so that Ardudwy and Penllyn were both under his sway.

Then these tidings reached Math the son of Mathonwy. And heaviness and grief came upon Math, and much more upon Gwydion than upon him. "Lord," said Gwydion, "I shall never rest until I have tidings of my nephew." "Verily," said Math, "may Heaven be thy strength." Then Gwydion set forth and began to go forward. And he went through Gwynedd and Powys to the confines. And when he had done so, he went into Arvon, and came to the house of a vassal, in Maenawr Penardd. And he alighted at the house, and stayed there that night. The man of the house and his household came in, and last of all came there the swineherd. Said the man of the house to the swineherd, "Well, youth, hath thy sow come in to-night?" "She hath," said he, "and is this instant returned to the pigs." "Where doth this sow go to?" said Gwydion. "Every day, when the sty is opened, she goeth forth and none can catch sight of her, neither is it known whither she goeth more than if she sank into the earth." "Wilt thou grant unto me," said Gwydion, "not to open the sty until I am beside the sty with thee?" "This will I do, right gladly," he answered.

That night they went to rest; and as soon as the swineherd saw the light of day, he awoke Gwydion. And Gwydion arose and dressed himself, and went with the swineherd, and stood beside the sty. Then the swineherd opened the sty. And as soon as he opened it, behold she leaped forth, and set off with great speed. And Gwydion followed her, and she went against the course of a river, and made for a brook, which is now called Nant y Llew. And there she halted and began feeding. And Gwydion came under the tree, and looked what it might be that the sow was feeding on. And he saw that she was eating putrid flesh and vermin. Then looked he up to the top of the tree, and as he looked he beheld on the top of the tree an eagle, and when the eagle shook itself, there fell vermin and putrid flesh from off it, and these the sow devoured. And it seemed to him that the eagle was Llew. And he sang an Englyn: —

"Oak that grows between the two banks;
Darkened is the sky and hill!
Shall I not tell him by his wounds,
That this is Llew?"

Upon this the eagle came down until he reached the centre of the tree. And Gwydion sang another Englyn: —

"Oak that grows in upland ground,
Is it not wetted by the rain? Has it not been drenched
By nine score tempests?
It bears in its branches Llew Llaw Gyffes!"

Then the eagle came down until he was on the lowest branch of the tree, and thereupon this Englyn did Gwydion sing: —

"Oak that grows beneath the steep;
Stately and majestic is its aspect!
Shall I not speak it?
That Llew will come to my lap?"

And the eagle came down upon Gwydion's knee. And Gwydion struck him with his magic wand, so that he returned to his own form. No one ever saw a more piteous sight, for he was nothing but skin and bone.

Then he went unto Caer Dathyl, and there were brought unto him good physicians that were in Gwynedd, and before the end of the year he was quite healed.

"Lord," said he unto Math the son of Mathonwy, "it is full time now that I have retribution of him by whom I have suffered all this woe." "Truly," said Math, "he will never be able to maintain himself in the possession of that which is thy right." "Well," said Llew, "the sooner I have my right, the better shall I be pleased."

Then they called together the whole of Gwynedd, and set forth to Ardudwy. And Gwydion went on before and proceeded to Mur y Castell. And when Blodeuwedd heard that he was coming, she took her maidens with her, and fled to the mountain. And they passed through the river Cynvael, and went towards a court that there was upon the mountain, and through fear they could not proceed except with their faces looking backwards, so that unawares they fell into the lake. And they were all drowned except Blodeuwedd herself, and her Gwydion overtook. And he said unto her, "I will not slay thee, but I will do unto thee worse than that. For I will turn thee into a bird; and because of the shame thou hast done unto Llew Llaw Gyffes, thou shalt never show thy face in the light of day henceforth; and that through fear of all the other birds. For it shall be their nature to attack thee, and to chase thee from wheresoever they may find thee. And thou shalt not lose thy name, but shalt be always called Blodeuwedd." Now Blodeuwedd is an owl in the language of this present time, and for this reason is the owl hateful unto all birds. And even now the owl is called Blodeuwedd.

Then Gronw Pebyr withdrew unto Penllyn, and he dispatched thence an embassy. And the messengers he sent asked Llew Llaw Gyffes if he would take land, or domain, or gold, or silver, for the injury he had received. "I will not, by my confession to Heaven," said he. "Behold this is the least that I will accept from him; that he come to the spot where I was when he wounded me with the dart, and that I stand where he did, and that with a dart I take my aim at him. And this is the very least that I will accept."

And this was told unto Gronw Pebyr. "Verily," said he, "is it needful for me to do thus? My faithful warriors, and my household, and my foster-brothers, is there not one among you who will stand the blow in my stead?" "There is not, verily," answered they. And because of their refusal to suffer one stroke for their lord, they are called the third disloyal tribe even unto this day. "Well," said he, "I will meet it."

Then they two went forth to the banks of the river Cynvael, and Gronw stood in the place where Llew Llaw Gyffes was when he struck him, and Llew in the place where Gronw was. Then said Gronw Pebyr unto Llew, "Since it was through the wiles of a woman that I did unto thee as I have done, I adjure thee by Heaven to let me place between me and the blow, the slab thou seest yonder on the river's bank." "Verily," said Llew, "I will not refuse thee this." "Ah," said he, "may Heaven reward thee." So Gronw took the slab and placed it between him and the blow.

Then Llew flung the dart at him, and it pierced the slab and went through Gronw likewise, so that it pierced through his back. And thus was Gronw Pebyr slain. And there is still the slab on the bank of the river Cynvael, in Ardudwy, having the hole through it. And therefore is it even now called Llech Gronw.

A second time did Llew Llaw Gyffes take possession of the land, and prosperously did he govern it. And, as the story relates, he was lord after this over Gwynedd. And thus ends this portion of the Mabinogi.

THE DREAM OF MAXEN WLEDIG

MAXEN WLEDIG was emperor of Rome, and he was a comelier man, and a better and a wiser than any emperor that had been before him. And one day he held a council of kings, and he said to his friends, "I desire to go to-morrow to hunt." And the next day in the morning he set forth with his retinue, and came to the valley of the river that flowed towards Rome. And he hunted through the valley until mid-day. And with him also were two-and-thirty crowned kings, that were his vassals; not for the delight of hunting went the emperor with them, but to put himself on equal terms with those kings.

And the sun was high in the sky over their heads and the heat was great. And sleep came upon Maxen Wledig. And his attendants stood and set up their shields around him upon the shafts of their spears to protect him from the sun, and they placed a gold enamelled shield under his head; and so Maxen slept.

And he saw a dream. And this is the dream that he saw. He was journeying along the valley of the river towards its source; and he came to the highest mountain in the world. And he thought that the mountain was as high as the sky; and when he came over the mountain, it seemed to him that he went through the fairest and most level regions that man ever yet beheld, on the other side of the mountain. And he saw large and mighty rivers descending from the mountain to the sea, and towards the mouths of the rivers he proceeded. And as he journeyed thus, he came to the mouth of the largest river ever seen. And he beheld a great city at the entrance of the river, and a vast castle in the city, and he saw many high towers of various colours in the castle. And he saw a fleet at the mouth of the river, the largest ever seen. And he saw one ship among the fleet; larger was it by far, and fairer than all the others. Of such part of the ship as he could see above the water, one plank was gilded and the other silvered over. He saw a bridge of the bone of a whale from the ship to the land, and he thought that he went along the bridge, and came into the ship. And a sail was hoisted on the ship, and along the sea and the ocean was it borne. Then it seemed that he came to the fairest island in the whole world, and he traversed the island from sea to sea, even to the furthest shore of the island. Valleys he saw, and steeps, and rocks of wondrous height, and rugged precipices. Never yet saw he the like. And thence he beheld an island in the sea, facing this rugged land. And between him and this island was a country of which the plain was as large as the sea, the mountain as vast as the wood. And from the mountain he saw a river that flowed through the land and fell into the sea. And at the mouth of the river he beheld a castle, the fairest that man ever saw, and the gate of the castle was open, and he went into the castle. And in the castle he saw a fair hall, of which the roof seemed to be all gold, the walls of the hall seemed to be entirely of glittering precious gems, the doors all seemed to be of gold. Golden seats he saw in the hall, and silver tables. And on a seat opposite to him he beheld two auburn-haired youths playing at chess. He saw a silver board for the chess, and golden pieces thereon. The garments of the youths were of jet-black satin, and chaplets of ruddy gold bound their hair, whereon were sparkling jewels of great price, rubies, and gems, alternately with imperial stones. Buskins of new Cordovan leather on their feet, fastened by slides of red gold.

And beside a pillar in the hall he saw a hoary-headed man, in a chair of ivory, with the figures of two eagles of ruddy gold thereon. Bracelets of gold were upon his arms, and many rings were on his hands, and a golden torque about his neck; and his hair was bound with a golden diadem. He was of powerful aspect. A chess-board of gold was before him, and a rod of gold, and a steel file in his hand. And he was carving out chessmen.

And he saw a maiden sitting before him in a chair of ruddy gold. Not more easy than to gaze upon the sun when brightest, was it to look upon her by reason of her beauty. A vest of white silk was upon the maiden, with clasps of red gold at the breast; and a surcoat of gold tissue upon her, and a frontlet of red gold upon her head, and rubies and gems were in the frontlet, alternating with pearls and imperial stones. And a girdle of ruddy gold was around her. She was the fairest sight that man ever beheld.

The maiden arose from her chair before him, and he threw his arms about the neck of the maiden, and they two sat down together in the chair of gold: and the chair was not less roomy for them both, than for the maiden alone. And as he had his arms about the maiden's neck, and his cheek by her cheek, behold, through the chafing of the dogs at their leashing, and the clashing of the shields as they struck against each other, and the beating together of the shafts of the spears, and the neighing of the horses and their prancing, the emperor awoke.

And when he awoke, nor spirit nor existence was left him, because of the maiden whom he had seen in his sleep, for the love of the maiden pervaded his whole frame. Then his household spake unto him. "Lord," said they, "is it not past the time for thee to take thy food?" Thereupon the emperor mounted his palfrey, the saddest man that mortal ever saw, and went forth towards Rome.

And thus he was during the space of a week. When they of the household went to drink wine and mead out of golden vessels, he went not with any of them. When they went to listen to songs and tales, he went not with them there; neither could he be persuaded to do anything but sleep. And as often as he slept, he beheld in his dreams the maiden he loved best; but except when he slept he saw nothing of her, for he knew not where in the world she was.

One day the page of the chamber spake unto him; now, although he was page of the chamber, he was king of the Romans. "Lord," said he, "all the people revile thee." "Wherefore do they revile me?" asked the emperor. "Because they can get neither message nor answer from thee as men should have from their lord. This is the cause why thou art spoken evil of." "Youth," said the emperor, "do thou bring unto me the wise men of Rome, and I will tell them wherefore I am sorrowful."

Then the wise men of Rome were brought to the emperor, and he spake to them. "Sages of Rome," said he, "I have seen a dream. And in the dream I beheld a maiden, and because of the maiden is there neither life, nor spirit, nor existence within me." "Lord," they answered, "since thou judgest us worthy to counsel thee, we will give thee counsel. And this is our counsel; that thou send messengers for three years to the three parts of the world to seek for thy dream. And as thou knowest not what day or what night good news may come to thee, the hope thereof will support thee."

So the messengers journeyed for the space of a year, wandering about the world, and seeking tidings concerning his dream. But when they came back at the end of the year, they knew not one word more than they did the day they set forth. And then was the emperor exceeding sorrowful, for he thought that he should never have tidings of her whom best he loved.

Then spoke the king of the Romans unto the emperor. "Lord," said he, "go forth to hunt by the way thou didst seem to go, whether it were to the east, or to the west." So the emperor went forth to the hunt, and he came to the bank of the river. "Behold," said he, "this is where I was when I saw the dream, and I went towards the source of the river westward."

And thereupon thirteen messengers of the emperor's set forth, and before them they saw a high mountain, which seemed to them to touch the sky. Now this was the guise in which the messengers journeyed; one sleeve was on the cap of each of them in front, as a sign that they were messengers, in order that through what hostile land soever they might pass no harm might be done them. And when they were come over this mountain, they beheld vast plains, and large rivers flowing there through. "Behold," said they, "the land which our master saw."

And they went along the mouths of the rivers, until they came to the mighty river which they saw flowing to the sea, and the vast city, and the many-coloured high towers in the castle. They saw the largest fleet in the world, in the harbour of the river, and one ship that was larger than any of the others. "Behold again," said they, "the dream that our master saw." And in the great ship they crossed the sea, and came to the Island of Britain. And they traversed the island until they came to Snowdon. "Behold," said they, "the rugged land that our master saw." And they went forward until they saw Anglesey before them, and until they saw Arvon likewise. "Behold," said they, "the land our master saw in his sleep." And they saw Aber Sain, and a castle at the mouth of the river. The portal of the castle saw they open, and into the castle they went, and they saw a hall in the castle. Then said they, "Behold, the hall which he saw in his sleep." They went into the hall, and they beheld two youths playing at chess on the golden bench. And they beheld the hoary-headed man beside the pillar, in the ivory chair, carving chessmen. And they beheld the maiden sitting on a chair of ruddy gold.

The messengers bent down upon their knees. "Empress of Rome, all hail!" "Ha, gentles," said the maiden, "ye bear the seeming of honourable men, and the badge of envoys, what mockery is this ye do to me?" "We mock thee not, lady; but the Emperor of Rome hath seen thee in his sleep, and he has neither life nor spirit left because of thee. Thou shalt have of us therefore the choice, lady, whether thou wilt go with us and be made empress of Rome, or that the emperor come hither and take thee for his wife?" "Ha, lords," said the maiden, "I will not deny what ye say, neither will I believe it too well. If the emperor love me, let him come here to seek me."

And by day and night the messengers hied them back. And when their horses failed, they bought other fresh ones. And when they came to Rome, they saluted the emperor, and asked their boon, which was given to them according as they named it. "We will be thy guides, lord," said they, "over sea and over land, to the place where is the woman whom best thou lovest, for we know her name, and her kindred, and her race."

And immediately the emperor set forth with his army. And these men were his guides. Towards the Island of Britain they went over the sea and the deep. And he conquered the Island from Beli the son of Manogan, and his sons, and drove them to the sea, and went forward even unto Arvon. And the emperor knew the land when he saw it. And when he beheld the castle of Aber Sain, "Look yonder," said he, "there is the castle wherein I saw the damsel whom I best love." And he went forward into the castle and into the hall, and there he saw Kynan the son of Eudav, and Adeon the son of Eudav, playing at chess. And he saw Eudav the son of Caradawc, sitting on a chair of ivory carving chessmen. And the maiden whom he had beheld in his sleep, he saw sitting on a chair of gold. "Empress of Rome," said he, "all hail!" And the emperor threw his arms about her neck; and that night she became his bride.

And the next day in the morning, the damsel asked her maiden portion. And he told her to name what she would. And she asked to have the Island of Britain for her father, from the Channel to the Irish Sea, together with the three adjacent Islands, to hold under the empress of Rome; and to have three chief castles made for her, in whatever places she might choose in the Island of Britain. And she chose to have the highest castle made at Arvon. And they brought thither earth from Rome that it might be more healthful for the emperor to sleep, and sit, and walk upon. After that the two other castles were made for her, which were Caerlleon and Caermarthen.

And one day the emperor went to hunt at Caermarthen, and he came so far as the top of Brevi Vawr, and there the emperor pitched his tent. And that encamping place is called Cadeir Maxen, even to this day. And because that he built the castle with a myriad of men, he called it Caervyrddin. Then Helen bethought her to make high roads from one castle to another throughout the Island of Britain. And the roads were made. And for this cause are they called the roads of Helen Luyddawc, that she was sprung from a native of this island, and the men of the Island of Britain would not have made these great roads for any save for her.

Seven years did the emperor tarry in this Island. Now, at that time, the men of Rome had a custom, that whatsoever emperor should remain in other lands more than seven years should remain to his own overthrow, and should never return to Rome again.

So they made a new emperor. And this one wrote a letter of threat to Maxen. There was nought in the letter but only this. "If thou comest, and if thou ever comest to Rome." And even unto Caerlleon came this letter to Maxen, and these tidings. Then sent he a letter to the man who styled himself emperor in Rome. There was nought in that letter also but only this. "If I come to Rome, and if I come."

And thereupon Maxen set forth towards Rome with his army, and vanquished France and Bugundy, and every land on the way, and sat down before the city of Rome.

A year was the emperor before the city, and he was no nearer taking it than the first day. And after him there came the brothers of Helen Luyddawc from the Island of Britain, and a small host with them, and better warriors were in that small host than twice as many Romans. And the emperor was told that a host was seen, halting close to his army and encamping, and no man ever saw a fairer or better appointed host for its size, nor more handsome standards.

And Helen went to see the hosts, and she knew the standards of her brothers. Then came Kynan the son of Eudav, and Adeon the son of Eudav, to meet the emperor. And the emperor was glad because of them, and embraced them.

Then they looked at the Romans as they attacked the city. Said Kynan to his brother, "We will try to attack the city more expertly than this." So they measured by night the height of the wall, and they sent their carpenters to the wood, and a ladder was made for every four men of their number. Now when these were ready, every day at mid-day the emperors went to meat, and they ceased to fight on both sides till all had finished eating. And in the morning the men of Britain took their food, and they drank until they were invigorated. And while the two emperors were at meat, the Britons came to the city, and placed their ladders against it, and forthwith they came in through the city.

The new emperor had no time to arm himself when they fell upon him, and slew him, and many others with him. And three nights and three days were they subduing the men that were in the city and taking the castle. And others of them kept the city, lest any of the host of Maxen should come therein, until they had subjected all to their will.

Then spake Maxen to Helen Luyddawc. "I marvel, lady," said he, "that thy brothers have not conquered this city for me." "Lord, emperor," she answered, "the wisest youths in the world are my brothers. Go thou thither and ask the city of them, and if it be in their possession thou shalt have it gladly." So the emperor and Helen went and demanded the city. And they told the emperor that none had taken the city, and that none could give it him, but the men of the Island of Britain. Then the gates of the city of Rome were opened, and the emperor sat on the throne, and all the men of Rome submitted themselves unto him.

The emperor then said unto Kynan and Adeon, "Lords," said he, "I have now had possession of the whole of my empire. This host give I unto you to vanquish whatever region ye may desire in the world."

So they set forth and conquered lands, and castles, and cities. And they slew all the men, but the women they kept alive. And thus they continued until the young men that had come with them were grown greyheaded, from the length of time they were upon this conquest.

Then spoke Kynan unto Adeon his brother, "Whether wilt thou rather," said he, "tarry in this land, or go back into the land whence thou didst come forth?" Now he chose to go back to his own land, and many with him. But Kynan tarried there with the other part and dwelt there.

And they took counsel and cut out the tongues of the women, lest they should corrupt their speech. And because of the silence of the women from their own speech, the men of Armorica are called Britons. From that time there came frequently, and still comes, that language from the Island of Britain.

And this dream is called the Dream of Maxen Wledig, emperor of Rome. And here it ends.

HERE IS THE STORY OF LLUDD AND LLEVELYS

BELI the Great, the son of Manogan, had three sons, Lludd, and Caswallawn, and Nynyaw; and according to the story he had a fourth son called Llevelys. And after the death of Beli, the kingdom of the Island of Britain fell into the hands of Lludd his eldest son; and Lludd ruled prosperously, and rebuilt the walls of London, and encompassed it about with numberless towers. And after that he bade the citizens build houses therein, such as no houses in the kingdoms could equal. And moreover he was a mighty warrior, and generous and liberal in giving meat and drink to all that sought them. And though he had many castles and cities this one loved he more than any. And he dwelt therein most part of the year, and therefore was it called Caer Lludd, and at last Caer London. And after the stranger-race came there, it was called London, or Lwndrys.

Lludd loved Llevelys best of all his brothers, because he was a wise and discreet man. Having heard that the king of France had died, leaving no heir except a daughter, and that he had left all his possessions in her hands, he came to Lludd his brother, to beseech his counsel and aid. And that not so much for his own welfare, as to seek to add to the glory and honour and dignity of his kindred, if he might go to France to woo the maiden for his wife. And forthwith his brother conferred with him, and this counsel was pleasing unto him.

So he prepared ships and filled them with armed knights, and set forth towards France. And as soon as they had landed, they sent messengers to show the nobles of France the cause of the embassy. And by the joint counsel of the nobles of France and of the princes, the maiden was given to Llevelys, and the crown of the kingdom with her. And thenceforth he ruled the land discreetly, and wisely, and happily, as long as his life lasted.

After a space of time had passed, three plagues fell on the Island of Britain, such as none in the islands had ever seen the like of. The first was a certain race that came, and was called the Coranians; and so great was their knowledge, that there was no discourse upon the face of the Island, however low it might be spoken, but what, if the wind met it, it was known to them. And through this they could not be injured.[1]

The second plague was a shriek which came on every May-eve, over every hearth in the Island of Britain. And this went through people's hearts, and so scared them, that the men lost their hue and their strength, and the women their children, and the young men and the maidens lost their senses, and all the animals and trees and the earth and the waters, were left barren.

The third plague was, that however much of provisions and food might be prepared in the king's courts, were there even so much as a year's provision of meat and drink, none of it could ever be found, except what was consumed in the first night. And two of these plagues, no one ever knew their cause, therefore was there better hope of being freed from the first than from the second and third.

[1] The version in the Greal [an untranslated collection of several Mabinogi, printed in 1806] adds, "And their coin was fairy money;" literally, dwarf's money: that is, money which, when received, appeared to be good coin, but which, if kept, turned into pieces of fungus, &c.

And thereupon King Lludd felt great sorrow and care, because that he knew not how he might be freed from these plagues. And he called to him all the nobles of his kingdom, and asked counsel of them what they should do against these afflictions. And by the common counsel of the nobles, Lludd the son of Beli went to Llevelys his brother, king of France, for he was a man great of counsel and wisdom, to seek his advice.

And they made ready a fleet, and that in secret and in silence, lest that race should know the cause of their errand, or any besides the king and his counsellors. And when they were made ready, they went into their ships, Lludd and those whom he chose with him. And they began to cleave the seas towards France.

And when these tidings came to Llevelys, seeing that he knew not the cause of his brother's ships, he came on the other side to meet him, and with him was a fleet vast of size. And when Lludd saw this, he left all the ships out upon the sea except one only; and in that one he came to meet his brother, and he likewise with a single ship came to meet him. And when they were come together, each put his arms about the other's neck, and they welcomed each other with brotherly love.

After that Lludd had shown his brother the cause of his errand, Llevelys said that he himself knew the cause of the coming to those lands. And they took counsel together to discourse on the matter otherwise than thus, in order that the wind might not catch their words, nor the Coranians know what they might say. Then Llevelys caused a long horn to be made of brass, and through this horn they discoursed. But whatsoever words they spoke through this horn, one to the other, neither of them could hear any other but harsh and hostile words. And when Llevelys saw this, and that there was a demon thwarting them and disturbing through this horn, he caused wine to be put therein to wash it. And through the virtue of the wine the demon was driven out of the horn. And when their discourse was unobstructed, Llevelys told his brother that he would give him some insects whereof he should keep some to breed, lest by chance the like affliction might come a second time. And other of these insects he should take and bruise in water. And he assured him that it would have power to destroy the race of the Coranians. That is to say, that when he came home to his kingdom he should call together all the people both of his own race and of the race of the Coranians for a conference, as though with the intent of making peace between them; and that when they were all together, he should take this charmed water, and cast it over all alike. And he assured him that the water would poison the race of the Coranians, but that it would not slay or harm those of his own race.

"And the second plague," said he, "that is in thy dominion, behold it is a dragon. And another dragon of a foreign race is fighting with it, and striving to overcome it. And therefore does your dragon make a fearful outcry. And on this wise mayest thou come to know this. After thou hast returned home, cause the Island to be measured in its length and breadth, and in the place where thou dost find the exact central point, there cause a pit to be dug, and cause a cauldron full of the best mead that can be made to be put in the pit, with a covering of satin over the face of the cauldron. And then, in thine own person do thou remain there watching, and thou wilt see the dragon fighting in the form of terrific animals. And at length they will take the form of dragons in the air. And last of all, after wearying themselves with fierce and furious fighting, they will fall in the form of two pigs upon the covering, and they will sink in, and the covering with them, and they will draw it down to the very bottom of the cauldron. And they will drink up the whole of the mead; and after that they will sleep. Thereupon do thou immediately fold the covering around them, and bury them in a kistvaen, in the strongest place thou hast in thy dominions, and hide them in the earth. And as long as they shall bide in that strong place no plague shall come to the Island of Britain from elsewhere.

"The cause of the third plague," said he, "is a mighty man of magic, who take thy meat and thy drink and thy store. And he through illusions and charms causes every one to sleep. Therefore it is needful for thee in thy own person to watch thy food and thy provisions. And lest he should overcome thee with sleep, be there a cauldron of cold water by thy side, and when thou art oppressed with sleep, plunge into the cauldron."

Then Lludd returned back unto his land. And immediately he summoned to him the whole of his own race and of the Coranians. And as Llevelys had taught him, he bruised the insects in water, the which he cast over them all together, and forthwith it destroyed the whole tribe of the Coranians, without hurt to any of the Britons.

And some time after this, Lludd caused the Island to be measured in its length and in its breadth. And in Oxford he found the central point, and in that place he caused the earth to be dug, and in that pit a cauldron to be set, full of the best mead that could be made, and a covering of satin over the face of it. And he himself watched that night. And while he was there, he beheld the dragons fighting. And when they were weary they fell, and came down upon the top of the satin, and drew it with them to the bottom of the cauldron. And when they had drunk the mead they slept. And in their sleep, Lludd folded the covering around them, and in the securest place he had in Snowdon, he hid them in a kistvaen.

Now after that this spot was called Dinas Emreis, but before that, Dinas Ffaraon. And thus the fierce outcry ceased in his dominions.

And when this was ended, King Lludd caused an exceeding great banquet to be prepared. And when it was ready, he placed a vessel of cold water by his side, and he in his own proper person watched it. And as he abode thus clad with arms, about the third watch of the night, lo, he heard many surpassing fascinations and various songs. And drowsiness urged him to sleep. Upon this, lest he should be hindered from his purpose and be overcome by sleep, he went often into the water. And at last, behold, a man of vast size, clad in strong, heavy armour, came in, bearing a hamper. And, as he was wont, he put all the food and provisions of meat and drink into the hamper, and proceeded to go with it forth. And nothing was ever more wonderful to Lludd, than that the hamper should hold so much.

And thereupon King Lludd went after him and spoke unto him thus. "Stop, stop," said he, "though thou hast done many insults and much spoil erewhile, thou shalt not do so any more, unless thy skill in arms and thy prowess be greater than mine."

Then he instantly put down the hamper on the floor, and awaited him. And a fierce encounter was between them, so that the glittering fire flew out from their arms. And at the last Lludd grappled with him, and fate bestowed the victory on Lludd. And he threw the plague to the earth. And after he had overcome him by strength and might, he besought his mercy. "How can I grant thee mercy," said the king, "after all the many injuries and wrongs that thou hast done me?" "All the losses that ever I have caused thee," said he, "I will make thee atonement for, equal to what I have taken. And I will never do the like from this time forth. But thy faithful vassal will I be." And the king accepted this from him.

And thus Lludd freed the Island of Britain from the three plagues. And from thenceforth until the end of his life, in prosperous peace did Lludd the son of Beli rule the Island of Britain. And this Tale is called the Story of Lludd and Llevelys. And thus it ends.

KILHWCH AND OLWEN
OR THE TWRCH TRWYTH

KILYDD the son of Prince Kelyddon desired a wife as a helpmate, and the wife that he chose was Goleuddydd, the daughter of Prince Anlawdd. And after their union, the people put up prayers that they might have an heir. And they had a son through the prayers of the people. From the time of her pregnancy Goleuddydd became wild, and wandered about, without habitation; but when her delivery was at hand, her reason came back to her. Then she went to a mountain where there was a swineherd, keeping a herd of swine. And through fear of the swine the queen was delivered. And the swineherd took the boy, and brought him to the palace; and he was christened, and they called him Kilhwch, because he had been found in a swine's burrow. Nevertheless the boy was of gentle lineage, and cousin unto Arthur; and they put him out to nurse.

After this the boy's mother, Goleuddydd, the daughter of Prince Anlawdd, fell sick. Then she called her husband unto her, and said to him, "Of this sickness I shall die, and thou wilt take another wife. Now wives are the gift of the Lord, but it would be wrong for thee to harm thy son. Therefore I charge thee that thou take not a wife until thou see a briar with two blossoms upon my grave." And this he promised her. Then she besought him to dress her grave every year, that nothing might grow thereon. So the queen died. Now the king sent an attendant every morning to see if anything were growing upon the grave. And at the end of the seventh year the master neglected that which he had promised to the queen.

One day the king went to hunt, and he rode to the place of burial to see the grave, and to know if it were time that he should take a wife; and the king saw the briar. And when he saw it, the king took counsel where he should find a wife. Said one of his counsellors, "I know a wife that will suit thee well, and she is the wife of King Doged." And they resolved to go to seek her; and they slew the king, and brought away his wife and one daughter that she had along with her. And they conquered the king's lands.

On a certain day, as the lady walked abroad, she came to the house of an old crone that dwelt in the town, and that had no tooth in her head. And the queen said to her, "Old woman, tell me that which I shall ask thee, for the love of Heaven. Where are the children of the man who has carried me away by violence?" Said the crone, "He has not children."

Said the queen, "Woe is me, that I should have come to one who is childless!" Then said the hag, "Thou needest not lament on account of that, for there is a prediction he shall have an heir by thee, and by none other. Moreover, be not sorrowful, for he has one son."

The lady returned home with joy; and she asked her consort, "Wherefore hast thou concealed thy children from me?" The king said, "I will do so no longer." And he sent messengers for his son, and he was brought to the Court. His stepmother said unto him, "It were well for thee to have a wife, and I have a daughter who is sought of every man of renown in the world." "I am not yet of an age to wed," answered the youth. Then said she unto him, "I declare to thee, that it is thy destiny not to be suited with a wife until thou obtain Olwen, the daughter of Yspaddaden Penkawr." And the youth blushed, and the love of the maiden diffused itself through all his frame, although he had never seen her. And his father inquired of him, "What has come over thee, my son, and what aileth thee?" "My stepmother has declared to me that I shall never have a wife until I obtain Olwen, the daughter of Yspaddaden Penkawr." "That will be easy for thee," answered his father. "Arthur is thy cousin. Go, therefore, unto Arthur, to cut thy hair, and ask this of him as a boon."

And the youth pricked forth upon a steed with head dappled grey, of four winters old, firm of limb, with shell-formed hoofs, having a bridle of linked gold on his head, and upon him a saddle of costly gold. And in the youth's hand were two spears of silver, sharp, well-tempered, headed with steel, three ells in length, of an edge to wound the wind, and cause blood to flow, and swifter than the fall of the dewdrop from the blade of reed-grass upon the earth when the dew of June is at the heaviest. A gold-hilted sword was upon his thigh, the blade of which was of gold, bearing a cross of inlaid gold of the hue of the lightning of heaven: his war-horn was of ivory. Before him were two brindled white-breasted greyhounds, having strong collars of rubies about their necks, reaching from the shoulder to the ear. And the one that was on the left side bounded across to the right side, and the one on the right to the left, and like two sea-swallows sported around him. And his courser cast up four sods with his four hoofs, like four swallows in the air, about his head, now above, now below. About him was a four-cornered cloth of purple, and an apple of gold was at each corner, and every one of the apples was of the value of an hundred kine. And there was precious gold of the value of three hundred kine upon his shoes, and upon his stirrups, from his knee to the tip of his toe. And the blade of grass bent not beneath him, so light was his courser's tread as he journeyed towards the gate of Arthur's Palace.

Spoke the youth, "Is there a porter?" "There is; and if thou holdest not thy peace, small will be thy welcome. I am Arthur's porter every first day of January. And during every other part of the year but this, the office is filled by Huandaw, and Gogigwc, and Llaeskenym, and Pennpingyon, who goes upon his head to save his feet, neither towards the sky nor towards the earth, but like a rolling stone upon the floor of the court." "Open the portal." "I will not open it." "Wherefore not?" "The knife is in the meat, and the drink is in the horn, and there is revelry in Arthur's Hall, and none may enter therein but the son of a king of a privileged country, or a craftsman bringing his craft. But there will be refreshment for thy dogs, and for thy horses; and for thee there will be collops cooked and peppered, and luscious wine and mirthful songs, and food for fifty men shall be brought unto thee in the guest chamber, where the stranger and the sons of other countries eat, who come not unto the precincts of the Palace of Arthur. Thou wilt fare no worse there than thou wouldest with Arthur in the Court. A lady shall smooth thy couch, and shall lull thee with songs; and early to-morrow morning, when the gate is open for the multitude that come hither to-day, for thee shall it be opened first, and thou mayest sit in the place that thou shalt choose in Arthur's Hall, from the upper end to the lower." Said the youth, "That will I not do. If thou openest the gate, it is well. If thou dost not open it, I will bring disgrace upon thy Lord, and evil report upon thee. And I will set up three shouts at this very gate, than which none were ever more deadly, from the top of Pengwaed in Cornwall to the bottom of Dinsol, in the North, and to Esgair Oervel, in Ireland. And all the women in this Palace that are pregnant shall lose their offspring; and such as are not pregnant, their hearts shall be turned by illness, so that they shall never bear children from this day forward." "What clamour soever thou mayest make," said Glewlwyd Gavaelvawr, "against the laws of Arthur's Palace shalt thou not enter therein, until I first go and speak with Arthur."

Then Glewlwyd went into the Hall. And Arthur said to him, "Hast thou news from the gate?" — "Half of my life is past, and half of thine. I was heretofore in Kaer Se and Asse, in Sach and Salach, in Lotor and Fotor; and I have been heretofore in India the Great and India the Lesser; and I was in the battle of Dau Ynyr, when the twelve hostages were brought from Llychlyn. And I have also been in Europe, and in Africa, and in the islands of Corsica, and in Caer Brythwch, and Brythach, and Verthach; and I was present when formerly thou didst slay the family of Clis the son of Merin, and when thou didst slay Mil Du the son of Ducum, and when thou didst conquer Greece in the East. And I have been in Caer Oeth and Annoeth, and in Caer Nevenhyr; nine supreme sovereigns, handsome men, saw we there, but never did I behold a man of equal dignity with him who is now at the door of the portal." Then said

Arthur, "If walking thou didst enter in here, return thou running. And every one that beholds the light, and every one that opens and shuts the eye, let them shew him respect, and serve him, some with gold-mounted drinking-horns, others with collops cooked and peppered, until food and drink can be prepared for him. It is unbecoming to keep such a man as thou sayest he is, in the wind and the rain." Said Kai, "By the hand of my friend, if thou wouldest follow my counsel, thou wouldest not break through the laws of the Court because of him." "Not so, blessed Kai. It is an honour to us to be resorted to, and the greater our courtesy the greater will be our renown, and our fame, and our glory."

And Glewlwyd came to the gate, and opened the gate before him; and although all dismounted upon the horseblock at the gate, yet did he not dismount, but rode in upon his charger. Then said Kilhwch, "Greeting be unto thee, Sovereign Ruler of this Island; and be this greeting no less unto the lowest than unto the highest, and be it equally unto thy guests, and thy warriors, and thy chieftains — let all partake of it as completely as thyself. And complete be thy favour, and thy fame, and thy glory, throughout all this Island." "Greeting unto thee also," said Arthur; "sit thou between two of my warriors, and thou shalt have minstrels before thee, and thou shalt enjoy the privileges of a king born to a throne, as long as thou remainest here. And when I dispense my presents to the visitors and strangers in this Court, they shall be in thy hand at my commencing." Said the youth, "I came not here to consume meat and drink; but if I obtain the boon that I seek, I will requite it thee, and extol thee; and if I have it not, I will bear forth thy dispraise to the four quarters of the world, as far as thy renown has extended." Then said Arthur, "Since thou wilt not remain here, chieftain, thou shalt receive the boon whatsoever thy tongue may name, as far as the wind dries, and the rain moistens, and the sun revolves, and the sea encircles, and the earth extends; save only my ship; and my mantle; and Caledvwlch, my sword; and Rhongomyant, my lance; and Wynebgwrthucher, my shield; and Carnwenhau, my dagger; and Gwenhwyvar, my wife. By the truth of Heaven, thou shalt have it cheerfully, name what thou wilt." "I would that thou bless my hair." "That shall be granted thee."

And Arthur took a golden comb, and scissors, whereof the loops were of silver, and he combed his hair. And Arthur inquired of him who he was. "For my heart warms unto thee, and I know that thou art come of my blood. Tell me, therefore, who thou art." "I will tell thee," said the youth. "I am Kilhwch, the son of Kilydd, the son of Prince Kelyddon, by Goleuddydd, my mother, the daughter of Prince Anlawdd." "That is true," said Arthur; "thou art my cousin. Whatsoever boon thou mayest ask, thou shalt receive, be it what it may that thy tongue shall name." "Pledge the truth of Heaven and the faith of thy kingdom thereof." "I pledge it thee, gladly." "I crave of thee then, that thou obtain for me Olwen, the daughter of Yspaddaden Penkawr; and this boon I likewise seek at the hands of thy warriors. I seek it from Kai, and Bedwyr, and Greidawl Galldonyd, and Gwythyr the son of Greidawl, and Greid the son of Eri, and Kynddelig Kyvarwydd, and Tathal Twyll Goleu, and Maelwys the son of Baeddan, and Crychwr the son of Nes, and Cubert the son of Daere, and Percos the son of Poch, and Lluber Beuthach, and Corvil Bervach, and Gwynn the son of Nudd, and Edeyrn the son of Nudd, and Gadwy the son of Geraint, and Prince Fflewddur Fflam, and Ruawn Pebyr the son of Dorath, and Bradwen the son of Moren Mynawc, and Moren Mynawc himself, and Dalldav the son of Kimin Côv, and the son of Alun Dyved, and the son of Saidi, and the son of Gwryon, and Uchtryd Ardywad Kad, and Kynwas Curvagyl, and Gwrhyr Gwarthegvras, and Isperyr Ewingath, and Gallcoyt Govynynat, and Duach, and Grathach, and Nerthach, the sons of Gwawrddur Kyrvach (these men came forth from the confines of hell), and Kilydd Canhastyr, and Canhastyr Canllaw, and Cors Cant-Ewin, and Esgeir Gulhwch Govynkawn, and Drustwrn Hayarn, and Glewlwyd Gavaelvawr, and Lloch Llawwynnyawc, and Aunwas Adeiniawc, and Sinnoch the son of Seithved, and Gwennwynwyn the son of Naw, and Bedyw the son of Seithved, and Gobrwy the son of Echel Vorddwyttwll, and Echel Vorddwyttwll himself, and Mael the son of Roycol, and Dadweir Dallpenn, and Garwyli the son of Gwythawc Gwyr, and Gwythawc Gwyr himself, and Gormant the son of Ricca, and Menw the son of Teirgwaedd, and Digon the son of Alar, and Selyf the son of Smoit, and Gusg the son of Atheu, and Nerth the son of Kedarn, and Drudwas the son of Tryffin, and Twrch the son of Perif, and Twrch the son of Annwas, and Iona king of France, and Sel the son of Selgi, and Teregud the son of Iaen, and Sulyen the son of Iaen, and Bradwen the son of Iaen, and Moren the son of Iaen, and Siawn the son of Iaen, and Cradawc the son of Iaen. (They were men of Caerdathal, of Arthur's kindred on his father's side.) Dirmyg the son of Kaw, and Justic the son of Kaw, and Etmic the son of Kaw, and Anghawd the son of Kaw, and Ovan the son of Kaw, and Kelin the son of Kaw, and Connyn the son of Kaw, and Mabsant the son of Kaw, and Gwyngad the son of Kaw, and Llwybyr the son of Kaw, and Coth the son of Kaw, and Meilic the son of Kaw, and Kynwas the son of Kaw, and Ardwyad the son of Kaw, and Ergyryad the son of Kaw, and Neb the son of Kaw, and Gilda the son of Kaw, and Calcas the son of Kaw, and Hueil the son of Kaw (he never yet made a request at the hand of any Lord). And Samson Vinsych, and Taliesin the chief of the bards, and Manawyddan the son of Llyr, and Llary the son of Prince Kasnar, and Ysperni the son of Fflergant king of Armorica, and Saranhon the son of Glythwyr, and Llawr Eilerw, and Annyanniawc the son of Menw the son of Teirgwaedd, and Gwynn the son of Nwyvre, and Fflam the son of Nwyvre, and Geraint the son of Erbin, and Ermid the son of Erbin, and Dyvel the son of Erbin, and Gwynn the son of Ermid, and Kyndrwyn the son of Ermid, and Hyveidd Unllenn, and Eiddon Vawr Vrydic, and Reidwn Arwy, and Gormant the son of Ricca (Arthur's brother by his mother's side; the Penhynev of Cornwall was his father), and Llawnrodded Varvawc, and Nodawl Varyf Twrch, and Berth the son of Kado, and Rheidwn the son of Beli, and Iscovan Hael, and Iscawin the son of Panon, and Morvran the son of Tegid (no one struck him in the battle of Camlan by reason of his ugliness; all thought he was an auxiliary devil. Hair had he upon him like the hair of a stag). And Sandde Bryd Angel (no one touched him with a spear in the battle of Camlan because of his beauty; all thought he was a ministering angel). And Kynwyl Sant (the third man that escaped from the battle of Camlan, and he was the last who parted from Arthur on Hengroen his horse). And Uchtryd the son of Erim, and Eus the son of Erim, and Henwas Adeinawg the son of Erim, and Henbedestyr the son of Erim, and Sgilti Yscawndroed the son of Erim. (Unto these three men belonged these three qualities,—With Henbedestyr there was not any one who could keep pace, either on horseback or on foot; with Henwas Adeinawg, no four-footed beast could run the distance of an acre, much less could it go beyond it; and as to Sgilti Yscawndroed, when he intended to go upon a message for his Lord, he never sought to find a path, but knowing whither he was to go, if his way lay through a wood he went along the tops of the trees. During his whole life, a blade of reed grass bent not beneath his feet, much less did one ever break, so lightly did he tread.) Teithi Hên the son of Gwynhan (his dominions were swallowed up by the sea, and he himself hardly escaped, and he came to Arthur; and his knife had this peculiarity, that from the time that he came there no haft would ever remain upon it, and owing to this a sickness came over him, and he pined away during the remainder of his life, and of this he died). And Carneddyr the son of Govynyon Hên, and Gwenwynwyn the son of Nav Gyssevin, Arthur's champion, and Llysgadrudd Emys, and Gwrbothu Hên (uncles unto Arthur were they, his mother's brothers). Kulvanawyd the son of Goryon, and Llenlleawg Wyddel from the headland of Ganion, and Dyvynwal Moel, and Dunard king of the North, Teirnon Twryf Bliant, and Tegvan Gloff, and Tegyr Talgellawg, Gwrdinal the son of Ebrei, and Morgant Hael, Gwystyl the son of Rhun the son of Nwython, and Llwyddeu the son of Nwython, and Gwydre the son of Llwyddeu (Gwenabwy the daughter of [Kaw] was his mother, Hueil his uncle stabbed him, and hatred was between Hueil and Arthur because of the wound). Drem the son of Dremidyd (when the gnat arose in the morning with the sun, he could see it from Gelli Wic in Cornwall, as far off as Pen Blathaon in North Britain). And Eidyol the son of Ner, and Glwyddyn Saer (who constructed Ehangwen, Arthur's Hall). Kynyr Keinvarvawc (when he was told he had a son born he said to his wife, 'Damsel, if thy son be mine, his heart will be always cold, and there will be no warmth in his hands; and he will have another peculiarity, if he is my son he will always be stubborn; and he will have another peculiarity, when he carries a burden, whether it be large or small, no one will be able to see it, either before him or at his back; and he will have another peculiarity, no one will be able to resist fire and water so well as he will; and he will have another peculiarity, there will never be a servant or an officer equal to him'). Henwas, and Henwyneb (an old companion to Arthur). Gwallgoyc (another; when he came to a town, though there were three hundred houses in it, if he wanted anything, he would not let sleep come to the eyes of any one whilst he remained there). Berwyn the son of Gerenhir, and Paris king of France, and Osla Gyllellvawr (who bore a short broad dagger. When Arthur and his hosts came before a torrent, they would seek for a narrow place where they might pass the water, and would lay the sheathed dagger across the torrent, and it would form a bridge sufficient for the armies of the three Islands of Britain, and of the three islands adjacent, with their spoil). Gwyddawg the son of Menestyr (who slew Kai, and whom Arthur slew, together with his brothers, to revenge Kai). Garanwyn the son of Kai, and Amren the son of Bedwyr, and Ely Amyr, and Rheu Rhwyd Dyrys, and Rhun Rhudwern, and Eli, and Trachmyr (Arthur's chief huntsmen). And Llwyddeu the son of Kelcoed, and Hunabwy the son of Gwryon, and Gwynn Godyvron, and Gweir Datharwenniddawg, and Gweir the son of Cadell the son of Talaryant, and Gweir Gwrhyd Ennwir, and Gweir Paladyr Hir (the uncles of Arthur, the brothers of his mother). The sons of Llwch Llawwynnyawg (from beyond the raging sea). Llenlleawg Wyddel, and Ardderchawg Prydain. Cas the son of Saidi, Gwrvan Gwallt Avwyn, and Gwyllennhin the king of France, and Gwittart the son of Oedd king of Ireland, Garselit Wyddel, Panawr Pen Bagad, and Ffleudor the son of Nav, Gwynnhyvar mayor of Cornwall and Devon (the ninth man that rallied the battle of Camlan). Keli and Kueli, and Gilla Coes Hydd (he would clear three hundred acres at one bound: the chief leaper of Ireland was he). Sol, and Gwadyn Ossol, and Gwadyn Odyeith. (Sol could stand all day upon one foot. Gwadyn Ossol, if he stood upon the top of the highest mountain in the world, it would become a level plain under his feet. Gwadyn Odyeith, the soles of his feet emitted sparks of fire when they struck upon things hard, like the heated mass when drawn out of the forge. He cleared the way for Arthur when he came to any stoppage.) Hirerwm and Hiratrwm. (The day they went on a visit three Cantrevs provided for their entertainment, and they feasted until noon and drank until night, when they went to sleep. And then they devoured the heads of the vermin through hunger, as if they had never eaten anything. When they made a visit they left neither the fat nor the lean, neither the hot nor the cold, the sour nor the sweet, the fresh nor the salt, the boiled nor the raw.) Huarwar the son of Aflawn (who asked Arthur such a boon as would satisfy him. It was the third great plague of Cornwall when he received it. None could get a smile from him but when he was satisfied). Gware Gwallt Euryn. The two cubs of Gast Rhymi, Gwyddrud and Gwyddneu Astrus. Sugyn the son of Sugnedydd (who would suck up the sea on which were three hundred ships so as to leave nothing but a dry strand. He was broad-chested). Rhacymwri, the attendant of Arthur (whatever barn he was shown, were there the produce of thirty ploughs within it, he would strike it with an iron flail until the rafters, the beams, and the boards were no better than the small oats in the mow upon the floor of the barn). Dygyflwng and Anoeth Veidawg. And Hir Eiddyl, and Hir Amreu (they were two attendants of Arthur). And Gwevyl the son of Gwestad (on the day that he was sad, he would let one of his lips drop below his waist, while he turned up the other like a cap upon his head). Uchtryd Varyf Draws (who spread his red untrimmed beard over the eight-and-forty rafters which were in Arthur's Hall). Elidyr Gyvarwydd. Yskyrdav and Yscudydd (two attendants of Gwenhwyvar were they. Their feet were swift as their thoughts when bearing a message). Brys the son of Bryssethach (from the Hill of the Black Fernbrake in North Britain). And Grudlwyn Gorr. Bwlch, and Kyfwlch, and Sefwlch, the sons of Cleddyf Kyfwlch, the grandsons of Cleddyf Difwlch. (Their three shields were three gleaming glitterers; their three spears were three pointed piercers; their three swords were three grinding gashers; Glas, Glessic, and Gleisad. Their three dogs, Call, Cuall, and Cavall. Their three horses, Hwyrdyddwd, and Drwgdyddwd, and Llwyrdyddwg. Their three wives, Och, and Garym, and Diaspad. Their three grandchildren, Lluched, and Neved, and Eissiwed. Their three daughters, Drwg, and Gwaeth, and Gwaethav Oll. Their three handmaids, Eheubryd the daughter of Kyfwlch, Gorascwrn the daughter of Nerth, Ewaedan the daughter of Kynvelyn Keudawd Pwyll the half-man.) Dwnn Diessic Unbenn, Eiladyr the son of Pen Llarcau, Kynedyr Wyllt the son of Hettwn Talaryant, Sawyl Ben Uchel, Gwalchmai the son of Gwyar, Gwalhaved the son of Gwyar, Gwrhyr Gwastawd Ieithoedd (to whom all tongues were known), and Kethcrwm the Priest. Clust the son of Clustveinad (though he were buried seven cubits beneath the earth, he would hear the ant fifty miles off rise from her nest in the morning). Medyr the son of Methredydd (from Gelli Wic he could, in a twinkling, shoot the wren through the two legs upon Esgeir Oervel in Ireland). Gwiawn Llygad Cath (who could cut a haw from the eye of the gnat without hurting him). Ol the son of Olwydd (seven years before he was born his father's swine were carried off, and when he grew up a man he tracked the swine, and brought them back in seven herds). Bedwini the Bishop (who blessed Arthur's meat and drink). For the sake of the golden-chained daughters of this island. For the sake of Gwenhwyvar its chief lady, and Gwennhwyach her sister, and Rathtyeu the only daughter of Clemenhill, and Rhelemon the daughter of Kai, and Tannwen the daughter of Gweir Datharwenîddawg. Gwenn Alarch the daughter of Kynwyl Canbwch. Eurneid the daughter of Clydno Eiddin. Encuawc the daughter of Bedwyr. Enrydreg the daughter of Tudvathar. Gwennwledyr the daughter of Gwaledyr Kyrvach. Erddudnid the daughter of Tryffin. Eurolwen the daughter of Gwdolwyn Gorr. Teleri the daughter of Peul. Indeg the daughter of Garwy Hir. Morvudd the daughter of Urien Rheged. Gwenllian Deg the majestic maiden. Creiddylad the daughter of Lludd Llaw Ereint. (She was the most splendid maiden in the three Islands of the mighty, and in the three Islands adjacent, and for her Gwythyr the son of Greidawl and Gwynn the son of Nudd fight every first of May until the day of doom.) Ellylw the daughter of Neol Kynn-Crog (she lived three ages). Essyllt Vinwen and Essyllt Vingul." And all these did Kilhwch the son of Kilydd adjure to obtain his boon.

Then said Arthur, "Oh! chieftain, I have never heard of the maiden of whom thou speakest, nor of her kindred, but I will gladly send messengers in search of her. Give me time to seek her." And the youth said, "I will willingly grant from this night to that at the end of the year to do so." Then Arthur sent messengers to every land within his dominions to seek for the maiden; and at the end of the year Arthur's messengers returned without having gained any knowledge or intelligence concerning Olwen more than on the first day. Then said Kilhwch, "Every one has received his boon, and I yet lack mine. I will depart and bear away thy honour with me." Then said Kai, "Rash chieftain! dost thou reproach Arthur?

Go with us, and we will not part until thou dost either confess that the maiden exists not in the world, or until we obtain her." Thereupon Kai rose up. Kai had this peculiarity, that his breath lasted nine nights and nine days under water, and he could exist nine nights and nine days without sleep. A wound from Kai's sword no physician could heal. Very subtle was Kai. When it pleased him he could render himself as tall as the highest tree in the forest. And he had another peculiarity, — so great was the heat of his nature, that, when it rained hardest, whatever he carried remained dry for a handbreadth above and a handbreadth below his hand; and when his companions were coldest, it was to them as fuel with which to light their fire.

And Arthur called Bedwyr, who never shrank from any enterprise upon which Kai was bound. None was equal to him in swiftness throughout this island except Arthur and Drych Ail Kibddar. And although he was one-handed, three warriors could not shed blood faster than he on the field of battle. Another property he had; his lance would produce a wound equal to those of nine opposing lances.

And Arthur called to Kynddelig the Guide, "Go thou upon this expedition with the chieftain." For as good a guide was he in a land which he had never seen as he was in his own.

He called Gwrhyr Gwalstawt Ieithoedd, because he knew all tongues.

He called Gwalchmai the son of Gwyar, because he never returned home without achieving the adventure of which he went in quest. He was the best of footmen and the best of knights. He was nephew to Arthur, the son of his sister, and his cousin.

And Arthur called Menw the son of Teirgwaedd, in order that if they went into a savage country, he might cast a charm and an illusion over them, so that none might see them whilst they could see every one.

They journeyed until they came to a vast open plain, wherein they saw a great castle, which was the fairest of the castles of the world. And they journeyed that day until the evening, and when they thought they were nigh to the castle, they were no nearer to it than they had been in the morning. And the second and the third day they journeyed, and even then scarcely could they reach so far. And when they came before the castle, they beheld a vast flock of sheep, which was boundless and without an end. And upon the top of a mound there was a herdsman, keeping the sheep. And a rug made of skins was upon him; and by his side was a shaggy mastiff, larger than a steed nine winters old. Never had he lost even a lamb from his flock, much less a large sheep. He let no occasion ever pass without doing some hurt and harm. All the dead trees and bushes in the plain he burnt with his breath down to the very ground.

Then said Kai, "Gwrhyr Gwalstawt Ieithoedd, go thou and salute yonder man." "Kai," said he, "I engaged not to go further than thou thyself." "Let us go then together," answered Kai. Said Menw the son of Teirgwaedd, "Fear not to go thither, for I will cast a spell upon the dog, so that he shall injure no one." And they went up to the mound whereon the herdsman was, and they said to him, "How dost thou fare, O herdsman?" "No less fair be it to you than to me." "Truly, art thou the chief?" "There is no hurt to injure me but my own."[1] "Whose are the sheep that thou dost keep, and to whom does yonder castle belong?" "Stupid are ye, truly! Through the whole world is it known that this is the castle of Yspaddaden Penkawr." "And who art thou?" "I am called Custennin the son of Dyfnedig, and my brother Yspaddaden Penkawr oppressed me because of my possessions. And ye also, who are ye?" "We are an embassy from Arthur, come to seek Olwen the daughter of Yspaddaden Penkawr." "Oh men! the mercy of Heaven be upon you, do not that for all the world. None who ever came hither on this quest has returned alive." And the herdsman rose up. And as he arose, Kilhwch gave unto him a ring of gold. And he sought to put on the ring, but it was too small for him, so he placed it in the finger of his glove. And he went home, and gave the glove to his spouse to keep. And she took the ring from the glove when it was given her, and she said, "Whence came this ring, for thou art not wont to have good fortune?" "I went," said he, "to the sea to seek for fish, and lo, I saw a corpse borne by the waves. And a fairer corpse than it did I never behold. And from its finger did I take this ring." "O man! does the sea permit its dead to wear jewels? Show me then this body." "Oh wife, him to whom this ring belonged thou shalt see here in the evening." "And who is he?" asked the woman. "Kilhwch the son of Kilydd, the son of Prince Kelyddon, by Goleuddydd the daughter of Prince Anlawdd, his mother, who is come to seek Olwen as his wife." And when she heard that, her feelings were divided between the joy that she had that her nephew, the son of her sister, was coming to her, and sorrow because she had never known any one depart alive who had come on that quest.

And they went forward to the gate of Custennin the herdsman's dwelling. And when she heard their footsteps approaching, she ran out with joy to meet them. And Kai snatched a billet out of the pile. And when she met them she sought to throw her arms about their necks. And Kai placed the log between her two hands, and she squeezed it so that it became a twisted coil. "Oh woman," said Kai, "if thou hadst squeezed

[1] This dialogue consists of a series of repartees with a play upon words, which it is impossible to follow in the translation.

me thus, none could ever again have set their affections on me. Evil love were this." They entered into the house, and were served; and soon after they all went forth to amuse themselves. Then the woman opened a stone chest that was before the chimney-corner, and out of it arose a youth with yellow curling hair. Said Gwrhyr, "It is a pity to hide this youth. I know that it is not his own crime that is thus visited upon him." "This is but a remnant," said the woman. "Three-and-twenty of my sons has Yspaddaden Penkawr slain, and I have no more hope of this one than of the others." Then said Kai, "Let him come and be a companion with me, and he shall not be slain unless I also am slain with him." And they ate. And the woman asked them, "Upon what errand come you here?" "We come to seek Olwen for this youth." Then said the woman, "In the name of Heaven, since no one from the castle hath yet seen you, return again whence you came." "Heaven is our witness, that we will not return until we have seen the maiden." Said Kai, "Does she ever come hither, so that she may be seen?" "She comes here every Saturday to wash her head, and in the vessel where she washes, she leaves all her rings, and she never either comes herself or sends any messengers to fetch them." "Will she come here if she is sent to?" "Heaven knows that I will not destroy my soul, nor will I betray those that trust me; unless you will pledge me your faith that you will not harm her, I will not send to her." "We pledge it," said they. So a message was sent, and she came.

The maiden was clothed in a robe of flame-coloured silk, and about her neck was a collar of ruddy gold, on which were precious emeralds and rubies. More yellow was her head than the flower of the broom, and her skin was whiter than the foam of the wave, and fairer were her hands and her fingers than the blossoms of the wood anemone amidst the spray of the meadow fountain. The eye of the trained hawk, the glance of the three-mewed falcon was not brighter than hers. Her bosom was more snowy than the breast of the white swan, her cheek was redder than the reddest roses. Whoso beheld her was filled with her love. Four white trefoils sprung up wherever she trod. And therefore was she called Olwen.

She entered the house, and sat beside Kilhwch upon the foremost bench; and as soon as he saw her he knew her. And Kilhwch said unto her, "Ah! maiden, thou art she whom I have loved; come away with me, lest they speak evil of thee and of me. Many a day have I loved thee." "I cannot do this, for I have pledged my faith to my father not to go without his counsel, for his life will last only until the time of my espousals. Whatever is, must be. But I will give thee advice if thou wilt take it. Go, ask me of my father, and that which he shall require of thee, grant it, and thou wilt obtain me; but if thou deny him anything, thou wilt not obtain me, and it will be well for thee if thou escape with thy life." "I promise all this, if occasion offer," said he.

She returned to her chamber, and they all rose up and followed her to the castle. And they slew the nine porters that were at the nine gates in silence. And they slew the nine watch-dogs without one of them barking. And they went forward to the hall.

"The greeting of Heaven and of man be unto thee, Yspaddaden Penkawr," said they. "And you, wherefore come you?" "We come to ask thy daughter Olwen, for Kilhwch the son of Kilydd, the son of Prince Kelyddon." "Where are my pages and my servants? Raise up the forks beneath my two eyebrows which have fallen over my eyes, that I may see the fashion of my son-in-law." And they did so. "Come hither to-morrow, and you shall have an answer."

They rose to go forth, and Yspaddaden Penkawr seized one of the three poisoned darts that lay beside him, and threw it after them. And Bedwyr caught it, and flung it, and pierced Yspaddaden Penkawr grievously with it through the knee. Then he said, "A cursed ungentle son-in-law, truly. I shall ever walk the worse for his rudeness, and shall ever be without a cure. This poisoned iron pains me like the bite of a gadfly. Cursed be the smith who forged it, and the anvil whereon it was wrought! So sharp is it!"

That night also they took up their abode in the house of Custennin the herdsman. The next day with the dawn they arrayed themselves in haste and proceeded to the castle, and entered the hall, and they said, "Yspaddaden Penkawr, give us thy daughter in consideration of her dower and her maiden fee, which we will pay to thee and to her two kinswomen likewise. And unless thou wilt do so, thou shalt meet with thy death on her account." Then he said, "Her four great-grandmothers, and her four great-grandsires are yet alive, it is needful that I take counsel of them." "Be it so," answered they, "we will go to meat." As they rose up, he took the second dart that was beside him, and cast it after them. And Menw the son of Gwaedd caught it, and flung it back at him, and wounded him in the centre of the breast, so that it came out at the small of his back. "A cursed ungentle son-in-law, truly," said he, "the hard iron pains me like the bite of a horse-leech. Cursed be the hearth whereon it was heated, and the smith who formed it! So sharp is it! Henceforth, whenever I go up a hill, I shall have a scant in my breath, and a pain in my chest, and I shall often loathe my food." And they went to meat.

And the third day they returned to the palace. And Yspaddaden Penkawr said to them, "Shoot not at me again unless you desire death. Where are my attendants? Lift up the forks of my eyebrows which have fallen over my eyeballs, that I may see the fashion of my son-in-law."

Then they arose, and, as they did so, Yspaddaden Penkawr took the third poisoned dart and cast it at them. And Kilhwch caught it and threw it vigorously, and wounded him through the eyeball, so that the dart came out at the back of his head. "A cursed ungentle son-in-law, truly! As long as I remain alive, my eyesight will be the worse. Whenever I go against the wind, my eyes will water; and peradventure my head will burn, and I shall have a giddiness every new moon. Cursed be the fire in which it was forged. Like the bite of a mad dog is the stroke of this poisoned iron." And they went to meat.

And the next day they came again to the palace, and they said, "Shoot not at us any more, unless thou desirest such hurt, and harm, and torture as thou now hast, and even more." "Give me thy daughter, and if thou wilt not give her, thou shalt receive thy death because of her." "Where is he that seeks my daughter? Come hither where I may see thee." And they placed him a chair face to face with him.

Said Yspaddaden Penkawr, "Is it thou that seekest my daughter?" "It is I," answered Kilhwch. "I must have thy pledge that thou wilt not do towards me otherwise than is just, and when I have gotten that which I shall name, my daughter thou shalt have." "I promise thee that willingly," said Kilhwch, "name what thou wilt." "I will do so," said he.

"Seest thou yonder vast hill?" "I see it." "I require that it be rooted up, and that the grubbings be burned for manure on the face of the land, and that it be ploughed and sown in one day, and in one day that the grain ripen. And of that wheat I intend to make food and liquor fit for the wedding of thee and my daughter. And all this I require done in one day."

"It will be easy for me to compass this, although thou mayest think that it will not be easy."

"Though this be easy for thee, there is yet that which will not be so. No husbandman can till or prepare this land, so wild is it, except Amaethon the son of Don, and he will not come with thee by his own free will, and thou wilt not be able to compel him."

"It will be easy for me to compass this, although thou mayest think that it will not be easy."

"Though thou get this, there is yet that which thou wilt not get. Govannon the son of Don to come to the headland to rid the iron, he will do no work of his own good will except for a lawful king, and thou wilt not be able to compel him."

"It will be easy for me to compass this."

"Though thou get this, there is yet that which thou wilt not get; the two dun oxen of Gwlwlyd, both yoked together, to plough the wild land yonder stoutly. He will not give them of his own free will, and thou wilt not be able to compel him."

"It will be easy for me to compass this."

"Though thou get this, there is yet that which thou wilt not get; the yellow and the brindled bull yoked together do I require."

"It will be easy for me to compass this."

"Though thou get this, there is yet that which thou wilt not get; the two horned oxen, one of which is beyond, and the other this side of the peaked mountain, yoked together in the same plough. And these are Nynniaw and Peibaw whom God turned into oxen on account of their sins."

"It will be easy for me to compass this."

"Though thou get this, there is yet that which thou wilt not get. Seest thou yonder red tilled ground?"

"I see it."

"When first I met the mother of this maiden, nine bushels of flax were sown therein, and none has yet sprung up, neither white nor black; and I have the measure by me still. I require to have the flax to sow in the new land yonder, that when it grows up it may make a white wimple for my daughter's head, on the day of thy wedding."

"It will be easy for me to compass this, although thou mayest think that it will not be easy."

"Though thou get this, there is yet that which thou wilt not get. Honey that is nine times sweeter than the honey of the virgin swarm, without scum and bees, do I require to make bragget for the feast."

"It will be easy for me to compass this, although thou mayest think that it will not be easy."

"The vessel of Llwyr the son of Llwyryon, which is of the utmost value. There is no other vessel in the world that can hold this drink. Of his free will thou wilt not get it, and thou canst not compel him."

"It will be easy for me to compass this, although thou mayest think that it will not be easy."

"Though thou get this, there is yet that which thou wilt not get. The basket of Gwyddneu Garanhir, if the whole world should come together, thrice nine men at a time, the meat that each of them desired would be found within it. I require to eat therefrom on the night that my daughter becomes thy bride. He will give it to no one of his own free will, and thou canst not compel him."

"It will be easy for me to compass this, although thou mayest think that it will not be easy."

"Though thou get this, there is yet that which thou wilt not get. The horn of Gwlgawd Gododin to serve us with liquor that night. He will not give it of his own free will, and thou wilt not be able to compel him."

"It will be easy for me to compass this, although thou mayest think that it will not be easy."

"Though thou get this, there is yet that which thou wilt not get. The harp of Teirtu to play to us that night. When a man desires that it should play, it does so of itself, and when he desires that it should cease, it ceases. And this he will not give of his own free will, and thou wilt not be able to compel him."

"It will be easy for me to compass this, although thou mayest think that it will not be easy."

"Though thou get this, there is yet that which thou wilt not get. The cauldron of Diwrnach Wyddel, the steward of Odgar the son of Aedd, king of Ireland, to boil the meat for thy marriage feast."

"It will be easy for me to compass this, although thou mayest think that it will not be easy."

"Though thou get this, there is yet that which thou wilt not get. It is needful for me to wash my head, and shave my beard, and I require the tusk of Yskithyrwyn Penbaedd to shave myself withal, neither shall I profit by its use if it be not plucked alive out of his head."

"It will be easy for me to compass this, although thou mayest think that it will not be easy."

"Though thou get this, there is yet that which thou wilt not get. There is no one in the world that can pluck it out of his head except Odgar the son of Aedd, king of Ireland."

"It will be easy for me to compass this."

"Though thou get this, there is yet that which thou wilt not get. I will not trust any one to keep the tusk except Gado of North Britain. Now the threescore Cantrevs of North Britain are under his sway, and of his own free will he will not come out of his kingdom, and thou wilt not be able to compel him."

"It will be easy for me to compass this, although thou mayest think that it will not be easy."

"Though thou get this, there is yet that which thou wilt not get. I must spread out my hair in order to shave it, and it will never be spread out unless I have the blood of the jet-black sorceress, the daughter of the pure white sorceress, from Pen Nant Govid, on the confines of Hell."

"It will be easy for me to compass this, although thou mayest think that it will not be easy."

"Though thou get this, there is yet that which thou wilt not get. I will not have the blood unless I have it warm, and no vessels will keep warm the liquid that is put therein except the bottles of Gwyddolwyd Gorr, which preserve the heat of the liquor that is put into them in the east, until they arrive at the west. And he will not give them of his own free will, and thou wilt not be able to compel him."

"It will be easy for me to compass this, although thou mayest think that it will not be easy."

"Though thou get this, there is yet that which thou wilt not get. Some will desire fresh milk, and it will not be possible to have fresh milk for all, unless we have the bottles of Rhinnon Rhin Barnawd, wherein no liquor ever turns sour. And he will not give them of his own free will, and thou wilt not be able to compel him."

"It will be easy for me to compass this, although thou mayest think that it will not be easy."

"Though thou get this, there is yet that which thou wilt not get. Throughout the world there is not a comb or scissors with which I can arrange my hair, on account of its rankness, except the comb and scissors that are between the two ears of Twrch Trwyth, the son of Prince Tared. He will not give them of his own free will, and thou wilt not be able to compel him."

"It will be easy for me to compass this, although thou mayest think that it will not be easy."

"Though thou get this, there is yet that which thou wilt not get. It will not be possible to hunt Twrch Trwyth without Drudwyn the whelp of Greid, the son of Eri."

"It will be easy for me to compass this, although thou mayest think that it will not be easy."

"Though thou get this, there is yet that which thou wilt not get. Throughout the world there is not a leash that can hold him, except the leash of Cwrs Cant Ewin."

"It will be easy for me to compass this, although thou mayest think that it will not be easy."

"Though thou get this, there is yet that which thou wilt not get. Throughout the world there is no collar that will hold the leash except the collar of Canhastyr Canllaw."

"It will be easy for me to compass this, although thou mayest think that it will not be easy."

"Though thou get this, there is yet that which thou wilt not get. The chain of Kilydd Canhastyr to fasten the collar to the leash."

"It will be easy for me to compass this, although thou mayest think that it will not be easy."

"Though thou get this, there is yet that which thou wilt not get.

Throughout the world there is not a huntsman who can hunt with this dog, except Mabon the son of Modron. He was taken from his mother when three nights old, and it is not known where he now is, nor whether he is living or dead."

"It will be easy for me to compass this, although thou mayest think that it will not be easy."

"Though thou get this, there is yet that which thou wilt not get. Gwynn Mygdwn, the horse of Gweddw, that is as swift as the wave, to carry Mabon the son of Modron to hunt the boar Trwyth. He will not give him of his own free will, and thou wilt not be able to compel him."

"It will be easy for me to compass this, although thou mayest think that it will not be easy."

"Though thou get this, there is yet that which thou wilt not get. Thou wilt not get Mabon, for it is not known where he is, unless thou find Eidoel, his kinsman in blood, the son of Aer. For it would be useless to seek for him. He is his cousin."

"It will be easy for me to compass this, although thou mayest think that it will not be easy."

"Though thou get this, there is yet that which thou wilt not get. Garselit the Gwyddelian is the chief huntsman of Ireland; the Twrch Trwyth can never be hunted without him."

"It will be easy for me to compass this, although thou mayest think that it will not be easy."

"Though thou get this, there is yet that which thou wilt not get. A leash made from the beard of Dillus Varvawc, for that is the only one that can hold those two cubs. And the leash will be of no avail unless it be plucked from his beard while he is alive, and twitched out with wooden tweezers. While he lives he will not suffer this to be done to him, and the leash will be of no use should he be dead, because it will be brittle."

"It will be easy for me to compass this, although thou mayest think that it will not be easy."

"Though thou get this, there is yet that which thou wilt not get. Throughout the world there is no huntsman that can hold those two whelps except Kynedyr Wyllt, the son of Hettwn Glafyrawc; he is nine times more wild than the wildest beast upon the mountains. Him wilt thou never get, neither wilt thou ever get my daughter."

"It will be easy for me to compass this, although thou mayest think that it will not be easy."

"Though thou get this, there is yet that which thou wilt not get. It is not possible to hunt the boar Trwyth without Gwynn the son of Nudd, whom God has placed over the brood of devils in Annwvyn, lest they should destroy the present race. He will never be spared thence."

"It will be easy for me to compass this, although thou mayest think that it will not be easy."

"Though thou get this, there is yet that which thou wilt not get. There is not a horse in the world that can carry Gwynn to hunt the Twrch Trwyth, except Du, the horse of Mor of Oerveddawg."

"It will be easy for me to compass this, although thou mayest think that it will not be easy."

"Though thou get this, there is yet that which thou wilt not get. Until Gilennhin the king of France shall come, the Twrch Trwyth cannot be hunted. It will be unseemly for him to leave his kingdom for thy sake, and he will never come hither."

"It will be easy for me to compass this, although thou mayest think that it will not be easy."

"Though thou get this, there is yet that which thou wilt not get. The Twrch Trwyth can never be hunted without the son of Alun Dyved; he is well skilled in letting loose the dogs."

"It will be easy for me to compass this, although thou mayest think that it will not be easy."

"Though thou get this, there is yet that which thou wilt not get. The Twrch Trwyth cannot be hunted unless thou get Aned and Aethlem. They are as swift as the gale of wind, and they were never let loose upon a beast that they did not kill him."

"It will be easy for me to compass this, although thou mayest think that it will not be easy."

"Though thou get this, there is yet that which thou wilt not get; Arthur and his companions to hunt the Twrch Trwyth. He is a mighty man, and he will not come for thee, neither wilt thou be able to compel him."

"It will be easy for me to compass this, although thou mayest think that it will not be easy."

"Though thou get this, there is yet that which thou wilt not get. The Twrch Trwyth cannot be hunted unless thou get Bwlch, and Kyfwlch [and Sefwlch], the grandsons of Cleddyf Difwlch. Their three shields are three gleaming glitterers. Their three spears are three pointed piercers. Their three swords are three griding gashers, Glas, Glessic, and Clersag. Their three dogs, Call, Cuall, and Cavall. Their three horses, Hwyrdydwg, and Drwgdydwg, and Llwyrdydwg. Their three wives, Och, and Garam, and Diaspad. Their three grandchildren, Lluched, and Vyned, and Eissiwed. Their three daughters, Drwg, and Gwaeth, and Gwaethav Oll. Their three handmaids [Eheubryd, the daughter of Kyfwlch; Gorasgwrn, the daughter of Nerth; and Gwaedan, the daughter of Kynvelyn]. These three men shall sound the horn, and all the others shall shout, so that all will think that the sky is falling to the earth."

"It will be easy for me to compass this, although thou mayest think that it will not be easy."

"Though thou get this, there is yet that which thou wilt not get. The sword of Gwrnach the Giant; he will never be slain except therewith. Of his own free will he will not give it, either for a price or as a gift, and thou wilt never be able to compel him."

"It will be easy for me to compass this, although thou mayest think that it will not be easy."

"Though thou get this, there is yet that which thou wilt not get. Difficulties shalt thou meet with, and nights without sleep, in seeking this, and if thou obtain it not, neither shalt thou obtain my daughter."

"Horses shall I have, and chivalry; and my lord and kinsman Arthur will obtain for me all these things. And I shall gain thy daughter, and thou shalt lose thy life."

"Go forward. And thou shalt not be chargeable for food or raiment for my daughter while thou art seeking these things; and when thou has compassed all these marvels, thou shalt have my daughter for thy wife."

All that day they journeyed until the evening, and then they beheld a vast castle, which was the largest in the world. And lo, a black man, huger than three of the men of this world, came out from the castle. And they spoke unto him, "Whence comest thou, O man?" "From the castle which you see yonder." "Whose castle is that?" asked they. "Stupid are ye truly, O men. There is no one in the world that does not know to whom this castle belongs. It is the castle of Gwrnach the Giant." "What treatment is there for guests and strangers that alight in that castle?" "Oh! Chieftain, Heaven protect thee. No guest ever returned thence alive, and no one may enter therein unless he brings with him his craft."

Then they proceeded towards the gate. Said Gwrhyr Gwalstawt Ieithoedd, "Is there a porter?" "There is. And thou, if thy tongue be not mute in thy head, wherefore dost thou call?" "Open the gate." "I will not open it." "Wherefore wilt thou not?" "The knife is in the meat, and the drink is in the horn, and there is revelry in the hall of Gwrnach the Giant, and except for a craftsman who brings his craft, the gate will not be opened to-night." "Verily, porter," then said Kai, "my craft bring I with me." "What is thy craft?" "The best burnisher of swords am I in the world." "I will go and tell this unto Gwrnach the Giant, and I will bring thee an answer."

So the porter went in, and Gwrnach said to him, "Hast thou any news from the gate?" "I have. There is a party at the door of the gate who desire to come in." "Didst thou inquire of them if they possessed any art?" "I did inquire," said he, "and one told me that he was well skilled in the burnishing of swords." "We have need of him then. For some time have I sought for some one to polish my sword, and could find no one. Let this man enter, since he brings with him his craft." The porter thereupon returned and opened the gate. And Kai went in by himself, and he saluted Gwrnach the Giant. And a chair was placed for him opposite to Gwrnach. And Gwrnach said to him, "Oh man! is it true that is reported of thee, that thou knowest how to burnish swords?" "I know full well how to do so," answered Kai. Then was the sword of Gwrnach brought to him. And Kai took a blue whetstone from under his arm, and asked him whether he would have it burnished white or blue. "Do with it as it seems good to thee, and as thou wouldest if it were thine own." Then Kai polished one half of the blade and put it in his hand. "Will this please thee?" asked he. "I would rather than all that is in my dominions that the whole of it were like unto this. It is a marvel to me that such a man as thou should be without a companion." "Oh! noble sir, I have a companion, albeit he is not skilled in this art." "Who may he be?" "Let the porter go forth, and I will tell him whereby he may know him. The head of his lance will leave its shaft, and draw blood from the wind, and will descend upon its shaft again." Then the gate was opened, and Bedwyr entered. And Kai said, "Bedwyr is very skillful, although he knows not this art."

And there was much discourse among those who were without, because that Kai and Bedwyr had gone in. And a young man who was with them, the only son of Custennin the herdsman, got in also. And he caused all his companions to keep close to him as he passed the three wards, and until he came into the midst of the castle. And his companions said unto the son of Custennin, "Thou hast done this! Thou art the best of all men." And thenceforth he was called Goreu, the son of Custennin. Then they dispersed to their lodgings, that they might slay those who lodged therein, unknown to the Giant.

The sword was now polished, and Kai gave it unto the hand of Gwrnach the Giant, to see if he were pleased with his work. And the Giant said, "The work is good, I am content therewith." Said Kai, "It is thy scabbard that hath rusted thy sword, give it to me that I may take out the wooden sides of it and put in new ones." And he took the scabbard from him, and the sword in the other hand. And he came and stood over against the Giant, as if he would have put the sword into the scabbard; and with it he struck at the head of the Giant, and cut off his head at one blow. Then they despoiled the castle, and took from it what goods and jewels they would. And again on the same day, at the beginning of the year, they came to Arthur's Court, bearing with them the sword of Gwrnach the Giant.

Now, when they told Arthur how they had sped, Arthur said, "Which of these marvels will it be best for us to seek first?" "It will be best," said they, "to seek Mabon the son of Modron; and he will not be found unless we first find Eidoel the son of Aer, his kinsman." Then Arthur rose up, and the warriors of the Islands of Britain with him, to seek for Eidoel; and they proceeded until they came before the Castle of Glivi, where Eidoel was imprisoned. Glivi stood on the summit of his castle, and he said, "Arthur, what requirest thou of me, since nothing remains to me in this fortress, and I have neither joy nor pleasure in it; neither wheat nor oats? Seek not therefore to do me harm." Said Arthur, "Not to injure thee came I hither, but to seek for the prisoner that is with thee." "I will give thee my prisoner, though I had not thought to give him up to any one; and therewith shalt thou have my support and my aid."

His followers said unto Arthur, "Lord, go thou home, thou canst not proceed with thy host in quest of such small adventures as these." Then said Arthur, "It were well for thee, Gwrhyr Gwalstawt Ieithoedd, to go upon this quest, for thou knowest all languages, and art familiar with those of the birds and the beasts. Thou, Eidoel, oughtest likewise to go with my men in search of thy cousin. And as for you, Kai and Bedwyr, I have hope of whatever adventure ye are in quest of, that ye will achieve it. Achieve ye this adventure for me."

They went forward until they came to the Ousel of Cilgwri. And Gwrhyr adjured her for the sake of Heaven, saying, "Tell me if thou knowest aught of Mabon the son of Modron, who was taken when three nights old from between his mother and the wall." And the Ousel answered, "When I first came here, there was a smith's anvil in this place, and I was then a young bird; and from that time no work has been done upon it, save the pecking of my beak every evening, and now there is not so much as the size of a nut remaining thereof; yet the vengeance of Heaven be upon me, if during all that time I have ever heard of the man for whom you inquire. Nevertheless I will do that which is right, and that which it is fitting that I should do for an embassy from Arthur. There is a race of animals who were formed before me, and I will be your guide to them."

So they proceeded to the place where was the Stag of Redynvre. "Stag of Redynvre, behold we are come to thee, an embassy from Arthur, for we have not heard of any animal older than thou. Say, knowest thou aught of Mabon the son of Modron, who was taken from his mother when three nights old?" The Stag said, "When first I came hither, there was a plain all around me, without any trees save one oak sapling, which grew up to be an oak with an hundred branches. And that oak has since perished, so that now nothing remains of it but the withered stump; and from that day to this I have been here, yet have I never heard of the man for whom you inquire. Nevertheless, being an embassy from Arthur, I will be your guide to the place where there is an animal which was formed before I was."

So they proceeded to the place where was the Owl of Cwm Cawlwyd. "Owl of Cwm Cawlwyd, here is an embassy from Arthur; knowest thou aught of Mabon the son of Modron, who was taken after three nights from his mother?" "If I knew I would tell you. When first I came hither, the wide valley you see was a wooded glen. And a race of men came and rooted it up. And there grew there a second wood; and this wood is the third. My wings, are they not withered stumps? Yet all this time, even until to-day, I have never heard of the man for whom you inquire. Nevertheless, I will be the guide of Arthur's embassy until you come to the place where is the oldest animal in this world, and the one that has travelled most, the Eagle of Gwern Abwy."

Gwrhyr said, "Eagle of Gwern Abwy, we have come to thee an embassy from Arthur, to ask thee if thou knowest of Mabon the son of Modron, who was taken from his mother when he was three nights old." The Eagle said, "I have been here for a great space of time, and when I first came hither there was a rock here, from the top of which I pecked at the stars every evening; and now it is not so much as a span high. From that day to this I have been here, and I have never heard of the man for whom you inquire, except once when I went in search of food as far as Llyn Llyw. And when I came there, I struck my talons into a salmon, thinking he would serve me as food for a long time. But he drew me into the deep, and I was scarcely able to escape from him. After that I went with my whole kindred to attack him, and to try to destroy him, but he sent messengers, and made peace with me; and came and besought me to take fifty fish spears out of his back. Unless he know something of him whom you seek, I cannot tell who may. However, I will guide you to the place where he is."

So they went thither; and the Eagle said, "Salmon of Llyn Llyw, I have come to thee with an embassy from Arthur, to ask thee if thou knowest aught concerning Mabon the son of Modron, who was taken away at three nights old from his mother." "As much as I know I will tell thee. With every tide I go along the river upwards, until I come near to the walls of Gloucester, and there have I found such wrong as I never found elsewhere; and to the end that ye may give credence thereto, let one of you go thither upon each of my two shoulders." So Kai and Gwrhyr Gwalstawt Ieithoedd went upon the two shoulders of the salmon, and they proceeded until they came unto the wall of the prison, and they heard a great wailing and lamenting from the dungeon. Said Gwrhyr, "Who is it that laments in this house of stone?" "Alas, there is reason enough for whoever is here to lament. It is Mabon the son of Modron who is here imprisoned; and no imprisonment was ever so grievous as mine, neither that of Llud Llaw Ereint, nor that of Greid the son of Eri." "Hast thou hope of being released for gold or for silver, or for any gifts of wealth, or through battle and fighting?" "By fighting will whatever I may gain be obtained."

Then they went thence, and returned to Arthur, and they told him where Mabon the son of Modron was imprisoned. And Arthur summoned the warriors of the Island, and they journeyed as far as Gloucester, to the place where Mabon was in prison. Kai and Bedwyr went upon the shoulders of the fish, whilst the warriors of Arthur attacked the castle. And Kai broke through the wall into the dungeon, and brought away the prisoner upon his back, whilst the fight was going on between the warriors. And Arthur returned home, and Mabon with him at liberty.

Said Arthur, "Which of the marvels will it be best for us now to seek first?" "It will be best to seek for the two cubs of Gast Rhymhi." "Is it known," asked Arthur, "where she is?" "She is in Aber Deu Cleddyf," said one. Then Arthur went to the house of Tringad, in Aber Cleddyf, and he inquired of him whether he had heard of her there. "In what form may she be?" "She is in the form of a she-wolf," said he; "and with her there are two cubs." "She has often slain my herds, and she is there below in a cave in Aber Cleddyf."

So Arthur went in his ship Prydwen by sea, and the others went by land, to hunt her. And they surrounded her and her two cubs, and God did change them again for Arthur into their own form. And the host of Arthur dispersed themselves into parties of one and two.

On a certain day, as Gwythyr the son of Greidawl was walking over a mountain, he heard a wailing and a grievous cry. And when he heard it, he sprang forward, and went towards it. And when he came there, he drew his sword, and smote off an ant-hill close to the earth, whereby it escaped being burned in the fire. And the ants said to him, "Receive from us the blessing of Heaven, and that which no man can give we will give thee." Then they fetched the nine bushels of flax-seed which

Yspaddaden Penkawr had required of Kilhwch, and they brought the full measure without lacking any, except one flax-seed, and that the lame pismire brought in before night.

As Kai and Bedwyr sat on a beacon carn on the summit of Plinlimmon, in the highest wind that ever was in the world, they looked around them, and saw a great smoke towards the south, afar off, which did not bend with the wind. Then said Kai, "By the hand of my friend, behold, yonder is the fire of a robber!" Then they hastened towards the smoke, and they came so near to it, that they could see Dillus Varvawc scorching a wild boar. "Behold, yonder is the greatest robber that ever fled from Arthur," said Bedwyr unto Kai. "Dost thou know him?" "I do know him," answered Kai, "he is Dillus Varvawc, and no leash in the world will be able to hold Drudwyn, the cub of Greid the son of Eri, save a leash made from the beard of him thou seest yonder. And even that will be useless, unless his beard be plucked alive with wooden tweezers; for if dead, it will be brittle." "What thinkest thou that we should do concerning this?" said Bedwyr. "Let us suffer him," said Kai, "to eat as much as he will of the meat, and after that he will fall asleep." And during that time they employed themselves in making the wooden tweezers. And when Kai knew certainly that he was asleep, he made a pit under his feet, the largest in the world, and he struck him a violent blow, and squeezed him into the pit. And there they twitched out his beard completely with the wooden tweezers; and after that they slew him altogether.

And from thence they both went to Gelli Wic, in Cornwall, and took the leash made of Dillus Varvawc's beard with them, and they gave it into Arthur's hand. Then Arthur composed this Englyn —

Kai made a leash
Of Dillus son of Eurei's beard.
Were he alive, thy death he'd be.

And thereupon Kai was wroth, so that the warriors of the Island could scarcely make peace between Kai and Arthur. And thenceforth, neither in Arthur's troubles, nor for the slaying of his men, would Kai come forward to his aid for ever after.

Said Arthur, "Which of the marvels is it best for us now to seek?" "It is best for us to seek Drudwyn, the cub of Greid the son of Eri."

A little while before this, Creiddylad the daughter of Lludd Llaw Ereint, and Gwythyr the son of Greidawl, were betrothed. And before she had become his bride, Gwyn ap Nudd came and carried her away by force; and Gwythyr the son of Greidawl gathered his host together, and went to fight with Gwyn ap Nudd. But Gwyn overcame him, and captured Greid the son of Eri, and Glinneu the son of Taran, and Gwrgwst Ledlwm, and Dynvarth his son. And he captured Penn the son of Nethawg, and Nwython, and Kyledyr Wyllt his son. And they slew Nwython, and took out his heart, and constrained Kyledyr to eat the heart of his father. And therefrom Kyledyr became mad. When Arthur heard of this, he went to the North, and summoned Gwyn ap Nudd before him, and set free the nobles whom he had put in prison, and made peace between Gwyn ap Nudd and Gwythyr the son of Griedawl. And this was the peace that was made: — that the maiden should remain in her father's house, without advantage to either of them, and that Gwyn ap Nudd and Gwythyr the son of Griedawl should fight for her every first of May, from thenceforth until the day of doom, and that whichever of them should then be conqueror should have the maiden.

And when Arthur had thus reconciled these chieftains, he obtained Mygdwn, Gweddw's horse, and the leash of Cwrs Cant Ewin.

And after that Arthur went into Armorica, and with him Mabon the son of Mellt, and Gware Gwallt Euryn, to seek the two dogs of Glythmyr Ledewic. And when he had got them, he went to the West of Ireland, in search of Gwrgi Severi; and Odgar the son of Aedd king of Ireland went with him. And thence went Arthur into the North, and captured Kyledyr Wyllt; and he went after Yskithyrwyn Penbaedd. And Mabon the son of Mellt came with the two dogs of Glythmyr Ledewic in his hand, and Drudwyn, the cub of Greid the son of Eri. And Arthur went himself to the chase, leading his own dog Cavall. And Kaw, of North Britain, mounted Arthur's mare Llamrei, and was first in the attack. Then Kaw, of North Britain, wielded a mighty axe, and absolutely daring he came valiantly up to the boar, and clave his head in twain. And Kaw took away the tusk. Now the boar was not slain by the dogs that Yspaddaden had mentioned, but by Cavall, Arthur's own dog.

And after Yskithyrwyn Penbaedd was killed, Arthur and his host departed to Gelli Wic in Cornwall. And thence he sent Menw the son of Teirgwaedd to see if the precious things were between the two ears of Twrch Trwyth, since it were useless to encounter him if they were not there. Albeit it was certain where he was, for he had laid waste the third part of Ireland. And Menw went to seek for him, and he met with him in Ireland, in Esgeir Oervel. And Menw took the form of a bird; and he descended upon the top of his lair, and strove to snatch away one of the precious things from him, but he carried away nothing but one of his bristles. And the boar rose up angrily and shook himself so that some of his venom fell upon Menw, and he was never well from that day forward.

After this Arthur sent an embassy to Odgar, the son of Aedd king of Ireland, to ask for the cauldron of Diwrnach Wyddel, his purveyor. And Odgar commanded him to give it. But Diwrnach said, "Heaven is my witness, if it would avail him anything even to look at it, he should not do so." And the embassy of Arthur returned from Ireland with this denial. And Arthur set forward with a small retinue, and entered into Prydwen, his ship, and went over to Ireland. And they proceeded into the house of Diwrnach Wyddel. And the hosts of Odgar saw their strength. When they had eaten and drunk as much as they desired, Arthur demanded to have the cauldron. And he answered, "If I would have given it to any one, I would have given it at the word of Odgar king of Ireland."

When he had given them this denial, Bedwyr arose and seized hold of the cauldron, and placed it upon the back of Hygwyd, Arthur's servant, who was brother, by the mother's side, to Arthur's servant, Cachamwri. His office was always to carry Arthur's cauldron, and to place fire under it. And Llenlleawg Wyddel seized Caledvwlch, and brandished it. And they slew Diwrnach Wyddel and his company. Then came the Irish and fought with them. And when he had put them to flight, Arthur with his men went forward to the ship, carrying away the cauldron full of Irish money. And he disembarked at the house of Llwydden the son of Kelcoed, at Porth Kerddin in Dyvcd. And there is the measure of the cauldron.

Then Arthur summoned unto him all the warriors that were in the three Islands of Britain, and in the three Islands adjacent, and all that were in France and in Armorica, in Normandy and in the Summer Country, and all that were chosen footmen and valiant horsemen. And with all these he went into Ireland. And in Ireland there was great fear and terror concerning him. And when Arthur had landed in the country, there came unto him the saints of Ireland and besought his protection. And he granted his protection unto them, and they gave him their blessing. Then the men of Ireland came unto Arthur, and brought him provisions. And Arthur went as far as Esgeir Oervel in Ireland, to the place where the Boar Trwyth was with his seven young pigs. And the dogs were let loose upon him from all sides. That day until evening the Irish fought with him, nevertheless he laid waste the fifth part of Ireland. And on the day following the household of Arthur fought with him, and they were worsted by him, and got no advantage. And the third day Arthur himself encountered him, and he fought with him nine nights and nine days without so much as killing even one little pig. The warriors inquired of

Arthur what was the origin of that swine; and he told them that he was once a king, and that God had transformed him into a swine for his sins.

Then Arthur sent Gwrhyr Gwalstawt Ieithoedd, to endeavour to speak with him. And Gwrhyr assumed the form of a bird, and alighted upon the top of the lair, where he was with the seven young pigs. And Gwrhyr Gwalstawt Ieithoedd asked him, "By him who turned you into this form, if you can speak, let some one of you, I beseech you, come and talk with Arthur." Grugyn Gwrych Ereint made answer to him. (Now his bristles were like silver wire, and whether he went through the wood or through the plain, he was to be traced by the glittering of his bristles.) And this was the answer that Grugyn made: "By him who turned us into this form, we will not do so, and we will not speak with Arthur. That we have been transformed thus is enough for us to suffer, without your coming here to fight with us." "I will tell you. Arthur comes but to fight for the comb, and the razor, and the scissors which are between the two ears of Twrch Trwyth." Said Grugyn, "Except he first take his life, he will never have those precious things. And to-morrow morning we will rise up hence, and we will go into Arthur's country, and there will we do all the mischief that we can."

So they set forth through the sea towards Wales. And Arthur and his hosts, and his horses and his dogs, entered Prydwen, that they might encounter them without delay. Twrch Trwyth landed in Porth Cleis in Dyved, and Arthur came to Mynyw. The next day it was told to Arthur that they had gone by, and he overtook them as they were killing the cattle of Kynnwas Kwrr y Vagyl, having slain all that were at Aber Gleddyf, of man and beast, before the coming of Arthur.

Now when Arthur approached, Twrch Trwyth went on as far as Preseleu, and Arthur and his hosts followed him thither, and Arthur sent men to hunt him; Eli and Trachmyr, leading Drudwyn the whelp of Greid the son of Eri, and Gwarthegyd the son of Kaw, in another quarter, with the two dogs of Glythmyr Ledewic, and Bedwyr leading Cavall, Arthur's own dog. And all the warriors ranged themselves around the Nyver. And there came there the three sons of Cleddyf Divwlch, men who had gained much fame at the slaying of Yskithyrwyn Penbaedd; and they went on from Glyn Nyver, and came to Cwm Kerwyn.

And there Twrch Trwyth made a stand, and slew four of Arthur's champions, Gwarthegyd the son of Kaw, and Tarawc of Allt Clwyd, and Rheidwn the son of Eli Atver, and Iscovan Hael. And after he had slain these men, he made a second stand in the same place. And there he slew Gwydre the son of Arthur, and Garselit Wyddel, and Glew the son of Ysgawd, and Iscawyn the son of Panon; and there he himself was wounded.

And the next morning before it was day, some of the men came up with him. And he slew Huandaw, and Gogigwr, and Penpingon, three attendants upon Glewlwyd Gavaelvawr, so that Heaven knows he had not an attendant remaining, excepting only Llaesgevyn, a man from whom no one ever derived any good. And together with these he slew many of the men of that country, and Gwlydyn Saer, Arthur's chief Architect.

Then Arthur overtook him at Pelumyawc, and there he slew Madawc the son of Teithyon, and Gwyn the son of Tringad, the son of Neved, and Eiryawn Penllorau. Thence he went to Aberteivi, where he made another stand, and where he slew Kyflas the son of Kynan, and Gwilenhin king of France. Then he went as far as Glyn Ystu, and there the men and the dogs lost him.

Then Arthur summoned unto him Gwyn ab Nudd, and he asked him if he knew aught of Twrch Trwyth. And he said that he did not.

And all the huntsmen went to hunt the swine as far as Dyffryn Llychwr. And Grugyn Gwallt Ereint and Llwydawg Govynnyad closed with them and killed all the huntsmen, so that there escaped but one man only. And Arthur and his hosts came to the place where Grugyn and Llwydawg were. And there he let loose the whole of the dogs upon them, and with the shout and barking that was set up, Twrch Trwyth came to their assistance.

And from the time that they came across the Irish sea, Arthur had never got sight of him until then. So he set men and dogs upon him, and thereupon he started off and went to Mynydd Amanw. And there one of his young pigs was killed. Then they set upon him life for life, and Twrch Llawin was slain, and then there was slain another of the swine, Gwys was his name. After that he went on to Dyffryn Amanw, and there Banw and Bennwig were killed. Of all his pigs there went with him alive from that place none save Grugyn Gwallt Ereint and Llwydawg Govynnyad.

Thence he went on to Llwch Ewin, and Arthur overtook him there, and he made a stand. And there he slew Echel Forddwytwll, and Garwyli the son of Gwyddawg Gwyr, and many men and dogs likewise. And thence they went to Llwch Tawy. Grugyn Gwrych Ereint parted from them there, and went to Din Tywi. And thence he proceeded to Ceredigiawn, and Eli and Trachmyr with him, and a multitude likewise. Then he came to Garth Gregyn, and there Llwydawg Govynnyad fought in the midst of them, and slew Rhudvyw Rhys and many others with him. Then Llwydawg went thence to Ystrad Yw, and there the men of Armorica met him, and there he slew Hirpeissawg the king of

Armorica, and Llygatrudd Emys, and Gwrbothu, Arthur's uncles, his mother's brothers, and there was he himself slain.

Twrch Trwyth went from there to between Tawy and Euyas, and Arthur summoned all Cornwall and Devon unto him, to the estuary of the Severn, and he said to the warriors of this Island, "Twrch Trwyth has slain many of my men, but, by the valour of warriors, while I live he shall not go into Cornwall. And I will not follow him any longer, but I will oppose him life to life. Do ye as ye will." And he resolved that he would send a body of knights, with the dogs of the Island, as far as Euyas, who should return thence to the Severn, and that tried warriors should traverse the Island, and force him into the Severn. And Mabon the son of Modron came up with him at the Severn, upon Gwynn Mygdwn, the horse of Gweddw, and Goreu the son of Custennin, and Menw the son of Teirgwaedd; this was betwixt Llyn Lliwan and Aber Gwy. And Arthur fell upon him together with the champions of Britain. And Osla Kyllellvawr drew near, and Manawyddan the son of Llyr, and Kacmwri the servant of Arthur, and Gwyngelli, and they seized hold of him, catching him first by his feet, and plunged him in the Severn, so that it overwhelmed him. On the one side, Mabon the son of Modron spurred his steed and snatched his razor from him, and Kyledyr Wyllt came up with him on the other side, upon another steed, in the Severn, and took from him the scissors. But before they could obtain the comb, he had regained the ground with his feet, and from the moment that he reached the shore, neither dog, nor man, nor horse could overtake him until he came to Cornwall. If they had had trouble in getting the jewels from him, much more had they in seeking to save the two men from being drowned. Kacmwri, as they drew him forth, was dragged by two millstones into the deep. And as Osla Kyllellvawr was running after the boar, his knife had dropped out of the sheath, and he had lost it, and after that, the sheath became full of water, and its weight drew him down into the deep, as they were drawing him forth.

Then Arthur and his hosts proceeded until they overtook the boar in Cornwall, and the trouble which they had met with before was mere play to what they encountered in seeking the comb. But from one difficulty to another, the comb was at length obtained. And then he was hunted from Cornwall, and driven straight forward into the deep sea. And thenceforth it was never known whither he went; and Aned and Aethlem with him. Then went Arthur to Gelli Wic, in Cornwall, to anoint himself, and to rest from his fatigues.

Said Arthur, "Is there any one of the marvels yet unobtained?" Said one of his men, "There is — the blood of the witch Orddu, the daughter of the witch Orwen, of Pen Nant Govid, on the confines of Hell." Arthur set forth towards the North, and came to the place where was the witch's cave. And Gwyn ab Nudd, and Gwythyr the son of Greidawl, counselled him to send Kacmwri, and Hygwyd his brother, to fight with the witch. And as they entered the cave, the witch seized upon them, and she caught Hygwyd by the hair of his head, and threw him on the floor beneath her. And Kacmwri caught her by the hair of her head, and dragged her to the earth from off Hygwyd, but she turned again upon them both, and drove them both out with kicks and with cuffs.

And Arthur was wroth at seeing his two attendants almost slain, and he sought to enter the cave; but Gwyn and Gwythyr said unto him, "It would not be fitting or seemly for us to see thee squabbling with a hag. Let Hiramreu and Hireidil go to the cave." So they went. But if great was the trouble of the first two that went, much greater was that of these two. And Heaven knows that not one of the four could move from the spot, until they placed them all upon Llamrei, Arthur's mare. And then Arthur rushed to the door of the cave, and at the door he struck at the witch, with Carnwennan his dagger, and clove her in twain, so that she fell in two parts. And Kaw, of North Britain, took the blood of the witch and kept it.

Then Kilhwch set forward, and Goreu the son of Custennin with him, and as many as wished ill to Yspaddaden Penkawr. And they took the marvels with them to his court. And Kaw of North Britain came and shaved his beard, skin, and flesh clean off to the very bone from ear to ear. "Art thou shaved, man?" said Kilhwch. "I am shaved," answered he. "Is thy daughter mine now?" "She is thine," said he, "but therefore needest thou not thank me, but Arthur who hath accomplished this for thee. By my free will thou shouldest never have had her, for with her I lose my life." Then Goreu the son of Custennin seized him by the hair of his head, and dragged him after him to the keep, and cut off his head and placed it on a stake on the citadel. Then they took possession of his castle, and of his treasures.

And that night Olwen became Kilhwch's bride, and she continued to be his wife as long as she lived. And the hosts of Arthur dispersed themselves, each man to his own country. And thus did Kilhwch obtain Olwen, the daughter of Yspaddaden Penkawr.

THE DREAM OF RHONABWY

MADAWC the son of Maredudd possessed Powys within its boundaries, from Porfoed to Gwauan in the uplands of Arwystli. And at that time he had a brother, Iorwerth the son of Maredudd, in rank not equal to himself. And Iorwerth had great sorrow and heaviness because of the honour and power that his brother enjoyed, which he shared not. And he sought his fellows and his foster-brothers, and took counsel with them what he should do in this matter. And they resolved to dispatch some of their number to go and seek a maintenance for him. Then Madawc offered him to become Master of the Household and to have horses, and arms, and honour, and to fare like as himself. But Iorwerth refused this.

And Iorwerth made an inroad into Loegria, slaying the inhabitants, and burning houses, and carrying away prisoners. And Madawc took counsel with the men of Powys, and they determined to place an hundred men in each of the three Commots of Powys to seek for him. And thus did they in the plains of Powys from Aber Ceirawc, and in Allictwn Ver, and in Rhyd Wilure, on the Vyrnwy, the three best Commots of Powys. So he was none the better, he nor his household, in Powys, nor in the plains thereof. And they spread these men over the plains as far as Nillystwn Trevan.

Now one of the men who was upon this quest was called Rhonabwy. And Rhonabwy and Kynwrig Vrychgoch, a man of Mawddwy, and Cadwgan Vras, a man of Moelvre in Kynlleith, came together to the house of Heilyn Goch the son of Cadwgan the son of Iddon. And when they came near to the house, they saw an old hall, very black and having an upright gable, whence issued a great smoke; and on entering, they found the floor full of puddles and mounds; and it was difficult to stand thereon, so slippery was it with the mire of cattle. And where the puddles were, a man might go up to his ankles in water and dirt. And there were boughs of holly spread over the floor, whereof the cattle had browsed the sprigs. When they came to the hall of the house, they beheld cells full of dust, and very gloomy, and on one side an old hag making a fire. And whenever she felt cold, she cast a lapful of chaff upon the fire, and raised such a smoke, that it was scarcely to be borne, as it rose up the nostrils. And on the other side was a yellow calf-skin on the floor; a main privilege was it to any one who should get upon that hide.

And when they had sat down, they asked the hag where were the people of the house. And the hag spoke not, but muttered. Thereupon behold the people of the house entered; a ruddy, clownish, curly-headed man, with a burthen of faggots on his back, and a pale slender woman, also carrying a bundle under her arm. And they barely welcomed the men, and kindled a fire with the boughs. And the woman cooked something, and gave them to eat, barley bread, and cheese, and milk and water.

And there arose a storm of wind and rain, so that it was hardly possible to go forth with safety. And being weary with their journey, they laid themselves down and sought to sleep. And when they looked at the couch, it seemed to be made but of a little coarse straw full of dust and vermin, with the stems of boughs sticking up therethrough, for the cattle had eaten all the straw that was placed at the head and the foot. And upon it was stretched an old russet-coloured rug, threadbare and ragged; and a coarse sheet, full of slits, was upon the rug, and an ill-stuffed pillow, and a worn-out cover upon the sheet. And after much suffering from the vermin, and from the discomfort of their couch, a heavy sleep fell on Rhonabwy's companions. But Rhonabwy, not being able either to sleep or to rest, thought he should suffer less if he went to lie upon the yellow calf-skin that was stretched out on the floor. And there he slept.

As soon as sleep had come upon his eyes, it seemed to him that he was journeying with his companions across the plain of Argyngroeg, and he thought that he went towards Rhyd y Groes on the Severn. As he journeyed, he heard a mighty noise, the like whereof heard he never before; and looking behind him, he beheld a youth with yellow curling hair, and with his beard newly trimmed, mounted on a chestnut horse, whereof the legs were grey from the top of the forelegs, and from the bend of the hindlegs downwards. And the rider wore a coat of yellow satin sewn with green silk, and on his thigh was a gold-hilted sword, with a scabbard of new leather of Cordova, belted with the skin of the deer, and clasped with gold. And over this was a scarf of yellow satin wrought with green silk, the borders whereof were likewise green. And the green of the caparison of the horse, and of his rider, was as green as the leaves of the fir-tree, and the yellow was as yellow as the blossom of the broom. So fierce was the aspect of the knight, that fear seized upon them, and they began to flee. And the knight pursued them. And when the horse breathed forth, the men became distant from him, and when he drew in his breath, they were drawn near to him, even to the horse's chest. And when he had overtaken them, they besought his mercy. "You have it gladly," said he, "fear nought." "Ha, chieftain, since thou hast mercy upon me, tell me also who thou art," said Rhonabwy. "I will not conceal my lineage from thee, I am Iddawc the son of Mynyo, yet not by my name, but by my nickname am I best known." "And wilt thou tell us what thy nickname is?" "I will tell you; it is Iddawc Cordd Prydain." "Ha, chieftain," said Rhonabwy, "why art thou called thus?" "I will tell thee. I was one of the messengers between Arthur and Medrawd his nephew, at the battle of Camlan; and I was then a reckless youth, and through my desire for battle, I kindled strife between them, and stirred up wrath, when I was sent by Arthur the Emperor to reason with Medrawd, and to show him, that he was his foster-father and his uncle, and to seek for peace, lest the sons of the Kings of the Island of Britain, and of the nobles, should be slain. And whereas Arthur charged me with the fairest sayings he could think of, I uttered unto Medrawd the harshest I could devise. And therefore am I called Iddawc Cordd Prydain, for from this did the battle of Camlan ensue. And three nights before the end of the battle of Camlan I left them, and went to the Llech Las in North Britain to do penance. And there I remained doing penance seven years, and after that I gained pardon."

Then lo! they heard a mighty sound which was much louder than that which they had heard before, and when they looked round towards the sound, they beheld a ruddy youth, without beard or whiskers, noble of mien, and mounted on a stately courser. And from the shoulders and the front of the knees downwards the horse was bay. And upon the man was a dress of red satin wrought with yellow silk, and yellow were the borders of his scarf. And such parts of his apparel and of the trappings of his horse as were yellow, as yellow were they as the blossom of the broom, and such as were red, were as ruddy as the ruddiest blood in the world.

Then, behold the horseman overtook them, and he asked of Iddawc a share of the little men that were with him. "That which is fitting for me to grant I will grant, and thou shalt be a companion to them as I have been." And the horseman went away. "Iddawc," inquired Rhonabwy, "who was that horseman?" "Rhuvawn Pebyr the son of Prince Deorthach."

And they journeyed over the plain of Argyngroeg as far as the ford of Rhyd y Groes on the Severn. And for a mile around the ford on both sides of the road, they saw tents and encampments, and there was the clamour of a mighty host. And they came to the edge of the ford, and there they beheld Arthur sitting on a flat island below the ford, having Bedwini the Bishop on one side of him, and Gwarthegyd the son of Kaw on the other. And a tall, auburn-haired youth stood before him, with his sheathed sword in his hand, and clad in a coat and cap of jet-black satin. And his face was white as ivory, and his eyebrows black as jet, and such part of his wrist as could be seen between his glove and his sleeve, was whiter than the lily, and thicker than a warrior's ankle.

Then came Iddawc and they that were with him, and stood before

Arthur and saluted him. "Heaven grant thee good," said Arthur. "And where, Iddawc, didst thou find these little men?" "I found them, lord, up yonder on the road." Then the Emperor smiled. "Lord," said Iddawc, "wherefore dost thou laugh?" "Iddawc," replied Arthur, "I laugh not; but it pitieth me that men of such stature as these should have this island in their keeping, after the men that guarded it of yore." Then said Iddawc, "Rhonabwy, dost thou see the ring with a stone set in it, that is upon the Emperor's hand?" "I see it," he answered. "It is one of the properties of that stone to enable thee to remember that thou seest here to-night, and hadst thou not seen the stone, thou wouldest never have been able to remember aught thereof."

After this they saw a troop coming towards the ford. "Iddawc," inquired Rhonabwy, "to whom does yonder troop belong?" "They are the fellows of Rhuvawn Pebyr the son of Prince Deorthach. And these men are honourably served with mead and bragget, and are freely beloved by the daughters of the kings of the Island of Britain. And this they merit, for they were ever in the front and the rear in every peril." And he saw but one hue upon the men and the horses of this troop, for they were all as red as blood. And when one of the knights rode forth from the troop, he looked like a pillar of fire glancing athwart the sky. And this troop encamped above the ford.

Then they beheld another troop coming towards the ford, and these from their horses' chests upwards were whiter than the lily, and below blacker than jet. And they saw one of these knights go before the rest, and spur his horse into the ford in such a manner that the water dashed over Arthur and the Bishop, and those holding counsel with them, so that they were as wet as if they had been drenched in the river. And as he turned the head of his horse, the youth who stood before Arthur struck the horse over the nostrils with his sheathed sword, so that, had it been with the bare blade, it would have been a marvel if the bone had not been wounded as well as the flesh. And the knight drew his sword half out of the scabbard, and asked of him, "Wherefore didst thou strike my horse? Whether was it in insult or in counsel unto me?" "Thou dost indeed lack counsel. What madness caused thee to ride so furiously as to dash the water of the ford over Arthur, and the consecrated Bishop, and their counsellors, so that they were as wet as if they had been dragged out of the river?" "As counsel then will I take it." So he turned his horse's head round towards his army.

"Iddawc," said Rhonabwy, "who was yonder knight?" "The most eloquent and the wisest youth that is in this island; Adaon, the son of Taliesin." "Who was the man that struck his horse?" "A youth of froward nature; Elphin, the son of Gwyddno."

Then spake a tall and stately man, of noble and flowing speech, saying that it was a marvel that so vast a host should be assembled in so narrow a space, and that it was a still greater marvel that those should be there at that time who had promised to be by mid-day in the battle of Badon, fighting with Osla Gyllellvawr. "Whether thou mayest choose to proceed or not, I will proceed." "Thou sayest well," said Arthur, "and we will go altogether." "Iddawc," said Rhonabwy, "who was the man who spoke so marvellously unto Arthur erewhile?" "A man who may speak as boldly as he listeth, Caradawc Vreichvras, the son of Llyr Marini, his chief counsellor and his cousin."

Then Iddawc took Rhonabwy behind him on his horse, and that mighty host moved forward, each troop in its order, towards Cevndigoll. And when they came to the middle of the ford of the Severn, Iddawc turned his horse's head, and Rhonabwy looked along the valley of the Severn. And he beheld two fair troops coming towards the ford. One troop there came of brilliant white, whereof every one of the men had a scarf of white satin with jet-black borders. And the knees and the tops of the shoulders of their horses were jet-black, though they were of a pure white in every other part. And their banners were pure white, with black points to them all.

"Iddawc," said Rhonabwy, "who are yonder pure white troop?" "They are the men of Norway, and March the son of Meirchion is their prince. And he is cousin unto Arthur." And further on he saw a troop, whereof each man wore garments of jet-black, with borders of pure white to every scarf; and the tops of the shoulders and the knees of their horses were pure white. And their banners were jet-black with pure white at the point of each.

"Iddawc," said Rhonabwy, "who are the jet-black troop yonder?" "They are the men of Denmark, and Edeyrn the son of Nudd is their prince."

And when they had overtaken the host, Arthur and his army of mighty ones dismounted below Caer Badou, and he perceived that he and Iddawc journeyed the same road as Arthur. And after they had dismounted he heard a great tumult and confusion amongst the host, and such as were then at the flanks turned to the centre, and such as had been in the centre moved to the flanks. And then, behold, he saw a knight coming, clad, both he and his horse, in mail, of which the rings were whiter than the whitest lily, and the rivets redder than the ruddiest blood. And he rode amongst the host.

"Iddawc," said Rhonabwy, "will yonder host flee?" "King Arthur never fled, and if this discourse of thine were heard, thou wert a lost man. But as to the knight whom thou seest yonder, it is Kai. The fairest horseman is Kai in all Arthur's Court; and the men who are at the front of the army hasten to the rear to see Kai ride, and the men who are in the centre flee to the side, from the shock of his horse. And this is the cause of the confusion of the host."

Thereupon they heard a call made for Kadwr, Earl of Cornwall, and behold he arose with the sword of Arthur in his hand. And the similitude of two serpents was upon the sword in gold. And when the sword was drawn from its scabbard, it seemed as if two flames of fire burst forth from the jaws of the serpents, and then, so wonderful was the sword, that it was hard for any one to look upon it. And the host became still, and the tumult ceased, and the Earl returned to the tent.

"Iddawc," said Rhonabwy, "who is the man who bore the sword of Arthur?" "Kadwr, the Earl of Cornwall, whose duty it is to arm the King on the days of battle and warfare."

And they heard a call made for Eirynwych Amheibyn, Arthur's servant, a red, rough, ill-favoured man, having red whiskers with bristly hairs. And behold he came upon a tall red horse with the mane parted on each side, and he brought with him a large and beautiful sumpter pack. And the huge red youth dismounted before Arthur, and he drew a golden chair out of the pack, and a carpet of diapered satin. And he spread the carpet before Arthur, and there was an apple of ruddy gold at each corner thereof, and he placed the chair upon the carpet. And so large was the chair that three armed warriors might have sat therein. Gwenn was the name of the carpet, and it was one of its properties that whoever was upon it no one could see him, and he could see every one. And it would retain no colour but its own.

And Arthur sat within the carpet, and Owain the son of Urien was standing before him. "Owain," said Arthur, "wilt thou play chess?" "I will, Lord," said Owain. And the red youth brought the chess for Arthur and Owain; golden pieces and a board of silver. And they began to play.

And while they were thus, and when they were best amused with their game, behold they saw a white tent with a red canopy, and the figure of a jet-black serpent on the top of the tent, and red glaring venomous eyes in the head of the serpent, and a red flaming tongue. And there came a young page with yellow curling hair, and blue eyes, and a newly-springing beard, wearing a coat and a surcoat of yellow satin, and hose of thin greenish-yellow cloth upon his feet, and over his hose shoes of parti-coloured leather, fastened at the insteps with golden clasps. And he bore a heavy three-edged sword with a golden hilt, in a scabbard of black leather tipped with fine gold. And he came to the place where the Emperor and Owain were playing at chess.

And the youth saluted Owain. And Owain marvelled that the youth should salute him and should not have saluted the Emperor Arthur. And Arthur knew what was in Owain's thought. And he said to Owain, "Marvel not that the youth salutes thee now, for he saluted me erewhile; and it is unto thee that his errand is." Then said the youth unto Owain, "Lord, is it with thy leave that the young pages and attendants of the Emperor harass and torment and worry thy Ravens? And if it be not with thy leave, cause the Emperor to forbid them." "Lord," said Owain, "thou hearest what the youth says; if it seem good to thee, forbid them from my Ravens." "Play thy game," said he. Then the youth returned to the tent.

That game did they finish, and another they began, and when they were in the midst of the game, behold, a ruddy young man with auburn curling hair and large eyes, well-grown, and having his beard new-shorn, came forth from a bright yellow tent, upon the summit of which was the figure of a bright red lion. And he was clad in a coat of yellow satin, falling as low as the small of his leg, and embroidered with threads of red silk. And on his feet were hose of fine white buckram, and buskins of black leather were over his hose, whereon were golden clasps. And in his hand a huge, heavy, three-edged sword, with a scabbard of red deer-hide, tipped with gold. And he came to the place where Arthur and Owain were playing at chess. And he saluted him. And Owain was troubled at his salutation, but Arthur minded it no more than before. And the youth said unto Owain, "Is it not against thy will that the attendants of the Emperor harass thy Ravens, killing some and worrying others? If against thy will it be, beseech him to forbid them." "Lord," said Owain, "forbid thy men, if it seem good to thee." "Play thy game," said the Emperor. And the youth returned to the tent.

And that game was ended and another begun. And as they were beginning the first move of the game, they beheld at a small distance from them a tent speckled yellow, the largest ever seen, and the figure of an eagle of gold upon it, and a precious stone on the eagle's head. And coming out of the tent, they saw a youth with thick yellow hair upon his head, fair and comely, and a scarf of blue satin upon him, and a brooch of gold in the scarf upon his right shoulder as large as a warrior's middle finger. And upon his feet were hose of fine Totness, and shoes of parti-coloured leather, clasped with gold, and the youth was of noble bearing, fair of face, with ruddy cheeks and large hawk's eyes. In the hand of the youth was a mighty lance, speckled yellow, with a newly-sharpened head; and upon the lance a banner displayed.

Fiercely angry, and with rapid pace, came the youth to the place where Arthur was playing at chess with Owain. And they perceived that he was wroth. And thereupon he saluted Owain, and told him that his Ravens had been killed, the chief part of them, and that such of them as were not slain were so wounded and bruised that not one of them could raise its wings a single fathom above the earth. "Lord," said Owain, "forbid thy men." "Play," said he, "if it please thee." Then said Owain to the youth, "Go back, and wherever thou findest the strife at the thickest, there lift up the banner, and let come what pleases Heaven."

So the youth returned back to the place where the strife bore hardest upon the Ravens, and he lifted up the banner; and as he did so they all rose up in the air, wrathful and fierce and high of spirit, clapping their wings in the wind, and shaking off the weariness that was upon them. And recovering their energy and courage, furiously and with exultation did they, with one sweep, descend upon the heads of the men, who had erewhile caused them anger and pain and damage, and they seized some by the heads and others by the eyes, and some by the ears, and others by the arms, and carried them up into the air; and in the air there was a mighty tumult with the flapping of the wings of the triumphant Ravens, and with their croaking; and there was another mighty tumult with the groaning of the men, that were being torn and wounded, and some of whom were slain.

And Arthur and Owain marvelled at the tumult as they played at chess; and, looking, they perceived a knight upon a dun-coloured horse coming towards them. And marvellous was the hue of the dun horse. Bright red was his right shoulder, and from the top of his legs to the centre of his hoof was bright yellow. Both the knight and his horse were fully equipped with heavy foreign armour. The clothing of the horse from the front opening upwards was of bright red sendal, and from thence opening downwards was of bright yellow sendal. A large gold-hilted one-edged sword had the youth upon his thigh, in a scabbard of light blue, and tipped with Spanish laton. The belt of the sword was of dark green leather with golden slides and a clasp of ivory upon it, and a buckle of jet-black upon the clasp. A helmet of gold was on the head of the knight, set with precious stones of great virtue, and at the top of the helmet was the image of a flame-coloured leopard with two ruby-red stones in its head, so that it was astounding for a warrior, however stout his heart, to look at the face of the leopard, much more at the face of the knight. He had in his hand a blue-shafted lance, but from the haft to the point it was stained crimson-red with the blood of the Ravens and their plumage.

The knight came to the place where Arthur and Owain were seated at chess. And they perceived that he was harassed and vexed and weary as he came towards them. And the youth saluted Arthur, and told him that the Ravens of Owain were slaying his young men and attendants. And Arthur looked at Owain and said, "Forbid thy Ravens." "Lord," answered Owain, "play thy game." And they played. And the knight returned back towards the strife, and the Ravens were not forbidden any more than before.

And when they had played awhile, they heard a mighty tumult, and a wailing of men, and a croaking of Ravens, as they carried the men in their strength into the air, and, tearing them betwixt them, let them fall piecemeal to the earth. And during the tumult they saw a knight coming towards them, on a light grey horse, and the left foreleg of the horse was jet-black to the centre of his hoof. And the knight and the horse were fully accoutred with huge heavy blue armour. And a robe of honour of yellow diapered satin was upon the knight, and the borders of the robe were blue. And the housings of the horse were jet-black, with borders of bright yellow. And on the thigh of the youth was a sword, long, and three-edged, and heavy. And the scabbard was of red cut leather, and the belt of new red deer-skin, having upon it many golden slides and a buckle of the bone of the seahorse, the tongue of which was jet-black. A golden helmet was upon the head of the knight, wherein were set sapphire-stones of great virtue. And at the top of the helmet was the figure of a flame-coloured lion, with a fiery-red tongue, issuing above a foot from his mouth, and with venomous eyes, crimson-red, in his head. And the knight came, bearing in his hand a thick ashen lance, the head whereof, which had been newly steeped in blood, was overlaid with silver.

And the youth saluted the Emperor: "Lord," said he, "carest thou not for the slaying of thy pages, and thy young men, and the sons of the nobles of the Island of Britain, whereby it will be difficult to defend this island from henceforward for ever?" "Owain," said Arthur, "forbid thy Ravens." "Play this game, Lord," said Owain.

So they finished the game and began another; and as they were finishing that game, lo, they heard a great tumult and a clamour of armed men, and a croaking of Ravens, and a flapping of wings in the air, as they flung down the armour entire to the ground, and the men and the horses piecemeal. Then they saw coming a knight on a lofty-headed piebald horse. And the left shoulder of the horse was of bright red, and its right leg from the chest to the hollow of the hoof was pure white. And the knight and horse were equipped with arms of speckled yellow, variegated with Spanish laton. And there was a robe of honour upon him, and upon his horse, divided in two parts, white and black, and the borders of the robe of honour were of golden purple. And above the robe he wore a sword three-edged and bright, with a golden hilt. And the belt of the sword was of yellow goldwork, having a clasp upon it of the eyelid of a black sea-horse, and a tongue of yellow gold to the clasp. Upon the head of the knight was a bright helmet of yellow laton, with sparkling stones of crystal in it, and at the crest of the helmet was the figure of a griffin, with a stone of many virtues in its head. And he had an ashen spear in his hand, with a round shaft, coloured with azure blue. And the head of the spear was newly stained with blood, and was overlaid with fine silver.

Wrathfully came the knight to the place where Arthur was, and he told him that the Ravens had slain his household and the sons of the chief men of this island, and he besought him to cause Owain to forbid his Ravens. And Arthur besought Owain to forbid them. Then Arthur took the golden chessmen that were upon the board, and crushed them until they became as dust. Then Owain ordered Gwres the son of Rheged to lower his banner. So it was lowered, and all was peace.

Then Rhonabwy inquired of Iddawc who were the first three men that came to Owain, to tell him his Ravens were being slain. Said Iddawc, "They were men who grieved that Owain should suffer loss, his fellow-chieftains and companions, Selyv the son of Kynan Garwyn of Powys, and Gwgawn Gleddyvrudd, and Gwres the son of Rheged, he who bears the banner in the day of battle and strife." "Who," said Rhonabwy, "were the last three men who came to Arthur, and told him that the Ravens were slaughtering his men?" "The best of men," said Iddawc, "and the bravest, and who would grieve exceedingly that Arthur should have damage in aught; Blathaon the son of Mawrheth, and Rhuvawn Pebyr the son of Prince Deorthach, and Hyveidd Unllenn."

And with that behold four-and-twenty knights came from Osla Gyllellvawr, to crave a truce of Arthur for a fortnight and a month. And Arthur rose and went to take counsel. And he came to where a tall, auburn, curly-headed man was a little way off, and there he assembled his counsellors. Bedwini, the Bishop, and Gwarthegyd the son of Kaw, and March the son of Meirchawn, and Caradawc Vreichvras, and Gwalchmai the son of Gwyar, and Edeyrn the son of Nudd, and Rhuvawn Pebyr the son of Prince Deorthach, and Rhiogan the son of the King of Ireland, and Gwenwynwyn the son of Nav, Howel the son of Emyr Llydaw, Gwilym the son of Rhwyf Freinc, and Daned the son of Ath, and Goreu Custennin, and Mabon the son of Modron, and Peredur Paladyr Hir, and Hyveidd Unllenn, and Twrch the son of Perif, and Nerth the son of Kadarn, and Gobrwy the son of Echel Vorddwyttwll, Gwair the son of Gwestyl, and Gadwy the son of Geraint, Trystan the son of Tallwch, Moryen Manawc, Granwen the son of Llyr, and Llacheu the son of Arthur, and Llawvrodedd Varvawc, and Kadwr Earl of Cornwall, Morvran the son of Tegid, and Rhyawd the son of Morgant, and Dyvyr the son of Alun Dyved, Gwrhyr Gwalstawd Ieithoedd, Adaon the son of Taliesin, Llary the son of Kasnar Wledig, and Fflewddur Fflam, and Greidawl Galldovydd, Gilbert the son of Kadgyffro, Menw the son of Teirgwaedd, Gwrthmwl Wledig, Cawrdav the son of Caradawc Vreichvras, Gildas the son of Kaw, Kadyriaith the son of Saidi, and many of the men of Norway and Denmark, and many of the men of Greece, and a crowd of the men of the host came to that council.

"Iddawc," said Rhonabwy, "who was the auburn-haired man to whom they came just now?" "Rhun the son of Maelgwn Gwynedd, a man whose prerogative it is, that he may join in counsel with all." "And wherefore did they admit into counsel with men of such dignity as are yonder a stripling so young as Kadyriaith the son of Saidi?" "Because there is not throughout Britain a man better skilled in counsel than he."

Thereupon, behold, bards came and recited verses before Arthur, and no man understood those verses but Kadyriaith only, save that they were in Arthur's praise.

And lo, there came four-and-twenty asses with their burdens of gold and of silver, and a tired way-worn man with each of them, bringing tribute to Arthur from the Islands of Greece. Then Kadyriaith the son of Saidi besought that a truce might be granted to Osla Gyllellvawr for the space of a fortnight and a month, and that the asses and the burdens they carried might be given to the bards, to be to them as the reward for their stay and that their verse might be recompensed during the time of the truce. And thus it was settled.

"Rhonabwy," said Iddawc, "would it not be wrong to forbid a youth who can give counsel so liberal as this from coming to the councils of his Lord?"

Then Kai arose, and he said, "Whosoever will follow Arthur, let him be with him to-night in Cornwall, and whosoever will not, let him be opposed to Arthur even during the truce." And through the greatness of the tumult that ensued, Rhonabwy awoke. And when he awoke he was upon the yellow calf-skin, having slept three nights and three days.

And this tale is called the Dream of Rhonabwy. And this is the reason that no one knows the dream without a book, neither bard nor gifted seer; because of the various colours that were upon the horses, and the many wondrous colours of the arms and of the panoply, and of the precious scarfs, and of the virtue-bearing stones.

THE LADY OF THE FOUNTAIN

KING ARTHUR was at Caerlleon upon Usk; and one day he sat in his chamber; and with him were Owain the son of Urien, and Kynon the son of Clydno, and Kai the son of Kyner; and Gwenhwyvar and her handmaidens at needlework by the window. And if it should be said that there was a porter at Arthur's palace, there was none. Glewlwyd Gavaelvawr was there, acting as porter, to welcome guests and strangers, and to receive them with honour, and to inform them of the manners and customs of the Court; and to direct those who came to the Hall or to the presence-chamber, and those who came to take up their lodging.

In the centre of the chamber King Arthur sat upon a seat of green rushes, over which was spread a covering of flame-coloured satin, and a cushion of red satin was under his elbow.

Then Arthur spoke, "If I thought you would not disparage me," said he, "I would sleep while I wait for my repast; and you can entertain one another with relating tales, and can obtain a flagon of mead and some meat from Kai." And the King went to sleep. And Kynon the son of Clydno asked Kai for that which Arthur had promised them. "I, too, will have the good tale which he promised to me," said Kai. "Nay," answered Kynon, "fairer will it be for thee to fulfill Arthur's behest, in the first place, and then we will tell thee the best tale that we know." So Kai went to the kitchen and to the mead-cellar, and returned bearing a flagon of mead and a golden goblet, and a handful of skewers, upon which were broiled collops of meat. Then they ate the collops and began to drink the mead. "Now," said Kai, "it is time for you to give me my story." "Kynon," said Owain, "do thou pay to Kai the tale that is his due." "Truly," said Kynon, "thou are older, and art a better teller of tales, and hast seen more marvellous things than I; do thou therefore pay Kai his tale." "Begin thyself," quoth Owain, "with the best that thou knowest." "I will do so," answered Kynon.

"I was the only son of my mother and father, and I was exceedingly aspiring, and my daring was very great. I thought there was no enterprise in the world too mighty for me, and after I had achieved all the adventures that were in my own country, I equipped myself, and set forth to journey through deserts and distant regions. And at length it chanced that I came to the fairest valley in the world, wherein were trees of equal growth; and a river ran through the valley, and a path was by the side of the river. And I followed the path until mid-day, and continued my journey along the remainder of the valley until the evening; and at the extremity of a plain I came to a large and lustrous Castle, at the foot of which was a torrent. And I approached the Castle, and there I beheld two youths with yellow curling hair, each with a frontlet of gold upon his head, and clad in a garment of yellow satin, and they had gold clasps upon their insteps. In the hand of each of them was an ivory bow, strung with the sinews of the stag; and their arrows had shafts of the bone of the whale, and were winged with peacock's feathers; the shafts also had golden heads. And they had daggers with blades of gold, and with hilts of the bone of the whale. And they were shooting their daggers.

"And a little way from them I saw a man in the prime of life, with his beard newly shorn, clad in a robe and a mantle of yellow satin; and round the top of his mantle was a band of gold lace. On his feet were shoes of variegated leather, fastened by two bosses of gold. When I saw him, I went towards him and saluted him, and such was his courtesy that he no sooner received my greeting than he returned it. And he went with me towards the Castle. Now there were no dwellers in the Castle except those who were in one hall. And there I saw four-and-twenty damsels, embroidering satin at a window. And this I tell thee, Kai, that the least fair of them was fairer than the fairest maid thou hast ever beheld in the Island of Britain, and the least lovely of them was more lovely than Gwenhwyvar, the wife of Arthur, when she has appeared loveliest at the Offering, on the day of the Nativity, or at the feast of Easter. They rose up at my coming, and six of them took my horse, and divested me of my armour; and six others took my arms, and washed them in a vessel until they were perfectly bright. And the third six spread cloths upon the tables and prepared meat. And the fourth six took off my soiled garments, and placed others upon me; namely, an under-vest and a doublet of fine linen, and a robe, and a surcoat, and a mantle of yellow satin with a broad gold band upon the mantle. And they placed cushions both beneath and around me, with coverings of red linen; and I sat down. Now the six maidens who had taken my horse, unharnessed him, as well as if they had been the best squires in the Island of Britain. Then, behold, they brought bowls of silver wherein was water to wash, and towels of linen, some green and some white; and I washed. And in a little while the man sat down to the table. And I sat next to him, and below me sat all the maidens, except those who waited on us. And the table was of silver, and the cloths upon the table were of linen; and no vessel was served upon the table that was not either of gold or of silver, or of buffalo-horn. And our meat was brought to us. And verily, Kai, I saw there every sort of meat and every sort of liquor that I have ever seen elsewhere; but the meat and the liquor were better served there than I have ever seen them in any other place.

"Until the repast was half over, neither the man nor any one of the damsels spoke a single word to me; but when the man perceived that it would be more agreeable to me to converse than to eat any more, he began to inquire of me who I was. I said I was glad to find that there was some one who would discourse with me, and that it was not considered so great a crime at that Court for people to hold converse together. 'Chieftain,' said the man, 'we would have talked to thee sooner, but we feared to disturb thee during thy repast; now, however, we will discourse.' Then I told the man who I was, and what was the cause of my journey; and said that I was seeking whether any one was superior to me, or whether I could gain the mastery over all. The man looked upon me, and he smiled and said, 'If I did not fear to distress thee too much, I would show thee that which thou seekest.' Upon this I became anxious and sorrowful, and when the man perceived it, he said, 'If thou wouldest rather that I should show thee thy disadvantage than thine advantage, I will do so. Sleep here to-night, and in the morning arise early, and take the road upwards through the valley until thou reachest the wood through which thou camest hither. A little way within the wood thou wilt meet with a road branching off to the right, by which thou must proceed, until thou comest to a large sheltered glade with a mound in the centre. And thou wilt see a black man of great stature on the top of the mound. He is not smaller in size than two of the men of this world. He has but one foot; and one eye in the middle of his forehead. And he has a club of iron, and it is certain that there are no two men in the world who would not find their burden in that club. And he is not a comely man, but on the contrary he is exceedingly ill-favoured; and he is the woodward of that wood. And thou wilt see a thousand wild animals grazing around him. Inquire of him the way out of the glade, and he will reply to thee briefly, and will point out the road by which thou shalt find that which thou art in quest of.'

"And long seemed that night to me. And the next morning I arose and equipped myself, and mounted my horse, and proceeded straight through the valley to the wood; and I followed the cross-road which the man had pointed out to me, till at length I arrived at the glade. And there was I three times more astonished at the number of wild animals that I beheld, than the man had said I should be. And the black man was there, sitting upon the top of the mound. Huge of stature as the man had told me that he was, I found him to exceed by far the description he had given me of him. As for the iron club which the man had told me was a burden for two men, I am certain, Kai, that it would be a heavy weight for four warriors to lift; and this was in the black man's hand. And he only spoke to me in answer to my questions. Then I asked him what power he held over those animals. 'I will show thee, little man,' said he. And he took his club in his hand, and with it he struck a stag a great blow so that he brayed vehemently, and at his braying the animals came together, as numerous as the stars in the sky, so that it was difficult for me to find room in the glade to stand among them. There were serpents, and dragons, and divers sorts of animals. And he looked at them, and bade them go and feed; and they bowed their heads, and did him homage as vassals to their lord.

"Then the black man said to me, 'Seest thou now, little man, what power I hold over these animals?' Then I inquired of him the way, and he became very rough in his manner to me; however, he asked me whither I would go? And when I told him who I was and what I sought, he directed me. 'Take,' said he, 'that path that leads towards the head of the glade, and ascend the wooded steep until thou comest to its summit; and there thou wilt find an open space like to a large valley, and in the midst of it a tall tree, whose branches are greener than the greenest pine-trees. Under this tree is a fountain, and by the side of the fountain a marble slab, and on the marble slab a silver bowl, attached by a chain of silver, so that it may not be carried away. Take the bowl and throw a bowlful of water upon the slab, and thou wilt hear a mighty peal of thunder, so that thou wilt think that heaven and earth are trembling with its fury. With the thunder there will come a shower so severe that it will be scarce possible for thee to endure it and live. And the shower will be of hailstones; and after the shower, the weather will become fair, but every leaf that was upon the tree will have been carried away by the shower. Then a flight of birds will come and alight upon the tree; and in thine own country thou didst never hear a strain so sweet as that which they will sing. And at the moment thou art most delighted with the song of the birds, thou wilt hear a murmuring and complaining coming towards thee along the valley. And thou wilt see a knight upon a coal-black horse, clothed in black velvet, and with a pennon of black linen upon his lance; and he will ride unto thee to encounter thee with the utmost speed. If thou fleest from him he will overtake thee, and if thou abidest there, as sure as thou art a mounted knight, he will leave thee on foot. And if thou dost not find trouble in that adventure, thou needest not seek it during the rest of thy life.'

"So I journeyed on, until I reached the summit of the steep, and there I found everything as the black man had described it to me. And I went up to the tree, and beneath it I saw the fountain, and by its side the marble slab, and the silver bowl fastened by the chain. Then I took the bowl, and cast a bowlful of water upon the slab; and thereupon, behold, the thunder came, much more violent than the black man had led me to expect; and after the thunder came the shower; and of a truth I tell thee, Kai, that there is neither man nor beast that can endure that shower and live. For not one of those hailstones would be stopped, either by the flesh or by the skin, until it had reached the bone. I turned my horse's flank towards the shower, and placed the beak of my shield over his head and neck, while I held the upper part of it over my own head. And thus I withstood the shower. When I looked on the tree there was not a single leaf upon it, and then the sky became clear, and with that, behold the birds lighted upon the tree, and sang. And truly, Kai, I never heard any melody equal to that, either before or since. And when I was most charmed with listening to the birds, lo, a murmuring voice was heard through the valley, approaching me and saying, 'Oh, Knight, what has brought thee hither? What evil have I done to thee, that thou shouldst act towards me and my possessions as thou hast this day? Dost thou not know that the shower to-day has left in my dominions neither man nor beast alive that was exposed to it?' And thereupon, behold, a Knight on a black horse appeared, clothed in jet-black velvet, and with a tabard of black linen about him. And we charged each other, and, as the onset was furious, it was not long before I was overthrown. Then the Knight passed the shaft of his lance through the bridle rein of my horse, and rode off with the two horses, leaving me where I was. And he did not even bestow so much notice upon me as to imprison me, nor did he despoil me of my arms. So I returned along the road by which I had come. And when I reached the glade where the black man was, I confess to thee, Kai, it is a marvel that I did not melt down into a liquid pool, through the shame that I felt at the black man's derision. And that night I came to the same castle where I had spent the night preceding. And I was more agreeably entertained that night than I had been the night before; and I was better feasted, and I conversed freely with the inmates of the castle, and none of them alluded to my expedition to the fountain, neither did I mention it to any; and I remained there that night. When I arose on the morrow, I found, ready saddled, a dark bay palfrey, with nostrils as red as scarlet; and after putting on my armour, and leaving there my blessing, I returned to my own Court. And that horse I still possess, and he is in the stable yonder. And I declare that I would not part with him for the best palfrey in the Island of Britain.

"Now of a truth, Kai, no man ever before confessed to an adventure so much to his own discredit, and verily it seems strange to me, that neither before nor since have I heard of any person besides myself who knew of this adventure, and that the subject of it should exist within King Arthur's dominions, without any other person lighting upon it."

"Now," quoth Owain, "would it not be well to go and endeavour to discover that place?"

"By the hand of my friend," said Kai, "often dost thou utter that with thy tongue which thou wouldst not make good with thy deeds."

"In very truth," said Gwenhwyvar, "it were better thou wert hanged, Kai, than to use such uncourteous speech towards a man like Owain."

"By the hand of my friend, good Lady," said Kai, "thy praise of Owain is not greater than mine."

With that Arthur awoke, and asked if he had not been sleeping a little.

"Yes, Lord," answered Owain, "thou hast slept awhile."

"Is it time for us to go to meat?"

"It is, Lord," said Owain.

Then the horn for washing was sounded, and the King and all his household sat down to eat. And when the meal was ended, Owain withdrew to his lodging, and made ready his horse and his arms.

On the morrow, with the dawn of day, he put on his armour, and mounted his charger, and travelled through distant lands and over desert mountains. And at length he arrived at the valley which Kynon had described to him; and he was certain that it was the same that he sought. And journeying along the valley by the side of the river, he followed its course till he came to the plain and within sight of the Castle. When he approached the Castle, he saw the youths shooting their daggers in the place where Kynon had seen them, and the yellow man, to whom the Castle belonged, standing hard by. And no sooner had Owain saluted the yellow man than he was saluted by him in return.

And he went forward towards the Castle, and there he saw the chamber, and when he had entered the chamber he beheld the maidens working at satin embroidery, in chairs of gold. And their beauty and their comeliness seemed to Owain far greater than Kynon had represented to him. And they rose to wait upon Owain, as they had done to Kynon, and the meal which they set before him gave more satisfaction to Owain than it had done to Kynon.

About the middle of the repast, the yellow man asked Owain the object of his journey. And Owain made it known to him, and said, "I am in quest of the Knight who guards the fountain." Upon this the yellow man smiled, and said that he was as loth to point out that adventure to Owain as he had been to Kynon. However, he described the whole to Owain, and they retired to rest.

The next morning Owain found his horse made ready for him by the damsels, and he set forward and came to the glade where the black man was. And the stature of the black man seemed more wonderful to Owain than it had done to Kynon, and Owain asked of him his road, and he showed it to him. And Owain followed the road, as Kynon had done, till he came to the green tree; and he beheld the fountain, and the slab beside the fountain, with the bowl upon it. And Owain took the bowl, and threw a bowlful of water upon the slab. And, lo, the thunder was heard, and after the thunder came the shower, much more violent than Kynon had described, and after the shower the sky became bright. And when Owain looked at the tree, there was not one leaf upon it. And immediately the birds came, and settled upon the tree, and sang. And when their song was most pleasing to Owain, he beheld a Knight coming towards him through the valley, and he prepared to receive him; and encountered him violently. Having broken both their lances, they drew their swords, and fought blade to blade. Then Owain struck the Knight a blow through his helmet, head-piece and visor, and through the skin, and the flesh, and the bone, until it wounded the very brain. Then the black Knight felt that he had received a mortal wound, upon which he turned his horse's head, and fled. And Owain pursued him, and followed close upon him, although he was not near enough to strike him with his sword. Thereupon Owain descried a vast and resplendent Castle. And they came to the Castle gate. And the black Knight was allowed to enter, and the portcullis was let fall upon Owain; and it struck his horse behind the saddle, and cut him in two, and carried away the rowels of the spurs that were upon Owain's heels. And the portcullis descended to the floor. And the rowels of the spurs and part of the horse were without, and Owain with the other part of the horse remained between the two gates, and the inner gate was closed, so that Owain could not go thence; and Owain was in a perplexing situation. And while he was in this state, he could see through an aperture in the gate, a street facing him, with a row of houses on each side. And he beheld a maiden, with yellow curling hair, and a frontlet of gold upon her head; and she was clad in a dress of yellow satin, and on her feet were shoes of variegated leather. And she approached the gate, and desired that it should be opened. "Heaven knows, Lady," said Owain, "it is no more possible for me to open to thee from hence, than it is for thee to set me free." "Truly," said the damsel, "it is very sad that thou canst not be released, and every woman ought to succour thee, for I never saw one more faithful in the service of ladies than thou. As a friend thou art the most sincere, and as a lover the most devoted. Therefore," quoth she, "whatever is in my power to do for thy release, I will do it. Take this ring and put it on thy finger, with the stone inside thy hand; and close thy hand upon the stone. And as long as thou concealest it, it will conceal thee. When they have consulted together, they will come forth to fetch thee, in order to put thee to death; and they will be much grieved that they cannot find thee. And I will await thee on the horseblock yonder; and thou wilt be able to see me, though I cannot see thee; therefore come and place thy hand upon my shoulder, that I may know that thou art near me. And by the way that I go hence, do thou accompany me."

Then she went away from Owain, and he did all that the maiden had told him. And the people of the Castle came to seek Owain, to put him to death, and when they found nothing but the half of his horse, they were sorely grieved.

And Owain vanished from among them, and went to the maiden, and placed his hand upon her shoulder; whereupon she set off, and Owain followed her, until they came to the door of a large and beautiful chamber, and the maiden opened it, and they went in, and closed the door. And Owain looked around the chamber, and behold there was not even a single nail in it that was not painted with gorgeous colours; and there was not a single panel that had not sundry images in gold portrayed upon it.

The maiden kindled a fire, and took water in a silver bowl, and put a towel of white linen on her shoulder, and gave Owain water to wash. Then she placed before him a silver table, inlaid with gold; upon which was a cloth of yellow linen; and she brought him food. And of a truth, Owain had never seen any kind of meat that was not there in abundance, but it was better cooked there than he had ever found it in any other place. Nor did he ever see so excellent a display of meat and drink, as there. And there was not one vessel from which he was served, that was not of gold or of silver. And Owain ate and drank, until late in the afternoon, when lo, they heard a mighty clamour in the Castle; and Owain asked the maiden what that outcry was. "They are administering extreme unction," said she, "to the Nobleman who owns the Castle." And Owain went to sleep.

The couch which the maiden had prepared for him was meet for Arthur himself; it was of scarlet, and fur, and satin, and sendal, and fine linen. In the middle of the night they heard a woeful outcry. "What outcry again is this?" said Owain. "The Nobleman who owned the Castle is now dead," said the maiden. And a little after daybreak, they heard an exceeding loud clamour and wailing. And Owain asked the maiden what was the cause of it. "They are bearing to the church the body of the Nobleman who owned the Castle."

And Owain rose up, and clothed himself, and opened a window of the chamber, and looked towards the Castle; and he could see neither the bounds, nor the extent of the hosts that filled the streets. And they were fully armed; and a vast number of women were with them, both on horseback and on foot; and all the ecclesiastics in the city, singing. And it seemed to Owain that the sky resounded with the vehemence of their cries, and with the noise of the trumpets, and with the singing of the ecclesiastics. In the midst of the throng, he beheld the bier, over which was a veil of white linen; and wax tapers were burning beside and around it, and none that supported the bier was lower in rank than a powerful Baron.

Never did Owain see an assemblage so gorgeous with satin, and silk, and sendal. And following the train, he beheld a lady with yellow hair falling over her shoulders, and stained with blood; and about her a dress of yellow satin, which was torn. Upon her feet were shoes of variegated leather. And it was a marvel that the ends of her fingers were not bruised, from the violence with which she smote her hands together. Truly she would have been the fairest lady Owain ever saw, had she been in her usual guise. And her cry was louder than the shout of the men, or the clamour of the trumpets. No sooner had he beheld the lady, than he became inflamed with her love, so that it took entire possession of him.

Then he inquired of the maiden who the lady was. "Heaven knows," replied the maiden, "she may be said to be the fairest, and the most chaste, and the most liberal, and the wisest, and the most noble of women. And she is my mistress; and she is called the Countess of the Fountain, the wife of him whom thou didst slay yesterday." "Verily," said Owain, "she is the woman that I love best." "Verily," said the maiden, "she shall also love thee not a little."

And with that the maid arose, and kindled a fire, and filled a pot with water, and placed it to warm; and she brought a towel of white linen, and placed it around Owain's neck; and she took a goblet of ivory, and a silver basin, and filled them with warm water, wherewith she washed Owain's head. Then she opened a wooden casket, and drew forth a razor, whose haft was of ivory, and upon which were two rivets of gold. And she shaved his beard, and she dried his head, and his throat, with the towel. Then she rose up from before Owain, and brought him to eat. And truly Owain had never so good a meal, nor was he ever so well served.

When he had finished his repast, the maiden arranged his couch. "Come here," said she, "and sleep, and I will go and woo for thee." And Owain went to sleep, and the maiden shut the door of the chamber after her, and went towards the Castle. When she came there, she found nothing but mourning, and sorrow; and the Countess in her chamber could not bear the sight of any one through grief. Luned came and saluted her, but the Countess answered her not. And the maiden bent down towards her, and said, "What aileth thee, that thou answerest no one to-day?" "Luned," said the Countess, "what change hath befallen thee, that thou hast not come to visit me in my grief? It was wrong in thee, and I having made thee rich; it was wrong in thee that thou didst not come to see me in my distress. That was wrong in thee." "Truly," said Luned, "I thought thy good sense was greater than I find it to be. Is it well for thee to mourn after that good man, or for anything else, that thou canst not have?" "I declare to heaven," said the Countess, "that in the whole world there is not a man equal to him." "Not so," said Luned, "for an ugly man would be as good as, or better than he." "I declare to heaven," said the Countess, "that were it not repugnant to me to cause to be put to death one whom I have brought up, I would have thee executed, for making such a comparison to me. As it is, I will banish thee." "I am glad," said Luned, "that thou hast no other cause to do so, than that I would have been of service to thee where thou didst not know what was to thine advantage. And henceforth evil betide whichever of us shall make the first advance towards reconciliation to the other; whether I should seek an invitation from thee, or thou of thine own accord shouldst send to invite me."

With that Luned went forth: and the Countess arose and followed her to the door of the chamber, and began coughing loudly. And when Luned looked back, the Countess beckoned to her; and she returned to the Countess. "In truth," said the Countess, "evil is thy disposition; but if thou knowest what is to my advantage, declare it to me." "I will do so," quoth she.

"Thou knowest that except by warfare and arms it is impossible for thee to preserve thy possessions; delay not, therefore, to seek some one who can defend them." "And how can I do that?" said the Countess. "I will tell thee," said Luned. "Unless thou canst defend the fountain, thou canst not maintain thy dominions; and no one can defend the fountain, except it be a knight of Arthur's household; and I will go to Arthur's Court, and ill betide me, if I return thence without a warrior who can guard the fountain as well as, or even better than, he who defended it formerly." "That will be hard to perform," said the Countess. "Go, however, and make proof of that which thou hast promised."

Luned set out, under the pretence of going to Arthur's Court; but she went back to the chamber where she had left Owain; and she tarried there with him as long as it might have taken her to have travelled to the Court of King Arthur. And at the end of that time, she apparelled herself and went to visit the Countess. And the Countess was much rejoiced when she saw her, and inquired what news she brought from the Court. "I bring thee the best of news," said Luned, "for I have compassed the object of my mission. When wilt thou, that I should present to thee the chieftain who has come with me hither?" "Bring him here to visit me to-morrow, at mid-day," said the Countess, "and I will cause the town to be assembled by that time."

And Luned returned home. And the next day, at noon, Owain arrayed himself in a coat, and a surcoat, and a mantle of yellow satin, upon which was a broad band of gold lace; and on his feet were high shoes of variegated leather, which were fastened by golden clasps, in the form of lions. And they proceeded to the chamber of the Countess.

Right glad was the Countess of their coming, and she gazed steadfastly upon Owain, and said, "Luned, this knight has not the look of a traveller." "What harm is there in that, lady?" said Luned. "I am certain," said the Countess, "that no other man than this chased the soul from the body of my lord." "So much the better for thee, lady," said Luned, "for had he not been stronger than thy lord he could not have deprived him of life. There is no remedy for that which is past, be it as it may." "Go back to thine abode," said the Countess, "and I will take counsel."

The next day the Countess caused all her subjects to assemble, and showed them that her earldom was left defenceless, and that it could not be protected but with horse and arms, and military skill. "Therefore," said she, "this is what I offer for your choice: either let one of you take me, or give your consent for me to take a husband from elsewhere to defend my dominions."

So they came to the determination that it was better that she should have permission to marry some one from elsewhere; and, thereupon, she sent for the bishops and archbishops to celebrate her nuptials with Owain. And the men of the earldom did Owain homage.

And Owain defended the Fountain with lance and sword. And this is the manner in which he defended it: Whensoever a knight came there he overthrew him, and sold him for his full worth, and what he thus gained he divided among his barons and his knights; and no man in the whole world could be more beloved than he was by his subjects. And it was thus for the space of three years.

It befell that as Gwalchmai went forth one day with King Arthur, he perceived him to be very sad and sorrowful. And Gwalchmai was much grieved to see Arthur in this state; and he questioned him, saying, "Oh, my lord! what has befallen thee?" "In sooth, Gwalchmai," said Arthur, "I am grieved concerning Owain, whom I have lost these three years, and I shall certainly die if the fourth year passes without my seeing him. Now I am sure, that it is through the tale which Kynon the son of Clydno related, that I have lost Owain." "There is no need for thee," said Gwalchmai, "to summon to arms thy whole dominions on this account, for thou thyself and the men of thy household will be able to avenge Owain, if he be slain; or to set him free, if he be in prison; and, if alive, to bring him back with thee." And it was settled according to what Gwalchmai had said.

Then Arthur and the men of his household prepared to go and seek Owain, and their number was three thousand, besides their attendants. And Kynon the son of Clydno acted as their guide. And Arthur came to the Castle where Kynon had been before, and when he came there the youths were shooting in the same place, and the yellow man was standing hard by. When the yellow man saw Arthur he greeted him, and invited him to the Castle; and Arthur accepted his invitation, and they entered the Castle together. And great as was the number of his retinue, their presence was scarcely observed in the Castle, so vast was its extent. And the maidens rose up to wait on them, and the service of the maidens appeared to them all to excel any attendance they had ever met with; and even the pages who had charge of the horses were no worse served, that night, than Arthur himself would have been in his own palace.

The next morning Arthur set out thence, with Kynon for his guide, and came to the place where the black man was. And the stature of the black man was more surprising to Arthur than it had been represented to him. And they came to the top of the wooded steep, and traversed the valley till they reached the green tree, where they saw the fountain, and the bowl, and the slab. And upon that, Kai came to Arthur and spoke to him. "My lord," said he, "I know the meaning of all this, and my request is, that thou wilt permit me to throw the water on the slab, and to receive the first adventure that may befall." And Arthur gave him leave.

Then Kai threw a bowlful of water upon the slab, and immediately there came the thunder, and after the thunder the shower. And such a thunderstorm they had never known before, and many of the attendants who were in Arthur's train were killed by the shower. After the shower had ceased the sky became clear; and on looking at the tree they beheld it completely leafless. Then the birds descended upon the tree, and the song of the birds was far sweeter than any strain they had ever heard before. Then they beheld a knight on a coal-black horse, clothed in black satin, coming rapidly towards them. And Kai met him and encountered him, and it was not long before Kai was overthrown. And the knight withdrew, and Arthur and his host encamped for the night.

And when they arose in the morning, they perceived the signal of combat upon the lance of the Knight. And Kai came to Arthur, and spoke to him: "My lord," said he, "though I was overthrown yesterday, if it seem good to thee, I would gladly meet the Knight again to-day." "Thou mayst do so," said Arthur. And Kai went towards the Knight. And on the spot he overthrew Kai, and struck him with the head of his lance in the forehead, so that it broke his helmet and the head-piece, and pierced the skin and the flesh, the breadth of the spear-head, even to the bone. And Kai returned to his companions.

After this, all the household of Arthur went forth, one after the other, to combat the Knight, until there was not one that was not overthrown by him, except Arthur and Gwalchmai. And Arthur armed himself to encounter the Knight. "Oh, my lord," said Gwalchmai, "permit me to fight with him first." And Arthur permitted him. And he went forth to meet the Knight, having over himself and his horse a satin robe of honour which had been sent him by the daughter of the Earl of Rhangyw, and in this dress he was not known by any of the host. And they charged each other, and fought all that day until the evening, and neither of them was able to unhorse the other.

The next day they fought with strong lances, and neither of them could obtain the mastery.

And the third day they fought with exceeding strong lances. And they were incensed with rage, and fought furiously, even until noon. And they gave each other such a shock that the girths of their horses were broken, so that they fell over their horses' cruppers to the ground. And they rose up speedily, and drew their swords, and resumed the combat; and the multitude that witnessed their encounter felt assured that they had never before seen two men so valiant or so powerful. And had it been midnight, it would have been light from the fire that flashed from their weapons. And the Knight gave Gwalchmai a blow that turned his helmet from off his face, so that the Knight knew that it was Gwalchmai. Then Owain said, "My lord Gwalchmai, I did not know thee for my cousin, owing to the robe of honour that enveloped thee; take my sword and my arms." Said Gwalchmai, "Thou, Owain, art the victor; take thou my sword." And with that Arthur saw that they were conversing, and advanced towards them. "My lord Arthur," said Gwalchmai, "here is Owain, who has vanquished me, and will not take my arms." "My lord," said Owain, "it is he that has vanquished me, and he will not take my sword." "Give me your swords," said Arthur, "and then neither of you has vanquished the other." Then Owain put his arms around Arthur's neck, and they embraced. And all the host hurried forward to see Owain, and to embrace him; and there was nigh being a loss of life, so great was the press.

And they retired that night, and the next day Arthur prepared to depart. "My lord," said Owain, "this is not well of thee; for I have been absent from thee these three years, and during all that time, up to this very day, I have been preparing a banquet for thee, knowing that thou wouldst come to seek me. Tarry with me, therefore, until thou and thy attendants have recovered the fatigues of the journey, and have been anointed."

And they all proceeded to the Castle of the Countess of the Fountain, and the banquet which had been three years preparing was consumed in three months. Never had they a more delicious or agreeable banquet. And Arthur prepared to depart. Then he sent an embassy to the Countess, to beseech her to permit Owain to go with him for the space of three months, that he might show him to the nobles and the fair dames of the Island of Britain. And the Countess gave her consent, although it was very painful to her. So Owain came with Arthur to the Island of Britain. And when he was once more amongst his kindred and friends, he remained three years, instead of three months, with them.

And as Owain one day sat at meat, in the city of Caerlleon upon Usk, behold a damsel entered upon a bay horse, with a curling mane and covered with foam, and the bridle and so much as was seen of the saddle were of gold. And the damsel was arrayed in a dress of yellow satin. And she came up to Owain, and took the ring from off his hand. "Thus," said she, "shall be treated the deceiver, the traitor, the faithless, the disgraced, and the beardless." And she turned her horse's head and departed.

Then his adventure came to Owain's remembrance, and he was sorrowful; and having finished eating he went to his own abode and made preparations that night. And the next day he arose but did not go to the Court, but wandered to the distant parts of the earth and to uncultivated mountains. And he remained there until all his apparel was worn out, and his body was wasted away, and his hair was grown long. And he went about with the wild beasts and fed with them, until they became familiar with him; but at length he grew so weak that he could no longer bear them company. Then he descended from the mountains to the valley, and came to a park that was the fairest in the world, and belonged to a widowed Countess.

One day the Countess and her maidens went forth to walk by a lake, that was in the middle of the park. And they saw the form of a man. And they were terrified. Nevertheless they went near him, and touched him, and looked at him. And they saw that there was life in him, though he was exhausted by the heat of the sun. And the Countess returned to the Castle, and took a flask full of precious ointment, and gave it to one of her maidens. "Go with this," said she, "and take with thee yonder horse and clothing, and place them near the man we saw just now. And anoint him with this balsam, near his heart; and if there is life in him, he will arise through the efficacy of this balsam. Then watch what he will do."

And the maiden departed from her, and poured the whole of the balsam upon Owain, and left the horse and the garments hard by, and went a little way off, and hid herself to watch him. In a short time she saw him begin to move his arms; and he rose up, and looked at his person, and became ashamed of the unseemliness of his appearance. Then he perceived the horse and the garments that were near him. And he crept forward till he was able to draw the garments to him from off the saddle. And he clothed himself, and with difficulty mounted the horse. Then the damsel discovered herself to him, and saluted him. And he was rejoiced when he saw her, and inquired of her, what land and what territory that was. "Truly," said the maiden, "a widowed Countess owns yonder Castle; at the death of her husband, he left her two Earldoms, but at this day she has but this one dwelling that has not been wrested from her by a young Earl, who is her neighbour, because she refused to become his wife." "That is a pity," said Owain. And he and the maiden proceeded to the Castle; and he alighted there, and the maiden conducted him to a pleasant chamber, and kindled a fire and left him.

And the maiden came to the Countess, and gave the flask into her hand. "Ha! maiden," said the Countess, "where is all the balsam?" "Have I not used it all?" said she. "Oh, maiden," said the Countess, "I cannot easily forgive thee this; it is sad for me to have wasted seven-score pounds' worth of precious ointment upon a stranger whom I know not. However, maiden, wait thou upon him, until he is quite recovered."

And the maiden did so, and furnished him with meat and drink, and fire, and lodging, and medicaments, until he was well again. And in three months he was restored to his former guise, and became even more comely than he had ever been before.

One day Owain heard a great tumult, and a sound of arms in the Castle, and he inquired of the maiden the cause thereof. "The Earl," said she, "whom I mentioned to thee, has come before the Castle, with a numerous army, to subdue the Countess." And Owain inquired of her whether the Countess had a horse and arms in her possession. "She has the best in the world," said the maiden. "Wilt thou go and request the loan of a horse and arms for me," said Owain, "that I may go and look at this army?" "I will," said the maiden.

And she came to the Countess, and told her what Owain had said. And the Countess laughed. "Truly," said she, "I will even give him a horse and arms for ever; such a horse and such arms had he never yet, and I am glad that they should be taken by him to-day, lest my enemies should have them against my will to-morrow. Yet I know not what he would do with them."

The Countess bade them bring out a beautiful black steed, upon which was a beechen saddle, and a suit of armour, for man and horse. And Owain armed himself, and mounted the horse, and went forth, attended by two pages completely equipped, with horses and arms. And when they came near to the Earl's army, they could see neither its extent nor its extremity. And Owain asked the pages in which troop the Earl was. "In yonder troop," said they, "in which are four yellow standards. Two of them are before, and two behind him." "Now," said Owain, "do you return and await me near the portal of the Castle." So they returned, and Owain pressed forward until he met the Earl. And Owain drew him completely out of his saddle, and turned his horse's head towards the Castle, and though it was with difficulty, he brought the Earl to the portal, where the pages awaited him. And in they came. And Owain presented the Earl as a gift to the Countess. And said to her, "Behold a requital to thee for thy blessed balsam."

The army encamped around the Castle. And the Earl restored to the Countess the two Earldoms he had taken from her, as a ransom for his life; and for his freedom he gave her the half of his own dominions, and all his gold, and his silver, and his jewels, besides hostages.

And Owain took his departure. And the Countess and all her subjects besought him to remain, but Owain chose rather to wander through distant lands and deserts.

And as he journeyed, he heard a loud yelling in a wood. And it was repeated a second and a third time. And Owain went towards the spot, and beheld a huge craggy mound, in the middle of the wood; on the side of which was a grey rock. And there was a cleft in the rock, and a serpent was within the cleft. And near the rock stood a black lion, and every time the lion sought to go thence, the serpent darted towards him to attack him. And Owain unsheathed his sword, and drew near to the rock; and as the serpent sprang out, he struck him with his sword, and cut him in two. And he dried his sword, and went on his way, as before. But behold the lion followed him, and played about him, as though it had been a greyhound that he had reared.

They proceeded thus throughout the day, until the evening. And when it was time for Owain to take his rest, he dismounted, and turned his horse loose in a flat and wooded meadow. And he struck fire, and when the fire was kindled, the lion brought him fuel enough to last for three nights. And the lion disappeared. And presently the lion returned, bearing a fine large roebuck. And he threw it down before Owain, who went towards the fire with it.

And Owain took the roebuck, and skinned it, and placed collops of its flesh upon skewers, around the fire. The rest of the buck he gave to the lion to devour. While he was doing this, he heard a deep sigh near him, and a second, and a third. And Owain called out to know whether the sigh he heard proceeded from a mortal; and he received answer that it did. "Who art thou?" said Owain. "Truly," said the voice, "I am Luned, the handmaiden of the Countess of the Fountain." "And what dost thou here?" said Owain. "I am imprisoned," said she, "on account of the knight who came from Arthur's Court, and married the Countess. And he stayed a short time with her, but he afterwards departed for the Court of Arthur, and has not returned since. And he was the friend I loved best in the world. And two of the pages in the Countess's chamber traduced him, and called him a deceiver. And I told them that they two were not a match for him alone. So they imprisoned me in the stone vault, and said that I should be put to death, unless he came himself to deliver me, by a certain day; and that is no further off than the day after to-morrow. And I have no one to send to seek him for me. And his name is Owain the son of Urien." "And art thou certain that if that knight knew all this, he would come to thy rescue?" "I am most certain of it," said she.

When the collops were cooked, Owain divided them into two parts, between himself and the maiden; and after they had eaten, they talked together, until the day dawned. And the next morning Owain inquired of the damsel, if there was any place where he could get food and entertainment for that night. "There is, Lord," said she; "cross over yonder, and go along the side of the river, and in a short time thou wilt see a great Castle, in which are many towers, and the Earl who owns that Castle is the most hospitable man in the world. There thou mayst spend the night."

Never did sentinel keep stricter watch over his lord, than the lion that night over Owain.

And Owain accoutred his horse, and passed across by the ford, and came in sight of the Castle. And he entered it, and was honourably received. And his horse was well cared for, and plenty of fodder was placed before him. Then the lion went and lay down in the horse's manger; so that none of the people of the Castle dared to approach him. The treatment which Owain met with there was such as he had never known elsewhere, for every one was as sorrowful as though death had been upon him. And they went to meat; and the Earl sat upon one side of Owain, and on the other side his only daughter. And Owain had never seen any more lovely than she. Then the lion came and placed himself between Owain's feet, and he fed him with every kind of food that he took himself. And he never saw anything equal to the sadness of the people.

In the middle of the repast the Earl began to bid Owain welcome. "Then," said Owain, "behold, it is time for thee to be cheerful." "Heaven knows," said the Earl, "that it is not thy coming that makes us sorrowful, but we have cause enough for sadness and care." "What is that?" said Owain. "I have two sons," replied the Earl, "and yesterday they went to the mountains to hunt. Now there is on the mountain a monster who kills men and devours them, and he seized my sons; and to-morrow is the time he has fixed to be here, and he threatens that he will then slay my sons before my eyes, unless I will deliver into his hands this my daughter. He has the form of a man, but in stature he is no less than a giant."

"Truly," said Owain, "that is lamentable. And which wilt thou do?" "Heaven knows," said the Earl, "it will be better that my sons should be slain against my will, than that I should voluntarily give up my daughter to him to ill-treat and destroy." Then they talked about other things, and Owain stayed there that night.

The next morning they heard an exceeding great clamour, which was caused by the coming of the giant with the two youths. And the Earl was anxious both to protect his Castle and to release his two sons. Then Owain put on his armour and went forth to encounter the giant, and the lion followed him. And when the giant saw that Owain was armed, he rushed towards him and attacked him. And the lion fought with the giant much more fiercely than Owain did. "Truly," said the giant, "I should find no difficulty in fighting with thee, were it not for the animal that is with thee." Upon that Owain took the lion back to the Castle and shut the gate upon him, and then he returned to fight the giant, as before. And the lion roared very loud, for he heard that it went hard with Owain. And he climbed up till he reached the top of the Earl's hall, and thence he got to the top of the Castle, and he sprang down from the walls and went and joined Owain. And the lion gave the giant a stroke with his paw, which tore him from his shoulder to his hip, and his heart was laid bare, and the giant fell down dead. Then Owain restored the two youths to their father.

The Earl besought Owain to remain with him, and he would not, but set forward towards the meadow where Luned was. And when he came there he saw a great fire kindled, and two youths with beautiful curling auburn hair were leading the maiden to cast her into the fire. And Owain asked them what charge they had against her. And they told him of the compact that was between them, as the maiden had done the night before. "And," said they, "Owain has failed her, therefore we are taking her to be burnt." "Truly," said Owain, "he is a good knight, and if he knew that the maiden was in such peril, I marvel that he came not to her rescue; but if you will accept me in his stead, I will do battle with you." "We will," said the youths, "by him who made us."

And they attacked Owain, and he was hard beset by them. And with that the lion came to Owain's assistance, and they two got the better of the young men. And they said to him, "Chieftain, it was not agreed that we should fight save with thyself alone, and it is harder for us to contend with yonder animal than with thee." And Owain put the lion in the place where the maiden had been imprisoned, and blocked up the door with stones, and he went to fight with the young men, as before. But Owain had not his usual strength, and the two youths pressed hard upon him. And the lion roared incessantly at seeing Owain in trouble; and he burst through the wall until he found a way out, and rushed upon the young men, and instantly slew them. So Luned was saved from being burned.

Then Owain returned with Luned to the dominions of the Countess of the Fountain. And when he went thence he took the Countess with him to Arthur's Court, and she was his wife as long as she lived.

And then he took the road that led to the Court of the savage black man, and Owain fought with him, and the lion did not quit Owain until he had vanquished him. And when he reached the Court of the savage black man he entered the hall, and beheld four-and-twenty ladies, the fairest that could be seen. And the garments which they had on were not worth four-and-twenty pence, and they were as sorrowful as death. And Owain asked them the cause of their sadness. And they said, "We are the daughters of Earls, and we all came here with our husbands, whom we dearly loved. And we were received with honour and rejoicing. And we were thrown into a state of stupor, and while we were thus, the demon who owns this Castle slew all our husbands, and took from us our horses, and our raiment, and our gold, and our silver; and the corpses of our husbands are still in this house, and many others with them. And this, Chieftain, is the cause of our grief, and we are sorry that thou art come hither, lest harm should befall thee."

And Owain was grieved when he heard this. And he went forth from the Castle, and he beheld a knight approaching him, who saluted him in a friendly and cheerful manner, as if he had been a brother. And this was the savage black man. "In very sooth," said Owain, "it is not to seek thy friendship that I am here." "In sooth," said he, "thou shalt find it then." And with that they charged each other, and fought furiously. And Owain overcame him, and bound his hands behind his back. Then the black savage besought Owain to spare his life, and spoke thus: "My lord Owain," said he, "it was foretold that thou shouldst come hither and vanquish me, and thou hast done so. I was a robber here, and my house was a house of spoil; but grant me my life, and I will become the keeper of an Hospice, and I will maintain this house as an Hospice for weak and for strong, as long as I live, for the good of thy soul." And Owain accepted this proposal of him, and remained there that night.

And the next day he took the four-and-twenty ladies, and their horses, and their raiment, and what they possessed of goods and jewels, and proceeded with them to Arthur's Court. And if Arthur was rejoiced when he saw him, after he had lost him the first time, his joy was now much greater. And of those ladies, such as wished to remain in Arthur's Court remained there, and such as wished to depart departed.

And thenceforward Owain dwelt at Arthur's Court greatly beloved, as the head of his household, until he went away with his followers; and those were the army of three hundred ravens which Kenverchyn had left him. And wherever Owain went with these he was victorious.

And this is the tale of the Lady of the Fountain.

PEREDUR THE SON OF EVRAWC

EARL EVRAWC owned the Earldom of the North. And he had seven sons. And Evrawc maintained himself not so much by his own possessions as by attending tournaments, and wars, and combats. And, as it often befalls those who join in encounters and wars, he was slain, and six of his sons likewise. Now the name of his seventh son was Peredur, and he was the youngest of them. And he was not of an age to go to wars and encounters, otherwise he might have been slain as well as his father and brothers. His mother was a scheming and thoughtful woman, and she was very solicitous concerning this her only son and his possessions. So she took counsel with herself to leave the inhabited country, and to flee to the deserts and unfrequented wildernesses. And she permitted none to bear her company thither but women and boys, and spiritless men, who were both unaccustomed and unequal to war and fighting. And none dared to bring either horses or arms where her son was, lest he should set his mind upon them. And the youth went daily to divert himself in the forest, by flinging sticks and staves. And one day he saw his mother's flock of goats, and near the goats two hinds were standing. And he marvelled greatly that these two should be without horns, while the others had them. And he thought they had long run wild, and on that account they had lost their horns. And by activity and swiftness of foot, he drove the hinds and the goats together into the house which there was for the goats at the extremity of the forest. Then Peredur returned to his mother. "Ah, mother," said he, "a marvellous thing have I seen in the wood; two of thy goats have run wild, and lost their horns, through their having been so long missing in the wood. And no man had ever more trouble than I had to drive them in." Then they all arose and went to see. And when they beheld the hinds they were greatly astonished.

And one day they saw three knights coming along the horse-road on the borders of the forest. And the three knights were Gwalchmai the son of Gwyar, and Geneir Gwystyl, and Owain the son of Urien. And Owain kept on the track of the knight who had divided the apples in Arthur's Court, whom they were in pursuit of. "Mother," said Peredur, "what are those yonder?" "They are angels, my son," said she. "By my faith," said Peredur, "I will go and become an angel with them." And Peredur went to the road, and met them. "Tell me, good soul," said Owain, "sawest thou a knight pass this way, either to-day or yesterday?" "I know not," answered he, "what a knight is." "Such an one as I am," said Owain. "If thou wilt tell me what I ask thee, I will tell thee that which thou askest me." "Gladly will I do so," replied Owain. "What is this?" demanded Peredur, concerning the saddle. "It is a saddle," said Owain. Then he asked about all the accoutrements which he saw upon the men, and the horses, and the arms, and what they were for, and how they were used. And Owain shewed him all these things fully, and told him what use was made of them. "Go forward," said Peredur, "for I saw such an one as thou inquirest for, and I will follow thee."

Then Peredur returned to his mother and her company, and he said to her, "Mother, those were not angels, but honourable knights." Then his mother swooned away. And Peredur went to the place where they kept the horses that carried firewood, and that brought meat and drink from the inhabited country to the desert. And he took a bony piebald horse, which seemed to him the strongest of them. And he pressed a pack into the form of a saddle, and with twisted twigs he imitated the trappings which he had seen upon the horses. And when Peredur came again to his mother, the Countess had recovered from her swoon. "My son," said she, "desirest thou to ride forth?" "Yes, with thy leave," said he. "Wait, then, that I may counsel thee before thou goest." "Willingly," he answered; "speak quickly." "Go forward, then," she said, "to the Court of Arthur, where there are the best, and the boldest, and the most bountiful of men. And wherever thou seest a church, repeat there thy Paternoster unto it. And if thou see meat and drink, and have need of them, and none have the kindness or the courtesy to give them to thee, take them thyself. If thou hear an outcry, proceed towards it, especially if it be the outcry of a woman. If thou see a fair jewel, possess thyself of it, and give it to another, for thus thou shalt obtain praise. If thou see a fair woman, pay thy court to her, whether she will or no; for thus thou wilt render thyself a better and more esteemed man than thou wast before."

After this discourse, Peredur mounted the horse, and taking a handful of sharp-pointed forks in his hand, he rode forth. And he journeyed two days and two nights in the woody wildernesses, and in desert places, without food and without drink. And then he came to a vast wild wood, and far within the wood he saw a fair even glade, and in the glade he saw a tent, and the tent seeming to him to be a church, he repeated his Paternoster to it. And he went towards it, and the door of the tent was open. And a golden chair was near the door. And on the chair sat a lovely auburn-haired maiden, with a golden frontlet on her forehead, and sparkling stones in the frontlet, and with a large gold ring on her hand. And Peredur dismounted, and entered the tent. And the maiden was glad at his coming, and bade him welcome. At the entrance of the tent he saw food, and two flasks full of wine, and two loaves of fine wheaten flour, and collops of the flesh of the wild boar. "My mother told me," said Peredur, "wheresoever I saw meat and drink, to take it." "Take the meat and welcome, chieftain," said she. So Peredur took half of the meat and of the liquor himself, and left the rest to the maiden. And when Peredur had finished eating, he bent upon his knee before the maiden. "My mother," said he, "told me, wheresoever I saw a fair jewel, to take it." "Do so, my soul," said she. So Peredur took the ring. And he mounted his horse, and proceeded on his journey.

After this, behold the knight came to whom the tent belonged; and he was the Lord of the Glade. And he saw the track of the horse, and he said to the maiden, "Tell me who has been here since I departed." "A man," said she, "of wonderful demeanour." And she described to him what Peredur's appearance and conduct had been. "Tell me," said he, "did he offer thee any wrong?" "No," answered the maiden, "by my faith, he harmed me not." "By my faith, I do not believe thee; and until I can meet with him, and revenge the insult he has done me, and wreak my vengeance upon him, thou shalt not remain two nights in the same house." And the knight arose, and set forth to seek Peredur.

Meanwhile Peredur journeyed on towards Arthur's Court. And before he reached it, another knight had been there, who gave a ring of thick gold at the door of the gate for holding his horse, and went into the Hall where Arthur and his household, and Gwenhwyvar and her maidens, were assembled. And the page of the chamber was serving Gwenhwyvar with a golden goblet. Then the knight dashed the liquor that was therein upon her face, and upon her stomacher, and gave her a violent blow on the face, and said, "If any have the boldness to dispute this goblet with me, and to revenge the insult to Gwenhwyvar, let him follow me to the meadow, and there I will await him." So the knight took his horse, and rode to the meadow. And all the household hung down their heads, lest any of them should be requested to go and avenge the insult to Gwenhwyvar. For it seemed to them, that no one would have ventured on so daring an outrage, unless he possessed such powers, through magic or charms, that none could be able to take vengeance upon him. Then, behold, Peredur entered the Hall, upon the bony piebald horse, with the uncouth trappings upon it; and in this way he traversed the whole length of the Hall. In the centre of the Hall stood Kai. "Tell me, tall man," said Peredur, "is that Arthur yonder?" "What wouldest thou with Arthur?" asked Kai. "My mother told me to go to Arthur, and receive the honour of knighthood." "By my faith," said he, "thou art all too meanly equipped with horse and with arms." Thereupon he was perceived by all the household, and they threw sticks at him. Then, behold, a dwarf came forward. He had already been a year at Arthur's Court, both he and a female dwarf. They had craved harbourage of Arthur, and had obtained it; and during the whole year, neither of them had spoken a single word to any one. When the dwarf beheld Peredur, "Haha!" said he, "the welcome of Heaven be unto thee, goodly Peredur, son of Evrawc, the chief of warriors, and flower of knighthood." "Truly," said Kai, "thou art ill-taught to remain a year mute at Arthur's Court, with choice of society; and now, before the face of Arthur and all his household, to call out, and declare such a man as this the chief of warriors, and the flower of knighthood." And he gave him such a box on the ear that he fell senseless to the ground. Then exclaimed the female dwarf, "Haha! goodly Peredur, son of Evrawc; the welcome of Heaven be unto thee, flower of knights, and light of chivalry." "Of a truth, maiden," said Kai, "thou art ill-bred to remain mute for a year at the Court of Arthur, and then to speak as thou dost of such a man as this." And Kai kicked her with his foot, so that she fell to the ground senseless. "Tall man," said Peredur, "shew me which is Arthur." "Hold thy peace," said Kai, "and go after the knight who went hence to the meadow, and take from him the goblet, and overthrow him, and possess thyself of his horse and arms, and then thou shalt receive the order of knighthood." "I will do so, tall man," said Peredur. So he turned his horse's head towards the meadow. And when he came there, the knight was riding up and down, proud of his strength, and valour, and noble mien. "Tell me," said the knight, "didst thou see any one coming after me from the Court?" "The tall man that was there," said he, "desired me to come, and overthrow thee, and to take from thee the goblet, and thy horse and thy armour for myself." "Silence!" said the knight; "go back to the Court, and tell Arthur, from me, either to come himself, or to send some other to fight with me; and unless he do so quickly, I will not wait for him." "By my faith," said Peredur, "choose thou whether it shall be willingly or unwillingly, but I will have the horse, and the arms, and the goblet." And upon this the knight ran at him furiously, and struck him a violent blow with the shaft of his spear, between the neck and the shoulder. "Haha! lad," said Peredur, "my mother's servants were not used to play with me in this wise; therefore, thus will I play with thee." And thereupon he struck him with a sharp-pointed fork, and it hit him in the eye, and came out at the back of his neck, so that he instantly fell down lifeless.

"Verily," said Owain the son of Urien to Kai, "thou wert ill-advised, when thou didst send that madman after the knight. For one of two things must befall him. He must either be overthrown, or slain. If he is overthrown by the knight, he will be counted by him to be an honourable person of the Court, and an eternal disgrace will it be to Arthur and his warriors. And if he is slain, the disgrace will be the same, and moreover, his sin will be upon him; therefore will I go to see what has befallen him." So Owain went to the meadow, and he found Peredur dragging the man about. "What art thou doing thus?" said Owain. "This iron coat," said Peredur, "will never come from off him; not by my efforts, at any rate." And Owain unfastened his armour and his clothes. "Here, my good soul," said he, "is a horse and armour better than thine. Take them joyfully, and come with me to Arthur, to receive the order of knighthood, for thou dost merit it." "May I never shew my face again if I go," said Peredur; "but take thou the goblet to Gwenhwyvar, and tell Arthur, that wherever I am, I will be his vassal, and will do him what profit and service I am able. And say that I will not come to his Court until I have encountered the tall man that is there, to revenge the injury he did to the dwarf and dwarfess." And Owain went back to the Court, and related all these things to Arthur and Gwenhwyvar, and to all the household.

And Peredur rode forward. And as he proceeded, behold a knight met him. "Whence comest thou?" said the knight. "I come from Arthur's Court," said Peredur. "Art thou one of his men?" asked he. "Yes, by my faith," he answered. "A good service, truly, is that of Arthur." "Wherefore sayest thou so?" said Peredur. "I will tell thee," said he; "I have always been Arthur's enemy, and all such of his men as I have ever encountered I have slain." And without further parlance they fought, and it was not long before Peredur brought him to the ground, over his horse's crupper. Then the knight besought his mercy. "Mercy thou shalt have," said Peredur, "if thou wilt make oath to me, that thou wilt go to Arthur's Court, and tell him that it was I that overthrew thee, for the honour of his service; and say, that I will never come to the Court until I have avenged the insult offered to the dwarf and dwarfess." The knight pledged him his faith of this, and proceeded to the Court of Arthur, and said as he had promised, and conveyed the threat to Kai.

And Peredur rode forward. And within that week he encountered sixteen knights, and overthrew them all shamefully. And they all went to Arthur's Court, taking with them the same message which the first knight had conveyed from Peredur, and the same threat which he had sent to Kai. And thereupon Kai was reproved by Arthur; and Kai was greatly grieved thereat.

And Peredur rode forward. And he came to a vast and desert wood, on the confines of which was a lake. And on the other side was a fair castle. And on the border of the lake he saw a venerable, hoary-headed man, sitting upon a velvet cushion, and having a garment of velvet upon him. And his attendants were fishing in the lake. When the hoary-headed man beheld Peredur approaching, he arose and went towards the castle. And the old man was lame. Peredur rode to the palace, and the door was open, and he entered the hall. And there was the hoary-headed man sitting on a cushion, and a large blazing fire burning before him. And the household and the company arose to meet Peredur, and disarrayed him. And the man asked the youth to sit on the cushion; and they sat down, and conversed together. When it was time, the tables were laid, and they went to meat. And when they had finished their meal, the man inquired of Peredur if he knew well how to fight with the sword. "I know not," said Peredur, "but were I to be taught, doubtless I should." "Whoever can play well with the cudgel and shield, will also be able to fight with a sword." And the man had two sons; the one had yellow hair, and the other auburn. "Arise, youths," said he, "and play with the cudgel and the shield." And so did they. "Tell me, my soul," said the man, "which of the youths thinkest thou plays best." "I think," said Peredur, "that the yellow-haired youth could draw blood from the other, if he chose." "Arise thou, my life, and take the cudgel and the shield from the hand of the youth with the auburn hair, and draw blood from the yellow-haired youth if thou canst." So Peredur arose, and went to play with the yellow-haired youth; and he lifted up his arm, and struck him such a mighty blow, that his brow fell over his eye, and the blood flowed forth. "Ah, my life," said the man, "come now, and sit down, for thou wilt become the best fighter with the sword of any in this island; and I am thy uncle, thy mother's brother. And with me shalt thou remain a space, in order to learn the manners and customs of different countries, and courtesy, and gentleness, and noble bearing. Leave, then, the habits and the discourse of thy mother, and I will be thy teacher; and I will raise thee to the rank of knight from this time forward. And thus do thou. If thou seest aught to cause thee wonder, ask not the meaning of it; if no one has the courtesy to inform thee, the reproach will not fall upon thee, but upon me that am thy teacher." And they had abundance of honour and service. And when it was time they went to sleep. At the break of day, Peredur arose, and took his horse, and with his uncle's permission he rode forth. And he came to a vast desert wood, and at the further end of the wood was a meadow, and on the other side of the meadow he saw a large castle. And thitherward Peredur bent his way, and he found the gate open, and he proceeded to the hall. And he beheld a stately hoary-headed man sitting on one side of the hall, and many pages around him, who arose to receive and to honour Peredur. And they placed him by the side of the owner of the palace. Then they discoursed together; and when it was time to eat, they caused Peredur to sit beside the nobleman during the repast. And when they had eaten and drunk as much as they desired, the nobleman asked Peredur whether he could fight with a sword? "Were I to receive instruction," said Peredur, "I think I could." Now, there was on the floor of the hall a huge staple, as large as a warrior could grasp. "Take yonder sword," said the man to Peredur, "and strike the iron staple." So Peredur arose and struck the staple, so that he cut it in two; and the sword broke into two parts also. "Place the two parts together, and reunite them," and Peredur placed them together, and they became entire as they were before. And a second time he struck upon the staple, so that both it and the sword broke in two, and as before they reunited. And the third time he gave a like blow, and placed the broken parts together, and neither the staple nor the sword would unite as before. "Youth," said the nobleman, "come now, and sit down, and my blessing be upon thee. Thou fightest best with the sword of any man in the kingdom. Thou hast arrived at two-thirds of thy strength, and the other third thou hast not yet obtained, and when thou attainest to thy full power, none will be able to contend with thee. I am thy uncle, thy mother's brother, and I am brother to the man in whose house thou wast last night." Then Peredur and his uncle discoursed together, and he beheld two youths enter the hall, and proceed up to the chamber, bearing a spear of mighty size, with three streams of blood flowing from the point to the ground. And when all the company saw this, they began wailing and lamenting. But for all that, the man did not break off his discourse with Peredur. And as he did not tell Peredur the meaning of what he saw, he forbore to ask him concerning it. And when the clamour had a little subsided, behold two maidens entered, with a large salver between them, in which was a man's head, surrounded by a profusion of blood. And thereupon the company of the court made so great an outcry, that it was irksome to be in the same hall with them. But at length they were silent. And when time was that they should sleep, Peredur was brought into a fair chamber.

And the next day, with his uncle's permission, he rode forth. And he came to a wood, and far within the wood he heard a loud cry, and he saw a beautiful woman with auburn hair, and a horse with a saddle upon it, standing near her, and a corpse by her side. And as she strove to place the corpse upon the horse, it fell to the ground, and thereupon she made a great lamentation. "Tell me, sister," said Peredur, "wherefore art thou bewailing?" "Oh! accursed Peredur, little pity has my ill-fortune ever met with from thee." "Wherefore," said Peredur, "am I accursed?" "Because thou wast the cause of thy mother's death; for when thou didst ride forth against her will, anguish seized upon her heart, so that she died; and therefore art thou accursed. And the dwarf and the dwarfess that thou sawest at Arthur's Court were the dwarfs of thy father and mother; and I am thy foster-sister, and this was my wedded husband, and he was slain by the knight that is in the glade in the wood; and do not thou go near him, lest thou shouldest be slain by him likewise." "My sister, thou dost reproach me wrongfully; through my having so long remained amongst you, I shall scarcely vanquish him; and had I continued longer, it would, indeed, be difficult for me to succeed. Cease, therefore, thy lamenting, for it is of no avail, and I will bury the body, and then I will go in quest of the knight, and see if I can do vengeance upon him." And when he had buried the body, they went to the place where the knight was, and found him riding proudly along the glade; and he inquired of Peredur whence he came. "I come from Arthur's Court." "And art thou one of Arthur's men?" "Yes, by my faith." "A profitable alliance, truly, is that of

Arthur." And without further parlance, they encountered one another, and immediately Peredur overthrew the knight, and he besought mercy of Peredur. "Mercy shalt thou have," said he, "upon these terms, that thou take this woman in marriage, and do her all the honour and reverence in thy power, seeing thou hast, without cause, slain her wedded husband; and that thou go to Arthur's Court, and shew him that it was I that overthrew thee, to do him honour and service; and that thou tell him that I will never come to his Court again until I have met with the tall man that is there, to take vengeance upon him for his insult to the dwarf and dwarfess." And he took the knight's assurance, that he would perform all this. Then the knight provided the lady with a horse and garments that were suitable for her, and took her with him to Arthur's Court. And he told Arthur all that had occurred, and gave the defiance to Kai. And Arthur and all his household reproved Kai, for having driven such a youth as Peredur from his Court.

Said Owain the son of Urien, "This youth will never come into the Court until Kai has gone forth from it." "By my faith," said Arthur, "I will search all the deserts in the Island of Britain, until I find Peredur, and then let him and his adversary do their utmost to each other."

Then Peredur rode forward. And he came to a desert wood, where he saw not the track either of men or animals, and where there was nothing but bushes and weeds. And at the upper end of the wood he saw a vast castle, wherein were many strong towers; and when he came near the gate, he found the weeds taller than he had seen them elsewhere. And he struck the gate with the shaft of his lance, and thereupon behold a lean, auburn-haired youth came to an opening in the battlements. "Choose thou, chieftain," said he, "whether shall I open the gate unto thee, or shall I announce unto those that are chief, that thou art at the gateway?" "Say that I am here," said Peredur, "and if it is desired that I should enter, I will go in." And the youth came back, and opened the gate for Peredur. And when he went into the hall, he beheld eighteen youths, lean and redheaded, of the same height, and of the same aspect, and of the same dress, and of the same age as the one who had opened the gate for him. And they were well skilled in courtesy and in service. And they disarrayed him. Then they sat down to discourse. Thereupon, behold five maidens came from the chamber into the hall. And Peredur was certain that he had never seen another of so fair an aspect as the chief of the maidens. And she had an old garment of satin upon her, which had once been handsome, but was then so tattered, that her skin could be seen through it. And whiter was her skin than the bloom of crystal, and her hair and her two eyebrows were blacker than jet, and on her cheeks were two red spots, redder than whatever is reddest. And the maiden welcomed Peredur, and put her arms about his neck, and made him sit down beside her. Not long after this he saw two nuns enter, and a flask full of wine was borne by one, and six loaves of white bread by the other. "Lady," said they, "Heaven is witness, that there is not so much of food and liquor as this left in yonder Convent this night." Then they went to meat, and Peredur observed that the maiden wished to give more of the food and of the liquor to him than to any of the others. "My sister," said Peredur, "I will share out the food and the liquor." "Not so, my soul," said she. "By my faith but I will." So Peredur took the bread, and he gave an equal portion of it to each alike, as well as a cup full of the liquor. And when it was time for them to sleep, a chamber was prepared for Peredur, and he went to rest.

"Behold, sister," said the youths to the fairest and most exalted of the maidens, "we have counsel for thee." "What may it be?" she inquired. "Go to the youth that is in the upper chamber, and offer to become his wife, or the lady of his love, if it seem well to him." "That were indeed unfitting," said she. "Hitherto I have not been the lady-love of any knight, and to make him such an offer before I am wooed by him, that, truly, can I not do." "By our confession to Heaven, unless thou attest thus, we will leave thee here to thy enemies, to do as they will with thee." And through fear of this, the maiden went forth; and shedding tears, she proceeded to the chamber. And with the noise of the door opening, Peredur awoke; and the maiden was weeping and lamenting. "Tell me, my sister," said Peredur, "wherefore dost thou weep?" "I will tell thee, lord," said she. "My father possessed these dominions as their chief, and this palace was his, and with it he held the best earldom in the kingdom; then the son of another earl sought me of my father, and I was not willing to be given unto him, and my father would not give me against my will, either to him or any earl in the world. And my father had no child except myself. And after my father's death, these dominions came into my own hands, and then was I less willing to accept him than before. So he made war upon me, and conquered all my possessions, except this one house. And through the valour of the men whom thou hast seen, who are my foster-brothers, and the strength of the house, it can never be taken while food and drink remain. And now our provisions are exhausted; but, as thou hast seen, we have been fed by the nuns, to whom the country is free. And at length they also are without supply of food or liquor. And at no later date than to-morrow, the earl will come against this place with all his forces; and if I fall into his power, my fate will be no better than to be given over to the grooms of his horses. Therefore, lord, I am come to offer to place myself in thy hands, that thou mayest succour me, either by taking me hence, or by defending me here, whichever may seem best unto thee." "Go, my sister," said he, "and sleep; nor will I depart from thee until I do that which thou requirest, or prove whether I can assist thee or not." The maiden went again to rest; and the next morning she came to Peredur, and saluted him. "Heaven prosper thee, my soul, and what tidings dost thou bring?" "None other, than that the earl and all his forces have alighted at the gate, and I never beheld any place so covered with tents, and thronged with knights challenging others to the combat." "Truly," said Peredur, "let my horse be made ready." So his horse was accoutred, and he arose and sallied forth to the meadow. And there was a knight riding proudly along the meadow, having raised the signal for battle. And they encountered, and Peredur threw the knight over his horse's crupper to the ground. And at the close of the day, one of the chief knights came to fight with him, and he overthrew him also, so that he besought his mercy. "Who art thou?" said Peredur. "Verily," said he, "I am Master of the Household to the earl." "And how much of the countess's possessions is there in thy power?" "The third part, verily," answered he. "Then," said Peredur, "restore to her the third of her possessions in full, and all the profit thou hast made by them, and bring meat and drink for a hundred men, with their horses and arms, to her court this night. And thou shalt remain her captive, unless she wish to take thy life." And this he did forthwith. And that night the maiden was right joyful, and they fared plenteously.

And the next day Peredur rode forth to the meadow; and that day he vanquished a multitude of the host. And at the close of the day, there came a proud and stately knight, and Peredur overthrew him, and he besought his mercy. "Who art thou?" said Peredur. "I am Steward of the Palace," said he. "And how much of the maiden's possessions are under thy control?" "One-third part," answered he. "Verily," said Peredur, "thou shalt fully restore to the maiden her possessions, and, moreover, thou shalt give her meat and drink for two hundred men, and their horses and their arms. And for thyself, thou shalt be her captive." And immediately it was so done.

And the third day Peredur rode forth to the meadow; and he vanquished more that day than on either of the preceding. And at the close of the day, an earl came to encounter him, and he overthrew him, and he besought his mercy. "Who art thou?" said Peredur. "I am the earl," said he. "I will not conceal it from thee." "Verily," said Peredur, "thou shalt restore the whole of the maiden's earldom, and shalt give her thine own earldom in addition thereto, and meat and drink for three hundred men, and their horses and arms, and thou thyself shalt remain in her power." And thus it was fulfilled. And Peredur tarried three weeks in the country, causing tribute and obedience to be paid to the maiden, and the government to be placed in her hands. "With thy leave," said Peredur, "I will go hence." "Verily, my brother, desirest thou this?" "Yes, by my faith; and had it not been for love of thee, I should not have been here thus long." "My soul," said she, "who art thou?" "I am Peredur the son of Evrawc from the North; and if ever thou art in trouble or in danger, acquaint me therewith, and if I can, I will protect thee."

So Peredur rode forth. And far thence there met him a lady, mounted on a horse that was lean, and covered with sweat; and she saluted the youth. "Whence comest thou, my sister?" Then she told him the cause of her journey. Now she was the wife of the Lord of the Glade. "Behold," said he, "I am the knight through whom thou art in trouble, and he shall repent it, who has treated thee thus." Thereupon, behold a knight rode up, and he inquired of Peredur, if he had seen a knight such as he was seeking. "Hold thy peace," said Peredur, "I am he whom thou seekest; and by my faith, thou deservest ill of thy household for thy treatment of the maiden, for she is innocent concerning me." So they encountered, and they were not long in combat ere Peredur overthrew the knight, and he besought his mercy. "Mercy thou shalt have," said Peredur, "so thou wilt return by the way thou camest, and declare that thou holdest the maiden innocent, and so that thou wilt acknowledge unto her the reverse thou hast sustained at my hands." And the knight plighted him his faith thereto.

Then Peredur rode forward. And above him he beheld a castle, and thitherward he went. And he struck upon the gate with his lance, and then, behold, a comely auburn-haired youth opened the gate, and he had the stature of a warrior, and the years of a boy. And when Peredur came into the hall, there was a tall and stately lady sitting in a chair, and many handmaidens around her; and the lady rejoiced at his coming. And when it was time, they went to meat. And after their repast was finished, "It were well for thee, chieftain," said she, "to go elsewhere to sleep." "Wherefore can I not sleep here?" said Peredur. "Nine sorceresses are here, my soul, of the sorceresses of Gloucester, and their father and their mother are with them; and unless we can make our escape before daybreak, we shall be slain; and already they have conquered and laid waste all the country, except this one dwelling." "Behold," said Peredur, "I will remain here to-night, and if you are in trouble, I will do you what service I can; but harm shall you not receive from me." So they went to rest. And with the break of day, Peredur heard a dreadful outcry. And he hastily arose, and went forth in his vest and his doublet, with his sword about his neck, and he saw a sorceress overtake one of the watch, who cried out violently. Peredur attacked the sorceress, and struck her upon the head with his sword, so that he flattened her helmet and her head-piece like a dish upon her head. "Thy mercy, goodly Peredur, son of Evrawc, and the mercy of Heaven." "How knowest thou, hag, that I am Peredur?" "By destiny, and the foreknowledge that I should suffer harm from thee. And thou shalt take a horse and armour of me; and with me thou shalt go to learn chivalry and the use of thy arms." Said Peredur, "Thou shalt have mercy, if thou pledge thy faith thou wilt never more injure the dominions of the Countess." And Peredur took surety of this, and with permission of the Countess, he set forth with the sorceress to the palace of the sorceresses. And there he remained for three weeks, and then he made choice of a horse and arms, and went his way.

And in the evening he entered a valley, and at the head of the valley he came to a hermit's cell, and the hermit welcomed him gladly, and there he spent the night. And in the morning he arose, and when he went forth, behold a shower of snow had fallen the night before, and a hawk had killed a wild fowl in front of the cell. And the noise of the horse scared the hawk away, and a raven alighted upon the bird. And Peredur stood, and compared the blackness of the raven and the whiteness of the snow, and the redness of the blood, to the hair of the lady that best he loved, which was blacker than jet, and to her skin which was whiter than the snow, and to the two red spots upon her cheeks, which were redder than the blood upon the snow appeared to be.

Now Arthur and his household were in search of Peredur. "Know ye," said Arthur, "who is the knight with the long spear that stands by the brook up yonder?" "Lord," said one of them, "I will go and learn who he is." So the youth came to the place where Peredur was, and asked him what he did thus, and who he was. And from the intensity with which he thought upon the lady whom best he loved, he gave him no answer. Then the youth thrust at Peredur with his lance, and Peredur turned upon him, and struck him over his horse's crupper to the ground. And after this, four-and-twenty youths came to him, and he did not answer one more than another, but gave the same reception to all, bringing them with one single thrust to the ground. And then came Kai, and spoke to Peredur rudely and angrily; and Peredur took him with his lance under the jaw, and cast him from him with a thrust, so that he broke his arm and his shoulder-blade, and he rode over him one-and-twenty times. And while he lay thus, stunned with the violence of the pain that he had suffered, his horse returned back at a wild and prancing pace. And when the household saw the horse come back without his rider, they rode forth in haste to the place where the encounter had been. And when they first came there, they thought that Kai was slain; but they found that if he had a skilful physician, he yet might live. And Peredur moved not from his meditation, on seeing the concourse that was around Kai. And Kai was brought to Arthur's tent, and Arthur caused skilful physicians to come to him. And Arthur was grieved that Kai had met with this reverse, for he loved him greatly.

"Then," said Gwalchmai, "it is not fitting that any should disturb an honourable knight from his thought unadvisedly; for either he is pondering some damage that he has sustained, or he is thinking of the lady whom best he loves. And through such ill-advised proceeding, perchance this misadventure has befallen him who last met with him. And if it seem well to thee, lord, I will go and see if this knight hath changed from his thought; and if he has, I will ask him courteously to come and visit thee." Then Kai was wroth, and he spoke angry and spiteful words. "Gwalchmai," said he, "I know that thou wilt bring him because he is fatigued. Little praise and honour, nevertheless, wilt thou have from vanquishing a weary knight, who is tired with fighting. Yet thus hast thou gained the advantage over many. And while thy speech and thy soft words last, a coat of thin linen were armour sufficient for thee, and thou wilt not need to break either lance or sword in fighting with the knight in the state he is in." Then said Gwalchmai to Kai, "Thou mightest use more pleasant words, wert thou so minded: and it behoves thee not upon me to wreak thy wrath and thy displeasure. Methinks I shall bring the knight hither with me without breaking either my arm or my shoulder." Then said Arthur to Gwalchmai, "Thou speakest like a wise and prudent man; go, and take enough of armour about thee, and choose thy horse." And Gwalchmai accoutred himself, and rode forward hastily to the place where Peredur was.

And Peredur was resting on the shaft of his spear, pondering the same thought, and Gwalchmai came to him without any signs of hostility, and said to him, "If I thought that it would be as agreeable to thee as it would be to me, I would converse with thee. I have also a message from Arthur unto thee, to pray thee to come and visit him. And two men have been before on this errand." "That is true," said Peredur, "and uncourteously they came. They attacked me, and I was annoyed thereat, for it was not pleasing to me to be drawn from the thought that I was in, for I was thinking of the lady whom best I love, and thus was she brought to my mind: — I was looking upon the snow, and upon the raven, and upon the drops of the blood of the bird that the hawk had killed upon the snow. And I bethought me that her whiteness was like that of the snow, and that the blackness of her hair and her eyebrows like that of the raven, and that the two red spots upon her cheeks were like the two drops of blood." Said Gwalchmai, "This was not an ungentle thought, and I should marvel if it were pleasant to thee to be drawn from it." "Tell me," said Peredur, "is Kai in Arthur's Court?" "He is," said he, "and behold he is the knight that fought with thee last; and it would have been better for him had he not come, for his arm and his shoulder-blade were broken with the fall which he had from thy spear." "Verily," said Peredur, "I am not sorry to have thus begun to avenge the insult to the dwarf and dwarfess." Then Gwalchmai marvelled to hear him speak of the dwarf and the dwarfess; and he approached him, and threw his arms around his neck, and asked him what was his name. "Peredur the son of Evrawc am I called," said he; "and thou, Who art thou?" "I am called Gwalchmai," he replied. "I am right glad to meet with thee," said Peredur, "for in every country where I have been I have heard of thy fame for prowess and uprightness, and I solicit thy fellowship." "Thou shalt have it, by my faith, and grant me thine," said he. "Gladly will I do so," answered Peredur.

So they rode forth together joyfully towards the place where Arthur was, and when Kai saw them coming, he said, "I knew that Gwalchmai needed not to fight the knight. And it is no wonder that he should gain fame; more can he do by his fair words than I by the strength of my arm." And Peredur went with Gwalchmai to his tent, and they took off their armour. And Peredur put on garments like those that Gwalchmai wore, and they went together unto Arthur, and saluted him. "Behold, lord," said Gwalchmai, "him whom thou hast sought so long." "Welcome unto thee, chieftain," said Arthur. "With me thou shalt remain; and had I known thy valour had been such, thou shouldst not have left me as thou didst; nevertheless, this was predicted of thee by the dwarf and the dwarfess, whom Kai ill-treated and whom thou hast avenged." And hereupon, behold there came the Queen and her handmaidens, and Peredur saluted them. And they were rejoiced to see him, and bade him welcome. And Arthur did him great honour and respect, and they returned towards Caerlleon.

And the first night Peredur came to Caerlleon to Arthur's Court, and as he walked in the city after his repast, behold, there met him Angharad Law Eurawc. "By my faith, sister," said Peredur, "thou art a beauteous and lovely maiden; and, were it pleasing to thee, I could love thee above all women." "I pledge my faith," said she, "that I do not love thee, nor will I ever do so." "I also pledge my faith," said Peredur, "that I will never speak a word to any Christian again, until thou come to love me above all men."

The next day Peredur went forth by the high road, along a mountain-ridge, and he saw a valley of a circular form, the confines of which were rocky and wooded. And the flat part of the valley was in meadows, and there were fields betwixt the meadows and the wood. And in the bosom of the wood he saw large black houses of uncouth workmanship. And he dismounted, and led his horse towards the wood. And a little way within the wood he saw a rocky ledge, along which the road lay. And upon the ledge was a lion bound by a chain, and sleeping. And beneath the lion he saw a deep pit of immense size, full of the bones of men and animals. And Peredur drew his sword and struck the lion, so that he fell into the mouth of the pit and hung there by the chain; and with a second blow he struck the chain and broke it, and the lion fell into the pit; and Peredur led his horse over the rocky ledge, until he came into the valley. And in the centre of the valley he saw a fair castle, and he went towards it. And in the meadow by the castle he beheld a huge grey man sitting, who was larger than any man he had ever before seen. And two young pages were shooting the hilts of their daggers, of the bone of the sea-horse. And one of the pages had red hair, and the other auburn. And they went before him to the place where the grey man was, and Peredur saluted him. And the grey man said, "Disgrace to the beard of my porter." Then Peredur understood that the porter was the lion. — And the grey man and the pages went together into the castle, and Peredur accompanied them; and he found it a fair and noble place. And they proceeded to the hall, and the tables were already laid, and upon them was abundance of food and liquor. And thereupon he saw an aged woman and a young woman come from the chamber; and they were the most stately women he had ever seen. Then they washed and went to meat, and the grey man sat in the upper seat at the head of the table, and the aged woman next to him. And Peredur and the maiden were placed together, and the two young pages served them. And the maiden gazed sorrowfully upon Peredur, and Peredur asked the maiden wherefore she was sad. "For thee, my soul; for, from when I first beheld thee, I have loved thee above all men. And it pains me to know that so gentle a youth as thou should have such a doom as awaits thee to-morrow. Sawest thou the numerous black houses in the bosom of the wood? All these belong to the vassals of the grey man yonder, who is my father. And they are all giants. And to-morrow they will rise up against thee, and will slay thee. And the Round Valley is this valley called." "Listen, fair maiden, wilt thou contrive that my horse and arms be in the same lodging with me to-night?" "Gladly will I cause it so to be, by Heaven, if I can."

And when it was time for them to sleep rather than to carouse, they went to rest. And the maiden caused Peredur's horse and arms to be in the same lodging with him. And the next morning Peredur heard a great tumult of men and horses around the castle. And Peredur arose, and armed himself and his horse, and went to the meadow. Then the aged woman and the maiden came to the grey man: "Lord," said they, "take the word of the youth, that he will never disclose what he has seen in this place, and we will be his sureties that he keep it." "I will not do so, by my faith," said the grey man. So Peredur fought with the host, and towards evening he had slain the one-third of them without receiving any hurt himself. Then said the aged woman, "Behold, many of thy host have been slain by the youth; do thou, therefore, grant him mercy." "I will not grant it, by my faith," said he. And the aged woman and the fair maiden were upon the battlements of the castle, looking forth. And at that juncture, Peredur encountered the yellow-haired youth and slew him. "Lord," said the maiden, "grant the young man mercy." "That will I not do, by Heaven," he replied; and thereupon Peredur attacked the auburn-haired youth, and slew him likewise. "It were better that thou hadst accorded mercy to the youth before he had slain thy two sons; for now scarcely wilt thou thyself escape from him." "Go, maiden, and beseech the youth to grant mercy unto us, for we yield ourselves into his hands." So the maiden came to the place where Peredur was, and besought mercy for her father, and for all such of his vassals as had escaped alive. "Thou shalt have it, on condition that thy father and all that are under him go and render homage to Arthur, and tell him that it was his vassal Peredur that did him this service." "This will we do willingly, by Heaven." "And you shall also receive baptism; and I will send to Arthur, and beseech him to bestow this valley upon thee and upon thy heirs after thee for ever." Then they went in, and the grey man and the tall woman saluted Peredur. And the grey man said unto him, "Since I have possessed this valley I have not seen any Christian depart with his life, save thyself. And we will go to do homage to Arthur, and to embrace the faith and be baptized." Then said Peredur, "To Heaven I render thanks that I have not broken my vow to the lady that best I love, which was, that I would not speak one word unto any Christian."

That night they tarried there. And the next day, in the morning, the grey man, with his company, set forth to Arthur's Court; and they did homage unto Arthur, and he caused them to be baptized. And the grey man told Arthur that it was Peredur that had vanquished them. And

Arthur gave the valley to the grey man and his company, to hold it of him as Peredur had besought. And with Arthur's permission, the grey man went back to the Round Valley.

Peredur rode forward next day, and he traversed a vast tract of desert, in which no dwellings were. And at length he came to a habitation, mean and small. And there he heard that there was a serpent that lay upon a gold ring, and suffered none to inhabit the country for seven miles around. And Peredur came to the place where he heard the serpent was. And angrily, furiously, and desperately fought he with the serpent; and at last he killed it, and took away the ring. And thus he was for a long time without speaking a word to any Christian. And therefrom he lost his colour and his aspect, through extreme longing after the Court of Arthur, and the society of the lady whom best he loved, and of his companions. Then he proceeded forward to Arthur's Court, and on the road there met him Arthur's household going on a particular errand, with Kai at their head. And Peredur knew them all, but none of the household recognized him. "Whence comest thou, chieftain?" said Kai. And this he asked him twice and three times, and he answered him not. And Kai thrust him through the thigh with his lance. And lest he should be compelled to speak, and to break his vow, he went on without stopping. "Then," said Gwalchmai, "I declare to Heaven, Kai, that thou hast acted ill in committing such an outrage on a youth like this, who cannot speak." And Gwalchmai returned back to Arthur's Court. "Lady," said he to Gwenhwyvar, "seest thou how wicked an outrage Kai has committed upon this youth who cannot speak; for Heaven's sake, and for mine, cause him to have medical care before I come back, and I will repay thee the charge."

And before the men returned from their errand, a knight came to the meadow beside Arthur's Palace, to dare some one to the encounter. And his challenge was accepted; and Peredur fought with him, and overthrew him. And for a week he overthrew one knight every day.

And one day, Arthur and his household were going to Church, and they beheld a knight who had raised the signal for combat. "Verily," said Arthur, "by the valour of men, I will not go hence until I have my horse and my arms to overthrow yonder boor." Then went the attendants to fetch Arthur's horse and arms. And Peredur met the attendants as they were going back, and he took the horse and arms from them, and proceeded to the meadow; and all those who saw him arise and go to do battle with the knight, went upon the tops of the houses, and the mounds, and the high places, to behold the combat. And Peredur beckoned with his hand to the knight to commence the fight. And the knight thrust at him, but he was not thereby moved from where he stood. And Peredur spurred his horse, and ran at him wrathfully, furiously, fiercely, desperately, and with mighty rage, and he gave him a thrust, deadly-wounding, severe, furious, adroit, and strong, under his jaw, and raised him out of his saddle, and cast him a long way from him. And Peredur went back, and left the horse and the arms with the attendant as before, and he went on foot to the Palace.

Then Peredur went by the name of the Dumb Youth. And behold, Angharad Law Eurawc met him. "I declare to Heaven, chieftain," said she, "woful is it that thou canst not speak; for couldst thou speak, I would love thee best of all men; and by my faith, although thou canst not, I do love thee above all." "Heaven reward thee, my sister," said Peredur, "by my faith I also do love thee." Thereupon it was known that he was Peredur. And then he held fellowship with Gwalchmai, and Owain the son of Urien, and all the household, and he remained in Arthur's Court.

Arthur was in Caerlleon upon Usk; and he went to hunt, and Peredur went with him. And Peredur let loose his dog upon a hart, and the dog killed the hart in a desert place. And a short space from him he saw signs of a dwelling, and towards the dwelling he went, and he beheld a hall, and at the door of the hall he found bald swarthy youths playing at chess. And when he entered, he beheld three maidens sitting on a bench, and they were all clothed alike, as became persons of high rank. And he came, and sat by them upon the bench; and one of the maidens looked steadfastly upon Peredur, and wept. And Peredur asked her wherefore she was weeping. "Through grief, that I should see so fair a youth as thou art, slain." "Who will slay me?" inquired Peredur. "If thou art so daring as to remain here to-night, I will tell thee." "How great soever my danger may be from remaining here, I will listen unto thee." "This Palace is owned by him who is my father," said the maiden, "and he slays every one who comes hither without his leave." "What sort of a man is thy father, that he is able to slay every one thus?" "A man who does violence and wrong unto his neighbours, and who renders justice unto none." And hereupon he saw the youths arise and clear the chessmen from the board. And he heard a great tumult; and after the tumult there came in a huge black one-eyed man, and the maidens arose to meet him. And they disarrayed him, and he went and sat down; and after he had rested and pondered awhile, he looked at Peredur, and asked who the knight was. "Lord," said one of the maidens, "he is the fairest and gentlest youth that ever thou didst see. And for the sake of Heaven, and of thine own dignity, have patience with him." "For thy sake I will have patience, and

I will grant him his life this night." Then Peredur came towards them to the fire, and partook of food and liquor, and entered into discourse with the ladies. And being elated with the liquor, he said to the black man, "It is a marvel to me, so mighty as thou sayest thou art, who could have put out thine eye." "It is one of my habits," said the black man, "that whosoever puts to me the question which thou hast asked, shall not escape with his life, either as a free gift or for a price." "Lord," said the maiden, "whatsoever he may say to thee in jest, and through the excitement of liquor, make good that which thou saidst and didst promise me just now." "I will do so, gladly, for thy sake," said he. "Willingly will I grant him his life this night." And that night thus they remained.

And the next day the black man got up, and put on his armour, and said to Peredur, "Arise, man, and suffer death." And Peredur said unto him, "Do one of two things, black man; if thou wilt fight with me, either throw off thy own armour, or give arms to me, that I may encounter thee." "Ha, man," said he, "couldst thou fight, if thou hadst arms? Take, then, what arms thou dost choose." And thereupon the maiden came to Peredur with such arms as pleased him; and he fought with the black man, and forced him to crave his mercy. "Black man, thou shalt have mercy, provided thou tell me who thou art, and who put out thine eye." "Lord, I will tell thee; I lost it in fighting with the Black Serpent of the Carn. There is a mound, which is called the Mound of Mourning; and on the mound there is a carn, and in the carn there is a serpent, and on the tail of the serpent there is a stone, and the virtues of the stone are such, that whosoever should hold it in one hand, in the other he will have as much gold as he may desire. And in fighting with this serpent was it that I lost my eye. And the Black Oppressor am I called. And for this reason I am called the Black Oppressor, that there is not a single man around me whom I have not oppressed, and justice have I done unto none." "Tell me," said Peredur, "how far is it hence?" "The same day that thou settest forth, thou wilt come to the Palace of the Sons of the King of the Tortures." "Wherefore are they called thus?" "The Addanc of the Lake slays them once every day. When thou goest thence, thou wilt come to the Court of the Countess of the Achievements." "What achievements are there?" asked Peredur. "Three hundred men there are in her household, and unto every stranger that comes to the Court, the achievements of her household are related. And this is the manner of it, — the three hundred men of the household sit next unto the Lady; and that not through disrespect unto the guests, but that they may relate the achievements of the household. And the day that thou goest thence, thou wilt reach the Mound of Mourning, and round about the mound there are the owners of three hundred tents guarding the serpent." "Since thou hast, indeed, been an oppressor so long," said Peredur, "I will cause that thou continue so no longer." So he slew him.

Then the maiden spoke, and began to converse with him. "If thou wast poor when thou camest here, henceforth thou wilt be rich through the treasure of the black man whom thou hast slain. Thou seest the many lovely maidens that there are in this Court; thou shalt have her whom thou best likest for the lady of thy love." "Lady, I came not hither from my country to woo; but match yourselves as it liketh you with the comely youths I see here; and none of your goods do I desire, for I need them not." Then Peredur rode forward, and he came to the Palace of the Sons of the King of the Tortures; and when he entered the Palace, he saw none but women; and they rose up, and were joyful at his coming; and as they began to discourse with him, he beheld a charger arrive, with a saddle upon it, and a corpse in the saddle. And one of the women arose, and took the corpse from the saddle, and anointed it in a vessel of warm water, which was below the door, and placed precious balsam upon it; and the man rose up alive, and came to the place where Peredur was, and greeted him, and was joyful to see him. And two other men came in upon their saddles, and the maiden treated these two in the same manner as she had done the first. Then Peredur asked the chieftain wherefore it was thus. And they told him, that there was an Addanc in a cave, which slew them once every day. And thus they remained that night.

And next morning the youths arose to sally forth, and Peredur besought them, for the sake of the ladies of their love, to permit him to go with them; but they refused him, saying, "If thou shouldst be slain there, thou hast none to bring thee back to life again." And they rode forward, and Peredur followed after them; and, after they had disappeared out of his sight, he came to a mound, whereon sat the fairest lady he had ever beheld. "I know thy quest," said she; "thou art going to encounter the Addanc, and he will slay thee, and that not by courage, but by craft. He has a cave, and at the entrance of the cave there is a stone pillar, and he sees every one that enters, and none see him; and from behind the pillar he slays every one with a poisonous dart. And if thou wouldst pledge me thy faith to love me above all women, I would give thee a stone, by which thou shouldst see him when thou goest in, and he should not see thee." "I will, by my troth," said Peredur, "for when first I beheld thee I loved thee; and where shall I seek thee?" "When thou seekest me, seek towards India." And the maiden vanished, after placing the stone in Peredur's hand.

And he came towards a valley, through which ran a river; and the borders of the valley were wooded, and on each side of the river were level meadows. And on one side of the river he saw a flock of white sheep, and on the other a flock of black sheep. And whenever one of the white sheep bleated, one of the black sheep would cross over and become white; and when one of the black sheep bleated, one of the white sheep would cross over and become black. And he saw a tall tree by the side of the river, one half of which was in flames from the root to the top, and the other half was green and in full leaf. And nigh thereto he saw a youth sitting upon a mound, and two greyhounds, white-breasted and spotted, in leashes, lying by his side. And certain was he that he had never seen a youth of so royal a bearing as he. And in the wood opposite he heard hounds raising a herd of deer. And Peredur saluted the youth, and the youth greeted him in return. And there were three roads leading from the mound; two of them were wide roads, and the third was more narrow. And Peredur inquired where the three roads went. "One of them goes to my palace," said the youth; "and one of two things I counsel thee to do; either to proceed to my palace, which is before thee, and where thou wilt find my wife, or else to remain here to see the hounds chasing the roused deer from the wood to the plain. And thou shalt see the best greyhounds thou didst ever behold, and the boldest in the chase, kill them by the water beside us; and when it is time to go to meat, my page will come with my horse to meet me, and thou shalt rest in my palace to-night." "Heaven reward thee; but I cannot tarry, for onward must I go." "The other road leads to the town, which is near here, and wherein food and liquor may be bought; and the road which is narrower than the others goes towards the cave of the Addanc." "With thy permission, young man, I will go that way."

And Peredur went towards the cave. And he took the stone in his left hand, and his lance in his right. And as he went in he perceived the Addanc, and he pierced him through with his lance, and cut off his head. And as he came from the cave, behold the three companions were at the entrance; and they saluted Peredur, and told him that there was a prediction that he should slay that monster. And Peredur gave the head to the young men, and they offered him in marriage whichever of the three sisters he might choose, and half their kingdom with her. "I came not hither to woo," said Peredur, "but if peradventure I took a wife, I should prefer your sister to all others." And Peredur rode forward, and he heard a noise behind him. And he looked back, and saw a man upon a red horse, with red armour upon him; and the man rode up by his side, and saluted him, and wished him the favour of Heaven and of man. And Peredur greeted the youth kindly. "Lord, I come to make a request unto thee." "What wouldest thou?" "That thou shouldest take me as thine attendant." "Whom then should I take as my attendant, if I did so?" "I will not conceal from thee what kindred I am of. Etlym Gleddyv Coch am I called, an Earl from the East Country." "I marvel that thou shouldest offer to become attendant to a man whose possessions are no greater than thine own; for I have but an earldom like thyself. But since thou desirest to be my attendant, I will take thee joyfully."

And they went forward to the Court of the Countess, and all they of the Court were glad at their coming; and they were told it was not through disrespect they were placed below the household, but that such was the usage of the Court. For, whoever should overthrow the three hundred men of her household, would sit next the Countess, and she would love him above all men. And Peredur having overthrown the three hundred men of her household, sat down beside her, and the Countess said, "I thank Heaven that I have a youth so fair and so valiant as thou, since I have not obtained the man whom best I love." "Who is he whom best thou lovest?" "By my faith, Etlym Gleddyv Coch is the man whom I love best, and I have never seen him." "Of a truth, Etlym is my companion; and behold here he is, and for his sake did I come to joust with thy household. And he could have done so better than I, had it pleased him. And I do give thee unto him." "Heaven reward thee, fair youth, and I will take the man whom I love above all others." And the Countess became Etlym's bride from that moment.

And the next day Peredur set forth towards the Mound of Mourning. "By thy hand, lord, but I will go with thee," said Etlym. Then they went forwards till they came in sight of the mound and the tents. "Go unto yonder men," said Peredur to Etlym, "and desire them to come and do me homage." So Etlym went unto them, and said unto them thus, — "Come and do homage to my lord." "Who is thy lord?" said they. "Peredur with the long lance is my lord," said Etlym. "Were it permitted to slay a messenger, thou shouldest not go back to thy lord alive, for making unto Kings, and Earls, and Barons so arrogant a demand as to go and do him homage." Peredur desired him to go back to them, and to give them their choice, either to do him homage, or to do battle with him. And they chose rather to do battle. And that day Peredur overthrew the owners of a hundred tents; and the next day he overthrew the owners of a hundred more; and the third day the remaining hundred took counsel to do homage to Peredur. And Peredur inquired of them, wherefore they were there. And they told him they were guarding the serpent until he should die. "For then should we fight for the stone among ourselves, and whoever should be conqueror among us would have the stone." "Await here," said Peredur, "and I will go to encounter the serpent." "Not so, lord," said they; "we will go altogether to encounter the serpent."

"Verily," said Peredur, "that will I not permit; for if the serpent be slain, I shall derive no more fame therefrom than one of you." Then he went to the place where the serpent was, and slew it, and came back to them, and said, "Reckon up what you have spent since you have been here, and I will repay you to the full." And he paid to each what he said was his claim. And he required of them only that they should acknowledge themselves his vassals. And he said to Etlym, "Go back unto her whom thou lovest best, and I will go forwards, and I will reward thee for having been my attendant." And he gave Etlym the stone. "Heaven repay thee and prosper thee," said Etlym.

And Peredur rode thence, and he came to the fairest valley he had ever seen, through which ran a river; and there he beheld many tents of various colours. And he marvelled still more at the number of water-mills and of wind-mills that he saw. And there rode up with him a tall auburn-haired man, in a workman's garb, and Peredur inquired of him who he was. "I am the chief miller," said he, "of all the mills yonder." "Wilt thou give me lodging?" said Peredur. "I will, gladly," he answered. And Peredur came to the miller's house, and the miller had a fair and pleasant dwelling. And Peredur asked money as a loan from the miller, that he might buy meat and liquor for himself and for the household, and he promised that he would pay him again ere he went thence. And he inquired of the miller, wherefore such a multitude was there assembled. Said the miller to Peredur, "One thing is certain: either thou art a man from afar, or thou art beside thyself. The Empress of Cristinobyl the Great is here; and she will have no one but the man who is most valiant; for riches does she not require. And it was impossible to bring food for so many thousands as are here, therefore were all these mills constructed." And that night they took their rest.

And the next day Peredur arose, and he equipped himself and his horse for the tournament. And among the other tents he beheld one, which was the fairest he had ever seen. And he saw a beauteous maiden leaning her head out of a window of the tent, and he had never seen a maiden more lovely than she. And upon her was a garment of satin. And he gazed fixedly on the maiden, and began to love her greatly. And he remained there, gazing upon the maiden from morning until mid-day, and from mid-day until evening; and then the tournament was ended and he went to his lodging and drew off his armour. Then he asked money of the miller as a loan, and the miller's wife was wroth with Peredur; nevertheless, the miller lent him the money. And the next day he did in like manner as he had done the day before. And at night he came to his lodging, and took money as a loan from the miller. And the third day, as he was in the same place, gazing upon the maiden, he felt a hard blow between the neck and the shoulder, from the edge of an axe. And when he looked behind him, he saw that it was the miller; and the miller said to him, "Do one of two things: either turn thy head from hence, or go to the tournament." And Peredur smiled on the miller, and went to the tournament; and all that encountered him that day he overthrew. And as many as he vanquished he sent as a gift to the Empress, and their horses and arms he sent as a gift to the wife of the miller, in payment of the borrowed money. Peredur attended the tournament until all were overthrown, and he sent all the men to the prison of the Empress, and the horses and arms to the wife of the miller, in payment of the borrowed money. And the Empress sent to the Knight of the Mill, to ask him to come and visit her. And Peredur went not for the first nor for the second message. And the third time she sent a hundred knights to bring him against his will, and they went to him and told him their mission from the Empress. And Peredur fought well with them, and caused them to be bound like stags, and thrown into the mill-dyke. And the Empress sought advice of a wise man who was in her counsel; and he said to her, "With thy permission, I will go to him myself." So he came to Peredur, and saluted him, and besought him, for the sake of the lady of his love, to come and visit the Empress. And they went, together with the miller. And Peredur went and sat down in the outer chamber of the tent, and she came and placed herself by his side. And there was but little discourse between them. And Peredur took his leave, and went to his lodging.

And the next day he came to visit her, and when he came into the tent there was no one chamber less decorated than the others. And they knew not where he would sit. And Peredur went and sat beside the Empress, and discoursed with her courteously. And while they were thus, they beheld a black man enter with a goblet full of wine in his hand. And he dropped upon his knee before the Empress, and besought her to give it to no one who would not fight with him for it. And she looked upon Peredur. "Lady," said he, "bestow on me the goblet." And Peredur drank the wine, and gave the goblet to the miller's wife. And while they were thus, behold there entered a black man of larger stature than the other, with a wild beast's claw in his hand, wrought into the form of a goblet and filled with wine. And he presented it to the Empress, and besought her to give it to no one but the man who would fight with him. "Lady," said Peredur, "bestow it on me." And she gave it to him. And Peredur drank the wine, and sent the goblet to the wife of the miller. And while they were thus, behold a rough-looking, crisp-haired man, taller than either of the others, came in with a bowl in his hand full of wine; and he bent upon his knee, and gave it into the hands of the Empress, and he besought her to give it to none but him who would fight with him for it; and she gave it to Peredur, and he sent it to the miller's wife. And that night Peredur returned to his lodging; and the next day he accoutred himself and his horse, and went to the meadow and slew the three men. Then Peredur proceeded to the tent, and the Empress said to him, "Goodly Peredur, remember the faith thou didst pledge me when I gave thee the stone, and thou didst kill the Addanc." "Lady," answered he, "thou sayest truth, I do remember it." And Peredur was entertained by the Empress fourteen years, as the story relates.

Arthur was at Caerlleon upon Usk, his principal palace; and in the centre of the floor of the hall were four men sitting on a carpet of velvet, Owain the son of Urien, and Gwalchmai the son of Gwyar, and Howel the son of Emyr Llydaw, and Peredur of the long lance. And thereupon they saw a black curly-headed maiden enter, riding upon a yellow mule, with jagged thongs in her hand to urge it on; and having a rough and hideous aspect. Blacker were her face and her two hands than the blackest iron covered with pitch; and her hue was not more frightful than her form. High cheeks had she, and a face lengthened downwards, and a short nose with distended nostrils. And one eye was of a piercing mottled grey, and the other was as black as jet, deep-sunk in her head. And her teeth were long and yellow, more yellow were they than the flower of the broom. And her stomach rose from the breast-bone, higher than her chin. And her back was in the shape of a crook, and her legs were large and bony. And her figure was very thin and spare, except her feet and her legs, which were of huge size. And she greeted Arthur and all his household except Peredur. And to Peredur she spoke harsh and angry words. "Peredur, I greet thee not, seeing that thou dost not merit it. Blind was fate in giving thee fame and favour. When thou wast in the Court of the Lame King, and didst see there the youth bearing the streaming spear, from the points of which were drops of blood flowing in streams, even to the hand of the youth, and many other wonders likewise, thou didst not inquire their meaning nor their cause. Hadst thou done so, the King would have been restored to health, and his dominions to peace. Whereas from henceforth, he will have to endure battles and conflicts, and his knights will perish, and wives will be widowed, and maidens will be left portionless, and all this is because of thee." Then said she unto Arthur, "May it please thee, lord, my dwelling is far hence, in the stately castle of which thou hast heard, and therein are five hundred and sixty-six knights of the order of Chivalry, and the lady whom best he loves with each; and whoever would acquire fame in arms, and encounters, and conflicts, he will gain it there, if he deserve it. And whoso would reach the summit of fame and of honour, I know where he may find it. There is a castle on a lofty mountain, and there is a maiden therein, and she is detained a prisoner there, and whoever shall set her free will attain the summit of the fame of the world." And thereupon she rode away.

Said Gwalchmai, "By my faith, I will not rest tranquilly until I have proved if I can release the maiden." And many of Arthur's household joined themselves with him. Then, likewise, said Peredur, "By my faith, I will not rest tranquilly until I know the story and the meaning of the lance whereof the black maiden spoke." And while they were equipping themselves, behold a knight came to the gate. And he had the size and the strength of a warrior, and was equipped with arms and habiliments. And he went forward, and saluted Arthur and all his household, except Gwalchmai. And the knight had upon his shoulder a shield, ingrained with gold, with a fesse of azure blue upon it, and his whole armour was of the same hue. And he said to Gwalchmai, "Thou didst slay my lord by thy treachery and deceit, and that will I prove upon thee." Then Gwalchmai rose up. "Behold," said he, "here is my gage against thee, to maintain, either in this place or wherever else thou wilt, that I am not a traitor or deceiver." "Before the King whom I obey, will I that my encounter with thee take place," said the knight. "Willingly," said Gwalchmai; "go forward, and I will follow thee." So the knight went forth, and Gwalchmai accoutred himself, and there was offered unto him abundance of armour, but he would take none but his own. And when Gwalchmai and Peredur were equipped, they set forth to follow him, by reason of their fellowship and of the great friendship that was between them. And they did not go after him in company together, but each went his own way.

At the dawn of day Gwalchmai came to a valley, and in the valley he saw a fortress, and within the fortress a vast palace and lofty towers around it. And he beheld a knight coming out to hunt from the other side, mounted on a spirited black snorting palfrey, that advanced at a prancing pace, proudly stepping, and nimbly bounding, and sure of foot; and this was the man to whom the palace belonged. And Gwalchmai saluted him. "Heaven prosper thee, chieftain," said he, "and whence comest thou?" "I come," answered Gwalchmai, "from the Court of Arthur." "And art thou Arthur's vassal?" "Yes, by my faith," said Gwalchmai. "I will give thee good counsel," said the knight. "I see that thou art tired and weary; go unto my palace, if it may please thee, and tarry there to-night." "Willingly, lord," said he, "and Heaven reward thee." "Take this ring as a token to the porter, and go forward to yonder tower, and therein thou wilt find my sister." And Gwalchmai went to the gate, and showed the ring, and proceeded to the tower. And on entering he beheld a large blazing fire, burning without smoke and with a bright and lofty flame, and a beauteous and stately maiden was sitting on a chair by the fire. And the maiden was glad at his coming, and welcomed him, and advanced to meet him. And he went and sat beside the maiden, and they took their repast. And when their repast was over, they discoursed pleasantly together. And while they were thus, behold there entered a venerable hoary-headed man. "Ah! base girl," said he, "if thou didst think it was right for thee to entertain and to sit by yonder man, thou wouldest not do so." And he withdrew his head, and went forth. "Ah! chieftain," said the maiden, "if thou wilt do as I counsel thee, thou wilt shut the door, lest the man should have a plot against thee." Upon that Gwalchmai arose, and when he came near unto the door, the man, with sixty others, fully armed, were ascending the tower. And Gwalchmai defended the door with a chessboard, that none might enter until the man should return from the chase. And thereupon, behold the Earl arrived. "What is all this?" asked he. "It is a sad thing," said the hoary-headed man; "the young girl yonder has been sitting and eating with him who slew your father. He is Gwalchmai, the son of Gwyar." "Hold thy peace, then," said the Earl, "I will go in." And the Earl was joyful concerning Gwalchmai. "Ha! chieftain," said he, "it was wrong of thee to come to my court, when thou knewest that thou didst slay my father; and though we cannot avenge him, Heaven will avenge him upon thee." "My soul," said Gwalchmai, "thus it is: I came not here either to acknowledge or to deny having slain thy father; but I am on a message from Arthur, and therefore do I crave the space of a year until I shall return from my embassy, and then, upon my faith, I will come back unto this palace, and do one of two things, either acknowledge it, or deny it." And the time was granted him willingly; and he remained there that night. And the next morning he rode forth. And the story relates nothing further of Gwalchmai respecting this adventure.

And Peredur rode forward. And he wandered over the whole island, seeking tidings of the black maiden, and he could meet with none. And he came to an unknown land, in the centre of a valley, watered by a river. And as he traversed the valley he beheld a horseman coming towards him, and wearing the garments of a priest; and he besought his blessing. "Wretched man," said he, "thou meritest no blessing, and thou wouldest not be profited by one, seeing that thou art clad in armour on such a day as this." "And what day is to-day?" said Peredur. "To-day is Good Friday," he answered. "Chide me not that I knew not this, seeing that it is a year to-day since I journeyed forth from my country." Then he dismounted, and led his horse in his hand. And he had not proceeded far along the high road before he came to a cross road, and the cross road traversed a wood. And on the other side of the wood he saw an unfortified castle, which appeared to be inhabited. And at the gate of the castle there met him the priest whom he had seen before, and he asked his blessing. "The blessing of Heaven be unto thee," said he, "it is more fitting to travel in thy present guise than as thou wast erewhile; and this night thou shalt tarry with me." So he remained there that night.

And the next day Peredur sought to go forth. "To-day may no one journey. Thou shalt remain with me to-day and to-morrow, and the day following, and I will direct thee as best I may to the place which thou art seeking." And the fourth day Peredur sought to go forth, and he entreated the priest to tell him how he should find the Castle of Wonders. "What I know thereof I will tell thee," he replied. "Go over yonder mountain, and on the other side of the mountain thou wilt come to a river, and in the valley wherein the river runs is a King's palace, wherein the King sojourned during Easter. And if thou mayest have tidings anywhere of the Castle of Wonders, thou wilt have them there."

Then Peredur rode forward. And he came to the valley in which was the river, and there met him a number of men going to hunt, and in the midst of them was a man of exalted rank, and Peredur saluted him. "Choose, chieftain," said the man, "whether thou wilt go with me to the chase, or wilt proceed to my palace, and I will dispatch one of my household to commend thee to my daughter, who is there, and who will entertain thee with food and liquor until I return from hunting; and whatever may be thine errand, such as I can obtain for thee thou shalt gladly have." And the King sent a little yellow page with him as an attendant; and when they came to the palace the lady had arisen, and was about to wash before meat. Peredur went forward, and she saluted him joyfully, and placed him by her side. And they took their repast. And whatsoever Peredur said unto her, she laughed loudly, so that all in the palace could hear. Then spoke the yellow page to the lady. "By my faith," said he, "this youth is already thy husband; or if he be not, thy mind and thy thoughts are set upon him." And the little yellow page went unto the King, and told him that it seemed to him that the youth whom he had met with was his daughter's husband, or if he were not so already that he would shortly become so unless he were cautious. "What is thy counsel in this matter, youth?" said the King. "My counsel is," he replied, "that thou set strong men upon him, to seize him, until thou hast ascertained the truth respecting this." So he set strong men upon Peredur, who seized him and cast him into prison. And the maiden went before her father, and asked him wherefore he had caused the youth from Arthur's Court to be imprisoned. "In truth," he answered, "he shall not be free to-night, nor to-morrow, nor the day following, and he shall not come from where he is." She replied not to what the King had said, but she went to the youth. "Is it unpleasant to thee to be here?" said she. "I should not care if I were not," he replied. "Thy couch and thy treatment shall be in no wise inferior to that of the King himself, and thou shalt have the best entertainment that the palace affords. And if it were more pleasing to thee that my couch should be here, that I might discourse with thee, it should be so, cheerfully." "This can I not refuse," said Peredur. And he remained in prison that night. And the maiden provided all that she had promised him.

And the next day Peredur heard a tumult in the town. "Tell me, fair maiden, what is that tumult?" said Peredur. "All the King's hosts and his forces have come to the town to-day." "And what seek they here?" he inquired. "There is an Earl near this place who possesses two Earldoms, and is as powerful as a King; and an engagement will take place between them to-day." "I beseech thee," said Peredur, "to cause a horse and arms to be brought, that I may view the encounter, and I promise to come back to my prison again." "Gladly," said she, "will I provide thee with horse and arms." So she gave him a horse and arms, and a bright scarlet robe of honour over his armour, and a yellow shield upon his shoulder. And he went to the combat; and as many of the Earl's men as encountered him that day he overthrew; and he returned to his prison. And the maiden asked tidings of Peredur, and he answered her not a word. And she went and asked tidings of her father, and inquired who had acquitted himself best of the household. And he said that he knew not, but that it was a man with a scarlet robe of honour over his armour, and a yellow shield upon his shoulder. Then she smiled, and returned to where Peredur was, and did him great honour that night. And for three days did Peredur slay the Earl's men; and before any one could know who he was, he returned to his prison. And the fourth day Peredur slew the Earl himself. And the maiden went unto her father, and inquired of him the news. "I have good news for thee," said the King; "the Earl is slain, and I am the owner of his two Earldoms." "Knowest thou, lord, who slew him?" "I do not know," said the King. "It was the knight with the scarlet robe of honour and the yellow shield." "Lord," said she, "I know who that is." "By Heaven!" he exclaimed, "who is he?" "Lord," she replied, "he is the knight whom thou hast imprisoned." Then he went unto Peredur, and saluted him, and told him that he would reward the service he had done him, in any way he might desire. And when they went to meat, Peredur was placed beside the King, and the maiden on the other side of Peredur. "I will give thee," said the King, "my daughter in marriage, and half my kingdom with her, and the two Earldoms as a gift." "Heaven reward thee, lord," said Peredur, "but I came not here to woo." "What seekest thou then, chieftain?" "I am seeking tidings of the Castle of Wonders." "Thy enterprise is greater, chieftain, than thou wilt wish to pursue," said the maiden, "nevertheless, tidings shalt thou have of the Castle, and thou shalt have a guide through my father's dominions, and a sufficiency of provisions for thy journey, for thou art, O chieftain, the man whom best I love." Then she said to him, "Go over yonder mountain, and thou wilt find a lake, and in the middle of the lake there is a Castle, and that is the Castle that is called the Castle of Wonders; and we know not what wonders are therein, but thus is it called."

And Peredur proceeded towards the Castle, and the gate of the Castle was open. And when he came to the hall, the door was open, and he entered. And he beheld a chessboard in the hall, and the chessmen were playing against each other, by themselves. And the side that he favoured lost the game, and thereupon the others set up a shout, as though they had been living men. And Peredur was wroth, and took the chessmen in his lap, and cast the chessboard into the lake. And when he had done thus, behold the black maiden came in, and she said to him, "The welcome of Heaven be not unto thee. Thou hadst rather do evil than good." "What complaint hast thou against me, maiden?" said Peredur. "That thou hast occasioned unto the Empress the loss of her chessboard, which she would not have lost for all her empire. And the way in which thou mayest recover the chessboard is, to repair to the Castle of Ysbidinongyl, where is a black man, who lays waste the dominions of the Empress; and if thou canst slay him, thou wilt recover the chessboard. But if thou goest there, thou wilt not return alive." "Wilt thou direct me thither?" said Peredur. "I will show thee the way," she replied. So he went to the Castle of Ysbidinongyl, and he fought with the black man. And the black man besought mercy of Peredur. "Mercy will I grant thee," said he, "on condition that thou cause the chessboard to be restored to the place where it was when I entered the hall." Then the maiden came to him, and said, "The malediction of Heaven attend thee for thy work, since thou hast left that monster alive, who lays waste all the possessions of the Empress." "I granted him his life," said Peredur, "that he might cause the chessboard to be restored." "The chessboard is not in the place where thou didst find it; go back, therefore, and slay him," answered she. So Peredur went back, and slew the black man. And when he returned to the palace, he found the black maiden there. "Ah! maiden," said Peredur, "where is the Empress?" "I declare to Heaven that thou wilt not see her now, unless thou dost slay the monster that is in yonder forest." "What monster is there?" "It is a stag that is as swift as the swiftest bird; and he has one horn in his forehead, as long as the shaft of a spear, and as sharp as whatever is sharpest. And he destroys the branches of the best trees in the forest, and he kills every animal that he meets with therein; and those that he doth not slay perish of hunger. And what is worse than that, he comes every night, and drinks up the fish-pond, and leaves the fishes exposed, so that for the most part they die before the water returns again." "Maiden," said Peredur, "wilt thou come and show me this animal?" "Not so," said the maiden, "for he has not permitted any mortal to enter the forest for above a twelvemonth. Behold, here is a little dog belonging to the Empress, which will rouse the stag, and will chase him towards thee, and the stag will attack thee." Then the little dog went as a guide to Peredur, and roused the stag, and brought him towards the place where Peredur was. And the stag attacked Peredur, and he let him pass by him, and as he did so, he smote off his head with his sword. And while he was looking at the head of the stag, he saw a lady on horseback coming towards him. And she took the little dog in the lappet of her cap, and the head and the body of the stag lay before her. And around the stag's neck was a golden collar. "Ha! chieftain," said she, "uncourteously hast thou acted in slaying the fairest jewel that was in my dominions." "I was entreated so to do; and is there any way by which I can obtain thy friendship?" "There is," she replied. "Go thou forward unto yonder mountain, and there thou wilt find a grove; and in the grove there is a cromlech; do thou there challenge a man three times to fight, and thou shalt have my friendship."

So Peredur proceeded onward, and came to the side of the grove, and challenged any man to fight. And a black man arose from beneath the cromlech, mounted upon a bony horse, and both he and his horse were clad in huge rusty armour. And they fought. And as often as Peredur cast the black man to the earth, he would jump again into his saddle. And Peredur dismounted, and drew his sword; and thereupon the black man disappeared with Peredur's horse and his own, so that he could not gain sight of him a second time. And Peredur went along the mountain, and on the other side of the mountain he beheld a castle in the valley, wherein was a river. And he went to the castle; and as he entered it, he saw a hall, and the door of the hall was open, and he went in. And there he saw a lame grey-headed man sitting on one side of the hall, with Gwalchmai beside him. And Peredur beheld his horse, which the black man had taken, in the same stall with that of Gwalchmai. And they were glad concerning Peredur. And he went and seated himself on the other side of the hoary-headed man. Then, behold a yellow-haired youth came, and bent upon the knee before Peredur, and besought his friendship. "Lord," said the youth, "it was I that came in the form of the black maiden to Arthur's Court, and when thou didst throw down the chessboard, and when thou didst slay the black man of Ysbidinongyl, and when thou didst slay the stag, and when thou didst go to fight the black man of the cromlech. And I came with the bloody head in the salver, and with the lance that streamed with blood from the point to the hand, all along the shaft; and the head was thy cousin's, and he was killed by the sorceresses of Gloucester, who also lamed thine uncle; and I am thy cousin. And there is a prediction that thou art to avenge these things." Then Peredur and Gwalchmai took counsel, and sent to Arthur and his household, to beseech them to come against the sorceresses. And they began to fight with them; and one of the sorceresses slew one of Arthur's men before Peredur's face, and Peredur bade her forbear. And the sorceress slew a man before Peredur's face a second time, and a second time he forbad her. And the third time the sorceress slew a man before the face of Peredur; and then Peredur drew his sword, and smote the sorceress on the helmet; and all her head-armour was split in two parts. And she set up a cry, and desired the other sorceresses to flee, and told them that this was Peredur, the man who had learnt Chivalry with them, and by whom they were destined to be slain. Then Arthur and his household fell upon the sorceresses, and slew the sorceresses of Gloucester every one. And thus is it related concerning the Castle of Wonders.

GERAINT THE SON OF ERBIN

ARTHUR was accustomed to hold his Court at Caerlleon upon Usk. And there he held it seven Easters and five Christmases. And once upon a time he held his Court there at Whitsuntide. For Caerlleon was the place most easy of access in his dominions, both by sea and by land. And there were assembled nine crowned kings, who were his tributaries, and likewise earls and barons. For they were his invited guests at all the high festivals, unless they were prevented by any great hindrance. And when he was at Caerlleon, holding his Court, thirteen churches were set apart for mass. And thus were they appointed: one church for Arthur, and his kings, and his guests; and the second for Gwenhwyvar and her ladies; and the third for the Steward of the Household and the suitors; and the fourth for the Franks and the other officers; and the other nine churches were for the nine Masters of the Household and chiefly for Cwalchmai; for he, from the eminence of his warlike fame, and from the nobleness of his birth, was the most exalted of the nine. And there was no other arrangement respecting the churches than that which we have mentioned above.

Glewlwyd Gavaelvawr was the chief porter; but he did not himself perform the office, except at one of the three high festivals, for he had seven men to serve him, and they divided the year amongst them. They were Grynn, and Pen Pighon, and Llaes Cymyn, and Gogyfwlch, and Gwrdnei with cat's eyes, who could see as well by night as by day, and Drem the son of Dremhitid, and Clust the son of Clustveinyd; and these were Arthur's guards. And on Whit-Tuesday, as the King sat at the banquet, lo! there entered a tall, fair-headed youth, clad in a coat and a surcoat of diapered satin, and a golden-hilted sword about his neck, and low shoes of leather upon his feet. And he came, and stood before Arthur. "Hail to thee, Lord!" said he. "Heaven prosper thee," he answered, "and be thou welcome. Dost thou bring any new tidings?" "I do, Lord," he said. "I know thee not," said Arthur. "It is a marvel to me that thou dost not know me. I am one of thy foresters, Lord, in the Forest of Dean, and my name is Madawc, the son of Twrgadarn." "Tell me thine errand," said Arthur. "I will do so, Lord," said he. "In the Forest I saw a stag, the like of which beheld I never yet." "What is there about him," asked Arthur, "that thou never yet didst see his like?" "He is of pure white, Lord, and he does not herd with any other animal through stateliness and pride, so royal is his bearing. And I come to seek thy counsel, Lord, and to know thy will concerning him." "It seems best to me," said Arthur, "to go and hunt him to-morrow at break of day; and to cause general notice thereof to be given to-night in all quarters of the Court." And Arryfuerys was Arthur's chief huntsman, and Arelivri was his chief page. And all received notice; and thus it was arranged. And they sent the youth before them. Then Gwenhwyvar said to Arthur, "Wilt thou permit me, Lord," said she, "to go to-morrow to see and hear the hunt of the stag of which the young man spoke?" "I will gladly," said Arthur. "Then will I go," said she. And Gwalchmai said to Arthur, "Lord, if it seem well to thee, permit that into whose hunt soever the stag shall come, that one, be he a knight, or one on foot, may cut off his head, and give it to whom he pleases, whether to his own lady-love, or to the lady of his friend." "I grant it gladly," said Arthur, "and let the Steward of the Household be chastised, if all are not ready to-morrow for the chase."

And they passed the night with songs, and diversions, and discourse, and ample entertainment. And when it was time for them all to go to sleep, they went. And when the next day came, they arose; and Arthur called the attendants, who guarded his couch. And these were four pages, whose names were Cadyrnerth the son of Porthawr Gandwy, and Ambreu the son of Bedwor, and Amhar the son of Arthur, and Goreu the son of Custennin. And these men came to Arthur and saluted him, and arrayed him in his garments. And Arthur wondered that Gwenhwyvar did not awake, and did not move in her bed; and the attendants wished to awaken her. "Disturb her not," said Arthur, "for she had rather sleep than go to see the hunting."

Then Arthur went forth, and he heard two horns sounding, one from near the lodging of the chief huntsman, and the other from near that of the chief page. And the whole assembly of the multitudes came to Arthur, and they took the road to the Forest.

And after Arthur had gone forth from the palace, Gwenhwyvar awoke, and called to her maidens, and apparelled herself. "Maidens," said she, "I had leave last night to go and see the hunt. Go one of you to the stable, and order hither a horse such as a woman may ride." And one of them went, and she found but two horses in the stable, and Gwenhwyvar and one of her maidens mounted them, and went through the Usk, and followed the track of the men and the horses. And as they rode thus, they heard a loud and rushing sound; and they looked behind them, and beheld a knight upon a hunter foal of mighty size; and the rider was a fair-haired youth, bare-legged, and of princely mien, and a golden-hilted sword was at his side, and a robe and a surcoat of satin were upon him, and two low shoes of leather upon his feet; and around him was a scarf of blue purple, at each corner of which was a golden apple. And his horse stepped stately, and swift, and proud; and he overtook Gwenhwyvar, and saluted her. "Heaven prosper thee, Geraint," said she, "I knew thee when first I saw thee just now. And the welcome of Heaven be unto thee. And why didst thou not go with thy lord to hunt?" Because I knew not when he went," said he. "I marvel, too," said she, "how he could go unknown to me." "Indeed, lady," said he. "I was asleep, and knew not when he went; but thou, O young man, art the most agreeable companion I could have in the whole kingdom; and it may be, that I shall be more amused with the hunting than they; for we shall hear the horns when they sound, and we shall hear the dogs when they are let loose, and begin to cry." So they went to the edge of the Forest, and there they stood. "From this place," said she, "we shall hear when the dogs are let loose." And thereupon, they heard a loud noise, and they looked towards the spot whence it came, and they beheld a dwarf riding upon a horse, stately, and foaming, and prancing, and strong, and spirited. And in the hand of the dwarf was a whip. And near the dwarf they saw a lady upon a beautiful white horse, of steady and stately pace; and she was clothed in a garment of gold brocade. And near her was a knight upon a warhorse of large size, with heavy and bright armour both upon himself and upon his horse. And truly they never before saw a knight, or a horse, or armour, of such remarkable size. And they were all near to each other.

"Geraint," said Gwenhwyvar, "knowest thou the name of that tall knight yonder?" "I know him not," said he, "and the strange armour that he wears prevents my either seeing his face or his features." "Go, maiden," said Gwenhwyvar, "and ask the dwarf who that knight is." Then the maiden went up to the dwarf; and the dwarf waited for the maiden, when he saw her coming towards him. And the maiden inquired of the dwarf who the knight was. "I will not tell thee," he answered. "Since thou art so churlish as not to tell me," said she, "I will ask him himself." "Thou shalt not ask him, by my faith," said he. "Wherefore?" said she. "Because thou art not of honour sufficient to befit thee to speak to my Lord." Then the maiden turned her horse's head towards the knight, upon which the dwarf struck her with the whip that was in his hand across the face and the eyes, until the blood flowed forth. And the maiden, through the hurt she received from the blow, returned to Gwenhwyvar, complaining of the pain. "Very rudely has the dwarf treated thee," said Geraint. "I will go myself to know who the knight is." "Go," said Gwenhwyvar. And Geraint went up to the dwarf. "Who is yonder knight?" said Geraint. "I will not tell thee," said the dwarf. "Then will I ask him himself," said he. "That wilt thou not, by my faith," said the dwarf, "thou art not honourable enough to speak with my Lord." Said Geraint, "I have spoken with men of equal rank with him." And he turned his horse's head towards the knight; but the dwarf overtook him, and struck him as he had done the maiden, so that the blood coloured the scarf that Geraint wore. Then Geraint put his hand upon the hilt of his sword, but he took counsel with himself, and considered that it would be no vengeance for him to slay the dwarf, and to be attacked unarmed by the armed knight, so he returned to where Gwenhwyvar was.

"Thou hast acted wisely and discreetly," said she. "Lady," said he, "I will follow him yet, with thy permission; and at last he will come to some inhabited place, where I may have arms either as a loan or for a pledge, so that I may encounter the knight." "Go," said she, "and do not attack him until thou hast good arms, and I shall be very anxious concerning thee, until I hear tidings of thee." "If I am alive," said he, "thou shalt hear tidings of me by to-morrow afternoon;" and with that he departed.

And the road they took was below the palace of Caerlleon, and across the ford of the Usk; and they went along a fair, and even, and lofty ridge of ground, until they came to a town, and at the extremity of the town they saw a Fortress and a Castle. And they came to the extremity of the town. And as the knight passed through it, all the people arose, and saluted him, and bade him welcome. And when Geraint came into the town, he looked at every house, to see if he knew any of those whom he saw. But he knew none, and none knew him to do him the kindness to let him have arms either as a loan or for a pledge. And every house he saw was full of men, and arms, and horses. And they were polishing shields, and burnishing swords, and washing armour, and shoeing horses. And the knight, and the lady, and the dwarf rode up to the Castle that was in the town, and every one was glad in the Castle. And from the battlements and the gates they risked their necks, through their eagerness to greet them, and to show their joy.

Geraint stood there to see whether the knight would remain in the Castle; and when he was certain that he would do so, he looked around him; and at a little distance from the town he saw an old palace in ruins, wherein was a hall that was falling to decay. And as he knew not any one in the town, he went towards the old palace; and when he came near to the palace, he saw but one chamber, and a bridge of marble-stone leading to it. And upon the bridge he saw sitting a hoary-headed man, upon whom were tattered garments. And Geraint gazed steadfastly upon him for a long time. Then the hoary-headed man spoke to him. "Young man," he said, "wherefore art thou thoughtful?" "I am thoughtful," said he, "because I know not where to go to-night." "Wilt thou come forward this way, chieftain?" said he, "and thou shalt have of the best that can be procured for thee." So Geraint went forward. And the hoary-headed man preceded him into the hall. And in the hall he dismounted, and he left there his horse. Then he went on to the upper chamber with the hoary-headed man. And in the chamber he beheld an old decrepit woman, sitting on a cushion, with old, tattered garments of satin upon her; and it seemed to him that he had never seen a woman fairer than she must have been, when in the fulness of youth. And beside her was a maiden, upon whom were a vest and a veil, that were old, and beginning to be worn out. And truly, he never saw a maiden more full of comeliness, and grace, and beauty than she. And the hoary-headed man said to the maiden, "There is no attendant for the horse of this youth but thyself." "I will render the best service I am able," said she, "both to him and to his horse." And the maiden disarrayed the youth, and then she furnished his horse with straw and with corn. And she went to the hall as before, and then she returned to the chamber. And the hoary-headed man said to the maiden, "Go to the town," said he, "and bring hither the best that thou canst find both of food and of liquor." "I will, gladly, Lord," said she. And to the town went the maiden. And they conversed together while the maiden was at the town. And, behold! the maiden came back, and a youth with her, bearing on his back a costrel full of good purchased mead, and a quarter of a young bullock. And in the hands of the maiden was a quantity of white bread, and she had some manchet bread in her veil, and she came into the chamber. "I could not obtain better than this," said she, "nor with better should I have been trusted." "It is good enough," said Geraint. And they caused the meat to be boiled; and when their food was ready, they sat down. And it was on this wise; Geraint sat between the hoary-headed man and his wife, and the maiden served them. And they ate and drank.

And when they had finished eating, Geraint talked with the hoary-headed man, and he asked him in the first place, to whom belonged the palace that he was in. "Truly," said he, "it was I that built it, and to me also belonged the city and the castle which thou sawest." "Alas!" said Geraint, "how is it that thou hast lost them now?" "I lost a great Earldom as well as these," said he; "and this is how I lost them. I had a nephew, the son of my brother, and I took his possessions to myself; and when he came to his strength, he demanded of me his property, but I withheld it from him. So he made war upon me, and wrested from me all that I possessed." "Good Sir," said Geraint, "wilt thou tell me wherefore came the knight, and the lady, and the dwarf, just now into the town, and what is the preparation which I saw, and the putting of arms in order?" "I will do so," said he. "The preparations are for the game that is to be held to-morrow by the young Earl, which will be on this wise. In the midst of a meadow which is here, two forks will be set up, and upon the two forks a silver rod, and upon the silver rod a Sparrow-Hawk, and for the Sparrow-Hawk there will be a tournament. And to the tournament will go all the array thou didst see in the city, of men, and of horses, and of arms. And with each man will go the lady he loves best; and no man can joust for the Sparrow-Hawk, except the lady he loves best be with him. And the knight that thou sawest has gained the Sparrow-Hawk these two years;

and if he gains it the third year, they will, from that time, send it every year to him, and he himself will come here no more. And he will be called the Knight of the Sparrow-Hawk from that time forth." "Sir," said Geraint, "what is thy counsel to me concerning this knight, on account of the insult which I received from the dwarf, and that which was received by the maiden of Gwenhwyvar, the wife of Arthur?" And Geraint told the hoary-headed man what the insult was that he had received. "It is not easy to counsel thee, inasmuch as thou hast neither dame nor maiden belonging to thee, for whom thou canst joust. Yet, I have arms here, which thou couldest have; and there is my horse also, if he seem to thee better than thine own." "Ah! Sir," said he, "Heaven reward thee. But my own horse, to which I am accustomed, together with thy arms, will suffice me. And if, when the appointed time shall come to-morrow, thou wilt permit me, Sir, to challenge for yonder maiden that is thy daughter, I will engage, if I escape from the tournament, to love the maiden as long as I live; and if I do not escape, she will remain unsullied as before." "Gladly will I permit thee," said the hoary-headed man, "and since thou dost thus resolve, it is necessary that thy horse and arms should be ready to-morrow at break of day. For then the Knight of the Sparrow-Hawk will make proclamation, and ask the lady he loves best to take the Sparrow-Hawk. 'For,' will he say to her, 'thou art the fairest of women, and thou didst possess it last year, and the year previous; and if any deny it thee to-day, by force will I defend it for thee.' And therefore," said the hoary-headed man, "it is needful for thee to be there at daybreak; and we three will be with thee." And thus was it settled.

And at night, lo! they went to sleep; and before the dawn they arose, and arrayed themselves; and by the time that it was day, they were all four in the meadow. And there was the Knight of the Sparrow-Hawk making the proclamation, and asking his lady-love to fetch the Sparrow-Hawk. "Fetch it not," said Geraint, "for there is here a maiden, who is fairer, and more noble, and more comely, and who has a better claim to it than thou." "If thou maintainest the Sparrow-Hawk to be due to her, come forward, and do battle with me." And Geraint went forward to the top of the meadow, having upon himself and upon his horse armour which was heavy, and rusty, and worthless, and of uncouth shape. Then they encountered each other, and they broke a set of lances, and they broke a second set, and a third. And thus they did at every onset, and they broke as many lances as were brought to them. And when the Earl and his company saw the Knight of the Sparrow-Hawk gaining the mastery, there was shouting, and joy, and mirth amongst them. And the hoary-headed man, and his wife, and his daughter were sorrowful.

And the hoary-headed man served Geraint lances as often as he broke them, and the dwarf served the Knight of the Sparrow-Hawk. Then the hoary-headed man came to Geraint. "Oh! chieftain," said he, "since no other will hold with thee, behold, here is the lance which was in my hand on the day when I received the honour of knighthood; and from that time to this I never broke it. And it has an excellent point." Then Geraint took the lance, thanking the hoary-headed man. And thereupon the dwarf also brought a lance to his lord. "Behold, here is a lance for thee, not less good than his," said the dwarf. "And bethink thee, that no knight ever withstood thee before so long as this one has done." "I declare to Heaven," said Geraint, "that unless death takes me quickly hence, he shall fare never the better for thy service." And Geraint pricked his horse towards him from afar, and warning him, he rushed upon him, and gave him a blow so severe, and furious, and fierce, upon the face of his shield, that he cleft it in two, and broke his armour, and burst his girths, so that both he and his saddle were borne to the ground over the horse's crupper. And Geraint dismounted quickly. And he was wroth, and he drew his sword, and rushed fiercely upon him. Then the knight also arose, and drew his sword against Geraint. And they fought on foot with their swords until their arms struck sparks of fire like stars from one another; and thus they continued fighting until the blood and sweat obscured the light from their eyes. And when Geraint prevailed, the hoary-headed man, and his wife, and his daughter were glad; and when the knight prevailed, it rejoiced the Earl and his party. Then the hoary-headed man saw Geraint receive a severe stroke, and he went up to him quickly, and said to him, "Oh, chieftain, remember the treatment which thou hadst from the dwarf; and wilt thou not seek vengeance for the insult to thyself, and for the insult to Gwenhwyvar the wife of Arthur!" And Geraint was roused by what he said to him, and he called to him all his strength, and lifted up his sword, and struck the knight upon the crown of his head, so that he broke all his head-armour, and cut through all the flesh and the skin, even to the skull, until he wounded the bone.

Then the knight fell upon his knees, and cast his sword from his hand, and besought mercy of Geraint. "Of a truth," said he, "I relinquish my overdaring and my pride in craving thy mercy; and unless I have time to commit myself to Heaven for my sins, and to talk with a priest, thy mercy will avail me little." "I will grant thee grace upon this condition," said Geraint, "that thou wilt go to Gwenhwyvar the wife of Arthur, to do her satisfaction for the insult which her maiden received from thy dwarf. As to myself, for the insult which I received from thee and thy dwarf, I am content with that which I have done unto thee. Dismount not from the time thou goest hence until thou comest into the presence of Gwenhwyvar, to make her what atonement shall be adjudged at the Court of Arthur." "This will I do gladly. And who art thou?" said he. "I am Geraint the son of Erbin. And declare thou also who thou art." "I am Edeyrn the son of Nudd." Then he threw himself upon his horse, and went forward to Arthur's Court, and the lady he loved best went before him and the dwarf, with much lamentation. And thus far this story up to that time.

Then came the little Earl and his hosts to Geraint, and saluted him, and bade him to his castle. "I may not go," said Geraint, "but where I was last night, there will I be to-night also." "Since thou wilt none of my inviting, thou shalt have abundance of all that I can command for thee, in the place thou wast last night. And I will order ointment for thee, to recover thee from thy fatigues, and from the weariness that is upon thee." "Heaven reward thee," said Geraint, "and I will go to my lodging." And thus went Geraint, and Earl Ynywl, and his wife, and his daughter. And when they reached the chamber, the household servants and attendants of the young Earl had arrived at the Court, and they arranged all the houses, dressing them with straw and with fire; and in a short time the ointment was ready, and Geraint came there, and they washed his head. Then came the young Earl, with forty honourable knights from among his attendants, and those who were bidden to the tournament. And Geraint came from the anointing. And the Earl asked him to go to the hall to eat. "Where is the Earl Ynywl," said Geraint, "and his wife, and his daughter?" "They are in the chamber yonder," said the Earl's chamberlain, "arraying themselves in garments which the Earl has caused to be brought for them." "Let not the damsel array herself," said he, "except in her vest and her veil, until she come to the Court of Arthur, to be clad by Gwenhwyvar in such garments as she may choose." So the maiden did not array herself.

Then they all entered the hall, and they washed, and went, and sat down to meat. And thus were they seated. On one side of Geraint sat the young Earl, and Earl Ynywl beyond him; and on the other side of Geraint were the maiden and her mother. And after these all sat according to their precedence in honour. And they ate. And they were served abundantly, and they received a profusion of divers kind of gifts. Then they conversed together. And the young Earl invited Geraint to visit him next day. "I will not, by Heaven," said Geraint. "To the Court of Arthur will I go with this maiden to-morrow. And it is enough for me, as long as Earl Ynywl is in poverty and trouble; and I go chiefly to seek to add to his maintenance." "Ah, chieftain," said the young Earl, "it is not by my fault that Earl Ynywl is without his possessions." "By my faith," said Geraint, "he shall not remain without them, unless death quickly takes me hence." "Oh, chieftain," said he, "with regard to the disagreement between me and Ynywl, I will gladly abide by thy counsel, and agree to what thou mayest judge right between us." "I but ask thee," said Geraint, "to restore to him what is his, and what he should have received from the time he lost his possessions, even until this day." "That I will do gladly, for thee," answered he. "Then," said Geraint, "whosoever is here who owes homage to Ynywl, let him come forward, and perform it on the spot." And all the men did so. And by that treaty they abided. And his castle, and his town, and all his possessions were restored to Ynywl. And he received back all that he had lost, even to the smallest jewel.

Then spoke Earl Ynywl to Geraint. "Chieftain," said he, "behold the maiden for whom thou didst challenge at the tournament, I bestow her upon thee." "She shall go with me," said Geraint, "to the Court of Arthur; and Arthur and Gwenhwyvar they shall dispose of her as they will." And the next day they proceeded to Arthur's Court. So far concerning Geraint.

Now, this is how Arthur hunted the stag. The men and the dogs were divided into hunting parties, and the dogs were let loose upon the stag. And the last dog that was let loose was the favourite dog of Arthur. Cavall was his name. And he left all the other dogs behind him, and turned the stag. And at the second turn, the stag came towards the hunting party of Arthur. And Arthur set upon him. And before he could be slain by any other, Arthur cut off his head. Then they sounded the death horn for slaying, and they all gathered round.

Then came Kadyrieith to Arthur, and spoke to him. "Lord," said he, "behold, yonder is Gwenhwyvar, and none with her save only one maiden." "Command Gildas the son of Caw, and all the scholars of the Court," said Arthur, "to attend Gwenhwyvar to the palace." And they did so.

Then they all set forth, holding converse together concerning the head of the stag, to whom it should be given. One wished that it should be given to the lady best beloved by him, and another to the lady whom he loved best. And all they of the household, and the knights, disputed sharply concerning the head. And with that they came to the palace. And when Arthur and Gwenhwyvar heard them disputing about the head of the stag, Gwenhwyvar said to Arthur, "My lord, this is my counsel concerning the stag's head; let it not be given away until Geraint the son of

Erbin shall return from the errand he is upon." And Gwenhwyvar told Arthur what that errand was. "Right gladly shall it be so," said Arthur. And thus it was settled. And the next day Gwenhwyvar caused a watch to be set upon the ramparts for Geraint's coming. And after mid-day they beheld an unshapely little man upon a horse, and after him, as they supposed, a dame or a damsel, also on horseback, and after her a knight of large stature, bowed down, and hanging his head low and sorrowfully, and clad in broken and worthless armour.

And before they came near to the gate, one of the watch went to Gwenhwyvar, and told her what kind of people they saw, and what aspect they bore. "I know not who they are," said he. "But I know," said Gwenhwyvar; "this is the knight whom Geraint pursued, and methinks that he comes not here by his own free will. But Geraint has overtaken him, and avenged the insult to the maiden to the uttermost." And thereupon, behold a porter came to the spot where Gwenhwyvar was. "Lady," said he, "at the gate there is a knight, and I saw never a man of so pitiful an aspect to look upon as he. Miserable and broken is the armour that he wears, and the hue of blood is more conspicuous upon it than its own colour." "Knowest thou his name?" said she. "I do," said he; "he tells me that he is Edeyrn the son of Nudd." Then she replied, "I know him not."

So Gwenhwyvar went to the gate to meet him, and he entered. And Gwenhwyvar was sorry when she saw the condition he was in, even though he was accompanied by the churlish dwarf. Then Edeyrn saluted Gwenhwyvar. "Heaven protect thee," said she. "Lady," said he, "Geraint the son of Erbin, thy best and most valiant servant, greets thee." "Did he meet thee?" she asked. "Yes," said he, "and it was not to my advantage; and that was not his fault, but mine, Lady. And Geraint greets thee well; and in greeting thee he compelled me to come hither to do thy pleasure for the insult which thy maiden received from the dwarf. He forgives the insult to himself, in consideration of his having put me in peril of my life. And he imposed on me a condition, manly, and honourable, and warrior-like, which was to do thee justice, Lady." "Now, where did he overtake thee?" "At the place where we were jousting, and contending for the Sparrow-Hawk, in the town which is now called Cardiff. And there were none with him save three persons, of a mean and tattered condition. And these were an aged, hoary-headed man, and a woman advanced in years, and a fair young maiden, clad in worn-out garments. And it was for the avouchment of the love of that maiden that Geraint jousted for the Sparrow-Hawk at the tournament, for he said that that maiden was better entitled to the Sparrow-Hawk than this maiden who was with me. And thereupon we encountered each other, and he left me,

Lady, as thou seest." "Sir," said she, "when thinkest thou that Geraint will be here?" "To-morrow, Lady, I think he will be here with the maiden."

Then Arthur came to him, and he saluted Arthur; and Arthur gazed a long time upon him, and was amazed to see him thus. And thinking that he knew him, he inquired of him, "Art thou Edeyrn the son of Nudd?" "I am, Lord," said he, "and I have met with much trouble, and received wounds unsupportable." Then he told Arthur all his adventure. "Well," said Arthur, "from what I hear, it behoves Gwenhwyvar to be merciful towards thee." "The mercy which thou desirest, Lord," said she, "will I grant to him, since it is as insulting to thee that an insult should be offered to me as to thyself." "Thus will it be best to do," said Arthur; "let this man have medical care until it be known whether he may live. And if he live, he shall do such satisfaction as shall be judged best by the men of the Court; and take thou sureties to that effect. And if he die, too much will be the death of such a youth as Edeyrn for an insult to a maiden." "This pleases me," said Gwenhwyvar. And Arthur became surety for Edeyrn, and Caradawc the son of Llyr, Gwallawg the son of Llenawg, and Owain the son of Nudd, and Gwalchmai, and many others with them. And Arthur caused Morgan Tud to be called to him. He was the chief physician. "Take with thee Edeyrn the son of Nudd, and cause a chamber to be prepared for him, and let him have the aid of medicine as thou wouldst do unto myself, if I were wounded, and let none into his chamber to molest him, but thyself and thy disciples, to administer to him remedies." "I will do so gladly, Lord," said Morgan Tud. Then said the steward of the household, "Whither is it right, Lord, to order the maiden?" "To Gwenhwyvar and her handmaidens," said he. And the steward of the household so ordered her. Thus far concerning them.

The next day came Geraint towards the Court; and there was a watch set on the ramparts by Gwenhwyvar, lest he should arrive unawares. And one of the watch came to the place where Gwenhwyvar was. "Lady," said he, "methinks that I see Geraint, and the maiden with him. He is on horseback, but he has his walking gear upon him, and the maiden appears to be in white, seeming to be clad in a garment of linen." "Assemble all the women," said Gwenhwyvar, "and come to meet Geraint, to welcome him, and wish him joy." And Gwenhwyvar went to meet Geraint and the maiden. And when Geraint came to the place where Gwenhwyvar was, he saluted her. "Heaven prosper thee," said she, "and welcome to thee. And thy career has been successful, and fortunate, and resistless, and glorious. And Heaven reward thee, that thou hast so proudly caused me to have retribution." "Lady," said he, "I earnestly desired to obtain thee satisfaction according to thy will; and, behold, here is the maiden through whom thou hadst thy revenge." "Verily," said Gwenhwyvar, "the welcome of Heaven be unto her; and it is fitting that we should receive her joyfully." Then they went in, and dismounted. And Geraint came to where Arthur was, and saluted him. "Heaven protect thee," said Arthur, "and the welcome of Heaven be unto thee. And since Edeyrn the son of Nudd has received his overthrow and wounds from thy hands, thou hast had a prosperous career." "Not upon me be the blame," said Geraint, "it was through the arrogance of Edeyrn the son of Nudd himself that we were not friends. I would not quit him until I knew who he was, and until the one had vanquished the other." "Now," said Arthur, "where is the maiden for whom I heard thou didst give challenge?" "She is gone with Gwenhwyvar to her chamber."

Then went Arthur to see the maiden. And Arthur, and all his companions, and his whole Court, were glad concerning the maiden. And certain were they all, that had her array been suitable to her beauty, they had never seen a maid fairer than she. And Arthur gave away the maiden to Geraint. And the usual bond made between two persons was made between Geraint and the maiden, and the choicest of all Gwenhwyvar's apparel was given to the maiden; and thus arrayed, she appeared comely and graceful to all who beheld her. And that day and that night were spent in abundance of minstrelsy, and ample gifts of liquor, and a multitude of games. And when it was time for them to go to sleep, they went. And in the chamber where the couch of Arthur and Gwenhwyvar was, the couch of Geraint and Enid was prepared. And from that time she became his bride. And the next day Arthur satisfied all the claimants upon Geraint with bountiful gifts. And the maiden took up her abode in the palace; and she had many companions, both men and women, and there was no maiden more esteemed than she in the Island of Britain.

Then spake Gwenhwyvar. "Rightly did I judge," said she, "concerning the head of the stag, that it should not be given to any until Geraint's return; and, behold, here is a fit occasion for bestowing it. Let it be given to Enid the daughter of Ynywl, the most illustrious maiden. And I do not believe that any will begrudge it her, for between her and every one here there exists nothing but love and friendship." Much applauded was this by them all, and by Arthur also. And the head of the stag was given to Enid. And thereupon her fame increased, and her friends thenceforward became more in number than before. And Geraint from that time forth loved the stag, and the tournament, and hard encounters; and he came victorious from them all. And a year, and a second, and a third, he proceeded thus, until his fame had flown over the face of the kingdom.

* * *

And once upon a time Arthur was holding his Court at Caerlleon upon Usk, at Whitsuntide. And, behold, there came to him ambassadors, wise and prudent, full of knowledge, and eloquent of speech, and they saluted Arthur. "Heaven prosper you," said Arthur, "and the welcome of Heaven be unto you. And whence do you come?" "We come, Lord," said they, "from Cornwall; and we are ambassadors from Erbin the son of Custennin, thy uncle, and our mission is unto thee. And he greets thee well, as an uncle should greet his nephew, and as a vassal should greet his lord. And he represents unto thee that he waxes heavy and feeble, and is advancing in years. And the neighbouring chiefs, knowing this, grow insolent towards him, and covet his land and possessions. And he earnestly beseeches thee, Lord, to permit Geraint his son to return to him, to protect his possessions, and to become acquainted with his boundaries. And unto him he represents that it were better for him to spend the flower of his youth and the prime of his age in preserving his own boundaries, than in tournaments, which are productive of no profit, although he obtains glory in them."

"Well," said Arthur, "go, and divest yourselves of your accoutrements, and take food, and refresh yourselves after your fatigues; and before you go forth hence you shall have an answer." And they went to eat. And Arthur considered that it would go hard with him to let Geraint depart from him and from his Court; neither did he think it fair that his cousin should be restrained from going to protect his dominions and his boundaries, seeing that his father was unable to do so. No less was the grief and regret of Gwenhwyvar, and all her women, and all her damsels, through fear that the maiden would leave them. And that day and that night were spent in abundance of feasting. And Arthur showed Geraint the cause of the mission, and of the coming of the ambassadors to him out of Cornwall. "Truly," said Geraint, "be it to my advantage or disadvantage, Lord, I will do according to thy will concerning this embassy." "Behold," said Arthur, "though it grieves me to part with thee, it is my counsel that thou go to dwell in thine own dominions, and to defend thy boundaries, and to take with thee to accompany thee as many as thou wilt of those thou lovest best among my faithful ones, and among thy friends, and among thy companions in arms." "Heaven reward thee; and this will I do," said Geraint. "What discourse," said Gwenhwyvar, "do I hear between you? Is it of those who are to conduct Geraint to his country?" "It is," said Arthur. "Then it is needful for me to consider," said she, "concerning companions and a provision for the lady that is with me?" "Thou wilt do well," said Arthur.

And that night they went to sleep. And the next day the ambassadors were permitted to depart, and they were told that Geraint should follow them. And on the third day Geraint set forth, and many went with him. Gwalchmai the son of Gwyar, and Riogonedd the son of the king of Ireland, and Ondyaw the son of the duke of Burgundy, Gwilim the son of the ruler of the Franks, Howel the son of Emyr of Brittany, Elivry, and Nawkyrd, Gwynn the son of Tringad, Goreu the son of Custennin, Gweir Gwrhyd Vawr, Garannaw the son of Golithmer, Peredur the son of Evrawc, Gwynnllogell, Gwyr a judge in the Court of Arthur, Dyvyr the son of Alun of Dyved, Gwrei Gwalstawd Ieithoedd, Bedwyr the son of Bedrawd, Hadwry the son of Gwryon, Kai the son of Kynyr, Odyar the Frank, the Steward of Arthur's Court, and Edeyrn the son of Nudd. Said Geraint, "I think that I shall have enough of knighthood with me." "Yes," said Arthur, "but it will not be fitting for thee to take Edeyrn with thee, although he is well, until peace shall be made between him and Gwenhwyvar." "Gwenhwyvar can permit him to go with me, if he give sureties." "If she please, she can let him go without sureties, for enough of pain and affliction has he suffered for the insult which the maiden received from the dwarf." "Truly," said Gwenhwyvar, "since it seems well to thee and to Geraint, I will do this gladly, Lord." Then she permitted Edeyrn freely to depart. And many there were who accompanied Geraint, and they set forth; and never was there seen a fairer host journeying towards the Severn. And on the other side of the Severn were the nobles of Erbin the son of Custennin, and his foster-father at their head, to welcome Geraint with gladness; and many of the women of the Court, with his mother, came to receive Enid the daughter of Ynywl, his wife. And there was great rejoicing and gladness throughout the whole Court, and throughout all the country, concerning Geraint, because of the greatness of their love towards him, and of the greatness of the fame which he had gained since he went from amongst them, and because he was come to take possession of his dominions and to preserve his boundaries. And they came to the Court. And in the Court they had ample entertainment, and a multitude of gifts and abundance of liquor, and a sufficiency of service, and a variety of minstrelsy and of games. And to do honour to Geraint, all the chief men of the country were invited that night to visit him. And they passed that day and that night in the utmost enjoyment. And at dawn next day Erbin arose, and summoned to him Geraint, and the noble persons who had borne him company. And he said to Geraint, "I am a feeble and aged man, and whilst I was able to maintain the dominion for thee and for myself, I did so. But thou art young, and in the flower of thy vigour and of thy youth; henceforth do thou preserve thy possessions." "Truly," said Geraint, "with my consent thou shalt not give the power over thy dominions at this time into my hands, and thou shalt not take me from Arthur's Court." "Into thy hands will I give them," said Erbin, "and this day also shalt thou receive the homage of thy subjects."

Then said Gwalchmai, "It were better for thee to satisfy those who have boons to ask, to-day, and to-morrow thou canst receive the homage of thy dominions." So all that had boons to ask were summoned into one place. And Kadyrieith came to them, to know what were their requests. And every one asked that which he desired. And the followers of Arthur began to make gifts, and immediately the men of Cornwall came, and gave also. And they were not long in giving, so eager was every one to bestow gifts. And of those who came to ask gifts, none departed unsatisfied. And that day and that night were spent in the utmost enjoyment.

And the next day, at dawn, Erbin desired Geraint to send messengers to the men, to ask them whether it was displeasing to them that he should come to receive their homage, and whether they had anything to object to him. Then Geraint sent ambassadors to the men of Cornwall, to ask them this. And they all said that it would be the fulness of joy and honour to them for Geraint to come and receive their homage. So he received the homage of such as were there. And they remained with him till the third night. And the day after the followers of Arthur intended to go away. "It is too soon for you to go away yet," said he, "stay with me until I have finished receiving the homage of my chief men, who have agreed to come to me." And they remained with him until he had done so. Then they set forth towards the Court of Arthur; and Geraint went to bear them company, and Enid also, as far as Diganhwy: there they parted. Then Ondyaw the son of the duke of Burgundy said to Geraint, "Go first of all and visit the uppermost parts of thy dominions, and see well to the boundaries of thy territories, and if thou hast any trouble respecting them, send unto thy companions." "Heaven reward thee," said Geraint, "and this will I do." And Geraint journeyed to the uttermost part of his dominions. And experienced guides, and the chief men of his country, went with him. And the furthermost point that they showed him he kept possession of.

And, as he had been used to do when he was at Arthur's Court, he frequented tournaments. And he became acquainted with valiant and mighty men, until he had gained as much fame there as he had formerly done elsewhere. And he enriched his Court, and his companions, and his nobles, with the best horses and the best arms, and with the best and most valuable jewels, and he ceased not until his fame had flown over the face of the whole kingdom. And when he knew that it was thus, he began to love ease and pleasure, for there was no one who was worth his opposing. And he loved his wife, and liked to continue in the palace, with minstrelsy and diversions. And for a long time he abode at home. And after that he began to shut himself up in the chamber of his wife, and he took no delight in anything besides, insomuch that he gave up the friendship of his nobles, together with his hunting and his amusements, and lost the hearts of all the host in his Court; and there was murmuring and scoffing concerning him among the inhabitants of the palace, on account of his relinquishing so completely their companionship for the love of his wife. And these tidings came to Erbin. And when Erbin had heard these things, he spoke unto Enid, and inquired of her whether it was she that had caused Geraint to act thus, and to forsake his people and his hosts. "Not I, by my confession unto Heaven," said she, "there is nothing more hateful to me than this." And she knew not what she should do, for, although it was hard for her to own this to Geraint, yet was it not more easy for her to listen to what she heard, without warning Geraint concerning it. And she was very sorrowful.

And one morning in the summer time, they were upon their couch, and Geraint lay upon the edge of it. And Enid was without sleep in the apartment, which had windows of glass. And the sun shone upon the couch. And the clothes had slipped from off his arms and his breast, and he was asleep. Then she gazed upon the marvellous beauty of his appearance, and she said, "Alas, and am I the cause that these arms and this breast have lost their glory and the warlike fame which they once so richly enjoyed!" And as she said this, the tears dropped from her eyes, and they fell upon his breast. And the tears she shed, and the words she had spoken, awoke him; and another thing contributed to awaken him, and that was the idea that it was not in thinking of him that she spoke thus, but that it was because she loved some other man more than him, and that she wished for other society, and thereupon Geraint was troubled in his mind, and he called his squire; and when he came to him, "Go quickly," said he, "and prepare my horse and my arms, and make them ready. And do thou arise," said he to Enid, "and apparel thyself; and cause thy horse to be accoutred, and clothe thee in the worst riding-dress that thou hast in thy possession. And evil betide me," said he, "if thou returnest here until thou knowest whether I have lost my strength so completely as thou didst say. And if it be so, it will then be easy for thee to seek the society thou didst wish for of him of whom thou wast thinking." So she arose, and clothed herself in her meanest garments. "I know nothing, Lord," said she, "of thy meaning." "Neither wilt thou know at this time," said he.

Then Geraint went to see Erbin. "Sir," said he, "I am going upon a quest, and I am not certain when I may come back. Take heed, therefore, unto thy possessions, until my return." "I will do so," said he, "but it is strange to me that thou shouldest go so suddenly. And who will proceed with thee, since thou art not strong enough to traverse the land of Lloegyr alone?" "But one person only will go with me." "Heaven counsel thee, my son," said Erbin, "and may many attach themselves to thee in Lloegyr." Then went Geraint to the place where his horse was, and it was equipped with foreign armour, heavy and shining. And he desired Enid to mount her horse, and to ride forward, and to keep a long way before him. "And whatever thou mayest see, and whatever thou mayest hear concerning me," said he, "do thou not turn back. And unless I speak unto thee, say not thou one word either." And they set forward. And he did not choose the pleasantest and most frequented road, but that which was the wildest and most beset by thieves, and robbers, and venomous animals. And they came to a high road, which they followed till they saw a vast forest, and they went towards it, and they saw four armed horsemen come forth from the forest. When the horsemen had beheld them, one of them said to the others, "Behold, here is a good occasion for us to capture two horses and armour, and a lady likewise; for this we shall have no difficulty in doing against yonder single knight, who hangs his head so pensively and heavily." And Enid heard this discourse, and she knew not what she should do through fear of Geraint, who had told her to be silent. "The vengeance of Heaven be upon me," she said, "if I would not rather receive my death from his hand than from the hand of any other; and though he should slay me yet will I speak to him, lest I should have the misery to witness his death." So she waited for Geraint until he came near to her. "Lord," said she, "didst thou hear the words of those men concerning thee?" Then he lifted up his eyes, and looked at her angrily. "Thou hadst only," said he, "to hold thy peace as I bade thee. I wish but for silence, and not for warning. And though thou shouldest desire to see my defeat and my death by the hands of those men, yet do I feel no dread." Then the foremost of them couched his lance, and rushed upon Geraint. And he received him, and that not feebly. But he let the thrust go by him, while he struck the horseman upon the centre of his shield in such a manner that his shield was split, and his armour broken, and so that a cubit's length of the shaft of Geraint's lance passed through his body, and sent him to the earth, the length of the lance over his horse's crupper. Then the second horseman attacked him furiously, being wroth at the death of his companion. But with one thrust Geraint overthrew him also, and killed him as he had done the other. Then the third set upon him, and he killed him in like manner. And thus also he slew the fourth. Sad and sorrowful was the maiden as she saw all this. Geraint dismounted from his horse, and took the arms of the men he had slain, and placed them upon their saddles, and tied together the reins of their horses, and he mounted his horse again. "Behold what thou must do," said he; "take the four horses, and drive them before thee, and proceed forward, as I bade thee just now. And say not one word unto me, unless I speak first unto thee. And I declare unto Heaven," said he, "if thou doest not thus, it will be to thy cost." "I will do, as far as I can, Lord," said she, "according to thy desire." Then they went forward through the forest; and when they left the forest, they came to a vast plain, in the centre of which was a group of thickly tangled copse-wood; and from out thereof they beheld three horsemen coming towards them, well equipped with armour, both they and their horses. Then the maiden looked steadfastly upon them; and when they had come near, she heard them say one to another, "Behold, here is a good arrival for us; here are coming for us four horses and four suits of armour. We shall easily obtain them spite of yonder dolorous knight, and the maiden also will fall into our power." "This is but too true," said she to herself, "for my husband is tired with his former combat. The vengeance of Heaven will be upon me, unless I warn him of this." So the maiden waited until Geraint came up to her. "Lord," said she, "dost thou not hear the discourse of yonder men concerning thee?" "What was it?" asked he. "They say to one another, that they will easily obtain all this spoil." "I declare to Heaven," he answered, "that their words are less grievous to me than that thou wilt not be silent, and abide by my counsel." "My Lord," said she, "I feared lest they should surprise thee unawares." "Hold thy peace, then," said he, "do not I desire silence?" And thereupon one of the horsemen couched his lance, and attacked Geraint. And he made a thrust at him, which he thought would be very effective; but Geraint received it carelessly, and struck it aside, and then he rushed upon him, and aimed at the centre of his person, and from the shock of man and horse, the quantity of his armour did not avail him, and the head of the lance and part of the shaft passed through him, so that he was carried to the ground an arm and a spear's length over the crupper of his horse. And both the other horsemen came forward in their turn, but their onset was not more successful than that of their companion. And the maiden stood by, looking at all this; and on the one hand she was in trouble lest Geraint should be wounded in his encounter with the men, and on the other hand she was joyful to see him victorious. Then Geraint dismounted, and bound the three suits of armour upon the three saddles, and he fastened the reins of all the horses together, so that he had seven horses with him. And he mounted his own horse, and commanded the maiden to drive forward the others. "It is no more use for me to speak to thee than to refrain, for thou wilt not attend to my advice." "I will do so, as far as I am able, Lord," said she; "but I cannot conceal from thee the fierce and threatening words which I may hear against thee, Lord, from such strange people as those that haunt this wilderness." "I declare to Heaven," said he, "that I desire nought but silence; therefore, hold thy peace." "I will, Lord, while I can." And the maiden went on with the horses before her, and she pursued her way straight onwards. And from the copse-wood already mentioned, they journeyed over a vast and dreary open plain. And at a great distance from them they beheld a wood, and they could see neither end nor boundary to the wood, except on that side that was nearest to them, and they went towards it. Then there came from out the wood five horsemen, eager, and bold, and mighty, and strong, mounted upon chargers that were powerful, and large of bone, and high-mettled, and proudly snorting, and both the men and the horses were well equipped with arms. And when they drew near to them, Enid heard them say, "Behold, here is a fine booty coming to us, which we shall obtain easily and without labour, for we shall have no trouble in taking all those horses and arms, and the lady also, from yonder single knight, so doleful and sad."

Sorely grieved was the maiden upon hearing this discourse, so that she knew not in the world what she should do. At last, however, she determined to warn Geraint; so she turned her horse's head towards him. "Lord," said she, "if thou hadst heard as I did what yonder horsemen said concerning thee, thy heaviness would be greater than it is." Angrily and bitterly did Geraint smile upon her, and he said, "Thee do I hear doing everything that I forbade thee; but it may be that thou will repent this yet." And immediately, behold, the men met them, and victoriously and gallantly did Geraint overcome them all five. And he placed the five suits of armour upon the five saddles, and tied together the reins of the twelve horses, and gave them in charge to Enid. "I know not," said he, "what good it is for me to order thee; but this time I charge thee in an especial manner." So the maiden went forward towards the wood, keeping in advance of Geraint, as he had desired her; and it grieved him as much as his wrath would permit, to see a maiden so illustrious as she having so much trouble with the care of the horses. Then they reached the wood, and it was both deep and vast; and in the wood night overtook them. "Ah, maiden," said he, "it is vain to attempt proceeding forward!" "Well, Lord," said she, "whatsoever thou wishest, we will do."

"It will be best for us," he answered, "to turn out of the wood, and to rest, and wait for the day, in order to pursue our journey." "That will we, gladly," said she. And they did so. Having dismounted himself, he took her down from her horse. "I cannot, by any means, refrain from sleep, through weariness," said he. "Do thou, therefore, watch the horses, and sleep not." "I will, Lord," said she. Then he went to sleep in his armour, and thus passed the night, which was not long at that season. And when she saw the dawn of day appear, she looked around her, to see if he were waking, and thereupon he woke. "My Lord," she said, "I have desired to awake thee for some time." But he spake nothing to her about fatigue, as he had desired her to be silent. Then he arose, and said unto her, "Take the horses, and ride on; and keep straight on before thee as thou didst yesterday." And early in the day they left the wood, and they came to an open country, with meadows on one hand, and mowers mowing the meadows. And there was a river before them, and the horses bent down, and drank the water. And they went up out of the river by a lofty steep; and there they met a slender stripling, with a satchel about his neck, and they saw that there was something in the satchel, but they knew not what it was. And he had a small blue pitcher in his hand, and a bowl on the mouth of the pitcher. And the youth saluted Geraint. "Heaven prosper thee," said Geraint, "and whence dost thou come?" "I come," said he, "from the city that lies before thee. My Lord," he added, "will it be displeasing to thee if I ask whence thou comest also?" "By no means — through yonder wood did I come." "Thou camest not through the wood to-day." "No," he replied, "we were in the wood last night." "I warrant," said the youth, "that thy condition there last night was not the most pleasant, and that thou hadst neither meat nor drink." "No, by my faith," said he. "Wilt thou follow my counsel," said the youth, "and take thy meal from me?" "What sort of meal?" he inquired. "The breakfast which is sent for yonder mowers, nothing less than bread and meat and wine; and if thou wilt, Sir, they shall have none of it." "I will," said he, "and Heaven reward thee for it."

So Geraint alighted, and the youth took the maiden from off her horse. Then they washed, and took their repast. And the youth cut the bread in slices, and gave them drink, and served them withal. And when they had finished, the youth arose, and said to Geraint, "My Lord, with thy permission, I will now go and fetch some food for the mowers." "Go, first, to the town," said Geraint, "and take a lodging for me in the best place that thou knowest, and the most commodious one for the horses, and take thou whichever horse and arms thou choosest in payment for thy service and thy gift." "Heaven reward thee, Lord," said the youth, "and this would be ample to repay services much greater than those I have rendered unto thee." And to the town went the youth, and he took the best and the most pleasant lodgings that he knew; and after that he went to the palace, having the horse and armour with him, and proceeded to the place where the Earl was, and told him all his adventure. "I go now, Lord," said he, "to meet the young man, and to conduct him to his lodging." "Go, gladly," said the Earl, "and right joyfully shall he be received here, if he so come." And the youth went to meet Geraint, and told him that he would be received gladly by the Earl in his own palace; but he would go only to his lodgings. And he had a goodly chamber, in which was plenty of straw, and drapery, and a spacious and commodious place he had for the horses; and the youth prepared for them plenty of provender. And after they had disarrayed themselves, Geraint spoke thus to Enid: "Go," said he, "to the other side of the chamber, and come not to this side of the house; and thou mayest call to thee the woman of the house, if thou wilt." "I will do, Lord," said she, "as thou sayest." And thereupon the man of the house came to Geraint, and welcomed him. "Oh, chieftain," he said, "hast thou taken thy meal?" "I have," said he. Then the youth spoke to him, and inquired if he would not drink something before he met the Earl. "Truly I will," said he. So the youth went into the town, and brought them drink. And they drank. "I must needs sleep," said Geraint. "Well," said the youth; "and whilst thou sleepest, I will go to see the Earl." "Go, gladly," he said, "and come here again when I require thee." And Geraint went to sleep; and so did Enid also.

And the youth came to the place where the Earl was, and the Earl asked him where the lodgings of the knight were, and he told him. "I must go," said the youth, "to wait on him in the evening." "Go," answered the Earl, "and greet him well from me, and tell him that in the evening I will go to see him." "This will I do," said the youth. So he came when it was time for them to awake. And they arose, and went forth. And when it was time for them to take their food, they took it. And the youth served them. And Geraint inquired of the man of the house, whether there were any of his companions that he wished to invite to him, and he said that there were. "Bring them hither, and entertain them at my cost with the best thou canst buy in the town."

And the man of the house brought there those whom he chose, and feasted them at Geraint's expense. Thereupon, behold, the Earl came to visit Geraint, and his twelve honourable knights with him. And Geraint rose up, and welcomed him. "Heaven preserve thee," said the Earl. Then they all sat down according to their precedence in honour. And the Earl conversed with Geraint, and inquired of him the object of his journey.

"I have none," he replied, "but to seek adventures, and to follow my own inclination." Then the Earl cast his eye upon Enid, and he looked at her steadfastly. And he thought he had never seen a maiden fairer or more comely than she. And he set all his thoughts and his affections upon her. Then he asked of Geraint, "Have I thy permission to go and converse with yonder maiden, for I see that she is apart from thee?" "Thou hast it gladly," said he. So the Earl went to the place where the maiden was, and spake with her. "Ah, maiden," said he, "it cannot be pleasant to thee to journey thus with yonder man!" "It is not unpleasant to me," said she, "to journey the same road that he journeys." "Thou hast neither youths nor maidens to serve thee," said he. "Truly," she replied, "it is more pleasant for me to follow yonder man, than to be served by youths and maidens." "I will give thee good counsel," said he. "All my Earldom will I place in thy possession, if thou wilt dwell with me." "That will I not, by Heaven," she said; "yonder man was the first to whom my faith was ever pledged; and shall I prove inconstant to him!" "Thou art in the wrong," said the Earl; "if I slay the man yonder, I can keep thee with me as long as I choose; and when thou no longer pleasest me I can turn thee away. But if thou goest with me by thine own good will, I protest that our union shall continue eternal and undivided as long as I remain alive." Then she pondered these words of his, and she considered that it was advisable to encourage him in his request. "Behold, then, chieftain, this is most expedient for thee to do to save me any needless imputation; come here to-morrow, and take me away as though I knew nothing thereof." "I will do so," said he. So he arose, and took his leave, and went forth with his attendants. And she told not then to Geraint any of the conversation which she had had with the Earl, lest it should rouse his anger, and cause him uneasiness and care.

And at the usual hour they went to sleep. And at the beginning of the night Enid slept a little; and at midnight she arose, and placed all Geraint's armour together, so that it might be ready to put on. And although fearful of her errand, she came to the side of Geraint's bed; and she spoke to him softly and gently, saying, "My Lord, arise, and clothe thyself, for these were the words of the Earl to me, and his intention concerning me." So she told Geraint all that had passed. And although he was wroth with her, he took warning, and clothed himself. And she lighted a candle, that he might have light to do so. "Leave there the candle," said he, "and desire the man of the house to come here." Then she went, and the man of the house came to him. "Dost thou know how much I owe thee?" asked Geraint. "I think thou owest but little." "Take the eleven horses and the eleven suits of armour." "Heaven reward thee, lord," said he, "but I spent not the value of one suit of armour upon thee." "For that reason," said he, "thou wilt be the richer. And now, wilt thou come to guide me out of the town?" "I will, gladly," said he, "and in which direction dost thou intend to go?" "I wish to leave the town by a different way from that by which I entered it." So the man of the lodgings accompanied him as far as he desired. Then he bade the maiden to go on before him; and she did so, and went straight forward, and his host returned home. And he had only just reached his house, when, behold, the greatest tumult approached that was ever heard. And when he looked out, he saw fourscore knights in complete armour around the house, with the Earl Dwnn at their head. "Where is the knight that was here?" said the Earl. "By thy hand," said he, "he went hence some time ago." "Wherefore, villain," said he, "didst thou let him go without informing me?" "My Lord, thou didst not command me to do so, else would I not have allowed him to depart." "What way dost thou think that he took?" "I know not, except that he went along the high road." And they turned their horses' heads that way, and seeing the tracks of the horses upon the high road, they followed. And when the maiden beheld the dawning of the day, she looked behind her, and saw vast clouds of dust coming nearer and nearer to her. And thereupon she became uneasy, and she thought that it was the Earl and his host coming after them. And thereupon she beheld a knight appearing through the mist. "By my faith," said she, "though he should slay me, it were better for me to receive my death at his hands, than to see him killed without warning him. My Lord," she said to him, "seest thou yonder man hastening after thee, and many others with him?" "I do see him," said he; "and in despite of all my orders, I see that thou wilt never keep silence." Then he turned upon the knight, and with the first thrust he threw him down under his horse's feet. And as long as there remained one of the fourscore knights, he overthrew every one of them at the first onset. And from the weakest to the strongest, they all attacked him one after the other, except the Earl: and last of all the Earl came against him also. And he broke his lance, and then he broke a second. But Geraint turned upon him, and struck him with his lance upon the centre of his shield, so that by that single thrust the shield was split, and all his armour broken, and he himself was brought over his horse's crupper to the ground, and was in peril of his life. And Geraint drew near to him; and at the noise of the trampling of his horse the Earl revived. "Mercy, Lord," said he to Geraint. And Geraint granted him mercy. But through the hardness of the ground where they had fallen, and the violence of the stroke which they had received, there was not a single knight amongst them that escaped without receiving a fall, mortally severe, and grievously painful, and desperately wounding, from the hand of Geraint.

And Geraint journeyed along the high road that was before him, and the maiden went on first; and near them they beheld a valley which was the fairest ever seen, and which had a large river running through it; and there was a bridge over the river, and the high road led to the bridge. And above the bridge upon the opposite side of the river, they beheld a fortified town, the fairest ever seen. And as they approached the bridge, Geraint saw coming towards him from a thick copse a man mounted upon a large and lofty steed, even of pace and spirited though tractable. "Ah, knight," said Geraint, "whence comest thou?" "I come," said he, "from the valley below us." "Canst thou tell me," said Geraint, "who is the owner of this fair valley and yonder walled town?" "I will tell thee, willingly," said he. "Gwiffert Petit he is called by the Franks, but the Cymry call him the Little King." "Can I go by yonder bridge," said Geraint, "and by the lower highway that is beneath the town?" Said the knight, "Thou canst not go by his tower on the other side of the bridge, unless thou dost intend to combat him; because it is his custom to encounter every knight that comes upon his lands." "I declare to Heaven," said Geraint, "that I will, nevertheless, pursue my journey that way." "If thou dost so," said the knight, "thou wilt probably meet with shame and disgrace in reward for thy daring." Then Geraint proceeded along the road that led to the town, and the road brought him to a ground that was hard, and rugged, and high, and ridgy. And as he journeyed thus, he beheld a knight following him upon a warhorse, strong, and large, and proudly-stepping, and wide-hoofed, and broad-chested. And he never saw a man of smaller stature than he who was upon the horse. And both he and his horse were completely armed. When he had overtaken Geraint, he said to him, "Tell me, chieftain, whether it is through ignorance or through presumption that thou seekest to insult my dignity, and to infringe my rules." "Nay," answered Geraint, "I knew not this road was forbid to any." "Thou didst know it," said the other; "come with me to my Court, to give me satisfaction.' "That will I not, by my faith," said Geraint; "I would not go even to thy Lord's Court, excepting Arthur were thy Lord." "By the hand of Arthur himself," said the knight, "I will have satisfaction of thee, or receive my overthrow at thy hands." And immediately they charged one another. And a squire of his came to serve him with lances as he broke them. And they gave each other such hard and severe strokes that their shields lost all their colour. But it was very difficult for Geraint to fight with him on account of his small size, for he was hardly able to get a full aim at him with all the efforts he could make. And they fought thus until their horses were brought down upon their knees; and at length Geraint threw the knight headlong to the ground; and then they fought on foot, and they gave one another blows so boldly fierce, so frequent, and so severely powerful, that their helmets were pierced, and their skullcaps were broken, and their arms were shattered, and the light of their eyes was darkened by sweat and blood. At the last Geraint became enraged, and he called to him all his strength; and boldly angry, and swiftly resolute, and furiously determined, he lifted up his sword, and struck him on the crown of his head a blow so mortally painful, so violent, so fierce, and so penetrating, that it cut through all his head armour, and his skin, and his flesh, until it wounded the very bone, and the sword flew out of the hand of the Little King to the furthest end of the plain, and he besought Geraint that he would have mercy and compassion upon him. "Though thou hast been neither courteous nor just," said Geraint, "thou shalt have mercy, upon condition that thou wilt become my ally, and engage never to fight against me again, but to come to my assistance whenever thou hearest of my being in trouble." "This will I do, gladly, Lord," said he. So he pledged him his faith thereof. "And now, Lord, come with me," said he, "to my Court yonder, to recover from thy weariness and fatigue." "That will I not, by Heaven," said he.

Then Gwiffert Petit beheld Enid where she stood, and it grieved him to see one of her noble mien appear so deeply afflicted. And he said to Geraint, "My Lord, thou doest wrong not to take repose, and refresh thyself awhile; for, if thou meetest with any difficulty in thy present condition, it will not be easy for thee to surmount it." But Geraint would do no other than proceed on his journey, and he mounted his horse in pain, and all covered with blood. And the maiden went on first, and they proceeded towards the wood which they saw before them.

And the heat of the sun was very great, and through the blood and sweat, Geraint's armour cleaved to his flesh; and when they came into the wood, he stood under a tree, to avoid the sun's heat; and his wounds pained him more than they had done at the time when he received them. And the maiden stood under another tree. And lo! they heard the sound of horns, and a tumultuous noise; and the occasion of it was, that Arthur and his company had come down to the wood. And while Geraint was considering which way he should go to avoid them, behold, he was espied by a foot-page, who was an attendant on the Steward of the Household; and he went to the Steward, and told him what kind of man he had seen in the wood. Then the Steward caused his horse to be saddled, and he took his lance and his shield, and went to the place where Geraint was. "Ah, knight!" said he, "what dost thou here?" "I am standing under a shady tree, to avoid the heat and the rays of the sun." "Wherefore is thy journey, and who art thou?" "I seek adventures, and go where I list." "Indeed," said Kai; "then come with me to see Arthur, who is here hard by." "That will I not, by Heaven," said Geraint. "Thou must needs come," said Kai. Then Geraint knew who he was, but Kai did not know Geraint. And Kai attacked Geraint as best he could. And Geraint became wroth, and he struck him with the shaft of his lance, so that he rolled headlong to the ground. But chastisement worse than this would he not inflict on him.

Scared and wildly Kai arose, and he mounted his horse, and went back to his lodging. And thence he proceeded to Gwalchmai's tent. "Oh, Sir," said he to Gwalchmai, "I was told by one of the attendants, that he saw in the wood above a wounded knight, having on battered armour; and if thou dost right, thou wilt go and see if this be true." "I care not if I do so," said Gwalchmai. "Take, then, thy horse, and some of thy armour," said Kai; "for I hear that he is not over courteous to those who approach him." So Gwalchmai took his spear and his shield, and mounted his horse, and came to the spot where Geraint was. "Sir Knight," said he, "wherefore is thy journey?" "I journey for my own pleasure, and to seek the adventures of the world." "Wilt thou tell me who thou art; or wilt thou come and visit Arthur, who is near at hand?" "I will make no alliance with thee, nor will I go and visit Arthur," said he. And he knew that it was Gwalchmai, but Gwalchmai knew him not. "I purpose not to leave thee," said Gwalchmai, "till I know who thou art." And he charged him with his lance, and struck him on his shield, so that the shaft was shivered into splinters, and their horses were front to front. Then Gwalchmai gazed fixedly upon him, and he knew him. "Ah, Geraint," said he, "is it thou that art here?" "I am not Geraint," said he. "Geraint thou art, by Heaven," he replied, "and a wretched and insane expedition is this." Then he looked around, and beheld Enid, and he welcomed her gladly. "Geraint," said Gwalchmai, "come thou and see Arthur; he is thy lord and thy cousin." "I will not," said he, "for I am not in a fit state to go and see any one." Thereupon, behold, one of the pages came after Gwalchmai to speak to him. So he sent him to apprise Arthur that Geraint was there wounded, and that he would not go to visit him, and that it was pitiable to see the plight that he was in. And this he did without Geraint's knowledge, inasmuch as he spoke in a whisper to the page. "Entreat Arthur," said he, "to have his tent brought near to the road, for he will not meet him willingly, and it is not easy to compel him in the mood he is in." So the page came to Arthur, and told him this. And he caused his tent to be removed unto the side of the road. And the maiden rejoiced in her heart. And Gwalchmai led Geraint onwards along the road, till they came to the place where Arthur was encamped, and the pages were pitching his tent by the roadside. "Lord," said Geraint, "all hail unto thee." "Heaven prosper thee; and who art thou?" said Arthur. "It is Geraint," said Gwalchmai, "and of his own free will would he not come to meet thee." "Verily," said Arthur, "he is bereft of his reason." Then came Enid, and saluted Arthur. "Heaven protect thee," said he. And thereupon he caused one of the pages to take her from her horse. "Alas! Enid," said Arthur, "what expedition is this?" "I know not, Lord," said she, "save that it behoves me to journey by the same road that he journeys." "My Lord," said Geraint, "with thy permission we will depart." "Whither wilt thou go?" said Arthur. "Thou canst not proceed now, unless it be unto thy death." "He will not suffer himself to be invited by me," said Gwalchmai. "But by me he will," said Arthur; "and, moreover, he does not go from here until he is healed." "I had rather, Lord," said Geraint, "that thou wouldest let me go forth." "That will I not, I declare to Heaven," said he. Then he caused a maiden to be sent for to conduct Enid to the tent where Gwenhwyvar's chamber was. And Gwenhwyvar and all her women were joyful at her coming; and they took off her riding-dress, and placed other garments upon her. Arthur also called Kadyrieith, and ordered him to pitch a tent for Geraint and the physicians; and he enjoined him to provide him with abundance of all that might be requisite for him. And Kadyrieith did as he had commanded him. And Morgan Tud and his disciples were brought to Geraint.

And Arthur and his hosts remained there nearly a month, whilst Geraint was being healed. And when he was fully recovered, Geraint came to Arthur, and asked his permission to depart. "I know not if thou art quite well." "In truth I am, Lord," said Geraint. "I shall not believe thee concerning that, but the physicians that were with thee." So Arthur caused the physicians to be summoned to him, and asked them if it were true. "It is true, Lord," said Morgan Tud. So the next day Arthur permitted him to go forth, and he pursued his journey. And on the same day Arthur removed thence. And Geraint desired Enid to go on, and to keep before him, as she had formerly done. And she went forward along the high road. And as they journeyed thus, they heard an exceeding loud wailing near to them. "Stay thou here," said he, "and I will go and see what is the cause of this wailing." "I will," said she. Then he went forward unto an open glade that was near the road. And in the glade he saw two horses, one having a man's saddle, and the other a woman's saddle upon it. And, behold, there was a knight lying dead in his armour, and a young damsel in a riding-dress standing over him, lamenting. "Ah! Lady," said Geraint, "what hath befallen thee?" "Behold," she answered, "I journeyed here with my beloved husband, when, lo! three giants came upon us, and without any cause in the world, they slew him." "Which way went they hence?" said Geraint. "Yonder by the high road," she replied. So he returned to Enid. "Go," said he, "to the lady that is below yonder, and await me there till I come." She was sad when he ordered her to do thus, but nevertheless she went to the damsel, whom it was ruth to hear, and she felt certain that Geraint would never return. Meanwhile Geraint followed the giants, and overtook them. And each of them was greater of stature than three other men, and a huge club was on the shoulder of each. Then he rushed upon one of them, and thrust his lance through his body. And having drawn it forth again, he pierced another of them through likewise. But the third turned upon him, and struck him with his club, so that he split his shield, and crushed his shoulder, and opened his wounds anew, and all his blood began to flow from him. But Geraint drew his sword, and attacked the giant, and gave him a blow on the crown of his head so severe, and fierce, and violent, that his head and his neck were split down to his shoulders, and he fell dead. So Geraint left him thus, and returned to Enid. And when he saw her, he fell down lifeless from his horse. Piercing, and loud, and thrilling was the cry that Enid uttered. And she came and stood over him where he had fallen. And at the sound of her cries came the Earl of Limours, and the host that journeyed with him, whom her lamentations brought out of their road. And the Earl said to Enid, "Alas, Lady, what hath befallen thee?" "Ah! good Sir," said she, "the only man I have loved, or ever shall love, is slain." Then he said to the other, "And what is the cause of thy grief?" "They have slain my beloved husband also," said she. "And who was it that slew them?" "Some giants," she answered, "slew my best-beloved, and the other knight went in pursuit of them, and came back in the state thou seest, his blood flowing excessively; but it appears to me that he did not leave the giants without killing some of them, if not all." The Earl caused the knight that was dead to be buried, but he thought that there still remained some life in Geraint; and to see if he yet would live, he had him carried with him in the hollow of his shield, and upon a bier. And the two damsels went to the Court; and when they arrived there, Geraint was placed upon a litter-couch in front of the table that was in the hall. Then they all took off their travelling gear, and the Earl besought Enid to do the same, and to clothe herself in other garments. "I will not, by Heaven," said she. "Ah! Lady," said he, "be not so sorrowful for this matter." "It were hard to persuade me to be otherwise," said she.

"I will act towards thee in such wise, that thou needest not be sorrowful, whether yonder knight live or die. Behold, a good Earldom, together with myself, will I bestow on thee; be, therefore, happy and joyful." "I declare to Heaven," said she, "that henceforth I shall never be joyful while I live." "Come, then," said he, "and eat." "No, by Heaven, I will not," she answered. "But, by Heaven, thou shalt," said he. So he took her with him to the table against her will, and many times desired her to eat. "I call Heaven to witness," said she, "that I will not eat until the man that is upon yonder bier shall eat likewise." "Thou canst not fulfil that," said the Earl, "yonder man is dead already." "I will prove that I can," said she. Then he offered her a goblet of liquor. "Drink this goblet," he said, "and it will cause thee to change thy mind." "Evil betide me," she answered, "if I drink aught until he drink also." "Truly," said the Earl, "it is of no more avail for me to be gentle with thee than ungentle." And he gave her a box on the ear. Thereupon she raised a loud and piercing shriek, and her lamentations were much greater than they had been before, for she considered in her mind that had Geraint been alive, he durst not have struck her thus. But, behold, at the sound of her cry, Geraint revived from his swoon, and he sat up on the bier, and finding his sword in the hollow of his shield, he rushed to the place where the Earl was, and struck him a fiercely-wounding, severely-venomous, and sternly-smiting blow upon the crown of his head, so that he clove him in twain, until his sword was stayed by the table. Then all left the board, and fled away. And this was not so much through fear of the living as through the dread they felt at seeing the dead man rise up to slay them. And Geraint looked upon Enid, and he was grieved for two causes; one was, to see that Enid had lost her colour and her wonted aspect, and the other, to know that she was in the right. "Lady," said he, "knowest thou where our horses are?" "I know, Lord, where thy horse is," she replied, "but I know not where is the other. Thy horse is in the house yonder." So he went to the house, and brought forth his horse, and mounted him, and took up Enid from the ground, and placed her upon the horse with him. And he rode forward. And their road lay between two hedges. And the night was gaining on the day. And lo! they saw behind them the shafts of spears betwixt them and the sky, and they heard the trampling of horses, and the noise of a host approaching. "I hear something following us," said he, "and I will put thee on the other side of the hedge." And thus he did. And thereupon, behold, a knight pricked towards him, and couched his lance. When Enid saw this, she cried out, saying, "Oh! chieftain, whoever thou art, what renown wilt thou gain by slaying a dead man?" "Oh! Heaven," said he, "is it Geraint?" "Yes, in truth," said she. "And who art thou?" "I am the Little King," he answered, "coming to thy assistance, for I heard that thou wast in trouble. And if thou hadst followed my advice, none of these hardships would have befallen thee." "Nothing can happen," said Geraint, "without the will of Heaven, though much good results from counsel." "Yes," said the Little King, "and I know good counsel for thee now. Come with me to the court of a son-in-law of my sister, which is near here, and thou shalt have the best medical assistance in the kingdom." "I will do so gladly," said Geraint. And Enid was placed upon the horse of one of the Little King's squires, and they went forward to the Baron's palace. And they were received there with gladness, and they met with hospitality and attention. And the next morning they went to seek physicians; and it was not long before they came, and they attended Geraint until he was perfectly well. And while Geraint was under medical care, the Little King caused his armour to be repaired, until it was as good as it had ever been. And they remained there a fortnight and a month.

Then the Little King said to Geraint, "Now will we go towards my own Court, to take rest, and amuse ourselves." "Not so," said Geraint, "we will first journey for one day more, and return again." "With all my heart," said the Little King, "do thou go then." And early in the day they set forth. And more gladly and more joyfully did Enid journey with them that day than she had ever done. And they came to the main road. And when they reached a place where the road divided in two, they beheld a man on foot coming towards them along one of these roads, and Gwiffert asked the man whence he came. "I come," said he, "from an errand in the country." "Tell me," said Geraint, "which is the best for me to follow of these two roads?" "That is the best for thee to follow," answered he, "for if thou goest by this one, thou wilt never return. Below us," said he, "there is a hedge of mist, and within it are enchanted games, and no one who has gone there has ever returned. And the Court of the Earl Owain is there, and he permits no one to go to lodge in the town, except he will go to his Court." "I declare to Heaven," said Geraint, "that we will take the lower road." And they went along it until they came to the town. And they took the fairest and pleasantest place in the town for their lodging. And while they were thus, behold, a young man came to them, and greeted them. "Heaven be propitious to thee," said they. "Good Sirs," said he, "what preparations are you making here?" "We are taking up our lodging," said they, "to pass the night." "It is not the custom with him who owns the town," he answered, "to permit any of gentle birth, unless they come to stay in his Court, to abide here; therefore, come ye to the Court." "We will come, gladly," said Geraint. And they went with the page, and they were joyfully received. And the Earl came to the hall to meet them, and he commanded the tables to be laid. And they washed, and sat down. And this is the order in which they sat: Geraint on one side of the Earl, and Enid on the other side, and next to Enid the Little King, and then the Countess next to Geraint; and all after that as became their rank. Then Geraint recollected the games, and thought that he should not go to them; and on that account he did not eat. Then the Earl looked upon Geraint, and considered, and he bethought him that his not eating was because of the games, and it grieved him that he had ever established those games, were it only on account of losing such a youth as Geraint. And if Geraint had asked him to abolish the games, he would gladly have done so. Then the Earl said to Geraint, "What thought occupies thy mind, that thou dost not eat? If thou hesitatest about going to the games, thou shalt not go, and no other of thy rank shall ever go either." "Heaven reward thee," said Geraint, "but I wish nothing better than to go to the games, and to be shown the way thither." "If that is what thou dost prefer, thou shalt obtain it willingly." "I do prefer it, indeed," said he. Then they ate, and they were amply served, and they had a variety of gifts, and abundance of liquor. And when they had finished eating they arose. And Geraint called for his horse and his armour, and he accoutred both himself and his horse. And all the hosts went forth until they came to the side of the hedge, and the hedge was so lofty, that it reached as high as they could see in the air, and upon every stake in the hedge, except two, there was the head of a man, and the number of stakes throughout the hedge was very great. Then said the Little King, "May no one go in with the chieftain?" "No one may," said Earl Owain. "Which way can I enter?" inquired Geraint. "I know not," said Owain, "but enter by the way that thou wilt, and that seemeth easiest to thee."

Then fearlessly and unhesitatingly Geraint dashed forward into the mist. And on leaving the mist, he came to a large orchard; and in the orchard he saw an open space, wherein was a tent of red satin; and the door of the tent was open, and an apple-tree stood in front of the door of the tent; and on a branch of the apple-tree hung a huge hunting-horn. Then he dismounted, and went into the tent; and there was no one in the tent save one maiden sitting in a golden chair, and another chair was opposite to her, empty. And Geraint went to the empty chair, and sat down therein. "Ah! chieftain," said the maiden, "I would not counsel thee to sit in that chair." "Wherefore?" said Geraint. "The man to whom that chair belongs has never suffered another to sit in it." "I care not," said Geraint, "though it displease him that I sit in the chair." And thereupon they heard a mighty tumult around the tent. And Geraint looked to see what was the cause of the tumult. And he beheld without a knight mounted upon a warhorse, proudly snorting, high-mettled, and large of bone; and a robe of honour in two parts was upon him and upon his horse, and beneath it was plenty of armour. "Tell me, chieftain," said he to Geraint, "who it was that bade thee sit there?" "Myself," answered he. "It was wrong of thee to do me this shame and disgrace. Arise, and do me satisfaction for thine insolence." Then Geraint arose; and they encountered immediately; and they broke a set of lances, and a second set, and a third; and they gave each other fierce and frequent strokes; and at last Geraint became enraged, and he urged on his horse, and rushed upon him, and gave him a thrust on the centre of his shield, so that it was split, and so that the head of his lance went through his armour, and his girths were broken, and he himself was borne headlong to the ground the length of Geraint's lance and arm, over his horse's crupper. "Oh, my Lord!" said he, "thy mercy, and thou shalt have what thou wilt." "I only desire," said Geraint, "that this game shall no longer exist here, nor the hedge of mist, nor magic, nor enchantment." "Thou shalt have this gladly, Lord," he replied. "Cause, then, the mist to disappear from this place," said Geraint. "Sound yonder horn," said he, "and when thou soundest it, the mist will vanish; but it will not go hence unless the horn be blown by the knight by whom I am vanquished." And sad and sorrowful was Enid where she remained, through anxiety concerning Geraint. Then Geraint went and sounded the horn. And at the first blast he gave, the mist vanished. And all the hosts came together, and they all became reconciled to each other. And the Earl invited Geraint and the Little King to stay with him that night. And the next morning they separated. And Geraint went towards his own dominions; and thenceforth he reigned prosperously, and his warlike fame and splendour lasted with renown and honour both to him and to Enid from that time forth.

TALIESIN

IN times past there lived in Penllyn a man of gentle lineage, named Tegid Voel, and his dwelling was in the midst of the lake Tegid, and his wife was called Caridwen. And there was born to him of his wife a son named Morvran ab Tegid, and also a daughter named Creirwy, the fairest maiden in the world was she; and they had a brother, the most ill-favoured man in the world, Avagddu. Now Caridwen his mother thought that he was not likely to be admitted among men of noble birth, by reason of his ugliness, unless he had some exalted merits or knowledge. For it was in the beginning of Arthur's time and of the Round Table.

So she resolved, according to the arts of the books of the Fferyllt, to boil a cauldron of Inspiration and Science for her son, that his reception might be honourable because of his knowledge of the mysteries of the future state of the world.

Then she began to boil the cauldron, which from the beginning of its boiling might not cease to boil for a year and a day, until three blessed drops were obtained of the grace of Inspiration.

And she put Gwion Bach the son of Gwreang of Llanfair in Caereinion, in Powys, to stir the cauldron, and a blind man named Morda to kindle the fire beneath it, and she charged them that they should not suffer it to cease boiling for the space of a year and a day. And she herself, according to the books of the astronomers, and in planetary hours, gathered every day of all charm-bearing herbs. And one day, towards the end of the year, as Caridwen was culling plants and making incantations, it chanced that three drops of the charmed liquor flew out of the cauldron and fell upon the finger of Gwion Bach. And by reason of their great heat he put his finger to his mouth, and the instant he put those marvel-working drops into his mouth, he foresaw everything that was to come, and perceived that his chief care must be to guard against the wiles of Caridwen, for vast was her skill. And in very great fear he fled towards his own land. And the cauldron burst in two, because all the liquor within it except the three charm-bearing drops was poisonous, so that the horses of Gwyddno Garanhir were poisoned by the water of the stream into which the liquor of the cauldron ran, and the confluence of that stream was called the Poison of the Horses of Gwyddno from that time forth.

Thereupon came in Caridwen and saw all the toil of the whole year lost. And she seized a billet of wood and struck the blind Morda on the head until one of his eyes fell out upon his cheek. And he said, "Wrongfully hast thou disfigured me, for I am innocent. Thy loss was not because of me." "Thou speakest truth," said Caridwen, "it was Gwion Bach who robbed me."

And she went forth after him, running. And he saw her, and changed himself into a hare and fled. But she changed herself into a greyhound and turned him. And he ran towards a river, and became a fish. And she in the form of an otter-bitch chased him under the water, until he was fain to turn himself into a bird of the air. She, as a hawk, followed him and gave him no rest in the sky. And just as she was about to stoop upon him, and he was in fear of death, he espied a heap of winnowed wheat on the floor of a barn, and he dropped among the wheat, and turned himself into one of the grains. Then she transformed herself into a high-crested black hen, and went to the wheat and scratched it with her feet, and found him out and swallowed him. And, as the story says, she bore him nine months, and when she was delivered of him, she could not find it in her heart to kill him, by reason of his beauty. So she wrapped him in a leathern bag, and cast him into the sea to the mercy of God, on the twenty-ninth day of April.

And at that time the weir of Gwyddno was on the strand between Dyvi and Aberystwyth, near to his own castle, and the value of an hundred pounds was taken in that weir every May eve. And in those days Gwyddno had an only son named Elphin, the most hapless of youths, and the most needy. And it grieved his father sore, for he thought that he was born in an evil hour. And by the advice of his council, his father had granted him the drawing of the weir that year, to see if good luck would ever befall him, and to give him something wherewith to begin the world.

And the next day when Elphin went to look, there was nothing in the weir. But as he turned back he perceived the leathern bag upon a pole of the weir. Then said one of the weir-ward unto Elphin, "Thou wast never unlucky until to-night, and now thou hast destroyed the virtues of the weir, which always yielded the value of an hundred pounds every May eve, and to-night there is nothing but this leathern skin within it." "How now," said Elphin, "there may be therein the value of an hundred pounds." Well, they took up the leathern bag, and he who opened it saw the forehead of the boy, and said to Elphin, "Behold a radiant brow!"[1] "Taliesin be he called," said Elphin. And he lifted the boy in his arms, and lamenting his mischance, he placed him sorrowfully behind him. And he made his horse amble gently, that before had been trotting, and he carried him as softly as if he had been sitting in the easiest chair in the world. And presently the boy made a Consolation and praise to Elphin, and foretold honour to Elphin; and the Consolation was as you may see: —

"Fair Elphin, cease to lament!
Let no one be dissatisfied with his own,
To despair will bring no advantage.

[1] Taliesin.

No man sees what supports him;
The prayer of Cynllo will not be in vain;
God will not violate his promise.
Never in Gwyddno's weir
Was there such good luck as this night.
Fair Elphin, dry thy cheeks!
Being too sad will not avail.
Although thou thinkest thou hast no gain,
Too much grief will bring thee no good;
Nor doubt the miracles of the Almighty:
Although I am but little, I am highly gifted.
From seas, and from mountains,
And from the depths of rivers,
God brings wealth to the fortunate man.
Elphin of lively qualities,
Thy resolution is unmanly;
Thou must not be over sorrowful:
Better to trust in God than to forbode ill.
Weak and small as I am,
On the foaming beach of the ocean,
In the day of trouble I shall be
Of more service to thee than three hundred salmon.
Elphin of notable qualities,
Be not displeased at thy misfortune;
Although reclined thus weak in my bag,
There lies a virtue in my tongue.
While I continue thy protector
Thou hast not much to fear;
Remembering the names of the Trinity,
None shall be able to harm thee."

And this was the first poem that Taliesin ever sang, being to console Elphin in his grief for that the produce of the weir was lost, and, what was worse, that all the world would consider that it was through his fault and ill-luck. And then Gwyddno Garanhir[1] asked him what he was, whether man or spirit. Whereupon he sang this tale, and said: —

"First, I have been formed a comely person,
In the court of Caridwen I have done penance;

[1] The mention of Gwyddno Garanhir instead of Elphin ab Gwyddno in this place is evidently an error of some transcriber of the MS.

Though little I was seen, placidly received,
I was great on the floor of the place to where I was led;
I have been a prized defence, the sweet muse the cause,
And by law without speech I have been liberated
By a smiling black old hag, when irritated
Dreadful her claim when pursued:
I have fled with vigour, I have fled as a frog,
I have fled in the semblance of a crow, scarcely finding rest;
I have fled vehemently, I have fled as a chain,
I have fled as a roe into an entangled thicket;
I have fled as a wolf cub, I have fled as a wolf in a wilderness,
I have fled as a thrush of portending language;
I have fled as a fox, used to concurrent bounds of quirks;
I have fled as a martin, which did not avail;
I have fled as a squirrel, that vainly hides,
I have fled as a stag's antler, of ruddy course,
I have fled as iron in a glowing fire,
I have fled as a spear-head, of woe to such as has a wish for it;
I have fled as a fierce bull bitterly fighting,
I have fled as a bristly boar seen in a ravine,
I have fled as a white grain of pure wheat,
On the skirt of a hempen sheet entangled,
That seemed of the size of a mare's foal,
That is filling like a ship on the waters;
Into a dark leathern bag I was thrown,
And on a boundless sea I was sent adrift;
Which was to me an omen of being tenderly nursed,
And the Lord God then set me at liberty."

Then came Elphin to the house or court of Gwyddno his father, and Taliesin with him. And Gwyddno asked him if he had had a good haul at the weir, and he told him that he had got that which was better than fish. "What was that?" said Gwyddno. "A Bard," answered Elphin. Then said Gwyddno, "Alas, what will he profit thee?" And Taliesin himself replied and said, "He will profit him more than the weir ever profited thee." Asked Gwyddno, "Art thou able to speak, and thou so little?" And Taliesin answered him, "I am better able to speak than thou to question me." "Let me hear what thou canst say," quoth Gwyddno. Then Taliesin sang: —

"In water there is a quality endowed with a blessing;
On God it is most just to meditate aright;

To God it is proper to supplicate with seriousness,
Since no obstacle can there be to obtain a reward from him.
Three times have I been born, I know by meditation;
It were miserable for a person not to come and obtain
All the sciences of the world, collected together in my breast,
For I know what has been, what in future will occur.
I will supplicate my Lord that I get refuge in him,
A regard I may obtain in his grace;
The Son of Mary is my trust, great in him is my delight,
For in him is the world continually upholden.
God has been to instruct me and to raise my expectation,
The true Creator of heaven, who affords me protection;
It is rightly intended that the saints should daily pray,
For God, the renovator, will bring them to him."

* * * * *

And forthwith Elphin gave his haul to his wife, and she nursed him tenderly and lovingly. Thenceforward Elphin increased in riches more and more day after day, and in love and favour with the king, and there abode Taliesin until he was thirteen years old, when Elphin son of Gwyddno went by a Christmas invitation to his uncle, Maelgwn Gwynedd, who some time after this held open court at Christmastide in the castle of Dyganwy, for all the number of his lords of both degrees, both spiritual and temporal, with a vast and thronged host of knights and squires. And amongst them there arose a discourse and discussion. And thus was it said.

"Is there in the whole world a king so great as Maelgwn, or one on whom Heaven has bestowed so many spiritual gifts as upon him? First, form, and beauty, and meekness, and strength, besides all the powers of the soul!" And together with these they said that Heaven had given one gift that exceeded all the others, which was the beauty, and comeliness, and grace, and wisdom, and modesty of his queen, whose virtues surpassed those of all the ladies and noble maidens throughout the whole kingdom. And with this they put questions one to another amongst themselves: Who had braver men? Who had fairer or swifter horses or greyhounds? Who had more skilful or wiser bards — than Maelgwn?

Now at that time the bards were in great favour with the exalted of the kingdom; and then none performed the office of those who are now called heralds, unless they were learned men, not only expert in the service of kings and princes, but studious and well versed in the lineage, and arms, and exploits of princes and kings, and in discussions concerning foreign kingdoms, and the ancient things of this kingdom, and chiefly in the annals of the first nobles; and also were prepared always with their answers in various languages, Latin, French, Welsh, and English. And together with this they were great chroniclers, and recorders, and skilful in framing verses, and ready in making englyns in every one of those languages. Now of these there were at that feast within the palace of Maelgwn as many as four-and-twenty, and chief of them all was one named Heinin Vardd.

When they had all made an end of thus praising the king and his gifts, it befell that Elphin spoke in this wise. "Of a truth none but a king may vie with a king; but were he not a king, I would say that my wife was as virtuous as any lady in the kingdom, and also that I have a bard who is more skilful than all the king's bards." In a short space some of his fellows showed the king all the boastings of Elphin; and the king ordered him to be thrown into a strong prison, until he might know the truth as to the virtues of his wife, and the wisdom of his bard.

Now when Elphin had been put in a tower of the castle, with a thick chain about his feet (it is said that it was a silver chain, because he was of royal blood), the king, as the story relates, sent his son Rhun to inquire into the demeanour of Elphin's wife. Now Rhun was the most graceless man in the world, and there was neither wife nor maiden with whom he had held converse, but was evil spoken of. While Rhun went in haste towards Elphin's dwelling, being fully minded to bring disgrace upon his wife, Taliesin told his mistress how that the king had placed his master in durance in prison, and how that Rhun was coming in haste to strive to bring disgrace upon her. Wherefore he caused his mistress to array one of the maids of her kitchen in her apparel; which the noble lady gladly did; and she loaded her hands with the best rings that she and her husband possessed.

In this guise Taliesin caused his mistress to put the maiden to sit at the board in her room at supper, and he made her to seem as her mistress, and the mistress to seem as the maid. And when they were in due time seated at their supper in the manner that has been said, Rhun suddenly arrived at Elphin's dwelling, and was received with joy, for all the servants knew him plainly; and they brought him in haste to the room of their mistress, in the semblance of whom the maid rose up from supper and welcomed him gladly. And afterwards she sat down to supper again the second time, and Rhun with her. Then Rhun began jesting with the maid, who still kept the semblance of her mistress. And verily this story shows that the maiden became so intoxicated, that she fell asleep; and the story relates that it was a powder that Rhun put into the drink, that made her sleep so soundly that she never felt it when he cut from off her hand her little finger, whereupon was the signet ring of Elphin, which he had sent to his wife as a token, a short time before. And Rhun returned to the king with the finger and the ring as a proof, to show that he had cut it from off her hand, without her awaking from her sleep of intemperance.

The king rejoiced greatly at these tidings, and he sent for his councillors, to whom he told the whole story from the beginning. And he caused Elphin to be brought out of his prison, and he chided him because of his boast. And he spake unto Elphin on this wise. "Elphin, be it known to thee beyond a doubt that it is but folly for a man to trust in the virtues of his wife further than he can see her; and that thou mayest be certain of thy wife's vileness, behold her finger, with thy signet ring upon it, which was cut from her hand last night, while she slept the sleep of intoxication." Then thus spake Elphin. "With thy leave, mighty king, I cannot deny my ring, for it is known of many; but verily I assert strongly that the finger around which it is, was never attached to the hand of my wife, for in truth and certainty there are three notable things pertaining to it, none of which ever belonged to any of my wife's fingers. The first of the three is, that it is certain, by your grace's leave, that wheresoever my wife is at this present hour, whether sitting, or standing, or lying down, this ring would never remain upon her thumb, whereas you can plainly see that it was hard to draw it over the joint of the little finger of the hand whence this was cut; the second thing is, that my wife has never let pass one Saturday since I have known her without paring her nails before going to bed, and you can see fully that the nail of this little finger has not been pared for a month. The third is, truly, that the hand whence this finger came was kneading rye dough within three days before the finger was cut therefrom, and I can assure your goodness that my wife has never kneaded rye dough since my wife she has been."

Then the king was mightily wroth with Elphin for so stoutly withstanding him, respecting the goodness of his wife, wherefore he ordered him to his prison a second time, saying that he should not be loosed thence until he had proved the truth of his boast, as well concerning the wisdom of his bard as the virtues of his wife.

In the meantime his wife and Taliesin remained joyful at Elphin's dwelling. And Taliesin showed his mistress how that Elphin was in prison because of them, but he bade her be glad, for that he would go to Maelgwn's court to free his master. Then she asked him in what manner he would set him free. And he answered her: —

"A journey will I perform,
And to the gate I will come;
The hall I will enter,

And my song I will sing;
My speech I will pronounce
To silence royal bards,
In presence of their chief,
I will greet to deride,
Upon them I will break
And Elphin I will free.
Should contention arise,
In presence of the prince,
With summons to the bards,
For the sweet flowing song,
And wizards' posing lore
And wisdom of Druids,
In the court of the sons of the Distributor
Some are who did appear
Intent on wily schemes,
By craft and tricking means,
In pangs of affliction
To wrong the innocent,
Let the fools be silent,
As erst in Badon's fight, —
With Arthur of liberal ones
The head, with long red blades;
Through feats of testy men,
And a chief with his foes.
Woe be to them, the fools,
When revenge comes on them.
I Taliesin, chief of bards,
With a sapient Druid's words,
Will set kind Elphin free
From haughty tyrant's bonds.
To their fell and chilling cry,
By the act of a surprising steed,
From the far distant North,
There soon shall be an end.
Let neither grace nor health
Be to Maelgwn Gwynedd,
For this force and this wrong;
And be extremes of ills
And an avenged end
To Rhun and all his race:
Short be his course of life,
Be all his lands laid waste;
And long exile be assigned
To Maelgwn Gwynedd!"

After this he took leave of his mistress, and came at last to the Court of Maelgwn, who was going to sit in his hall and dine in his royal state, as it was the custom in those days for kings and princes to do at every chief feast. And as soon as Taliesin entered the hall, he placed himself in a quiet corner, near the place where the bards and the minstrels were wont to come in doing their service and duty to the king, as is the custom at the high festivals when the bounty is proclaimed. And so, when the bards and the heralds came to cry largess, and to proclaim the power of the king and his strength, at the moment that they passed by the corner wherein he was crouching, Taliesin pouted out his lips after them, and played "Blerwm, blerwm," with his finger upon his lips. Neither took they much notice of him as they went by, but proceeded forward till they came before the king, unto whom they made their obeisance with their bodies, as they were wont, without speaking a single word, but pouting out their lips, and making mouths at the king, playing "Blerwm, blerwm," upon their lips with their fingers, as they had seen the boy do elsewhere. This sight caused the king to wonder and to deem within himself that they were drunk with many liquors. Wherefore he commanded one of his lords, who served at the board, to go to them and desire them to collect their wits, and to consider where they stood, and what it was fitting for them to do. And this lord did so gladly. But they ceased not from their folly any more than before. Whereupon he sent to them a second time, and a third, desiring them to go forth from the hall. At the last the king ordered one of his squires to give a blow to the chief of them named Heinin Vardd; and the squire took a broom and struck him on the head, so that he fell back in his seat. Then he arose and went on his knees, and besought leave of the king's grace to show that this their fault was not through want of knowledge, neither through drunkenness, but by the influence of some spirit that was in the hall. And after this Heinin spoke on this wise. "Oh, honourable king, be it known to your grace, that not from the strength of drink, or of too much liquor, are we dumb, without power of speech like drunken men, but through the influence of a spirit that sits in the corner yonder in the form of a child." Forthwith the king commanded the squire to fetch him; and he went to the nook where Taliesin sat, and brought him before the king, who asked him what he was, and whence he came. And he answered the king in verse.

"Primary chief bard am I to Elphin,
And my original country is the region of the summer stars;
Idno and Heinin called me Merddin,
At length every king will call me Taliesin.

I was with my Lord in the highest sphere,
On the fall of Lucifer into the depth of hell
I have borne a banner before Alexander;
I know the names of the stars from north to south;
I have been on the galaxy at the throne of the Distributor;
I was in Canaan when Absalom was slain;
I conveyed the Divine Spirit to the level of the vale of Hebron;
I was in the court of Don before the birth of Gwdion.
I was instructor to Eli and Enoc;
I have been winged by the genius of the splendid crosier;
I have been loquacious prior to being gifted with speech;
I was at the place of the crucifixion of the merciful Son of God;
I have been three periods in the prison of Arianrod;
I have been the chief director of the work of the tower of Nimrod;
I am a wonder whose origin is not known.
I have been in Asia with Noah in the ark,
I have seen the destruction of Sodom and Gomorra;
I have been in India when Roma was built,
I am now come here to the remnant of Troia.

I have been with my Lord in the manger of the ass:
I strengthened Moses through the water of Jordan;
I have been in the firmament with Mary Magdalene;
I have obtained the muse from the cauldron of Caridwen;
I have been bard of the harp to Lleon of Lochlin.
I have been on the White Hill, in the court of Cynvelyn,
For a day and a year in stocks and fetters,
I have suffered hunger for the Son of the Virgin,
I have been fostered in the land of the Deity,
I have been teacher to all intelligences,
I am able to instruct the whole universe.
I shall be until the day of doom on the face of the earth;
And it is not known whether my body is flesh or fish.

Then I was for nine months
In the womb of the hag Caridwen;
I was originally little Gwion,
And at length I am Taliesin."

And when the king and his nobles had heard the song, they wondered much, for they had never heard the like from a boy so young as he. And when the king knew that he was the bard of Elphin, he bade Heinin, his first and wisest bard, to answer Taliesin and to strive with him. But when he came, he could do no other but play "blerwm" on his lips; and when he sent for the others of the four-and-twenty bards they all did likewise, and could do no other. And Maelgwn asked the boy Taliesin what was his errand, and he answered him in song.

"Puny bards, I am trying
To secure the prize, if I can;
By a gentle prophetic strain
I am endeavouring to retrieve
The loss I may have suffered;
Complete the attempt I hope,
Since Elphin endures trouble
In the fortress of Teganwy,
On him may there not be laid
Too many chains and fetters;
The Chair of the fortress of Teganwy
Will I again seek;
Strengthened by my muse I am powerful;
Mighty on my part is what I seek,
For three hundred songs and more
Are combined in the spell I sing.
There ought not to stand where I am
Neither stone, neither ring;
And there ought not to be about me
Any bard who may not know
That Elphin the son of Gwyddno
Is in the land of Artro,
Secured by thirteen locks,
For praising his instructor;
And then I Taliesin,
Chief of the bards of the west,
Shall loosen Elphin
Out of a golden fetter."

* * * * *

"If you be primary bards
To the master of sciences,
Declare ye mysteries
That relate to the inhabitants of the world;
There is a noxious creature,
From the rampart of Satanas,
Which has overcome all
Between the deep and the shallow;
Equally wide are his jaws

As the mountains of the Alps;
Him death will not subdue,
Nor hand or blades;
There is the load of nine hundred wagons
In the hair of his two paws;
There is in his head an eye
Green as the limpid sheet of icicle;
Three springs arise
In the nape of his neck;
Sea-roughs thereon
Swim through it;
There was the dissolution of the oxen
Of Deivrdonwy the water-gifted.
The names of the three springs
From the midst of the ocean;
One generated brine
Which is from the Corina,
To replenish the flood
Over seas disappearing;
The second, without injury
It will fall on us,
When there is rain abroad,
Through the whelming sky;
The third will appear
Through the mountain veins,
Like a flinty banquet,
The work of the King of kings,
You are blundering bards,
In too much solicitude;
You cannot celebrate
The kingdom of the Britons;
And I am Taliesin,
Chief of the bards of the west,
Who will loosen Elphin
Out of the golden fetter."

* * * * *

"Be silent, then, ye unlucky rhyming bards,
For you cannot judge between truth and falsehood.
If you be primary bards formed by heaven,
Tell your king what his fate will be.
It is I who am a diviner and a leading bard,
And know every passage in the country of your king;
I shall liberate Elphin from the belly of the stony tower;

And will tell your king what will befall him.
A most strange creature will come from the sea marsh of Rhianedd
As a punishment of iniquity on Maelgwn Gwynedd;
His hair, his teeth, and his eyes being as gold,
And this will bring destruction upon Maelgwn Gwynedd."

* * * * *

"Discover thou what is
The strong creature from before the flood,
Without flesh, without bone,
Without vein, without blood,
Without head, without feet,
It will neither be older nor younger
Than at the beginning;
For fear of a denial,
There are no rude wants
With creatures.
Great God! how the sea whitens
When first it comes!
Great are its gusts
When it comes from the south;
Great are its evaporations
When it strikes on coasts.
It is in the field, it is in the wood,
Without hand, and without foot,
Without signs of old age,
Though it be co-æval
With the five ages or periods
And older still,
Though they be numberless years.
It is also so wide
As the surface of the earth;
And it was not born,
Nor was it seen.
It will cause consternation
Wherever God willeth
On sea, and on land,
It neither sees, nor is seen.
Its course is devious,
And will not come when desired;
On land and on sea,
It is indispensable.
It is without an equal,
It is four-sided;

It is not confined,
It is incomparable;
It comes from four quarters;
It will not be advised,
It will not be without advice.
It commences its journey
Above the marble rock,
It is sonorous, it is dumb,
It is mild,
It is strong, it is bold,
When it glances over the land,
It is silent, it is vocal,
It is clamorous,
It is the most noisy
On the face of the earth.
It is good, it is bad,
It is extremely injurious.
It is concealed,
Because sight cannot perceive it.
It is noxious, it is beneficial;
It is yonder, it is here;
It will discompose,
But will not repair the injury;
It will not suffer for its doings,
Seeing it is blameless.
It is wet, it is dry,
It frequently comes,
Proceeding from the heat of the sun,
And the coldness of the moon.
The moon is less beneficial,
Inasmuch as her heat is less.
One Being has prepared it,
Out of all creatures,
By a tremendous blast,
To wreak vengeance
On Maelgwn Gwynedd."

And while he was thus singing his verse near the door, there arose a mighty storm of wind, so that the king and all his nobles thought that the castle would fall on their heads. And the king caused them to fetch Elphin in haste from his dungeon, and placed him before Taliesin. And it is said, that immediately he sang a verse, so that the chains opened from about his feet.

"I adore the Supreme, Lord of all animation, —
Him that supports the heavens, Ruler of every extreme,
Him that made the water good for all,
Him who has bestowed each gift, and blesses it; —
May abundance of mead be given Maelgwn of Anglesey, who supplies us,
From his foaming meadhorns, with the choicest pure liquor.
Since bees collect, and do not enjoy,
We have sparkling distilled mead, which is universally praised.
The multitude of creatures which the earth nourishes
God made for man, with a view to enrich him; —
Some are violent, some are mute, he enjoys them,
Some are wild, some are tame; the Lord makes them; —
Part of their produce becomes clothing;
For food and beverage till doom will they continue.
I entreat the Supreme, Sovereign of the region of peace,
To liberate Elphin from banishment,
The man who gave me wine, and ale, and mead,
With large princely steeds, of beautiful appearance;
May he yet give me; and at the end,
May God of his good will grant me, in honour,
A succession of numberless ages, in the retreat of tranquillity.
Elphin, knight of mead, late be thy dissolution!"

And afterwards he sang the ode which is called "The Excellence of the Bards."

"What was the first man
Made by the God of heaven;
What the fairest flattering speech
That was prepared by Ieuav;
What meat, what drink,
What roof his shelter;
What the first impression
Of his primary thinking;
What became his clothing;
Who carried on a disguise,
Owing to the wilds of the country,
In the beginning?
Wherefore should a stone be hard;
Why should a thorn be sharp-pointed?
Who is hard like a flint;
Who is salt like brine;
Who is sweet like honey;

Who rides on the gale;
Why ridged should be the nose;
Why should a wheel be round;
Why should the tongue be gifted with speech
Rather than another member?
If thy bards, Heinin, be competent,
Let them reply to me, Taliesin."

And after that he sang the address which is called "The Reproof of the Bards."

"If thou art a bard completely imbued
With genius not to be controlled,
Be thou not untractable
Within the court of thy king;
Until thy rigmarole shall be known,
Be thou silent, Heinin,
As to the name of thy verse,
And the name of thy vaunting;
And as to the name of thy grandsire
Prior to his being baptized.
And the name of the sphere,
And the name of the element,
And the name of thy language,
And the name of thy region.
Avaunt, ye bards above,
Avaunt, ye bards below!
My beloved is below,
In the fetter of Ariansod
It is certain you know not
How to understand the song I utter,
Nor clearly how to discriminate
Between the truth and what is false;
Puny bards, crows of the district,
Why do you not take to flight?
A bard that will not silence me,
Silence may he not obtain,
Till he goes to be covered
Under gravel and pebbles;
Such as shall listen to me,
May God listen to him."

Then sang he the piece called "The Spite of the Bards."

"Minstrels persevere in their false custom,
Immoral ditties are their delight;
Vain and tasteless praise they recite;
Falsehood at all times do they utter;
The innocent persons they ridicule;
Married women they destroy,
Innocent virgins of Mary they corrupt;
As they pass their lives away in vanity,
Poor innocent persons they ridicule;
At night they get drunk, they sleep the day;
In idleness without work they feed themselves;
The Church they hate, and the tavern they frequent;
With thieves and perjured fellows they associate;
At courts they inquire after feasts;
Every senseless word they bring forward;
Every deadly sin they praise;
Every vile course of life they lead;
Through every village, town, and country they stroll;
Concerning the gripe of death they think not;
Neither lodging nor charity do they give;
Indulging in victuals to excess.
Psalms or prayers they do not use,
Tithes or offerings to God they do not pay,
On holidays or Sundays they do not worship;
Vigils or festivals they do not heed.
The birds do fly, the fish do swim,
The bees collect honey, worms do crawl,
Every thing travails to obtain its food,
Except minstrels and lazy useless thieves.

I deride neither song nor minstrelsy,
For they are given by God to lighten thought;
But him who abuses them,
For blaspheming Jesus and his service."

Taliesin having set his master free from prison, and having protected the innocence of his wife, and silenced the Bards, so that not one of them dared to say a word, now brought Elphin's wife before them, and showed that she had not one finger wanting. Right glad was Elphin, right glad was Taliesin.

Then he bade Elphin wager the king, that he had a horse both better and swifter than the king's horses. And this Elphin did, and the day, and the time, and the place were fixed, and the place was that which at this day is called Morva Rhiannedd: and thither the king went with all his people, and four-and-twenty of the swiftest horses he possessed. And after a long process the course was marked, and the horses were placed for running. Then came Taliesin with four-and-twenty twigs of holly, which he had burnt black, and he caused the youth who was to ride his master's horse to place them in his belt, and he gave him orders to let all the king's horses get before him, and as he should overtake one horse after the other, to take one of the twigs and strike the horse with it over the crupper, and then let that twig fall; and after that to take another twig, and do in like manner to every one of the horses, as he should overtake them, enjoining the horseman strictly to watch when his own horse should stumble, and to throw down his cap on the spot. All these things did the youth fulfil, giving a blow to every one of the king's horses, and throwing down his cap on the spot where his horse stumbled. And to this spot Taliesin brought his master after his horse had won the race. And he caused Elphin to put workmen to dig a hole there; and when they had dug the ground deep enough, they found a large cauldron full of gold. And then said Taliesin, "Elphin, behold a payment and reward unto thee, for having taken me out of the weir, and for having reared me from that time until now." And on this spot stands a pool of water, which is to this time called Pwllbair.

After all this, the king caused Taliesin to be brought before him, and he asked him to recite concerning the creation of man from the beginning; and thereupon he made the poem which is now called "One of the Four Pillars of Song."

"The Almighty made,
Down the Hebron vale,
With his plastic hands,
  Adam's fair form:

And five hundred years,
Void of any help,
There he remained and lay
  Without a soul.

He again did form,
In calm paradise,
From a left-side rib,
  Bliss-throbbing Eve.

Seven hours they were
The orchard keeping,
Till Satan brought strife,
  With wiles from hell.

Thence were they driven,
Cold and shivering,
To gain their living,
  Into this world.

To bring forth with pain
Their sons and daughters,
To have possession
  Of Asia's land.

Twice five, ten and eight,
She was self-bearing,
The mixed burden
  Of man-woman.

And once, not hidden,
She brought forth Abel,
And Cain the forlorn,
  The homicide.

To him and his mate
Was given a spade,
To break up the soil,
  Thus to get bread.

The wheat pure and white,
Summer tilth to sow,
Every man to feed,
  Till great yule feast.

An angelic hand
From the high Father,
Brought seed for growing
  That Eve might sow;

But she then did hide
Of the gift a tenth,
And all did not sow
  Of what was dug.

Black rye then was found,
And not pure wheat grain,
To show the mischief
  Thus of thieving.

For this thievish act,
It is requisite,
That all men should pay
   Tithe unto God.

Of the ruddy wine,
Planted on sunny days,
And on new-moon nights;
   And the white wine.

The wheat rich in grain
And red flowing wine
Christ's pure body make,
   Son of Alpha.

The wafer is flesh,
The wine is spilt blood,
The Trinity's words
   Sanctify them.

The concealed books
From Emmanuel's hand
Were brought by Raphael
   As Adam's gift,

When in his old age,
To his chin immersed
In Jordan's water,
   Keeping a fast,

Moses did obtain
In Jordan's water,
The aid of the three
   Most special rods.

Solomon did obtain
In Babel's tower,
All the sciences
   In Asia land.

So did I obtain,
In my bardic books,
All the sciences
   Of Europe and Africa.

Their course, their bearing,
Their permitted way,
And their fate I know,
   Unto the end.

Oh! what misery,
Through extreme of woe,
Prophecy will show
  On Troia's race!

A coiling serpent
Proud and merciless,
On her golden wings,
  From Germany.

She will overrun
England and Scotland,
From Lychlyn sea-shore
  To the Severn.

Then will the Brython
Be as prisoners,
By strangers swayed,
  From Saxony.

Their Lord they will praise,
Their speech they will keep,
Their land they will lose,
  Except wild Walia.

Till some change shall come,
After long penance,
When equally rife
  The two crimes come.

Britons then shall have
Their land and their crown,
And the stranger swarm
  Shall disappear.

All the angel's words,
As to peace and war,
Will be fulfilled
  To Britain's race."

He further told the king various prophecies of things that should be in the world, in songs, as follows.

* * * * *

[The manuscript from which Lady Guest made her translation breaks off at this point.]